© AEBIE TRAYLER-SMITH

Andrew Miller's first novel, *Ingenious Pain*,
won the James Tait Black Memorial Prize, the
International IMPAC Dublin Literary Award
and the Grinzane Cavour Prize for the best
foreign novel published in Italy. It was followed
by *Casanova*, *Oxygen*, which was shortlisted for
the Booker Prize and Whitbread Novel of the
Year Award in 2001, *The Optimists*, *One Morning
Like A Bird*, *Pure*, which won the Costa Book
of the Year Award 2011, and *The Crossing*.

Andrew Miller's novels have been published in
translation in twenty countries. Born in Bristol
in 1960, he has lived in Spain, Japan, France
and Ireland and currently lives in Somerset.

'In his luminous prose, Costa Prize winner Andrew Miller conjures three very different men, but their experiences have all been traumatising. Manhunt and pilgrimage, the tale unfolds into a gripping and, ultimately, surprising exploration of the inner battleground.'

ELIZABETH BUCHAN, *DAILY MAIL*

'A novel of delicately shifting moods, a pastoral comedy and passionate romance story alternating with a blackly menacing thriller. It is also a book of ideas: about male violence, the impact of war and the price of freedom.'

JOHANNA THOMAS-CORR, *OBSERVER*

'A sort of *The 39 Steps* with added malice . . . pitch-perfect.'

MICHAEL PRODGER, BOOKS OF THE YEAR, *NEW STATESMAN*

'Both a ripping yarn and a skilful meditation on absence . . . The pacing of his story is excellent; his style is crisp; his apprehension of pain is arresting; and his ability to show people trembling at the edge of unreason is compelling.'

ANDREW MOTION, *GUARDIAN*

'The joy of reading an Andrew Miller novel is his obvious passion for story and sensual language, and his ability to interweave the two seamlessly . . . one of the most impressive novelists at work today.'

JOHN BOYNE, *IRISH TIMES*

ANDREW MILLER

Now
We
Shall Be
Entirely
Free

SCEPTRE

First published in Great Britain in 2018 by Sceptre
An Imprint of Hodder & Stoughton
An Hachette UK company

This paperback edition published in 2019

4

A CIP catalogue record for this title is available from the British Library

Paperback ISBN 978 1 444 78466 4

Typeset in Janson Text by Hewer Text UK Ltd, Edinburgh
Printed and bound in Great Britain by Clays Ltd, Elcograf S.p.A.

Hodder & Stoughton policy is to use papers that are natural, renewable
and recyclable products and made from wood grown in sustainable
forests. The logging and manufacturing processes are expected to
conform to the environmental regulations of the country of origin.

Hodder & Stoughton Ltd
Carmelite House
50 Victoria Embankment
London EC4Y 0DZ

www.sceptrebooks.co.uk

For Bill Parish, Jim Hodges, Howard Allen and Maurice Osbourne. Patient men all. *Salve!*

I attempted to pray and recommend myself to God but my mind was so confused I could not arrange my ideas. I almost think I was deranged . . .

Thomas Howell, 71st Regiment of Foot

. . . the only art worth learning but which can never be wholly mastered, the art of inhabiting the earth.

Luigi Barzini

ONE

1

It came through lanes crazy with rain, its sides slabbed with mud, its wheels throwing arcs of mud behind it. There were two horses rigged side by side and on the left-hand horse the postilion, a man of fifty, peered from under the brim of his hat at the outline of high hedges, arching trees. Somewhere there was a moon but you would do well to say where. The lantern on the cab had guttered out a mile back. The last light he had seen was a candle at a farmhouse window, some farmer up late at his accounts or prayers.

He called to his horses, 'Steady, steady . . .' The mud was liquid clay. More than once the animals had lost their footing in it. If he were to be thrown here! Thrown and bones cracked! Then he and the poor wretch in the cab would be discovered in the morning by milkmaid or tinker, dead as if they'd met the devil on the road.

Or was his passenger already dead? At the Swans he'd been carried out in the arms of servants, eyes shut and shadowed, head lolling, the landlord looking on like a man well pleased to be rid of what troubled him.

He reined in the horses, brought them to a halt. Here the road turned and descended – he could sense it more than see it – and he sat, pushed at by the rain, trying to think of what was best to do. He could get on to the cab and work the brake but the wheels had nothing to grip and he did not want to be up top if the thing started to glide. No, he would take his chances in the mud. He climbed down, stood in his stiff postilion's boots, took the collar of the horse he had been riding and began to walk.

Did he know this hill? He would know it in daylight but now, creeping forward, muttering to the horse, the cab swaying on its axle, he could not rid himself of the feeling he was walking down into the sea and would soon feel the surf break against his boots. Nonsense of course. There was no sea for a hundred miles, but somehow even a Somerset postilion carried with him a sea in his imagination.

For a span of seconds the moon came free of clouds and he saw the hill's character, saw moonlight on the yardarm bough of a big tree he thought he recognised. Another twenty yards and the road turned sharply right and down again. He turned with it, going a little quicker now. The rain was easing. He shook the drops from his hat, went on descending (long enough to begin to doubt this could be the hill he had believed it was), then, stretching out with his hand, he grazed a stone pillar that marked the edge of an open gateway. He led the horses through on to the drive – or not a drive but a courtyard, small stones underfoot, and beyond it the blackness and slate-shine of a large, square house. He left the horses and went up the three low steps to the front door. He felt around for a knocker or bell-pull, found none and beat against the door with the sodden leather of his gloved palm. Almost immediately, a dog began to bark. Another dog, down in the village, answered it. He waited. A voice, a woman's, called the dog to silence. When the dog was hushed she said, 'Who is it? What do you want here?'

He told her, and told her his business. He was still not certain he had come to the right place, that this was the address he carried tucked inside his glove.

'Wait,' she said, her voice made a little strange by the door between them. When she returned she had a light that he saw as a bloom of yellow through the narrow window at the side of the door. He stood back to show himself. The light shifted, bolts were drawn and the door, swollen from the rain perhaps – raining off and on for days – opened with a scraping sound. The woman stood there holding up her lamp. Not young, not old. She had a blanket around her shoulders and was holding the edges with her free hand against her chest.

'Where is he?' she asked, looking either side of the postilion.

'He's in the cab.'

'Why does he not come?'

'He will need to be lifted. He was lifted in.'

She took this in for a moment, then said, 'There is only me here.'

'I can manage him,' he said, 'I believe I can.'

He turned from her and walked to the cab. He tapped for politeness' sake on the sliding window, then opened the door, got on to the step and leaned inside. It did not smell good in there, nor was it obvious at first that the man was still breathing.

'I'll be gentle as I can,' he said. He pulled the man forward, just enough to slide an arm around his back. His other arm went under the man's knees. With a grunt he lifted him, stepped down backwards on to the courtyard stones and carried him quickly into the house.

The woman shut the door. 'Sweet heaven,' she said. 'Can you bring him up the stairs?'

'If you don't mind my boots,' he said.

The woman went first, the lamplight washing over paintings of horses, men, land. Behind the postilion came a dog, a hunting animal of some type, with a long snout and slender legs. He didn't hear it, it came so quietly.

At the top of the stairs he paused to find his breath, then followed the woman down a panelled corridor to a panelled door and past the door into a bedchamber, the chill of a room that had passed all winter unvisited and fireless.

'On there,' she said, nodding to the bed. Then, more to herself, added, 'If I had known. If I had been told. If I had been told *something . . .*'

She stood beside the postilion. By the light of the lamp they both looked down, silently, at the man on the bed. The woman moved the lamp down the length of his body. 'Those aren't his clothes,' she said.

'No?'

A brown civilian coat that had once belonged to a bigger man. A waistcoat that looked to have been cut from a blanket. Grey trousers patched with all sorts, with squares of leather and brown fustian and a dark material – red? – that might be oilcloth. Both his feet were wound with strips of cloth.

'Where are his boots?' she asked.

'He is as I had him from the Swans. No boots and no hat.'

'No bags?'

'One. A small one. Down in the cab.'

She looked at the postilion, took proper notice of him for the first time. He wasn't from the village or the next village or the next, though she might have seen him somewhere, going about his work. A thin face touched by weather and the strong drink all men in his trade needed and relished. But there was a keenness there, a kindness too, that put her in mind of the preacher she had seen riding past the house the end of last year's apple picking, one of the new sort who spoke in the open air to miners and field labourers and servants. Even in Radstock.

'The landlord,' said the postilion, 'told me he had come up from the coast the day before. From Portsmouth.'

'Portsmouth?'

'That's what he said. And that there were soldiers back from Spain, some without eyes or legs, just lying in the streets.'

'Sweet mercy,' she said. 'But not the officers, surely?'

'He didn't say.'

'Well, those are not his clothes,' she said. 'I know all his clothes.'

'You keep house here, I suppose.'

'I do,' she said. 'An empty house.'

She took the blanket off her shoulders and folded it over the man. She had on a gown of faded blue stuff and under that the white of her shift. The postilion had to be paid and she went down to the scullery where she had a locked box behind the brewing tubs. She took the coins out to him. He thanked her and went out to the cab to fetch the man's bag, a knapsack.

'Nothing more?' she asked.

'Nothing,' he said.

They stood at the door. The night now was breezy but dry, and where the clouds had broken there was a washed sky busy with stars. He wished her luck. She nodded and closed the door, put the bolts over. He went to his horses, rubbed their foreheads and led them to the gate and on to the road.

'Odd,' he said, speaking into the ear of the nearest horse. 'An odd night. Carrying some dying soldier back to an empty house.'

The tall-case clock in the hall said just past two in the morning and showed, on the tip of a strip of bent metal, the face of a dreaming moon. She looked up the stairs (the postilion's mud still wet on the carpet), then went through to the kitchen. The fire there was easy enough to excite. She swung the kettle over it, then carried a scuttle of glowing coals up to the room where the man lay in utter darkness. She tipped the coals into the grate, went down again for kindling and fresh coal and two candles. When she came back she laid the kindling on the live coals, lit the candles from the flames and put small pieces of fresh coal on the fire. The room would take hours to become properly warm but the fire's glow encouraged her and she hurried down to the kitchen again. The water in the kettle was hot and she half filled an earthenware mug with it, added a good measure of brandy, put a horn spoon in her apron pocket. The dog was with her, had followed her on each journey, up and down.

She sat on the edge of the bed. She needed to catch up with herself, to breathe, to understand what the night had brought her and might bring her yet. She tugged the pillow down towards the man's shoulders so that his head would be raised a little, filled the horn spoon with brandy and water, tasted it herself to know the heat of it, and carefully tipped a little between his lips. Most of it spilled down his chin but some went in, a few drops. Almost immediately he opened his eyes. He stared at her in a way that made her grateful when he closed them again. 'It's Nell,' she said. She had no idea if he had known her or not, if he had been truly awake. 'You are in your own bed,' she said. 'You are home now.'

She fed him more of the mixture until it seemed to her he scowled and she put the spoon back in her pocket. She spent a few minutes working with the fire, then went back to the kitchen to fill a basin with warm water. She would have to wash him. He stank. Sickroom smells, yet it seemed more than that, as if he had brought with him a gust from the workhouse. He would have lice on him, that was certain. She would need a good razor because a sharp blade was the surest way to be rid of lice. She wondered if he might have his own razor in the knapsack but it had seemed to contain so little. She would look for one of his father's. There would be one in a drawer somewhere, in the old room. Can an unused razor lose its edge? She did not think so.

She unwrapped his feet. Much of the skin from the soles seemed to have gone. She had to peel away the cloth with infinite care to keep herself from removing what was left. She washed them, patted them dry, then fetched her sewing scissors and cut up the legs of his trousers. She smoothed and sopped, cleaned the very white skin of his thighs, cleaned between his legs, dabbed the slightly darker skin of his cock (thought how it had, poor piece, a stunned look to it, like something – a glove – flung down and forgotten).

The shirt, she decided, was his, the only thing of all. She imagined she recognised the stitching – her own – but it was stained beyond any scrubbing and she cut it off too, dropping strips of material by her feet, a pile of rags she would burn on the kitchen fire until they were ashes and then nothing.

She washed his chest. He had lost a stone in weight or more than that, but it was still a soldier's chest and when she flattened her palm over his heart she could feel the heat of it and for the first time since he was carried into the house she did not fear for his life.

His face she washed last of all. The lugs of his ears, the tender skin around the closed eyes, his brow, his lips. The whiskers and moustaches he wore when he left (Lord, the trimming, the rubbing-in of ointments!) had, at some point, been removed, but he had a week's growth of beard on him, the hair on his chin looking younger than the hair on his head, no threads of grey in it. She leaned back from him hoping to see the boy's face in the man's, the face she had seen when she first came into service with the family, but she could not, and knew that whatever had happened to him between the June day last summer when he left and this February night, it had taken with it the last of his youth.

She fetched a second blanket to lay over him. The warmth of the fire was creeping closer to the bed but had not yet reached it. The dog was sprawled on the rug, belly to the flames. She put on more coals, snuffed one of the candles. She could see out the rest of the night in the armchair by the fire, but the moment she sat she was restless again and went back to the bed. She held her hand by his mouth, felt the come and go of his breath. Was he easier, quieter? It seemed to her his breath came more slowly and she could not decide if this was good or not. As soon as Tom came up with the milk she would send him for the doctor. She could not have the responsibility just on herself. And doctors were not entirely useless, not all of them, always. They had their tricks.

She fussed, adjusted his blankets, his pillows, then told herself to cease, to have done. How could he sleep unless she let him be? She stepped away and crossed to the old linen press opposite the end of the bed. She had set down the knapsack there and now, for the first time, she thought to examine it. Like the clothes he had arrived in, the pack was not his own. Officers did not have packs like this. This was to be worn on a private soldier's back. She had seen such packs often enough when the recruiting parties came through, though this one had the look of something raked out of a fire. Scorched, filthy. Black with tar or grease, the world's filth. And *this* was what he had come back with? This and nothing besides?

She had in her head a picture – vivid, detailed – of all his kit spread over the bed, over half the floor. Such things! And the expense! The boots alone were more than twenty pounds. She had found the receipt under the bed once he'd gone – George Hoby, Bootmaker of Piccadilly. Six shirts she had sewn herself. Six black neckties, twelve pairs of worsted half-stockings, two sets of overalls, four white waistcoats. A blue pelisse – blue as you might dream of blue – with a fur-lined collar he told her was from the pelt of a wolf. And then the rest – the pocket handkerchiefs, pillowcases, spare cuffs, spare collars, spare buttons. Not that all of it was new. He had been with the regiment three years, bought his commission the autumn after his father died, but he had not been on campaign before and had been free with money he perhaps did not have. The spyglass! The spyglass was new. He was pleased with it and had taken it from its leather case and said come over here, Nell, come to the window, and he had held it to her eye and after some fiddling with the lens she had seen, large as life, a farmer (she knew him) swaying down Water Lane on his mare, babbling to himself and scratching his hindquarters and not the least idea he was watched. It had made her laugh but made her uneasy too. Was that how God watched us? And if so, what must He think of us, seeing everything?

She moved the pack on to the floor and sat in its place on the press. She undid the straps, pulled them through the buckles, laid back the flap. She paused, then reached inside. The first thing she pulled out was a tin mug, dented and smoke-blackened as though used as a little saucepan. She set it on the floor next to the pack. Next out was two inches of tallow candle, then a curry comb, a clasp knife with a broken blade, and a lump of something the size of a walnut and hard as a walnut which, examined more closely, she decided was bread, very old bread. The dog had drifted over to her. She held the lump to his nose. He sniffed it, touched it with the tip of his tongue, looked up at her. 'Yes,' she said. 'And we'll burn this too.'

Last of all was the object that gave the pack what weight it had. A parcel wrapped in the same dull red oilskin that had been used to patch his trousers. She set it on her lap and carefully unwound the oilskin until it hung in red pleats down to her slippers. She guessed what it was before she saw it. Smooth wood, steel, a fold of scratched brass at the base of the handle. This alone, it seemed, had returned much as it had gone, the wood gleaming like the wood of the tables downstairs she circled beeswax into (did so still, despite no one ever sitting at them). Was it the oil in the cloth? Was that why he had chosen it? An oily swaddling that would feed what it held?

On the mechanism, below the hammer, was the stamp of a crown, and below the crown a G and another letter she was less sure of. There was no flint in the jaws of the hammer. She turned it, this way and that. She raised it. It weighed in her hand like a skillet. She had never fired a gun in her life and had only touched them to tidy them away, those mornings they came back from duck shooting mad for their breakfasts and propped the fowling pieces in the hall like walking sticks. But this was not a hunting gun. Its character was entirely different.

12

She saw then – a little thrill of horror – that she was pointing the pistol at the bed, at the man in the bed, and she quickly lowered it and laid it across her knees again, shook her head. What would it be to shoot this at someone? To put a ball the size of a quail's egg through another man's chest or head? Was that what the beautiful clothes were for? The boots, the fur collars? And she found herself hoping that he had not done it. That he had ridden and drilled and paraded with his men but had never shattered some poor stranger with this thing.

She wrapped it again in the cloth, settled it in the bottom of the pack, put back the mug and the comb and the candle, then stood, opened the lid of the press and settled the pack inside. One darkness swallowing another.

The doctor came in the afternoon. In places the mud on the road was a foot deep. The horse's black haunches were starred with it, and there were splashes right up to the waist of the doctor's horse-coat. At least the rain had held off; he would not have to shift about for half a day in damp clothes. This last winter he had noted the stiffening of his joints, pain at times in both knees, in the deep places of his hips. His wife rubbed him with embrocation, the same stuff they used on the horses, until the pair of them stank like stable hands. But a doctor who would not ride had better have a fancy practice in Bath or the Hotwells. Out here he would starve.

He came to the ridge above the village and looked down into the vale where the fields were bright with standing water. From here you could see for miles: farmland, woods, a glimpse of the river, brown between vivid green banks. And now that he could spy the roof of the church (grey and mossy green, like a stepping stone you might use to cross this waterlogged land) he turned his thoughts to his patient, to young Lacroix, back from the war.

He had treated his father for years – for rheumatics, lockjaw, gout. Mostly for melancholy. The boy and his sisters he had seen or heard without taking much notice of them, though he remembered looking in at the younger girl when she had scarlatina. As for the mother, he had not met her, did not think she had got much beyond her twenty-fifth year. His business had been with Lacroix (*old* Lacroix he should perhaps call him now), and once medical matters were out the way they had liked to sit together talking farming or philosophy but mostly speaking of their collections, for they were both among that portion of mankind who gather and hoard the things that delight them. Moths and beetles for the doctor; village music and village songs for Lacroix. Sometimes he would bring his patient a beetle to look at, something jewelled, the size of a fingernail, carried in an old snuff box. In return, Lacroix would open one of his books, tall like ledgers, where he wrote down what the old men and women of the parish sang for him. His own singing voice was only middling but the doctor encouraged him, if only because a man cannot die of much while he is singing, and even if he sheds tears it is better to have them out and riding on music than he should sit staring dryly at the floor.

And now he would see the son and perhaps hear something about the war, news the papers didn't have and wouldn't have for weeks. The whole country feeding on rumour! Half the people wild for a fight, half wanting peace at almost any price. Militias made up of clerks and apprentices and commanded by whoever was willing to purchase the uniforms. The notion that the heroes of Shepton Mallet might stop the army that crushed the Austrians and Russians at Austerlitz had long since ceased to be entirely funny. There were reports of hunger in the cities, the kind that had not been known in a generation. And from the north country came stories of men who dressed as women and burned down the very places where they were employed . . .

He tapped the horse with the heels of his boots. 'Go on, Ben,' he said. 'Let us go down and have our guinea.'

Until he was halfway up the stairs he could not remember the housekeeper's name, then it came to him and he said, 'It must have given you quite a shock, Nelly, woken out of your sleep like that. He has spoken to you at all?'

'Nothing,' she said. 'He has barely opened his eyes. If he was sitting up and talking I should not have sent for you.'

The room she led him to was not one he had seen before. Plain, comfortable, square like the house itself, a door at the far side to what was presumably a dressing room. One large window looking south. The doctor stood with the housekeeper at the side of the bed.

'He is John, is he not?'

'Yes,' she said.

'John? John? It is Dr Forbes. I have come on a visit to see you . . . Hmm. *Nihil dicit*. Well, he is dormant. He is deeply asleep. A little flushed. Some fever. A low fever. I shall listen to his heart, Nelly.'

That morning, with Tom's help, the housekeeper had got him into a nightshirt and under the covers. The doctor now drew down the covers and undid the ties at the neck of the shirt. From his bag he took a short listening trumpet. It was made of tin and he had had it for many years.

He listened for nearly half a minute then stood straight again, wincing and touching his back. 'I thought at first I heard something. Some obstruction. But no, I believe it is strong enough. What is his age?'

'He turned thirty-one the week before he went.'

'And that was?'

'Last June.'

'And he has been in Spain or Portugal all this while?'

'He went first to his sister's in Bristol.'

'I thought she married a farmer in Devonshire. Or was it Dorset?'

'I mean his younger sister. Mrs Lucy Swann. Her husband is something with the ships.'

'He is at sea?'

'No. But he has business with them. The ships and the captains.'

'It's a pretty name, Lucy Swann.' The doctor had moved to the bottom of the bed. He found himself a chair and sat down to examine the man's feet. 'She has children?'

'She has the twins. They are five now though I have not seen them in more than a year.'

'And John here was with our cavalry?'

'He was. He is, I suppose.' She told the doctor the regiment. She could, had she wished, have told him many interesting things about the regiment. The name of the colonel. The name of the colonel's horse.

'It would appear,' said the doctor, touching Lacroix's feet with a little wooden stick he had suddenly in his hand, 'that our cavalry were walking too. You do not get such wounds on the back of a horse. Do you have brimstone in the house? I will send you some. Make a solution with warm water and wash his feet with it three times a day. Has he opened his bowels?'

She shook her head.

'I will also send you canella bark. Have him sit up as soon as he is able. I do not like a patient to lie prone longer than is necessary.' He began to feel around Lacroix's neck and throat.

'The one who brought him here,' said the housekeeper, 'was told there were soldiers sleeping out on the street at Portsmouth. Sleeping rough in the street. Some without eyes or legs.'

'Yes?'

She shrugged. 'It's what he said.'

'Well, we must wait for John to tell us. When he is up to it. There will be news, Nelly, though I fear it will not be the sort we wish for. None of this' – he nodded to the bed – 'has the look of victory.'

He was done. He closed his bag. The housekeeper went with him into the corridor. Just before they reached the top of the stairs the doctor stopped at a painting, much newer than the others, a figure in a close blue jacket, a fur hat under one arm, the hand of his other arm holding a scroll. Brown whiskers, brown moustache. The pose (there was a pillar in the background, and foliage of the kind they must teach young artists to paint in the academies) was languorous, not really martial, almost hesitant, as if the scroll contained unwelcome news. Inevitable but unwelcome.

'They all have them done before they go,' said the housekeeper. 'Some man comes into the barracks and does five in a week. I suppose he only changes the faces.'

They walked down the stairs together. Flat afternoon light in the hall.

'I seem to remember,' began the doctor, into whose mind had come, quite unbidden, the image of old Lacroix's face the last time he had seen it, his last call, the bones of his jaw fragile like the parts of a bird, grey wisps of unshaved beard, eyes shut, the lids large and dark, 'that John was a music scholar at one time. Before the army. Isn't that so, Nelly? Or have I imagined it?'

Each day she bathed his feet with the solution of brimstone. She also smeared the soles with honey, which she knew to be good for wounds.

She fed him broths from the pursed china lips of a sickroom cup. When he was better able to manage she gave him bowls of creamy milk from the half-pail Tom collected each day from the field girls. He spoke only in whispers. One time he asked her the day of the week – he had perhaps heard the cranky tolling of the church bell. Another time he said, 'I do not want people to know I am here,' and not wishing to vex him she said she would keep it a secret though she supposed most in the village already knew.

He liked the dog being with him. More than once she came into the room to find the dog standing by the bed, the man's hand settled on the nap of its skull, the dog perfectly still, the man himself apparently sleeping.

She did not send for the doctor again. She did not think she needed him. She considered asking Tom to shave off the man's beard (he knew, after all, how to shear a sheep, a man should be simple) but in the end she did it herself, brown curls floating in the scum of the basin, until he was as smooth and plain-faced as in the days before he bought his commission.

She emptied the chamber pot. She cut his nails.

A week went by. The weather was cold and clear. Snowdrops stood in clumps beside the pillars of the gate. He was sitting up to eat now and eating solid food – eggs, bread, slices of cold pork. Finally – nine days after arriving at the house – he climbed out of bed, sat there a while, pale and breathless, then said, 'I'll need some clothes, Nell.'

She fetched things from his dressing room. Salt-and-pepper trousers, a moleskin waistcoat, a quilted housecoat that had belonged to his father and that she had managed to keep the moths away from with little linen bags of lavender in the pockets. He dressed in front of her and tottered as he put on his trousers so that she had to steady him. She pushed the armchair closer to the fire, and later brought up a folding table, an old card table, which she spread with a cloth and served his meals on. She chattered to him, asked him harmless questions – about his health, about what he wished to eat, how he had slept, if the room was cold at night. Sometimes these questions went unanswered and she began to notice this happened most commonly when she spoke without his looking at her. She stood behind him one afternoon, behind the armchair, and spoke his name, softly at first, then louder. At the fourth attempt he turned to her, looked up. It might improve, she thought, in time. It might recover with his strength.

As for the news the doctor had anticipated, it did not come from John Lacroix but from the brush seller, a pedlar who criss-crossed the county like some industrious insect and who had called at the house for years. He told the housekeeper (as he laid out his brushes like pieces of best porcelain along the kitchen table) that the army had been chased out of Spain, that there had been a battle at a place whose name he could not recall for the moment and that the British general had been killed by a cannonball that took off his shoulder. What was left of the army, which was little enough, the sweepings, had escaped in ships, though at least one of these had foundered in a storm, perhaps others.

The following Sunday the parson read them pieces out of his newspaper. It was a dark morning, the church dark, and he held the paper so close to the candles in the sconce beside the pulpit it seemed certain it must catch fire, as once before – the news of Admiral Nelson's death – it had, flying out of his hands, then swooping above the congregation, a small fiery angel that settled at last beside the font and was stamped on.

The army, he read, had retreated over the mountains of northern Spain, the enemy in close pursuit. There was snow, ice, very little food. The Spanish, defeated in battle and themselves in great need, were unable to offer any assistance. At the coast, by the port of Corunna, the army had fought a desperate battle in which the gallant commander, Sir John Moore, was wounded and carried from the field but could not be saved. That so many had escaped onto the waiting transports was both a testament to the valour and ingenuity of British arms and an example of providence at its most benign ('By providence,' said the parson, looking up at them, 'they mean to say the will of the Almighty'). There was a list of regiments – the housekeeper leaned forward in her pew, nodding when she heard the one she was listening for. There was no list of the dead, only the general himself. They prayed for the repose of his soul, for the king and his ministers. They prayed that God would not test them beyond what they could endure.

About all this, Lacroix remained silent. He sat by the fire. He read books he collected from his father's study, read them or glanced into them. A pile of them grew by the side of the armchair. She did not know what they were but was pleased his feet were healed enough for him to get about the house.

He asked her one morning to eat with him. He said he did not want to eat alone. He smiled at her – the first smile she could remember seeing since his return – and at two o'clock she brought up food for both of them and they ate across the card table from each other. She found it awkward at first. She had not eaten with him since he was a boy when he and his sisters were sometimes sent to have their suppers in the kitchen, but it became easier and she started to enjoy it. During the meals he would say things, remarks broken free from some chain of private thought. He asked her one time if she had ever eaten a fig, which she had not. She knew that the duke (who owned the village) had a fig tree in a heated room in his house but she had not eaten one, nor even seen one other than in a picture.

'We picked them from the saddle,' he said. 'We leaned into the trees and picked them as we passed. Oranges too.'

The next time they ate together he asked if she would find a newspaper for him. She had wondered when he might make such a request, when he would want to look out further than the room, the house (no spyglass now) and she knew where she would go. Not to the parson, who would make a great show of being disturbed, but to a farmer called Nicholls who had taught himself to read as a young man and now had a modest library of his own. His farm was a mile off and she walked through a wind scented with snow. When she arrived at the farm she found one of the Nicholls' boys standing with a pail in the midst of a crowd of pigs. He pointed with his chin to the house where she found the farmer drinking tea and taking his ease at a table that once, perhaps, had been a door.

'I am,' said the farmer, holding up a volume about the size and thickness of an eating apple, 'reading the words of a man who walks all over the country.'

'He must know things then,' said the housekeeper.

'It could be,' said the farmer, 'that a man standing still knows just as much and will have his boots less worn. The world will pass through him.'

She asked if he had a paper and he called to his wife to ask if she had seen the *Examiner*, then found it himself, underneath a sleeping cat. When he gave it to the housekeeper it was still warm.

'For John Lacroix, I suppose.'

'It is,' she said.

'Has he had enough of fighting?' asked the farmer.

'I can't say,' said the housekeeper. 'He has not said one way or the other.'

'There's a great many young men in a great hurry to die,' said the farmer. His middle son had taken the bounty and was serving in America.

'There's a great many as are doing their duty,' said the housekeeper. She respected the farmer but she was not afraid of him.

'Strange duty killing men whose names you do not know.'

'Would it be better,' asked the housekeeper – it was, in fact, a question – 'to know their names?'

'Knights used to know each other's names. *I* used to know the name of every man at market. Now I know half at best.'

'You live in your books,' she said.

He nodded and took up the book again, as if she had reminded him. 'It may be,' he said, as she turned to leave, 'he'll go back to music. John Lacroix. I think that it suited him. Did it not? Music?'

When she knocked at the bedroom door there was no answer. She thought he might not have heard her and she opened the door, slowly. He was lying on top of the bed, fully clothed. She was alarmed for a moment; there was something in his pose, his face turned to the side, one arm flung out across the bed, but going closer she heard the slow tiding of his breath and was easy again. She wanted to put a blanket over him but thought even a light touch might rouse him. She left the newspaper on the table, put coal on the fire (lifting, for quiet's sake, the nuggets from the scuttle), wiped her fingers on her apron and crept out of the room.

She saw him next when she brought up his supper. It was a pie she had made from a pair of pheasants that had been hanging all week from a peg in the cool of the scullery. He was standing by the window. The newspaper was lying open on the rug beside the armchair.

'I'll go out tomorrow,' he said.

'You feel strong enough?' she asked, then seeing he had not heard her, said, 'Your feet are healed then?'

He shrugged. He wanted to know who she had fetched the paper from and when she told him he asked what the farmer had said. He knew Farmer Nicholls and knew he would have said something.

'He asked,' said the housekeeper, 'if you had finished with fighting.'

'With fighting?' He looked for a moment as if he might laugh. 'I have lost my sword, Nell. My uniform. My boots.'

'Yes,' she said, nodding as though it all made sense to her.

'My horse too. Poor Ruffian. You remember him.' He turned to look out of the window. She did not think he could see anything out there. Perhaps a light in the village or the glow of a charcoal burner's fire in the woods. Most likely he saw only the shadow of his own face in the glass. 'At Corunna we did not embark more than twenty. The war was very hard on horses, Nell.'

She waited. Now, she thought, he might be ready to speak of it all. Horses, men, ships. The mountains they had crossed. The killing of the general. All of it. She waited but he said nothing else, only went on looking out of the window, letting the silence grow between them until she was ashamed of her curiosity and wished only that he would turn back, sit with her and eat.

He went out walking very early. It was barely light. From the kitchen she heard his boots on the stairs and a single joyous bark from the dog. By the time she had put on a cap and slippers and reached the hall he was already out on the drive. Through the narrow window beside the door she saw the dog dancing around him as he tightened his scarf and settled the brim of his hat. He had a stick with him, one of the ten or twelve that leaned against the panels in a corner of the hall, blackthorns and ash. She tapped on the glass – she would give him some breakfast to take with him – but though the dog heard her the man did not and walked out of her sight towards the gate at the side of the house that would lead him through the garden and then to the fields.

He had been gone more than two hours when Tom arrived, snow on his shoulders. He had spent the night with the hens waiting for a fox that did not come. She heated cider for him and gave him the last of the pheasant pie. She told him about the man, his setting off without a bite in his pockets, his first time out of the house. And now snow!

'But what can befall him?' said Tom. She made a face and he said it again. 'What can befall him, Nell? He knows his way.'

He drank his cider, ate the pie. It was good to see him take such pleasure in the things she gave. He was her friend, unmarried, more or less her own age. There was a time – a season – a few years back, when they might have made more of each other but the moment had passed. Or perhaps it had not, not quite. She liked to think a sensible woman became more valuable with the passage of time. And she felt strong.

'What is he going to do with himself now he's here?' asked Tom.

'He must make his life again,' she said. It was a phrase that had come to her the previous night or the night before. Those moments when words seep out of silence. 'There's the house. The land . . .'

'What's left of it,' said Tom. He had made his views plain to her before on the matter of selling land to buy a commission and pay mess bills.

'He might find a wife,' she said.

'A wife?'

'Why not? He is not old.'

'There's Widow Simpson,' said Tom.

'She's near sixty!'

'There's Widow Coombes.'

'It does not have to be a widow, Tom.'

He nodded. On a forefinger he collected the crumbs from the pie. The snow was heavier but fell unhurried, brushing the kitchen window, settling on the tops of the stone pillars, on the boughs of the ash trees across the lane.

'Has he said any more about the battle?'

'What battle?' she asked.

'Where the general was killed.'

'I do not even know he was in the battle.'

'No?'

'It's more than I know.'

'Must have done something.'

'Says you,' she said. She looked at him, one-eyed, as a black-bird looks at a worm. They grinned at each other.

'What *does* he say then?'

She shrugged. 'He asked if I had eaten a fig.'

'And have you?'

'I have not,' she said.

'Have you even seen one, Nell?'

'What? A fig?'

'Yes.'

'Why should I want to see a fig?' She was laughing now, light-headed.

'Well, I have seen one,' said Tom. 'But I didn't eat it.'

'Who did then?'

'I think it was Briffit.'

'Briffit!' For a moment she let herself imagine it, Briffit the pig-killer eating a fig! Ugly-face Briffit! Her eyes were tight shut. Tears of laughter spilled down her cheeks. He could kiss me now, she thought and be done with it. Then she sobered and opened her eyes. She looked to the window.

'You would go and look for him, Tom, if he was not back in an hour?'

'I will go if you wish me to.'

'He has the dog with him.'

'That's good.'

'He said the war was very hard on horses.'

'On horses? Yes. I believe it.'

He came back before anyone needed to search for him. He came in trailing the cold, his face very white. He was shaking slightly. When she said she would bring him up some hot milk and brandy he nodded, went up the stairs, paused halfway, then went on, as if with the last of his strength. She made his drink so quickly she scalded her hand. In the room he was sitting in the armchair with his eyes shut. The dog looked pleased with itself. There was mud in its fur. It smelled of the river.

She woke him and made him take a mouthful of the drink. Then she got his gaiters off and his boots, stoked the fire and left him to sleep. She went outside and pressed her scalded hand in the snow. The fall was very light now. A few flakes settled on her shoulders, the linen of her cap. She thought of the widows Tom had mentioned, and in particular the Widow Coombes who had an interest in a quarry, and only one child, a girl of ten or thereabouts who hardly spoke a word. If they married – and there was nothing unpleasant about Widow Coombes, nothing at all – the house could come to life again. She would cook for a family, and the widow's money could buy back the fields. There would be visitors, lights in the windows. They would go to church on a Sunday, sit in the old box pew. The front of the box still had the Lacroix arms on it, though so faint now the griffin might almost be anything – a fox, a hare, a hare on its hind legs. But a man could paint it back in a day – a dab of blue, a dab of gold. It only needed the giving of an order. All any of it needed was a little attention, a stirring-up.

But would the widow like him? And did he have any interest in a wife? She did not believe he had had much to do with women in the past. She could only remember one or two whose names had been mentioned to her. An Amelia somebody in Blandford when he rode with the hunt there. A Miss Catherine in Bath he went to the concerts with. Though surely there had been others she knew nothing about. He had, after all, been a soldier, and all the songs could not be wrong.

She straightened herself, examined her hand, the pink half-moon of the burn. Then she stood a while in the odd grey light of the snow, looking at the soft confusion of footprints by the door of the house.

It snowed off and on for a week, froze for a few days then began to thaw. Where the snow melted there were vivid green shoots below. The ruts in the road softened to mud again.

Lacroix left his room more frequently and would startle her, sometimes appearing in parts of the house where she was not expecting him, passages that never saw more than a glimmer of daylight, his mother's former dressing room (bitter cold in there), the steps up to the attic. From the attic, if you chose, you could get on to the roof, sit between chimney pots and see for miles.

He walked out most days with the dog, always – so far as she knew – keeping to the cross-country paths where he might meet a herdsman or a woodsman or a pedlar but no one else, no one of any standing.

Sometimes, outside his door with a tray in her hands, she heard him speak to himself. His deafness made him speak louder and what she heard frightened her. It was as if he had a secret visitor, some old intimate whose company was no longer welcome, who troubled him and seemed, with silences, to get the better of him.

Once when she came in she thought he had been weeping. He kept his face away from her and she said nothing. It was not her place to comfort him, not directly.

In body, however, he was much recovered. The body has its own rules. His old clothes began to fit him again; his hair had grown to the tops of his shoulders; most of the shadow had gone from around his eyes. When she saw him set out on his walks his stride was what she remembered it being in the days before, or near enough.

A letter came. To *Captain John Lacroix Esq.* She carried it up. Later she thought she saw part of it – a charred corner with a sweep of ink – at the edge of the fire. He did not mention it. She did not ask. Something, she thought, needs to happen. We cannot go on like this. If she herself could write she might send a note to one of his sisters, to Lucy, who had the more tender conscience when it came to family matters. But she could not write, could not read above ten or fifteen words. And what would she say? Your brother has returned from the war but in truth has not returned at all. He is home but he is lost. It would be like a letter from a madwoman.

The second week of April. It took, it seemed, a single morning to see off what was left of the winter, of pure winter. Perhaps it took no more than an hour. The housekeeper opened windows in rooms that had spent six months in stunned inward concentration, rooms where in January there were frost flowers on the inside of the glass. With the windows up on their sashes the world rolled in – cool air tipped with warmth, the noise of the rooks. A fly sunned itself at the edge of a mirror. A humble bee settled, exhausted, on a window sill.

She started heating water on the kitchen range for a wash day. She would soak things today, scrub and rinse tonight and hang in the morning. She went upstairs to collect his sheets. He was kneeling on the floor, on the rug. All around him were the old books of music that had belonged to his father. He looked up at her and for a moment his face was bright as a boy's.

'You've got them out then,' she said. The air in the room was stale. She noticed it after airing the other rooms. She went to the window and braced the heels of her palms against the bar, pushed until it shifted.

'I had a dream of them,' he said. 'Last night. And this morning I went to find them.'

'It was a spring dream,' she said. She was a countrywoman and knew perfectly well the importance of dreams.

'And look at this,' he said, holding up to her a pressed flower – a ragged purple head, a stem that had darkened from green to grey. He held it very gently. It looked as if, blown upon, it would scatter to dust.

'It's devil's-bit,' she said. 'The herbals use it.'

'I had forgotten he put flowers in the books. I have found campion, cuckoo flower, ox-eyes. But this one escapes me.'

'Devil's-bit,' she repeated, more loudly.

He nodded. 'Yes,' he said, 'but it has another name too, I think.'

She stripped the bed and took the linen down. An hour later she came back with a tray of lunch for them both and found him still on his knees with the books. He left them open on the floor and sat at the table with her. Lunch was a broth with the last of the chimney bacon. She served him. He cleared his plate and immediately spooned on more, pushed squabs of bread into the juice. The books have changed him, she thought. The music in the books, the memory of his father. She said it was good to see him eat so well.

'And drink,' he said, filling both their cups with cider. She had made the cider herself the previous autumn, the old press in the outhouse, wasps crawling over the pommy.

'It's all soldiers think about,' he said. 'Eating and drinking. Beef and beer.'

'And what did you eat,' she asked, 'when you were away?'

'Everything with garlic and oil. In Lisbon they live on fried fish. The city stinks of it.'

'They have bacon?' she asked.

'Bacon? Yes.' He paused.

She waited. She had not thought there could be anything difficult in asking about bacon.

'I saw one time,' he said, 'soldiers attack a herd of swine they
found in the woods. They were so in a rage from hunger they cut
pieces from them while they still lived then cooked the meat on
kettle lids, though I think most barely singed it before they
started to eat.'

'Mercy,' she said. 'And were they sick after?'

'I don't know. They were infantry. We were riding through. I
stopped to watch them. It was amusing at first.'

'Well,' she said, 'I hope the French were just as hungry.'

'Who?'

'The French. That they were hungry also.'

'The French we thought were better served. The men believed
it at least. They were always hopeful of finding something in a
Frenchman's pack.'

'And how would they have Frenchmen's packs?' she asked, but
understood the answer before the question was out of her mouth.

All afternoon there was a picture in her head of men in red coats
running at swine and hacking at them. She had watched Briffit
cut out a pig many times, knew the noise of it, knew how the
blood ran. But the men in the woods . . . the sheer *wildness* of it!
And it surprised her a little that she could imagine it at all, as
though she, a woman of forty-three, neat in her dress, knew more
about such things – wildness, savagery – than she could have
guessed. As if, perhaps, everyone did.

She was worried that the new mood had been spoiled, but that
night, drowsing on the chair in the kitchen, she woke to hear
music in the house. It was so faint she was not sure at first what
side of sleep it came from. She put on her slippers and went out

into the hall. The dog followed her and stood with her at the bottom of the stairs. Anything? Nothing. So, she had merely dreamed it. But after half a minute it started again, a little reel played stop-start, phrase by phrase, like a poem once had by heart but not, for long years, brought to mind.

He would, of course, have known where to find the fiddle. It was where he himself had left it, under the writing table in the study. His father's fiddle. *His* fiddle when he was mad for music and had a master in Wells, those days when the young men called at the house with instruments under their arms and disappeared for hours, not eating much, drinking a great deal, always playing. They even played on the roof when the mood was on them and it was a miracle none broke his neck in a fall. (A year after they came down for the last time, Tom, fixing slates, found a wine bottle full of rain.)

The fiddle would have needed tuning, and she was not sure, listening from the bottom of the stairs, if he had made all the strings as they should be, if his hearing, his damaged ears, had made it hard for him to do. She supposed it must have, but she had listened to enough village players in her time who did not trouble themselves with anything beyond the loudness of their playing and keeping the dancers' feet in time. A little sharp, a little flat, it was all music.

Then silence, a hush filled by the tick of the clock, her own breath, the dog's. Then it was back, and more confident now, freer. His fingers were warmed, he was remembering the old tricks. The tune was as familiar to her as her own face, and in the hall, where moonlight hung like a luminous dust, she moved one slippered foot, toe down, then heel down, toe then heel.

Through the week that followed he would play for an hour or two in the day, and at night, when she had settled herself in the kitchen, he would often play for another hour. She became used to hearing him as she went about her business. Tom came into the house, smiling, and said he had heard it as he crossed the back field and it had come on him like a memory, if she knew what he meant. She said she did.

'Are we as we were, then?' he asked. He had new gaiters on, red ones, in honour of the new season.

'It would seem we are,' she said, though she did not believe it. She had been too much in the man's company to believe in any simple restoration of easier times. She would not drop her guard and knew Lacroix had not dropped his, music or no. They were waiting for something, for the moon to crash through the tiles of the roof, for old Lacroix to shoulder his way out of his grave, for the French to show up on the ridge with their plumes and what-nots. Her sleeping thinned out to scraps. She listened to owls, to spring rain that seemed to fall *inside* the house. She began to imagine her blood was not quite right, that she was spoiling for something (she who had been ill, properly ill, twice in her adult life). It was, then, not so much a surprising thing as a necessary one when a gig pulled by a pair of grey horses swung into the yard and she answered the door to a stranger, a man who, while not in uniform, she immediately recognised as a soldier.

He smiled at her, wished her a good morning. 'Captain Wood,' he said, 'to see Captain Lacroix.'

He was about the same age as Lacroix or a little younger, spoke with a big-house voice, had the side whiskers and moustache the regiment favoured and perhaps demanded. Another man stood by the heads of the horses. This, she assumed, was his servant.

'We have brought his trunk,' said the captain. 'From Spain. Now the dust has settled things have been finding their way back to us. Though I dare say he'll be surprised to see it.'

'He's out,' she said.

'Oh?'

'He took the dog out. I can't say when he'll be back.'

'But he will not walk all day, I hope?'

'No,' she said. 'No. He'll be back before dinner.'

She led him through to the drawing room. The morning sun had been coming in the window for the last two hours and the air was warm, the room scented with the soft smell of itself – wood, old fabrics, the coal-breath of the fireplace.

'We were in the Peninsula together,' he said. 'Shared billets in Lisbon. An onion loft, believe it or not.'

She nodded, her hands clasped in front of her apron.

'I wasn't with him on the road to Corunna, worse luck. Broke my arm in Salamanca and found myself back in Lisbon again. I suppose he has told you all this. Old campaigners are fond of their stories.'

'He has not been well,' she said. 'He was very bad when he came.'

'Yes?' he said. 'Well, it is not to be wondered at. I wrote to him here but heard nothing back. Perhaps he was not well enough to write.'

'I expect not,' she said.

'But he is walking now. That must be a good sign.'

'It is,' she said.

'Yet I sense you would not declare him perfectly recovered. Not yet.'

'He cannot hear quite well,' said the housekeeper. 'When he comes in you will need to speak clearly and let him see your face.'

'I wonder what that could have been,' said the captain. 'The cause of it. He has been attended by an able doctor? We have a very good fellow at the depot. Luff. Looks after the colonel's wife. She's often indisposed.'

'He can hear well enough,' she said, 'if you speak up a little.'

Lacroix was back in less than an hour. The housekeeper met him at the door. He had already seen the carriage. She gave him his visitor's name, twice. He frowned. He was angry. Or not angry quite. He was irritable, ill at ease. She wondered if he was frightened.

She went with him to the door of the drawing room and stood aside as he went through. She expected to be told to bring something in, some refreshments, but he said nothing and shut the door behind him. She looked a while at the door then stepped closer to it. It was easy enough to hear them – the visitor speaking as she had advised him to. And it was her business, she thought, to know something of theirs. Certainly there was no one to catch her at it.

For men who had shared an onion loft, who had been in the war together, there was nothing in their voices to suggest any warmth between them, any ease of manners. Captain Wood made enquiries about Lacroix's health. Lacroix offered his assurances, though when Wood suggested there was still some way to go before he was perfectly his old self again he did not disagree. Wood mentioned a name – Clarke? – who was quite wasted away and in appearance like a man of sixty. Another, Lieutenant Vane, had lost the use of a leg and would perhaps lose the leg itself. Lacroix said he was sorry. They were quiet a moment. Wood spoke of the trunk.

'Is that why you've come?'

'You must have been eager for it?'

'Eager? I had given it up. All of it.'

'Well, now it has come back to you. You would be astonished

at what has come back to us. Even men. A pair from Broadhurst's lot sauntered in a fortnight ago. Both presumed dead or at least made prisoner. I suspect they had been drinking somewhere on the coast and simply ran out of funds. The colonel, by the way, was wondering when *you* might return?'

'Am I expected?'

'Let us say they are anxious to have all serving officers' – or did he say 'surviving'? – 'take up their duties as soon as possible. We're damn short-handed, Lacroix. They've been sending me all over the country to find people.'

'Have you found many?'

'Not enough to keep the old man happy. They also wish to hear all they can about the campaign. You know. Reliable accounts.'

'Why?'

'I imagine as we are a young regiment they are anxious to have a little history. Something to brag about.'

'And is there talk of going back?'

'It's all the talk there is. Back to Lisbon. We might have our old loft again. No doubt the rats will remember us.' He laughed, though Lacroix did not join him.

The housekeeper left to fetch glasses and a bottle of port. When she took the wine in, Captain Wood, she thought, looked relieved to see her. Lacroix poured for them both, spilling a little on the salver as he did so.

She took a mug of cider out to the soldier. He thanked her. 'Will he have to go?' she asked.

'If he can still sit a horse. They're in a funk. I had hopes of going home myself soon but home will have to do without me a while yet. Worse luck.'

She asked him where his home was.

'Four Ashes,' he said. 'In Buckinghamshire.'

It was as though he had spoken the name of his love.

When they came out of the drawing room they were high-coloured from the wine. Wood ordered the soldier to carry in the trunk. Perhaps he had imagined Lacroix had a man to take the other end but Lacroix took it himself. The trunk was a tin box ribbed with wood, and large enough for someone to curl up inside. It was battered, rusted, though seemingly intact. It was held shut by a pair of broad leather straps.

With Lacroix going first, they took it up to his room and set it on the floor by the side of the bed. Then they came down to the hall again where the officers shook hands, exchanged remarks about the road and the route.

'So we will look for you shortly,' said Wood.

'Yes,' said Lacroix.

'Something in May?'

'In what?'

'In May. A date to keep the old man happy.'

'I cannot say exactly when,' said the man. 'There are still matters . . . outstanding.'

'How about the 10th? He will expect me to tell him something.'

'Yes. Very well.'

'The 10th then. Excellent. Should give you time to find a new horse.'

They took their leave of each other. The gig – the soldier at the reins, Captain Wood starting a cigar – turned in the court-yard, turned slowly at the gate, and was gone.

The housekeeper and Lacroix stood on the steps to the house. She looked at him, the side of his face. She meant to ask him whether he would eat now – he had not had any dinner – but asked instead if Captain Wood was a friend.

'Eh?'

'A friend.'

'Wood?'

'Yes.'

'Not of mine,' he said, and went back into the house.

⎯⎯⎯ • ⎯⎯⎯

That night he stayed up in the room on his own. Two candles burning – one on the mantelpiece, one by the bed. It was a clear night, the temperature dropping sharply. The fire, lit late, did little to take the chill from the air.

He was drinking brandy, pouring double mouthfuls into a glass that had somehow survived from his grandfather's time, the glass tinged green and bubbled with the air of the old century. He had gone on drinking since the bottle of port with Wood (who, in Salamanca, fell backwards off his horse after a mess dinner) but instead of the brandy dispersing him, giving him some lightness, it had concentrated him, mind and body, like an iron peg hammered into dry earth. Now and then he spoke to the air, sentences beginning 'I . . .' But they did not progress beyond a word or two.

The trunk was where they had set it down, next to the bed. He had not touched it. There was nothing in it he thought he wished to see again. He tried to remember when he had lost contact with it. Lugo? Bembibre? It had been with the baggage train but the baggage train was God knows where. Ahead of them, behind them. It had become a common sight to see wagons pushed on to the side of the road and set alight. Nothing could be allowed to hold up the retreat, to let its pace slacken. Yet out of this – out of the chaos of it – his trunk had returned!

He looked at it, looked away, glanced back. Then, as though the effort of ignoring it was greater than any shock it might produce, he emptied his glass, placed it carefully on the mantelpiece, took the candle that was burning there, went to the trunk and began to tug at the straps. The steel catch was bent outwards – you could see where someone had slid a bar behind it, some manner of jemmy – and he assumed that anything of any value would have been taken, but when he swung up the lid the trunk looked full, quite as full as he remembered it.

On top was his blue pelisse. The spare one, the good one. He thought for a moment one of the sleeves was damaged, watermarked – then he moved and saw it was only his own shadow and that the cloth, the fur collar, the silver braiding, were almost as new. He could wear it in front of the colonel tomorrow. A light brushing perhaps, nothing more.

He started to dig. Under the pelisse was a boat cloak (that, God knows, he could have used) and beneath the cloak a pair of grey overalls, a flannel waistcoat, two of Nell's shirts. He found a mirror (broken), a pair of bronze spurs, a bar of Windsor soap still in its wrapping. He found the painted fans he had bought in Lisbon for his sisters, views of the Tagus. Then his fingers caught on a solid edge, a smooth right-angle of wood, and he took hold of it and dragged it out as if through the weeds of a pond. This, he had forgotten and he sat on the bed with it, a wooden box the size of a backgammon set, the lid and base bound with blue Russian leather. It was the writing case he had bought at the auction of a dead officer's effects (when they still had the luxury of such occasions). Two brass hooks kept the box closed. He slid them back and lifted the lid. A silver ink bottle, two patent pens, two quills, a dozen sheets of common notepaper. Also, folded flat, a pair of green solar glasses put there at the end of the summer for safe keeping, though one of the lenses had shaken loose and would need to be fitted again.

On the inside of the lid, in gothic lettering, was the dead officer's name. *Osbert George Lovall.*

Lovall!

He had died of frenzy fever before they even left Portugal. Sick one day, worse the next, dead the third. Twenty-two or -three, pale features. His father had made a fortune in brewing. The writing case might have been a farewell gift. He could not remember what he had paid for it at the auction; more, he thought, than it was worth. Lieutenant Ward bought Lovall's saddle for a very low price and it had to be explained to him later that finding bargains was not the intention of such auctions.

He put the case on the bed and went back to the trunk. Dress gloves, a barrel sash, a forage cap, a copy of Sime's *Military Guide for Young Officers*, the margins of many pages busy with his own handwriting. At the very bottom of the trunk, the fragrant dust of a cigar. As far as he could tell the only items missing were an embroidered sword belt, his DuBois and Wheeler watch (which had, anyway, ceased to work), and the spyglass with its leather case. So, a discerning thief or a careless one. Certainly a thief in a hurry.

For a few minutes he stood over the open trunk. A drop of wax spilled from his candle and splashed on to the sleeve of the pelisse. At one time, not very long ago, he would have cursed himself for such carelessness; now he simply watched it cool and whiten. Then he swung down the lid, blew out the candle and went to the window, leaned his forehead against the cold glass, shut his eyes.

That night he dreamed again of the Polish lancers in the snow, the dozen or so on the slope beneath the crown of the hill where they had fallen charging a Spanish artillery position. Dead horses too, their corpses mounted by crows that would not scare. Mountains soft as lace in the white light of the dusk. The crows lifting like cinders, hovering, then settling again . . .

He had had this dream five or six times since his return. It had no variation, no narrative beyond the barest, was nothing but a picture of nothing, of absence, nullity. But something else must have come to him in his sleep that night, something more useful, for when he woke, an hour or so after dawn, it seemed to him he knew exactly what he was about to do, and by the time Nell came up with his breakfast, he had, using the paper and ink in Lovall's case, almost finished a letter to his sister Lucy. It was his third attempt, the first saying things he had no right to burden her with, the next brief to the point of oddness. Finally, having burned the others, he wrote:

Dearest Lucy,

You must forgive me for not having written to you sooner and so, I fear, been the cause of unnecessary anxiety. I returned from Spain in February. You will have read by now something of what happened there. I was fit for nothing when I got home and do not know how I would have managed without Nell to nurse me. I am over the worst of it now but have decided, for the sake of my health, to make a small journey – a convalescent's tour – and have settled upon the Scottish islands, believing their remoteness, the grandeur of their scenery, will work a good change in me and make me ready for the world again. I

*have had thoughts on music too, and mean to try to collect some of the
old songs of the islands and so make a little coda or addendum to
Father's books. That, at least, is my scheme. I hope you will not think
it a bad or an idle one. I hoped you might ask William if he has any
ship on his books bound for northern ports. Glasgow? Aberdeen? (I
cannot find a good map in the house but William will know what is
best.) I will need very little in the way of comforts and am anxious to
start as soon as is practicable.*

Are the twins well? And you?

Ever affectionately,

John

He read it through then read it through again. The difficulty
of knowing if you are behaving correctly. The difficulty of knowing how what you say and do will appear to the others, if perhaps
you have lost some common, invisible thread of sense.

He folded, sealed and addressed the letter, handed it to Nell
who passed it to Tom who took it to the toll house where it
would be forwarded to the Cross Keys and loaded on to the
Bristol mail. The reply came in three days. Nell carried it up with
his lunch. She had recognised the hand and said how nice it was
to have a letter from Lucy. She said she hoped it might mean a
visit would soon follow.

He broke the seal and moved to the window. There were some
lines about her relief in hearing from him at last, a gentle admon-
ishment at his leaving them all so long without knowledge of
him. Some news of their sister Sarah (pregnant with her fifth),
some matter about the twins (childhood illnesses). Then, near
the bottom of the page, the information he was looking for. A
ship (*William is making me copy this most precisely for he does not
entirely believe a woman can be relied upon to be accurate in a matter*

42

of business . . .) was leaving Bristol on the 29th, bound for Glasgow. Was the 29th too soon? She was called the *Jenny*, and William undertook to speak to her master about a cabin. It was, however, likely to be a very small cabin as the *Jenny* was in no way a large or luxurious vessel!

The 29th. He looked at Nell. 'What day is it?' he asked.

'The day?'

'The date.'

She thought a moment. 'The 24th,' she said. 'Or it may be the 25th.'

He nodded. 'Nell,' he said, 'I shall be away a while. You will have the place to yourself again.'

'You are going back to the regiment? To the war?'

'I am going to see Lucy. Then I may . . . travel a while.'

'Travel?'

'You are disappointed in me, Nell.'

'I had hoped you would stay longer.'

'I will come back.'

'Are you in trouble?' she asked.

'What's that?'

'In trouble.'

He smiled at her, and for a moment rested a hand on her shoulder.

He would take only what he could carry himself. In that, at least, he would be a good soldier. He looked for a suitable bag, something stout, not too large, and found, in his father's dressing room, a leather holdall about the size of a hollowed dog-fox. Then, in the cupboard behind the steps to the attic, he pulled out another bag, slightly smaller, that had his mother's initials on it, and inside, in the empty leathery whiff of it, a copy of *Pilgrim's Progress*.

43

He took the bags to his room, opened them wide – two old mouths, gaping – then sat on the bed trying to picture the islands and what he might need there. He was a man of the south country. He had never been further north than Gloucester. The islands, he assumed, were places where 'north' achieved a sort of purity, a meaning it could never quite have in Somerset. But he knew *something* of them, of what they might be, had read in papers and quarterlies the reports of travellers, men made poetical by mountains and cataracts and such. Tours in the north had become quite the thing. Albion's own savage back room, its last true wilderness. And, more usefully, he had spent a week in column with the 71st on the way to Salamanca. He had heard their language, heard some of their songs. He had liked the look of them. They had seemed to him like men who might be trusted.

First into the larger bag went his boat cloak, then two plain shirts from the trunk, a pair of blue slops, some buckskin breeches. He packed two waistcoats and two white neckerchiefs. He packed Lovall's writing case in the smaller bag together with some nankeen trousers, his razor and strop, the Windsor soap, some small-clothes.

The fiddle had its own case, and the case a leather strap he could wear across his shoulder.

What else?

One of his father's books of music? But they were too large and too fragile. He would not be able to forgive himself if one was lost or destroyed.

He looked around the room, thought of things, rejected them. Then his gaze settled on the linen press by the window. Nell had told him what she put in there, what had remained there, untouched, for all the weeks he had been back. He raised the lid, reached down and lifted the pack, recoiling a little at the smell of it. There was only one thing he needed from it and he tugged the straps through the buckles, drew out the oilskin package and sat with it on top of the press, unwinding the oilskin until the pistol was in plain view. He moved his fingers about it in a kind of ghosting of the actions necessary for making it ready. Then he wrapped it in the cloth again and packed it in the smaller of the bags, next to Lovall's writing case. The day now was well advanced, the room swimming with late-afternoon light, and warm – warm for the first time without a fire. He sat on the bed. After a minute he lay back and stretched himself out. He did not dare to question what he was doing. Start to question it and he might find himself gazing through a tear in the skin of the world. There was no other plan. He shut his eyes, opened them. He stared up at the blue shadow of the ceiling, longing for his own boyhood until the longing shamed him.

2

Earlier, when the witnesses arrived, there had been a commotion. The gate of the courtyard unbarred, the witnesses – two men and a woman carrying a child – prodded towards a bench that was in the partial shade of a creeper that had grown thickly up the wall and was studded with blue flowers. Then the gate was closed and barred again, shutting out the ragged, curious children and returning the courtyard to its former stillness.

As always in this city, it was sun or shade, each as intense as the other. In one, your whole skull was packed with light, in the other you seemed only half born, a spirit or ghost whose real form was uncertain.

Close to where the witnesses were sitting – close enough to share the flies – four horses were tethered to rings in the wall. Three were English horses with docked tails; the fourth, a palomino, was smaller and fatter, and looked as if its main work in life was carrying its master out to supper and back. The horse that interested Calley was one of the English horses, a stallion of obvious beauty and strength, tethered where the shade was deepest. He was no horseman himself, did not care for the way horses looked at men and seemed to know them, but the stallion was something remarkable and he knew you would not find more than two or three such horses in the whole of the British army.

Across the city bells rang. Doves rose from the roof of the house overlooking the courtyard, wheeled and returned. It was somewhere near the middle of the day. A smell of frying fish drifted over the walls. The only other smell – other than the horses and horse dung – was the smoke from the cigar the Spanish officer was smoking as he leaned against a pillar on the other side of the courtyard. He and Calley had arrived at almost the same moment, though from different ends of the street. Coming in, each had silently chosen which side of the courtyard to wait on, had eyed each other, briefly, across the sheer fall of light between them, then ignored the other's existence. Time crawled, the hours passed. There was nowhere in the world, perhaps, where nothing could happen in quite the way it could in Lisbon.

Then, from above, came the sound of a door opening and the head and shoulders of a man looked at them from over the white parapet at the top of the steps. He came down the steps to the courtyard. When he arrived he looked suddenly lost, as though he had entered some new element, had slid into water or from water into air. He was wearing a black coat thick enough for the cool of an English April. He moved forward, cautiously, peering through his glasses at the figures on the bench under the blue flowers.

'Are these people the witnesses?' he asked. An English voice and a voice fresh from England. It was not clear who he was addressing. Perhaps he did not see very much through his glasses, was not yet accustomed to seeing life in the shadows.

The Spanish officer pushed himself away from his pillar. 'Yes,' he said. 'These are the witnesses.'

The man stared at him, this figure, half gorgeous, half absurd in the canary-yellow uniform of a Spanish cavalry regiment. He nodded, then hurried back to the stairs and hurried up them. At the top he paused to catch his breath, then disappeared through the double doors into the upper apartments.

The Spanish officer returned to his pillar, his smoking. Now that Calley had heard his voice he felt a new interest in him, and turning himself a little, shifting on the block of dressed stone he was using for a seat, he observed the man without seeming to. It was his habit, when looking at any stranger, to think first of how, in a fight, he would overcome him. His own build was slight – you do not grow tall, do not grow broad shoulders living as he had lived as a boy. Despite this, there were very few he thought he could not take, if only because of his willingness to start at a pitch most had no stomach for. He was not a fantasist. He had put himself to the test many times. The Spaniard, he was sure, would give him no trouble. But that voice. He had liked that voice. An accent, though not a strong one, not like those among them you could make no sense of even when they were speaking fluent English. He wondered if he might ask him for a cigar. Not wise, of course, to ask a British officer for a smoke, not wise at all, but Spanish officers were men in fancy dress. They did not need to be treated with the same care.

He was pondering this, picking his words, when he felt himself observed in turn, and flicking his gaze to the side he saw that it was the woman with the child. She looked down the moment he caught her, stared at the ground from beneath thick black brows. It did not trouble him, or it did not trouble him greatly. To her, surely, one English soldier was very like another. Even so. He stood up and walked to where, in the wall by the steps, water trickled into a basin. On the tiles above the basin there were images of birds in a kind of paradise. A tin scoop hung from a peg. He filled the scoop with water and walked over to the bench where the woman was sitting. Her head was covered with a cloth, a scarf, but from under its folds flowed a heavy plait of black hair that lay like a fish tail across her right breast. Only when he stood above her, did she look up at him. He offered her the scoop. He even leaned down a little so she could look hard into his face, so that she could not avoid it.

'Go on,' he said. Then a word they all knew, '*Agua.*'

She took the scoop, held it stupidly for a moment, as though she had no idea what it was, then gave some of the water to the child and took some for herself. Calley indicated that she should pass it to the men. The men drank from the scoop in turn. They had long, serious faces, like the faces of horses or mules. They uttered their thanks to Calley, spoke out of their chests. After a few seconds the woman added her own quiet, '*Gracias.*'

They were all watching him now. He had created a piece of theatre. He had shaped their thinking. He returned the scoop to its nail and went back to his stone in the shade, sat there, brushing the white dust from his boots with the side of his hand.

The doors to the apartments were opened again, and again the man in the black coat peered over the wall at them before descending on his errand. What was he? Some sort of lawyer's clerk? A scrivener? He stood on the bottom step. 'The inquiry,' he said, looking left and right as if Bonaparte himself might be lurking behind one of the potted lemon trees, 'calls Lieutenant Medina, Corporal Calley and the witnesses. If you please. Gentlemen.'

When Medina stepped out of the shade his uniform caught the light and for a moment he had no edges. He gestured to the witnesses. They stood. '*No tengan miedo,*' he said. Don't be afraid. Then he turned to Calley. There was, perhaps, a year or two between them in age, neither yet the far side of thirty. 'They have kept us waiting so long,' he said. 'Let us hope they will be brief.'

They went up – the black coat, Medina, the witnesses, Calley. At the top of the stairs both doors to the apartments were open. They filed inside. The man in the black coat pulled the doors shut.

It was a long room with a low, carved ceiling. A wooden floor, dark and old and polished. Three windows with shutters that let in small, complicated geometries of brightness. Between the windows were paintings. In one of them a woman held out a human heart or some version of a human heart.

The new arrivals stood by their chairs. Facing them – at a distance of three or four strides – was a table, and sitting behind it were three men, two in British army uniforms, the third in civilian dress. One of the army men Calley knew already, a captain called Henderson who had interviewed him a week ago at the barracks. A list of questions, Calley playing the respectful halfwit, the honest veteran recovering from his hardships, until he had begun to see what it was they wanted and that it wasn't him. After that they went on more quickly.

The man in the centre spoke first. 'I am Colonel Riviere. This is Captain Henderson. And this gentleman is Don Ignacio Alvarez, who is here to represent the interests of Junta Suprema. No one is on trial. This is an inquiry, not a court martial. There will be no written record. Our single intention' – he paused, as though the single intention had momentarily escaped him – 'is to know the truth, as far as we are able, of the events that took place at the village of Los Morales during the recent retreat of the British army to Corunna. We will hear from the witnesses. We will hear the testimony of Corporal Calley. Lieutenant Medina, who has served as a liaison officer with the British army, will act as our translator. Perhaps you would begin now, Lieutenant, by giving the witnesses the sense of what I have just said. Tell them please they should speak freely. They have nothing to fear from us. Be seated, all of you.'

They sat. Calley was nearest the door; next to him were the witnesses, then Medina, who leaned in towards the witnesses and spoke to them rapidly in a low voice. Calley sat with his right side turned a little towards the table to display his corporal's chevrons and the merit badge above them he had sewn on with meticulous care the previous evening.

The colonel was studying his papers, though the light must have made reading them difficult. He did not have the appearance of a man who revelled in his part. Henderson was impassive, a soldier waiting for orders. Don Ignacio examined his watch, then shut the watch and shut his eyes. It was only when Medina finished speaking that Calley noticed what he should have noticed the moment he entered the room. There was a door behind the table. It was part open, and though the place it led to was dark as night, why – in a matter where all were much concerned with secrecy – should the door be open at all?

The colonel looked up at Medina. 'Yes?' he asked.

'Yes, sir,' said Medina.

And so it began. Questions from the table to the witnesses, the questions translated by Medina and answered by one or other of the male witnesses. Then the process in reverse, a cumbersome business made less so by Medina's quickness, his fluency. Now and then his English had an old-world feel to it as if he had learned it from a speaker of the last century rather than the present one but there was no confusion and not once was he asked to repeat himself. Most tellingly, it seemed he made no attempt to alter or refine what the witnesses said, and as a consequence, as the questioning continued, those who spoke from behind the table, and those who answered from the chairs, no longer looked at Medina but only at each other.

There was an attempt by the colonel to establish a date. The best that could be managed was that the events took place at some point during the first week of January. Not a Sunday.

'It was still light when they arrived?'

'It was the time between the light and the dark.'

'It was dusk?'

'Yes.'

'And how many did you see? Did you count them?'

'No. But it looked like twenty.'

'Twenty?'

'Maybe more, maybe less.'

'They came on horses?'

A shake of the head. 'Only one with a horse.'

'Very well. We will come to that, the horseman, in due course. What was the first thing the men did in the village?'

'They shot Vitor Ramirez.'

'Why did they shoot him?'

'He would not give them bread.'

'He refused?'

'He had no bread.'

'What happened after the man was shot?'

'They burned his house.'

'And then?'

'They killed his son, Lino.'

'How old was he?'

The male witnesses conferred. 'Twelve years old.'

'And then?'

'They brought the people out of their houses. The men they killed. The women they took away.'

'How many men did they kill?'

'We have buried nineteen.'

'They were all shot?'

'Some they hanged.'

'Hanged? Where?'

'The tree in the plaza.'

'Were any of the women killed?'

'They were not killed.'

'Where were they taken?'

'Into the houses.'

'Their own houses?'

'To whatever house was near.'

'And they were attacked? They were outraged?'

Here Lieutenant Medina paused, or rather he held the gaze of the colonel half a second longer as if to be quite sure of what he meant. To the witnesses they heard him use the word *violar*. The men nodded.

'And how long,' asked the colonel, 'did the men, the soldiers, stay at the village?'

'They left two hours before it was light.'

'And before they left did they burn any more of the houses?'

'Nearly every one.'

'Is there a church in the village?'

'There is.'

'Did they burn the church?'

'Yes.'

'Then they left?'

'They left. Yes.'

'And how did you survive? The three of you?'

'We were hiding on the hill.'

'You could see the village clearly from the hill?'

'Yes.'

'Can you speak French?'

'No.'

'Can you tell the English language from the French language?'

'Yes.'

'You are certain?'

'Yes.'

'And the soldiers spoke English?'

'Yes.'

The colonel nodded. He ran a finger up the centre of his brow, smoothing it. He looked at Captain Henderson, then back to the witnesses. 'Was there a man who commanded the soldiers? One who led them?'

'There was.'

'He arrived on horseback?'

'Yes.'

'What colour was his coat?'

The men turned to each other. No one had explained what their relationship was or their relationship to the woman and child. 'A grey coat or a black coat. Brown perhaps.'

'And on his head?'

'A hat of fur.'

'Fur? You are sure? You could see that from the hill?'

'We were not on the hill when they arrived.'

'Can you describe this man? The commander?'

'He had a moustache.'

'Light? Dark? As light as Captain Henderson's hair?'

It was not, they thought, as light as the captain's hair. Nor as dark as their own.

'Did you see him attack anyone? Did the officer shoot at anyone or strike them with his sword?'

'We did not see that.'

'When the others were being killed, where was he?'

'He went into Benito's house.'

'And where was this Benito?'

'With us. On the hill.'

'His house was burned too?'

'It was not.'

'Did you at any time see the commander attempt to stop the killing of the men and the burning of the houses?'

'No.'

'He remained in the house? In Benito's house?'

'Yes.'

'From the house he would have heard the shooting?'

'Yes.'

'How long did he stay in the house?'

A shrug. 'Perhaps one hour.'

'And then he came out?'

'A soldier came to fetch him.'

'And he came out then?'

'Not the first time. The soldier called for him but he did not come out.'

'So the soldier went away?'

'Yes.'

'And came back later?'

'Yes.'

'And this time he came out? The officer?'

'He did.'

'And what did he do?'

'He went with the soldier to the priest's house.'

'The priest was there?'

'The priest left long ago.'

'Who lives in the house now?'

'A widow and her daughter.'

'And the officer went into this house? The priest's house?'

'He did.'

'He stayed there a long time?'

'A little time.'

'A minute? Five minutes? Ten?'

Here the witnesses seemed at a loss, as though minutes were a measure of time they had few dealings with. They began a discussion between themselves. It had a thoughtful, almost philosophical air.

'Lieutenant Medina,' said the colonel. 'All we are looking for is an estimate. Something to guide our thinking as to what may or may not have happened in the house.'

One of the witnesses, the younger man, held up a hand, thumb folded, fingers spread. Five minutes.

'And these women,' said the colonel. 'Where are these women? The widow and her daughter? I should like to hear what they have to say.'

'The widow,' said Henderson, 'is bedridden. Her daughter looks after her.'

'And the daughter. Has she made an accusation? Concerning the officer?'

'She has,' answered Henderson, 'said nothing at all.'

'Nothing?'

'Apparently not.'

'Well, let us move on.' The colonel looked across at the witnesses again. It was hard to say what his view of them was, how far he trusted them. It was hard to say what his view of any of it was, except that perhaps he wished himself elsewhere.

'So the officer was in the house for five minutes and then came out. Came out alone?'

'He came out with the one he went in with. Later the others came out.'

'There were other soldiers in the widow's house?'

'Yes.'

'How many?'

'Ten. Twelve.'

'And then they left?'

'Yes.'

'Did the officer seem to give orders to the men? Did the men obey him?'

The witnesses shrugged.

'Were the soldiers drunk?'

'Those who could find wine.'

'Do you think the officer was drunk?'

'He drank wine in Benito's house.'

'You know this?'

'He found Benito's wine.'

'It was hidden?'

'Yes.'

'What else was hidden in the village? Was food hidden?'

It was the younger man's answer that Medina translated. 'What we do not hide will be taken from us. Then we will have nothing. We will starve.'

'Thank you,' said the colonel, sitting back in his chair. 'I have no more questions. Don Ignacio. You wish to question the witnesses?'

Don Ignacio unlaced his long fingers. He had beautiful boots. Where the light fell on them you could see the leather was almost red. 'I am trying to imagine,' he said, 'how these people have suffered.'

'Indeed,' said the colonel. He waited, as though he assumed Don Ignacio's words were the preface to something. When nothing came he turned back to the witnesses. 'If you go with this gentleman' – he pointed to the man in the black coat – 'he will take you to where you can eat. I would like to thank you for the long journey you have made to answer our questions. And my thanks to you, Lieutenant. A most disagreeable task for all of us.'

He picked up the papers from the table but as Medina began the translation the woman interrupted him. It was a single sentence, vehement, and aimed at Don Ignacio, who visibly flinched.

The colonel looked at Medina. 'Lieutenant?'

'One moment, please . . .' said Medina. He spoke to the woman who answered him in a quieter voice. The child, who had been sleeping throughout the story of the massacre, had woken. It stared up at the carved ceiling, an expression of panic on its face.

'She says,' said Medina, 'that they cut her hair.'

'Her hair?' said the colonel. 'Her hair does not look to have been cut in years.'

'No,' said Medina. 'The girl in the priest's house. After she was violated they cut off her hair.'

'In God's name, *why*?' asked the colonel.

Medina glanced at the woman, then back to the colonel. 'To insult her,' he said.

When the witnesses had been led from the room, when those still in the room could no longer hear the child's crying and had endured together a full minute of silence, the heat pooling like oil on the wood of the floor, the colonel straightened himself in his chair.

'Corporal Calley?'

'Sir.'

'Stay seated. You are ready to give your testimony?'

'Yes, sir.'

'You were interviewed by Captain Henderson at the Convento barracks last . . .' He looked at Henderson.

'Six days ago,' said Henderson. 'The 5th of the month.'

'I'm afraid, Corporal, you will need to repeat yourself somewhat for the benefit of those of us who were not present. Now then. You told Captain Henderson you had become detached from your unit some forty-eight hours before you came upon the village. Morales, I mean.'

'Yes, sir. I had gone foraging with Private Withrington. We had gone a mile or more when we found a farm and made arrangements with the farmer to have some potatoes.'

'What sort of arrangement was that I wonder?'

'Well, sir, I had a clay pipe to give him, and Withrington had a handkerchief.'

'Very proper. So you obtained your potatoes.'

'Yes, sir. But when we set off back we met with the enemy who started sniping us from the woods. We returned fire and kept moving as best we could but we hadn't much in the way of cover and after a while Private Withrington was shot in the belly. Down here, on the right. I did what I could for him but I doubt the surgeon could have saved him and he was gone soon enough.'

'I am very sorry to hear it. How did you escape?'

'It was coming on dark, sir. I stayed where I was and kept my head down. I shot at any of the enemy who showed themselves. When it was properly dark I set off again to find the others but finding no sign of them and knowing the enemy was about I decided I should make my way as best I could.'

'And how did you know which way to go?'

'It was a clear night, sir. I found the North Star. I made that my guide.'

'And that was well done, Calley. Now let us come to the village.'

'That was the next night, sir. I saw the light of the fires.'

'You were still alone?'

'I was, sir.'

'You must have been wary. It could have been the enemy in the village.'

'I was wary, sir. I found a place I could look down on them without risk of being seen.'

'You were perhaps on the same hill as the witnesses.'

'It may be, sir. But I didn't see anyone else there.'

'What did you see?'

'Houses on fire. Men running to and fro.'

'The men were soldiers?'

'Yes, sir.'

'They were ours?'

'Yes, sir.'

'Did you speak to any?'

'No, sir.'

'Why not?'

'I didn't know how they would take to me.'

'So how did you know they were ours?'

'By their oaths, sir.'

'You could hear that from where you were?'

'I could.'

'And could you identify them? What were their uniforms?'

'With respect, sir, by this time men were wearing whatever they could find to keep them warm. There wasn't much red and white left. Long coats if they had them. Scarves round their heads. I'd say it was men from different regiments.'

'Men who had become lost like you?'

'I suppose so, sir.'

'Did you see them shooting the villagers?'

'I did hear shots, sir.'

'Did you see the hanged men?'

'I did, sir.'

'What did the village look like to you?'

'A place in hell, sir.'

'In hell?'

'Yes, sir.'

The colonel conferred in whispers with Captain Henderson. Henderson turned over a sheet of paper from among the small pile in front of the colonel and indicated a place about halfway down the page. The colonel nodded. Don Ignacio kept his gaze on Calley and for a moment Calley allowed himself to lock eyes with him.

The colonel cleared his throat. 'Very well. Let us come to the officer. You told Captain Henderson you saw an officer at the village. May we assume this was the same man the witnesses have just described to us?'

'It sounded right, sir.'

'The witnesses spoke of him wearing a fur hat.'

'Yes, sir. A busby.'

'So you identified him as a hussar.'

'From the busby, sir.'

'Though you have already stated that men wore whatever they could find that might defend them from the cold. This applied to officers too?'

'All, sir.'

'So this busby might have been acquired at some point on the retreat?'

'It's possible, sir.'

'Captain Henderson asked you if you had heard the officer addressed by name. You said you had.'

'Yes, sir. By rank and name.'

'From the hill?'

'I was not so far away, sir. And the man was shouting for him.'

'Very well. We have examined the army list, the relevant parts. We have a name that would seem to match the one you gave to Captain Henderson. Can you read, Corporal?'

'The Lord's Prayer, sir. The regiment's name. My own.'

'Then you will step outside this room with Captain Henderson. He will speak the name we have found and you will tell him if it is, to the best of your belief, the name you heard at Morales. You understand?'

'Yes, sir.'

The colonel turned to Don Ignacio. 'You will not take it amiss, I hope, if the name of this officer remains for the moment a matter exclusively for the army? It is a very delicate thing. The man may be entirely innocent.'

Don Ignacio moved a shoulder, a strangely expressive gesture that seemed to suggest he found the idea of an innocent British officer almost incredible.

'Thank you,' said the colonel. Then, 'Go ahead, Henderson.'

Calley and Henderson went outside. Henderson closed the doors and both men crossed the terrace to the top of the stairs, out of earshot. They stood in columns of heat, the light from the white walls dazzling them.

'Am I doing all right then, sir?'

'All right?'

'In there. With the colonel.'

'All we want from you is the name of the officer responsible for the massacre.'

'And that's all you want.'

'That is all.'

'And with this officer, whose name you want. I've been thinking, sir. What if it came down to his word against mine?'

'It won't.'

'It's just that I know the army, sir. I've been in uniform since I was fifteen. I know sometimes people get mashed up in the machine.'

'You have nothing to fear, Calley. I thought I made all this clear last time we spoke.'

'You did, sir. I just wanted to be sure I'd understood right.'

'The colonel is waiting for us. Are you ready?'

Calley nodded. From up here, between the tilting of red roofs you could see the blue-black mirror of the harbour. Henderson glanced at the paper in his hand, though the name there must have been in his head for days. He spoke it, carefully, twice.

'That sounds about right,' said Calley.

'About right?'

'That's the name I heard, sir.'

'You are sure?'

'Never been more so, sir.'

The inquiry was a drama that had reached its last act. The colonel asked Calley about his escape from Spain, the long walk with a detachment of stragglers to the Portuguese border, a place marked by nothing. Calley had commanded. He was the only one with rank. They walked with their feet wrapped in strips of blanket or they walked in bare feet, each step a print of red on the road. They ate grass, berries. Once they caught and ate a bird of a kind none of them had seen before. They had stones in their mouths. They crossed the empty hills like the last men left on earth and those who prayed at the beginning did not pray at the end. Once they realised they were across the border and no longer had to fear French patrols or Spanish guerrillas they entered settlements and begged from people who had almost as little as they did but who offered water or milk, a bite of bread.

The first British troops they met was a squadron of heavy cavalry outside the Torres Vedras lines. To begin with the troopers stared at them with hard, frightened faces, as if they had come across a company of the risen dead, then changed (high up on their shifting horses) and looked as if they might laugh at the sight of men so reduced. Calley took the stone from his mouth. He spoke to them and they listened like children. He could, he knew, have said anything then, that they would have believed him. I am Christ and these are my apostles. He could have tried that, it had been done before, and to good effect. A cart was found. They went to Lisbon on the back of it, sleeping, stinking, nearer to death than they had been on the walk. In the week that followed two of them died in the British military hospital. One, a sapper called Lower, was declared insane and sent back to an asylum in England. To this story, or those parts of it Calley chose to tell, even Don Ignacio paid close attention.

'It was a first-class effort, Corporal,' said the colonel. He looked relieved, as if something had been salvaged. The honour of the army. Men's decency. He brought the proceedings to a close. Lieutenant Medina was requested to go to the witnesses and arrange with them for their return to the village. All necessary funds, of course, would be drawn on the British commissariat. The lieutenant was thanked again. He was excused. Calley was also excused or – after a whispered exchange with Captain Henderson – he was *not* excused but asked to wait in the courtyard. The board would discuss the day's findings. When that was concluded he would, no doubt, be free to return to barracks. Calley stood, saluted, and left the room. Behind him, the man in the black coat closed the doors.

In the courtyard there were only the horses for company, the horses and the flies. He settled himself in the shade, his back to the cool of the wall, his shako on his lap. The air seemed to hold the echo of voices, his own among them. Then he heard bells again, and what sounded like a woman singing. He shut his eyes. Someone, he thought, someone like that cunt Henderson, could come down now and shoot him in the face and they could throw his body in the sea tonight. He often pictured such things. Assassinations, ambushes. How to set them, how to foil them. The one you couldn't foil. That one. He slept anyway – the walk out of the mountains was no distant memory. It had taken it out of him, drained off, he supposed, some of the vital fluids. But even in sleep he was vigilant and when he felt the weight of a man's shadow on his face he was on his feet in an instant, nicely tensed. It was the Spanish officer, Medina. 'The fuck,' said Calley.

The officer smiled. Rather than a blade he was holding out a small, fragrant box.

'*Un puro?*'

Calley took one, rustled it between his fingers, sniffed it. Medina let him light it from the tip of his own cigar, then they sat together, side by side, smoking.

'So where'd you learn to speak English?' asked Calley.

'My family are in the wine trade. We have sent wine to England for three generations. My grandfather was even married to an

Englishwoman, Doña Anna, and when I was a small boy I would visit her and she would speak to me in English. But I learned the language from my father and from the English who work in the town. In Cordoba. It is a part of our business. We must know it.'

'So you've been there then?'

'England? No. I was to go for the first time in the same month General Dupont crossed the Pyrenees. I decided England must wait for a while.'

'And you joined up. Bought yourself a commission.'

'I have an uncle in the *regimiento* El Rey. As a favour to my father . . .' He made a little movement with his hand. The clearing of a path, the flowing of a river.

'See much action?'

'Not, I think, as much as you.'

'But you like it, do you? Soldiering?'

'Not, I think, as much as you.'

And Calley might have said, you don't know what I like, do you? How do you know what I like? But hearing the doors of the apartment open they fell silent and looked up. It was Don Ignacio. They watched him settle a broad-brimmed hat the colour of mouse fur on his head. He came down the steps. Medina and Calley stood as he passed them. He looked at them both. Medina made a shallow bow. Don Ignacio beckoned him and they walked together to the horses, heads together. When they had finished, Don Ignacio looked over at Calley, made the slightest of nods. Medina handed him the reins of the palomino then went to the gate, lifted the bar and pulled the gate open. A barefooted man was waiting outside, a beggar or perhaps one of Don Ignacio's servants. Seeing Don Ignacio, he crouched down and let him mount the horse from his back. Red boots on a torn shirt. Medina swung the gate shut.

'I am free to go,' said Medina. He picked up his hat (it was at least black rather than yellow). 'Though I am to remain in Lisbon at the Junta's disposal.'

'What sort of man is he?' asked Calley.

'Don Ignacio? A powerful man. Or one who serves powerful men.'

'We all do that,' said Calley.

Medina smiled at him. 'Good luck to you, Corporal Calley.'

Calley nodded. 'One of those horses yours?' he asked. He knew none was.

Medina smiled again. 'For the moment, the Spanish cavalry is without horses.'

He left; Calley barred the gate behind him. 'Just me then,' he said softly. He sat again. He was not short of patience. He breathed upon and gently polished the brass plate on his shako; he combed out the feathers of the plume. He was in the process of retying his sash when the colonel appeared on the terrace above and some seconds later was joined by Captain Henderson and the man in the black coat. They came down together. Calley got to his feet again. As the colonel passed he glanced at Calley, made a little noise in his throat, the meaning of which was anyone's guess, and went on to where the man in the black coat was readying his horse for him. Henderson, however, had stopped by the bottom of the steps next to the tiled basin. He gestured with his head. Calley went to him.

'When we are gone,' said Henderson, 'you will return to the room and wait there until you are called.'

'Who is going to call me, sir? When you've all gone?'

'Just wait in the room. And see that you shut the doors behind you. Is that clear?'

'Yes, sir. Perfectly clear.'

Henderson brushed past him. The gate to the courtyard stood open. The colonel and the man in the black coat had already passed through it. Calley watched Henderson free his horse, lead it around out of the shade. Only one horse remained there now.

He stood in the doorway, examining the room carefully. The table (cleared of papers), the chairs, the part-shuttered windows, the paintings, the woman with the heart in her hand. As if. He stepped in to the room, closed the doors, and not knowing what else to do, went to stand in front of the chair he had been sitting on during the inquiry. He waited. It was like waiting as a boy to be summoned by the overlooker. He told himself to be steady, to trust in what was reckless in himself, and lucky.

'Calley? Corporal Calley?'

The voice came from the open doorway behind the table. It was not an unexpected source but the suddenness of it, a voice reaching out for him, invisibly, in the midst of the city's long afternoon drowse, made him almost cringe.

'Come to the door,' said the voice. 'Once you have entered the room you may close the door behind you. There is nothing to fear.'

Calley placed his shako on the seat of the chair. He went around the end of the table, paused by the opening of the door, listening for sounds of breathing, for anything at all that might betray what was on the far side, if it was one man or more than one, how close they were. Then he stepped inside and shut the door. The room now glittered with its own darkness, and on that darkness images appeared, curiously, of winter apples dangling on pieces of string such as he had seen hanging from the ceiling of the kitchen where he and Private Withrington had done for the farmer and his wife.

'Three strides to me,' said the voice. 'There is nothing in your way.'

Calley stepped forward. Three strides. When next the voice spoke it was just ahead of him. Ahead and below. The man was sitting!

'Here we are, Corporal. Meeting like sweethearts in the dark. You are not one of those timid souls troubled by darkness?'

'No, sir.'

'Hold out your hand.'

Calley held out his left hand; another hand met it; there was something maddening in that contact. The grip was light but it overwhelmed him, took all his strength.

'So that you know something of whom you are speaking with. So you know enough.'

The hand led Calley's down until his fingers grazed metal, an object, cool and intricate and shaped into a kind of . . . star. The man wore it on his chest. Calley could feel the slight warmth of him, his heart-blood.

'There now,' said the voice, removing Calley's hand. 'You have my credentials. And I, of course, have yours.'

'Yes, sir.'

'We are both soldiers, you and I. Unfortunately my duties are no longer all of a purely military type. I am required to play the politician. Do you know what a politician is? It is a man who must compromise his character in the service of power. Irksome for one who has put on the king's uniform. Would you agree?'

'Yes, sir.'

'You were on the retreat.'

'I was, sir.'

'That was a bloody mess.'

'Yes, sir.'

'The gallant Sir John described the army's conduct as infamous beyond belief. Those were his exact words. Infamous. Beyond belief. But perhaps Sir John himself was responsible?'

'I couldn't say, sir.'

'Forced the pace of the retreat. Pushed men beyond what they could bear. Made them strange to themselves. Wild. Well, Sir John is killed. The army, the most part of it, has escaped to lick its wounds in England. Time, you may think, to draw a veil. After all, it is not as if such things are unknown. No ancient and honourable institution without its ancient and honourable crimes. But our Spanish friends are in a dither. They are striking attitudes. They say they would be better off with the French. It is fanciful, of course, a childish rage, but the trust between us has suffered and must be recovered. There is, I can tell you, no more talk in London of peace treaties. The war will go on, must do. And because of this we must all be firm friends again. You are still following me, Corporal?'

'Yes, sir.'

'So let us come to particulars. The village of Morales belonged, before it was burned to the ground, to a certain high-strung gentleman with a seat on the great council, the Junta Suprema. He is, I fear, unimaginably offended by what became of his village. And though the village was perhaps one he rarely set foot in, the offence cannot be simply put aside. His voice in the Junta is influential and his voice in this matter has become the voice of the Junta itself. There will be gifts of money, naturally, but something more than that is required. Indeed, it has been insisted upon. They want a man. A guilty man or one who can be taken as such. Who do you think we should offer them?'

'I don't know, sir.'

'No idea?'

70

'No, sir.'

'Why, Calley, do I find myself wondering exactly when, during the destruction of this most unfortunate village, you arrived upon the scene?'

'You heard how it was, sir.'

'Oh yes, I heard. And you can rest easy. The Spanish do not, I fear, recognise the value of a British infantry corporal. What they require is an *officer*, and that is what we shall give them. For the sake of the alliance. For the sake of the war. But there cannot be a court martial. Any such affair would inevitably become public. The news of it would spill out. Imagine, please, certain of our papers, their pages full of stories of British soldiers assaulting defenceless women and dangling their menfolk from a tree. Or, in different papers, a different story, one about a British officer, doubtless a hero, being sacrificed to soothe the pride of a Spanish *conde*. Either way we have a scandal we cannot afford. The public are weary of the war. They feel it in their pockets. Trade falters. They lose their farm boys, their apprentices, their sons and brothers. The tale of Morales might just be the straw that breaks the camel's back. Have you ever seen a camel?'

'No, sir.'

'You were not on the campaign in Egypt?'

'No, sir.'

'We cannot fight a war without the support of the people. That is the truth of it. It did not used to matter. People did not know what went on. They did not know, they did not care. But England now is enamoured of the printed word. Gentlemen, ladies too, are all either writing or reading. We are adrift in a sea of opinions, language, ink. So we must proceed in the only way left open to us. We will give the Junta what it demands but none, other than the few of us to whom this unpleasant business falls, shall know of it. Now then, I *feel* you understand what I am saying but I need to hear you say so.'

'Yes, sir.'

'Yes?'

'I believe I do, sir.'

'What is the first rule of a soldier's life, Calley?'

'Orders, sir.'

'The first rule of warfare?'

'Killing the enemy.'

'And?'

'Not getting killed yourself.'

'And?'

'Tidiness?'

'Well, I like a tidy soldier. A tidy soldier has not forgotten himself. But I was thinking rather of necessity. Of doing what is necessary. When were you last in England?'

'June last year, sir.'

'Then you will be pleased to see it again.'

'I'm going back?'

'You will be shipped on the first suitable transport. You will find the officer whose name you confirmed to the inquiry. Having found him you will do what your country requires of you.'

There was a silence between them. Three, four seconds.

'There are always those, Calley, who are called upon to do what others prefer not even to contemplate. Think of it like this. You will be continuing the war in a private and unofficial capacity. You will not wear a uniform but you will still be a soldier.'

Another silence. Calley shifted his weight. A board squeaked.

'He might already be dead, sir.'

'He is listed as embarking at Corunna. His ship arrived.'

72

'And how do I find him?'

'Captain Henderson will supply you with what is necessary. Beyond that you must use your nose. Whatever else you are I believe you are a resourceful man.'

'You will need some proof of it?'

'Of it having been done? I don't, God forbid, need any. But the Junta will.'

'Like a ring?'

'Yes. Good. I see your practical nature at work. But the Junta trusts us so little that a ring could be one we picked off the ground. It could be one of mine. They require what you do to be witnessed. To that end you will travel with one of their own.'

'Now I don't quite follow you, sir.'

'You will be accompanied by someone whose word they will accept.'

'Like a Spaniard?'

'I would assume so, wouldn't you? The estimable Don Ignacio is taking care of the arrangements.'

'I'd rather go alone, sir, if it's all the same.'

'But it is not the same. Not at all. Alone is nothing. It is useless. Alone and the whole business is entirely sordid. Witnessed, it becomes an act of statecraft. It is important you understand that.'

'Yes, sir.'

'You have a question?'

'What if I'm taken? If I do as you say and I'm taken?'

'When you stand in the line waiting to receive the enemy, what are your thoughts? That you will live? That you will die? That you may be maimed? All of this, of course. Everyone the same, officer or private soldier. But all that matters is that we do our duty. The risk is something we put on with our jackets and boots. If you are taken you must do as well as you can. Reporting a conversation you had in the dark with an unnamed personage is unlikely to assist you. But the advantage will all be yours. The officer you are going to find might be wary. He might very well be expecting some call to account. What he will not be expecting is you.'

The voice. In the darkness it seemed to Calley the voice was half his own.

'You will be back inside a month. You will have served your country. And I will see to it that Captain Henderson has some appropriate reward waiting. Another stripe for your shoulder perhaps. What were your beginnings, Calley?'

'The house on Saffron Hill, sir. Near the Fleet.'

'By house you mean workhouse?'

'Yes, sir.'

'Well, Moses was a foundling, was he not? And there are many men who might have done better without the burden of a family. Now, about face and return to the door. Do not look back. You and I will neither meet nor speak to each other again. Not in this world.'

Calley turned. The door showed itself with outlines of grey light. He crossed to it, left the room, entered the lit shadows of the second room, collected his shako from the chair and went out into the true brightness, that glare that seemed to erase him. He stood a while at the top of the steps letting his eyes adjust. There was a great noise inside him, a clashing of voices, like the sound of a riot or the sound of men screaming in battle. Then he felt a breeze on his cheek, something blowing up from the shore, and he felt refreshed, calm. Below him, the courtyard was empty of everything but the stallion, though once he had descended and was making his way to the gate he saw that there *was* someone, a servant presumably, squatting in the shade by the side of the horse. For a moment he thought of asking who he waited for but that, he knew, would be a poor beginning. He put on his shako, adjusted the chin-scales, let himself out into the street. Boys followed him, impersonating his walk, his bandy legs. It did not unsettle him; he had received such attention all his life and always from those as poor as himself. He thought, those fuckers could have hanged me! Then nearly laughed out loud at the pleasure of recalling the voice in the room, the power it had given him, and to him alone. Like a secret spring drunk from in darkness.

3

The steps from the quayside were steep and narrow, and Lacroix's bags brushed against the blackened walls. A big herring gull watched him come, stood its ground, then flew off low over his head. He winced, felt foolish, kept climbing. The higher he went the better the houses. His sister's place was a little over halfway up and would in time, no doubt, be higher still. Her husband, William Swann, was the son of a man who had run a team of drays in the city, an intemperate man, a notorious brawler, but William was sober, industrious, a respected shipping agent who combined a sure knowledge of his Bible with a sure grasp of book-keeping and the life of money. And having Lucy for a wife made his rise more certain. A gentleman's daughter counted for something, even in a city like Bristol where old money meant the slavers whose ships lay idle now but who still lived on the city's heights like nabobs.

It was almost a year since he was last at the house. When the servant girl answered his ringing he did not recognise her, nor she him. He left his bags in the hall and followed her up to the first floor where he was shown through to the room at the front.

The twins were playing by the fire. With their dolls in their hands they looked at him coldly until their mother embraced him. She squeezed his fingers, gazed at him with such directness he was glad to have the distraction of the children. He touched their heads, the silk of their hair. 'Hello, young friends,' he said. He had no hope of telling them apart.

Lucy laughed at him. 'I suppose young friends will do for now,' she said.

They spent the heart of the afternoon together, the four of them. The room, ample with light, smelled of coal smoke and some floral scent of his sister's, violets he thought. There was a mirror above the fire, a clock with a sturdy tick. It was good to remember such places existed, were common even.

The children, once they knew he was theirs, would not allow him to have any interest but themselves. He played on his knees with them, answering his sister's questions over his shoulder, the ones that he heard. She asked about the house, about Nell, about their country neighbours. She asked, in a general way, about his return from Spain, though did not press him as their sister Sarah would have done, wanting details, specifics. He answered her in the same spirit – lightly, vaguely – while wondering what she knew of the world beyond this warm, safe house, the tea-parties, the Sunday psalm singing at the new chapel. When he was able to, when she was drawn into the children's game (they had posed her a riddle) and he was released for a while, he studied her, a woman of thirty-three in a long-sleeved dress that suggested propriety more than fashion, her figure angular, sharp, slight as a girl's, her thin fingers white and cold-looking. She had suffered with chilblains as a girl, from coughs that lingered for months. Was she naive? Ignorant? What could she possibly know of the things he had seen, of how things *could* be? And yet she had almost died when the twins were born, was – so he had heard from Sarah – given over by the doctor attending her, and in the years since then had lost at least one child before its term, probably more. He had not ever paid it much heed. He had not, he feared, paid it any. Now the image of his sister sweating on a bloody sheet became muddled in his head with things he would do well to keep at a distance, certainly here, in a room where children played.

She turned to him, caught him at his staring. 'What is it, John? I shall begin to think I have a blemish.'

He dropped his gaze to the rug and shook his head 'No,' he said. 'Not at all.'

The family sat for their supper in the green-painted dining room. Plain food plainly done, a decanter of wine on the cloth for the sake of their guest. William Swann, from the head of the table, explained to Lacroix that the *Jenny* was a small brig that had seen better days but was strongly built with northern waters in mind and quite able to ride out a blow. He spoke to Lacroix with a respectful sense of the difference between their beginnings, but also with the confidence of one whose place in life was perhaps more correct, more assured. Certainly his place with God.

'Hopefully there will be no blow,' said Lucy. She was sitting between the children, picking spilled food from the cloth, wiping mouths with her thumb. The little maid stood by the door, still as a horse.

'I trust there will not,' said William. 'But the Irish Sea is no millpond.'

'Was you ever in a storm before, brother? At sea, I mean?'

'Once,' said Lacroix, 'and not long after I last saw you. In the Bay of Biscay on our way out to Lisbon. Waves such that we could not, in a trough, see the mastheads of any other ship, though we were in close convoy.'

'Did your vessel have a good master?' asked William.

'He remained in his cabin,' said Lacroix. 'I saw him twice in the entire voyage.'

'Well, I am sure the master of the *Jenny* will do better for you,' said Lucy. She looked anxiously at her husband.

'Have no worry on that score,' said William. 'Browne is a man of experience. He knows his work.'

'I suppose you had horses on the ship?' asked Lucy. 'The storm must have frightened them.'

'It did. Men and horses.'

'How do they convey them?' asked William.

'How . . .?'

'How do they carry the horses?' Both William and his wife had been steadily increasing the volume of their remarks as Lacroix's deafness became more apparent to them.

'They are in stalls under the deck. Canvas slings about their middles.'

'Well, they are valuable animals,' said William. 'I dare say a cavalry horse is worth more than . . . what? Twenty-five guineas?'

'You might have a three-year-old for such a price,' said Lacroix, 'but such a horse is not fit for service for another year. A horse ready for service is closer to forty.'

'And many must be lost,' said William.

'Yes,' said Lacroix.

'Then I am astonished there is money enough in the country,' said William. 'I am astonished it can be paid for.'

'John,' said Lucy, who had silenced her husband with a quick frown, who knew his views on the war, the profligacy of it, 'you spoke of music in your letter. Of finding music in the islands.'

'Yes. I have some thought of that.'

'And I saw you had the old fiddle with you.'

'It is not so old for a fiddle, Lucy. I think Father bought it new in seventy-something. A maker in Salisbury.'

'And you studied,' said William. 'Was it in Bath?'

'Banks,' said Lacroix, thinking he had been asked the name of the maker. 'Benjamin Banks.'

'John studied in Wells,' said Lucy. 'He was several years at it. He played beautifully and I am sure he still could.'

'I never played beautifully.'

'I would say it was so,' she insisted. 'And I had a thousand times rather see you with a fiddle in your hands than a sword, John. A thousand times.' She too had her views on the war. She flushed a little as she spoke. The children looked up at her.

William Swann put a piece of beef into his mouth, laid down his knife and fork. He had noticed that his brother-in-law was not entirely clean. His hair. His neck. 'But won't the army miss you?' he asked. 'Does your regiment not want you back?'

'In time,' said Lacroix. 'When I am fully strong again.'

He was given his usual room at the top of the house, the same floor as William's office. The room was small but had a good view over the quay and the water. Bristol looked better at night. A rich scatter of lights, some of them on ships. And at night you could not see the kilns and furnace chimneys that all day poured their filth into the air.

Lucy had come up with him on the pretext of seeing he had all he might need. Now she lingered by the door, candle in hand. He knew he should turn to her, talk to her; knew she understood there was, in this journey of his, something unexplained. He should try to set her mind at ease, though he had no real sense of how to do it and was aching with tiredness. Why had he not stayed in a hotel or a lodging house? Family always saw too much. Family could not be fooled, not for long, not entirely. But surely there was *something* he could tell her, some anecdote of the kind that might appear in a newspaper under the heading 'The Campaigning Life'? If he could make her laugh! He would love to hear her laugh. And he could recall moments of comedy, of comic confusion. An impromptu band of pots and kettles at a bivouac outside Vila Franca, two officers waltzing together like lovers. Or how, on cold evenings in their billets in Salamanca the ladies of the house sat with charcoal braziers under their skirts so that it seemed likely – if they did not actually combust – they might rise suddenly into the air and float over the furniture. Or that time a young trooper in Murray's squadron, coming in off piquet duty, somehow shot his own horse and for days afterwards any mention of it provoked gales of laughter – laughter that seemed now beyond comprehension. What was comical about the shooting of a horse?

He heard her speak his name and he turned away from the window. The candle rather hid her face than showed it. He wondered if she had been calling him for some time.

'A penny for your thoughts,' she said.

'I was thinking . . . how glad I am at your way of life here. How settled you are.'

'I am,' she said. 'I have much to give thanks for.'

'Well, I am pleased for it,' he said.

'John,' she said, 'are you well enough for a sea journey? You could stay here a while. A week or two. Learn to tell the children from each other. And there will be other ships.'

He made himself smile at her. 'I have set my heart on the *Jenny*,' he said.

She took a step deeper into the room. He saw her face now, balanced on the light. More their father's face than their mother's, though his memory of their mother's face was, each year, a little less convincing.

'I wonder,' she said, 'if in all this soldiering you have sometimes forgotten our Comforter?'

For a second or two he was perplexed, as if the comforter might be an item of gear, something worn under the shirt or laid across a saddle.

'Jesus Christ,' she said.

'Yes,' he said.

'If you would like to pray with William and me, the children are asleep. And Martha has gone to her bed. We would be quite undisturbed.'

'I know you would like it,' he said.

'You should not do it for me, John.'

'But you would love me better if I learned to say my prayers again.'

'No,' she said, 'that would be a poor sort of love. But you might be happier. Or you would find again a quietness you may have lost. Prayer is balm for troubled hearts. I know this.'

'You have had your own troubles,' he said.

'I have had some.'

'And you are uncomplaining.'

'If I am it is because I do not have to bear them alone.'

'You have William.'

'Yes. William, of course. But I mean He that is greater than any mortal man.'

'I know you do.'

'Alone we can do nothing.'

'Faith is a gift,' he said.

'It is a gift we can choose, John. Our Saviour does not care how we come to Him, only that we do. We are His children. He wants only that we should lay our hand in His. And when we do He cares for us like a father.'

Lacroix nodded. 'One trick,' he said, 'the Spanish irregulars liked to perform when they caught a Frenchman out on his own was to crucify him upside down on a barn door. Then they would build a little fire under his head.'

She said nothing. He apologised. It was not even a thing he had seen. He had heard of it but not seen it. It might not even have been true.

'You are going away to forget such things,' she said.

'I am going away,' he answered. 'That much I know.'

'I can see the sense of it now, John. I can see it is what you need. I should have known better than to speak to you like this.'

'Dear Lucy, if you will not speak to me openly I cannot think who will.'

'A wife perhaps.'

'A what?'

'A wife.'

'I somehow doubt,' he said, 'there will be many marriageable young women on the *Jenny*.'

She nodded, smiled at him, the smile resigned and grave. 'I will put a lamp in our window,' she said. 'The room we played in with the children. I will put a lamp there, and each night until you are back I will light it for you.'

Though he would have preferred to sleep on for hours – had not arrived at sleep at all until three or four in the morning – he rose at six and breakfasted with Lucy and the twins. William was already at work and when Lacroix had finished his coffee he went up to see him.

An office at the top of the house was convenient. Men calling on business could use a door from the alley that ran at the level of the upper storeys and so enter the office without disturbing Lucy and the children. William was at his desk, coatless, a pair of false sleeves tied by his elbows to guard against ruining a good shirt with ink. There was a map of the coast on the wall beside him, and next to it a lithographic portrait of John Wesley, preacher's bands around his neck, one hand raised in a gesture of blessing or witness.

'The *Jenny* will not leave early,' said William. 'They are taking on their cargo this morning, though you should make yourself known to the master.'

'Browne?'

'Yes.'

'May I ask what you have told him about me?' asked Lacroix.

'Only that you are family, and that you wish to travel to Glasgow.'

'You said perhaps I was on business.'

'He did not ask. I did not say. He is not an intrusive man. Nor will he overcharge you. You can have confidence in him.'

Lacroix was thanking him and might have tried to find out more about the *Jenny*, about Browne, the journey north, but there was a rap at the office door and a moment later a man came in, pulling aside the curtain that hung in front of the door. He had papers tied in ribbon under his arm. First caller of the day. Business to be done.

In the hall downstairs he took his leave of his sister. She did not cry but he thought she would do when he had gone.

'Find some beautiful songs,' she said. 'Then come and play them to us.'

'I will,' he said.

'Do you have warm clothes with you? It is always cold at sea. Though of course you know that already.'

He embraced her. The children gazed up at him like the envoys of another world. He touched their hair again. He wasn't sure if they would let him kiss them. He thought it might be wiser not to try.

Outside, descending the steps with his bags, he felt freer. Whatever was to become of him, whatever it was he would not be able to outpace, whatever form that took, he did not want it to happen in the presence of Lucy or the children. Better to be around strangers. Better, infinitely, to be around men. Men who did not know him, who would be – must be – indifferent to him. If he had to fall – and this was how he dimly imagined it, a sudden, passionate floundering through air – they would let him do so, they would not interfere . . .

He asked directions from a boy carrying a cage of goldfinches. Fifteen minutes later he found the *Jenny* alongside a stone jetty, much larger ships tied fore and aft of her. She was, at a guess, no more than a quarter the size of the ship he had sailed in to Lisbon. Two masts, a high prow, her deck cluttered with ropes and gear and stores. Certainly you would not get much cavalry inside the *Jenny*.

On the jetty beside her, a crane on small iron wheels was hoisting wooden crates, the ropes hauled by a pair of blinkered horses, sad-looking creatures, their ribs showing through dull hides. Overseeing the work, and giving out at frequent intervals the order 'Careful there!', was a broad-backed man in a short black jacket, his head bare, his hair, what was left of it, curled around his ears and the collar of his jacket, some strands dark still, most of it grey.

Lacroix approached him and said he was looking for the master of the *Jenny*.

'You have found him,' said the other, his attention on the hooking of a crate. When the hook was snug, the horses were walked until the rope tautened.

'I am your passenger for Glasgow. I hope William Swann told you to expect me?'

The man nodded. The crate was at rest between gravity and the strength of the horses. Then it began to rise.

'What are you loading?'

'Glass.'

On the deck, the crew eased the crate towards them by means of a trailing rope. The horses stopped. They had the burden of what they couldn't see. Then they were walked slowly backwards, and the crate descended into a nest of arms.

'You have dunnage?' asked the master, looking at Lacroix for the first time.

'Just what I carry.'

'What's in there?' He pointed.

'A violin. A fiddle.'

'I don't much care for music at sea,' said the master, though something in his face made it hard to know how serious he was.

'We should agree on a price,' said Lacroix.

'To Glasgow it is five.'

'It is . . .?'

'Five.'

'Pounds?'

'Guineas. You have a servant with you?'

'No.'

'Then you have a cabin to yourself. You will eat with the crew. If you want liquor you must speak to the cook and pay him by the bottle. You will not give drink to any of the crew.'

Lacroix nodded. He had caught most of this, not all. 'You wish for the money now?'

'It can come later.'

'And when should I board?'

'Wait over in the Star there. I'll send for you when we're ready.'

'My luggage?'

'Leave it where you are. We will bring it on when we have the leisure.'

'It will be safe here?'

'Why?' said the master. 'Do you not trust sailors?'

He crossed to the Star and looked in. Though it was no later than ten in the morning the place was full of trade. Men drinking with their shadows, men in a huddle. He did not want to go in and perhaps have to spend hours in the place. He would stroll while he was still free to do so, and he set off, walking away from the water and turning into a narrow street of gabled buildings, part of the city's medieval guts. Through cellar windows he saw backs bent over benches, cutting, sewing. He saw through two windows – the whole body of a house – a garden where men were twisting rope. At the gates of a yard he saw three giants stripped to the waist, their skin blushed blue from some process they were resting from. They watched him as he passed. They looked like men made almost mad by what they did.

He imagined the street would lead somewhere – a market square, a crossroads – but it wound on, blindly, and he was at the point of deciding he must turn back when he noticed, slung above the entrance of a shop some twenty yards ahead, a wooden blunderbuss big as a drummer boy. He went to the window and leaned close. The place looked shut, lifeless, but when he tried the door it opened with the singing of a small bell and he stepped inside.

So little daylight found its way into the shop it took him a while to see how big it was, that it extended back beyond its own rear walls and seemed to burrow into the side of the hill, a sort of cave. Everywhere, there were guns. A rack of Baker rifles (with folding rear sights), a half-dozen Ferguson breech-loaders, a cabinet of assorted carbines – Elliots, Pagets. A second cabinet displayed volley guns of the type intended to clear a room with a single pull of the trigger but more likely to take off the shooter's hand. He was admiring a box of long-barrelled sea-pistols with all their gear around them – powder-flask, flints, wads, patches and greasers – when the gunsmith appeared from the depths of the cave and hung his lantern from a hook over the counter. He was stout, cheerful as a butcher, immediately full of talk, of little courtesies. His shirtsleeves were rolled to the elbows, his forearms hairless and mottled with the scars of old burns.

Lacroix explained what he had and what he wanted.

'Private manufacture or military issue?'

'Military.'

'Tower stamp?'

'Yes.'

The gunsmith moved among his wares, dipped down to open a drawer and lifted out a sacking pouch of shot. He poured some into his hand. 'Bristol-made,' he said. 'Very exact. You won't find better.'

He offered one to Lacroix, who took it and turned its coolness between his fingers.

'The dog's particulars, sir, if you'll allow it. And you'll want some powder too?'

'Yes.'

'If you are content to wait, sir, I can make up some cartridges for you.'

'I will do that myself,' said Lacroix. 'I will have the time.'

'Very proper,' said the gunsmith. 'But they don't all know how, sir. Some of the young gentlemen of the militia. *You* will know, of course. I shall place everything in a little parcel for you, then you shall do it all as you please.'

He made himself busy. As he measured out the powder – a job done on scales by the window, no flickering candle nearby – he said, 'Are you cavalry, sir?'

After a pause, 'Yes.'

The gunsmith nodded, concentrating. 'I can usually guess that right.'

'How so?'

'Many things. The weapons. Also the way a man stands and moves. Infantry officers are always trying to see over the top of something.' He laughed. It was perhaps an old joke of his. Presumably he had a different joke to tell to infantrymen. 'On your way back, are you?'

'What's that?'

'Going back. You've been on leave, I think.'

'Yes,' said Lacroix. 'On my way back.'

'Well,' said the gunsmith, tying off the parcel, 'I wish you good fortune. I'm sure we all do. And with this' – he lifted the parcel with both hands – 'they will not find you undefended. You have the means here to bring down a wall, let alone a man.'

In the Star he found space for himself at one end of a table near a window that let him see the cross-trees of the *Jenny*. A woman came by and he ordered a glass of brandy and water. The man on the bench beside him was dressed in the striped costume of a Scaramouche. He had a drink in front of him but seemed to be sleeping. On the floor, under the bench, Lacroix found part of a newspaper. It was two weeks old and was, in places, damp from spilled beer, but he spread it out on the table and began to study it. Bristol news. The coming and going of ships: *Swallow*, *Briton*, *Hero*, *Kate*. The sale of goods, the sale of land. A patented method for fattening swine. Over the page (and beneath the strangely exact imprint of a hobnail boot sole) was the story of two women found dead in a room in Bedminster, victims of hunger. No one seemed sure of their names or how long they had lived in the room. Below this was a paragraph describing the stoning of an alderman's house by a mob that had smashed the windows then sung 'Millions be Free' and other revolutionary songs.

The last page of the paper – or the last of what he had – offered news of the larger world. A report of the French entry into Vienna, and in the neighbouring column – the paper so sodden it was mostly illegible – a letter from a gentleman in Lisbon where they were awaiting the return of Wellesley. (*Already we are wearing our summer costumes and broadest brims. Veterans of the last campaign can be seen strolling in the squares of the city with visages almost as pitchy as those of the inhabitants, whilst newcomers from England blink in the sunshine like so many owls . . .*)

The woman came by again. He ordered more brandy. He thought of Lisbon, its roofs and shadows, its beggars, its sudden glimpses of the sea. He remembered the onion loft he shared with Wood. How bored they were, how excited! In the cool of early morning they exercised the horses, winding up a hill out of the city, the clink-clink of a troop of cavalry moving at walking pace between silent houses. For the first time since his father's death he had experienced a simple contentment, one with its roots in the body, in riding and eating and sleeping. Even in dancing, for they were invited several times into the better houses to dance in painted rooms, to dance sometimes on painted floors.

And there was that girl, Lucia de something. Bad teeth, beautiful eyes. Clumsy attempts to communicate. Much laughter. Two dances to the guitar. He had bowed to her like a German when he left the party, said he hoped they would meet again. She might have said something similar. Everybody had a sweetheart then, a girl to mention in conversation. Even Lovall.

When he looked up from the paper he saw the Scaramouche had been replaced by a black man who wore on his head the model of a ship. He was looking at Lacroix – had, it seemed, been looking at him for some time – and the moment their eyes met the man began to speak, though in the din of the place, that low human roar, Lacroix could hear no more than one word in five. It did not seem to matter much. The man was telling a story, the story involved the ship, what had passed on the ship, what he, the storyteller, had suffered. He was a human theatre and this was his performance. His only one? Or did he have other hats, other stories?

Lacroix bought him a drink and another for himself. 'I admire your ship,' he said.

The man held up a finger. He began to move his head so as to make the ship travel an imaginary sea, to make her roll and pitch on the swell. The others at the table heckled him, blew noisily at the little sails. The man was not distracted. He was used to it. He went on, dipping his head, tilting it, until Lacroix, staring at the ship, no longer saw the man's head at all . . .

Once it was over, Lacroix felt in his coat pocket for coins. Their audience – for the show now had become both of them – waited to see what he would give and when he gave it there was laughter, as if the man had cheated him. He did not feel cheated. He shifted closer to the man. He wanted him to start again, wanted this time to try to *hear* his story, for he had some idea it would instruct him, and that if he could gather things – could gather, specifically, the last twelve months of his existence – into a story of his own, he could, if it was demanded of him (when?), provide an account of himself that would satisfy. He would be coherent. He would make sense. Was that not how stories served us? But before it could begin again a child appeared at his shoulder and in an accent that came from somewhere up the country, told Lacroix the *Jenny* would sail within the hour and that Captain Browne wished him to come aboard at once.

He stood, steadied himself against the table. Brandy on an empty stomach. Brandy in the system of a man who was less strong than he had been. He followed the boy outside. The day was bigger than he had left it, more uncontained, more real. He blinked, then noticed the slick surface of the cobbles and realised it was raining. Ahead of him, the boy, on bare feet, was threading the crowd but Lacroix stopped and turned up his face to feel the rain. He was still there, tilt-faced, the skin of his brow and cheeks growing brighter, when he felt his sleeve tugged, and looking down saw it was the man from the Star, his ship now sheltered under an umbrella of tattered yellow silk.

'What?' asked Lacroix.

The man smiled. In his free hand he held out the gunsmith's parcel. Lacroix stared at it a moment as though he could not understand how it had got there, could not understand at all. Then he took the parcel and placed it under his coat to keep it dry.

'Thank you,' he said.

TWO

4

From Portsdown Hill, the wind in their faces, they watched the fleet at anchor. Pennants, flags, here and there the streaked cream belly of a sail. The big ships were constantly visited by boats that fought their way, awkwardly but unerringly, across the swell. Further off, beyond the human work (the flogging of malefactors, the swabbing and coiling, the learning of stars, the difficult Arab maths), rain in columns of faint shadow drifted landwards.

The outing to the viewing place – the trudge out of Portsmouth, the trudge up the hill – was, Medina understood, intended to instruct him, and for the sake of politeness he asked questions about the ships, the town, the history of it all. But Corporal Calley either did not know or did not see fit to trouble himself with answers. They looked out in silence, the Spanish officer of cavalry, the English corporal of foot, both in mufti, both in long horse-coats bought that morning in the Charlotte Street market, until the column of rain advancing up the hill in a series of brightenings engulfed them.

They started down – the sheep-cropped grass, the London

road, then into the town with its low roof of brown smoke, its gangs of sailors in bum-freezer jackets, its herds of cattle aimed at the dockside slaughter houses, the salting rooms, the sea.

Their boarding house was off the High Street. It was called Mrs Cooke's Place, a tall, precarious-looking building opposite a bottle shop in an alley with an open drain down its middle. The house had been Calley's choice. They had come up yesterday from their ship, the *Medusa*, had entered Portsmouth through the pewter light of evening, had found themselves on the High Street, and after walking a little one way and a little the other, had turned into the alley. There had been no discussion. Medina followed where Calley led. Calley was an Englishman, they were in England, it made sense that he should take the lead. Also – more decisively, more troublingly – it was Calley who had the money, the whatever it was Captain Henderson had provided. There was a rule perhaps, a law even, that prohibited British army money being put into the hands of anyone other than a serving member of that army. No one had said so but it was likely. Anyway, Medina preferred to think it so. For his own needs he would have to manage with the shillings he had borrowed at the last minute from an English military surgeon for whom, in Lisbon, he had acted as a translator and go-between in an affair of the heart. Later, Calley might offer him money, something for cigars, miscellaneous expenses, though there was little, after eleven days at sea with him, to suggest that he would.

Their room was on the top floor of the house. They had a view of a bricked-up window, of a ledge where pigeons carried on their ceaseless courting. There was a table, a chair, a bed big enough for two, though Calley made it clear there would be no sharing, that Medina could have the bed to himself. The impression he gave was that a bed – or just lying down – was something for weaker men, men who would, ultimately, come to no good. He spent the night on the chair facing the door, and though he must have slept at some hour, he was awake when Medina closed his eyes and awake when he opened them again in the morning.

They had horse-coats but no horses. They went back to the market to look for someone they might do business with. Calley picked men out. He clearly had a type in mind – watchful men, men who stood, feet apart, like boxers, who, when they spoke to you, looked at you once, made their judgement, then returned their attention to the street behind you. Men like Calley himself. At the third attempt he found one who would serve, a young blood with a branding scar on his cheek, a bristling, pink-eyed dog by his boots. They followed him to a farm, a place that had been swallowed up by the town, the old farmhouse derelict, the field it stood on converted into a waste ground where small fires burned and men and women camped, cooked, hung out their washing and observed the arrival of strangers.

Grazing between the fires were horses, a dozen or so in loose groupings, a pair of foals among them, upright as furniture. The man whistled up a boy. The boy fetched two mares, led them without the use of ropes or halters. Calley walked around them. He did not touch them. The man and the boy and the pink-eyed dog watched him. It took them less than a minute to realise he knew nothing about horses. Medina stepped forward. He ran a hand down the horses' backs, stroked down the backs of their legs.

'Not these,' he said.

'Why?' said Calley.

'This one will be lame in a week. This one is blind in its right eye.'

97

The man denied the blindness but had the boy fetch two more. Of these, one was sound, the other had swollen glands in its neck. The fifth horse was too flighty, the sixth had bad teeth, but the seventh, a bay with one white sock, Medina liked. A good top line, a balanced walk, a steady gaze. He stayed with the horses while Calley went to another part of the field to barter. He talked to the bay, murmured to her, as he had, in better times, whispered to girls through the iron grille-work of windows in narrow Cordovan streets. For tack, there was another man, a hoard of stolen leather tumbled out of sacks on to the grass. They bought what they needed. Medina made the horses ready, kept them calm, then he and Calley rode back to the High Street, found a farrier's behind one of the inns, left the horses there for shoeing.

It was three o'clock when they returned to the boarding house. Time for dinner. The food was served in a basement refectory by Mrs Cooke herself, an elderly woman with red hair, a pipe smoker, who dipped her ladle into an iron pot and dribbled the food into bowls. While they ate she read from the Bible, a large edition with a cracked leather binding that she balanced on top of the empty pot. The company, all of them men, sat in rows, the only sounds the working of their jaws and the language of the Gospels. ('What *is* this?' hissed Medina, pointing with his knife to what lay under a thin shroud of dark gravy. He thought it might be an ear. 'Slink,' answered Calley without looking up. End of conversation.)

The others, when they had finished their food, crossed to the bottle shop, ran there some of them, but Calley did not care for liquor. He had in his pack what he called 'a screw of tea' and with this and water from the basement he made, in their room, his afternoon refreshment.

'Here's something else you don't know about,' he said, when he had done with the fussy work of making the tea, when he had broken off the nose of a little sugar-loaf, then turned his back to hide the tea in some compartment of his pack.

'I know what tea is,' said Medina.

Calley grimaced. 'I'm not talking about if you know what it *is*. I know you know what it *is*. It's fucking tea. That's not what I'm saying.'

Medina understood, of course. Tea, the proper making of it, the knowledgeable enjoyment, was, like British sea power, a mystery a foreigner could only gaze upon, awed and confused, an idiot at High Mass. It was not personal. Medina did not think Calley disliked him, or disliked him particularly, it was simply that he loved his country. Or it was not love he felt, but a feverish insistence that seemed to Medina not easily told apart from despair. The cattle, the buildings, the ships, the clothes, the roads, the food, the sky itself, all were the first of their kind. And at the centre of this tangled passion was the army, or more particularly, Calley's own regiment of foot, whose history he knew from its first being raised in northern shires for the purpose of killing Jacobites. Every battle, every honour, the good colonels and the ones who ought to swing, who ought to be stuck on a fucking pole. When he spoke about the army he was serious, and what he had to say he had considered, on long marches, on long nights squatting at the side of green-wood fires in the rain. Infantry was what counted. Sappers he respected. He did not object to artillery. Cavalry, however, he did not like. Cavalry did not win battles. Cavalry did not know what it was to stand in line while the enemy guns swept away the men on either side of you, made them non-men, butcher's trash. They thought war was a fox hunt. They were barely soldiers at all.

To amuse himself, Medina sometimes asked Calley his opinion of the Spanish army. In the last two weeks it had become almost a game between them. Medina would ask and Calley would shake his head as though he could not find the loose end of his derision, did not know how to start. When he did begin he was fluent and looked grateful to have a target worthy of his contempt, relieved, though once – they were on the deck of the *Medusa*, the English coast newly in view – he said, 'At least you're not Portuguese,' and this, some while later (he was learning, slowly, to translate this man) Medina understood as kindness.

The next morning when he woke, Medina was alone in the room. He looked quickly to see if Calley's pack was gone but it was on the seat of the chair, arranged there with a casual precision, so he would know, when he came back, if it had been touched.

What was it like to trust no one? Was it wise? Or was there a small file, like a watchmaker's file, that rasped away at the heart until, one day, in the crossing of a street, the middle of a sentence, you ceased to be human at all?

He lay back in the bed, treated himself to a groan. If Calley had flown off like one of those red-eyed pigeons (he could hear them through the window, their sad, mechanical lust) he would be free. Nothing to do but gather his things and walk out, go down to the water, find a ship for Lisbon or Cadiz. Then make his way back to his regiment – or home? Why not? Had he not earned it? A month with his family, two months perhaps; to hell with the war. As for Don Ignacio Alvarez, why should he ever see him again? And if he did, would Don Ignacio even recognise him?

When he was summoned to Don Ignacio's house in Lisbon (or the one he had use of; it belonged, perhaps, to a more powerful man) he had imagined he was about to be thanked for his work at the inquiry, even, conceivably, offered a staff job with the Junta in Seville, aide-de-camp to one of those gentlemen who pretended to run the country while the country's true rulers sat in the Buen Retiro in Madrid, speaking French. He had followed a servant up a flight of marble steps to a room whose windows, twice the height of a man, were shuttered against the midday sun. In the shade of the room there was the glimmer of a chandelier, and above the double doors the gilded dome of a large clock that either ran soundlessly or had stopped. The servant crossed to the right-hand window, opened the shutters. The house was near the water and the light seemed doubled by reflection. Dazzled, Medina looked down at the polished boards of the floor. When he looked up again Don Ignacio was present, had, presumably, been waiting for him in the shadows.

This house we are in, said Don Ignacio (the curtain had risen, the opera had begun), was completely destroyed in the great earthquake of '55. It was rebuilt from its own rubble, all of it, down to the last detail, a perfect replica of what stood before. Is it, then, the same house, or a different one? He cocked an eyebrow, spread his fingers, then, in his gorgeous boots, he stepped towards Medina, close enough to share the scent of the cologne he was wearing. He said he wished they had time to sit down together, drink wine, eat a dish of almonds. Unfortunately he had many, many matters to attend to and he knew the *teniente* would understand. These days he slept in the saddle, his life was not his own. But while Spain lay on the rack what were they supposed to do? Play cards? Sing songs? So, to business. Your thoughts, please, on the inquiry. You may speak quite openly. There is no one here but ourselves.

Medina spoke. He *had* thoughts, but after half a minute Don Ignacio interrupted him. What he wanted to hear, he said, was what the *teniente* thought should be done about it. How was the insult of Morales to be answered?

Again, Medina began to speak; again Don Ignacio cut him off.

I have something for you, he said. An opportunity I can offer only to one I have the most perfect trust in . . .

Medina, after the briefest of pauses, assured him that he was, in fact, that person.

You are of course, said Don Ignacio, or I should not have brought you here. He glanced at the doors, or at the clock over the doors. Now that there was light in the room Medina could see the clock was hours out and must, indeed, have ceased to run. Had it too been rebuilt? Did it mark the hour of the earthquake? But the mere sight of a clock seemed to remind Don Ignacio of his many duties. He touched the point of his beard, possessed for an instant the eyes of a cutpurse in some filthy *posada* in the south, then informed Medina, in three or four sentences, the tone you might use to order your dinner, what exactly was required of him. When he had finished he said, you are astonished. Perhaps you do not think the people of Morales deserve such an effort.

Medina denied it. The people of Morales deserved whatever justice could be found for them. But surely, he said, the French had done as much, and more than once. In Cordoba . . .

Don Ignacio waved him to silence. He looked pained, angry even. Did the young *teniente* think he had forgotten the French? Did he suppose there was a day, an hour, when the names of sacked Spanish towns did not pass through his head?

Medina apologised. Don Ignacio, with a brief closing of his eyes, forgave him. He called Medina by his given name. Strange how powerful it was, in that room, at that moment. You need, he said, only to accompany the one they send. You have only to see that he does what they have promised us.

But can we be certain, asked Medina, that this English officer is the one responsible? Was there not some doubt?

As for that, said Don Ignacio with a shrug, it is for the English to concern themselves with.

A fly came in. It flew a circuit of the room. The men stood, unspeaking, as if waiting to see if it would find its way out again. It did. Medina drew himself up, stood to attention. He asked, formally, that he might be excused this particular honour. His wish, his only wish, was to meet the enemy in open battle, to fight and if necessary, to die for Spain, as so many of his ancestors had (they had not; they had grown white grapes; they had been thin, hardy, long-lived, gentle). He made a little speech of it, concluding with some flattering references to Don Ignacio and to the people he supposed Don Ignacio served. When he finished, Don Ignacio nodded. He glanced again at the stopped clock, then gestured to the tapestry that hung on the wall between the windows. It was very old, Flemish perhaps, and its colours had faded. In places you could make out only the weave.

What do you see there? he asked.

Is it a hunt? asked Medina.

It may be, said Don Ignacio. Or a procession or a wedding party or an army on the march. He smiled. Someone would know. He reached up and touched Medina's cheek.

The honour is yours, he said. If there was someone else who could go, well, that someone would be here now and the *teniente* . . . somewhere else. Anyway, he was only passing on the orders of another. He was only the messenger. Everything had already been decided. Go and come back, he said. Make us proud. Make your family proud. *El honor es tuyo.*

At this (it was a short opera, one act, perhaps a pantomime), the doors were opened and the servant announced a visitor. A

103

woman, of course. Don Ignacio spread his arms. Here was the world again, beating at his door! He smiled once more, then turned away and walked into the depths of the room. Medina bowed to his back. There was no more to be said. Everything had already been decided. He went down the stairs, the heels of his boots clack-clacking on the marble steps, his yellow jacket floating in mirrors that he now saw were riddled with fine cracks as though covered in a film of cobwebs. Outside, in the shade of a flowering jacaranda tree, the English captain, Henderson, was waiting for him. Medina followed him like a lamb. It was the time of day when shadows are more real than the men who cast them.

Though it was tempting simply to stay in bed, to lounge there listening to the pigeons and watching the pale light exhaust itself, Medina decided to dress and go out. Some sense that the world might speak to him, might have something interesting to say. He nodded to Mrs Cooke, who was sitting on the front steps of the house, tamping the bowl of her pipe. He walked out of the alley, crossed the High Street, then picked streets at random until he came out at the shore. He was standing on a wall. Below him was a beach, or rather a shelf of black-veined mud that ended in a fringe of foam and the greasy rumpled green of the sea. A man was down there, sliding over the shining mud on a pair of narrow boards strapped to his feet. He had a sack and into it he placed whatever valuable things he could pull out of the mud, bottles mostly. Medina studied him. There was comedy here but he did not laugh. The sight of this man, who moved over the mud so cleverly, who had found a place, ten yards of stinking foreshore, to make his own, impressed him more than the fleet he had seen from the hill. *This* was the real English genius. This was why, for a hundred years, they would be irresistible. Eventually, of course, they would grow lazy. They would have somebody else strap on the boards. They would become interested in comfort, would lose their barbarian vitality. But for now, everyone else could simply rest in subservience, wait their turn.

He was still watching (the man was trying to tug something large from under the mud, the rib, perhaps, of a drowned colossus) when a woman came up and stood beside him on the wall.

'You look like a nice one,' she said. He thanked her. She was young, ruined. Lie with her and you would wake up with a fever you would not get better from. They talked about the man on the mud. She said he was always out there. She said she thought he would sink into the mud one day or that the tide would catch him.

'Would he not float?' asked Medina.

She said he would, but upside down.

He smiled at her. Even the whores, he thought, are exact, practical. She wanted to know where he was from and he told her. He asked her (for he was longing to ask someone) if she had ever heard of a city called Cordoba, and when she said she could name all the principal towns of Hampshire and Devon and knew the names of three or four cities in India but had never heard of Cordoba, he told her about walled gardens with fountains, the scent of jasmine, about roofs where you lay all the summer night an arm's reach under the stars. He wanted to build a city in her head. After all, she knew what a wall was, a fountain, had seen stars even in Portsmouth, and that was all imagination required, but the day was progressing and the woman had other things on her mind.

'Are we going for a walk,' she said, 'or what?'

Sharing the sea wall with them were two hawkers, one with a basket of yellow flowers, one with a wooden bucket of small flat fish that bubbled and squirmed over each other's bodies. He asked her which she preferred, and after examining both flowers and fish and putting a finger sweetly to her chin, she chose the fish. He bought her a half-dozen. The hawker wrapped them in newspaper. He handed the parcel to Medina who presented it to the woman.

'You will remember Cordoba?' he called as he backed away. She nodded but he had already lost her. Another man was standing in his place on the wall looking out to sea, and the woman, her parcel of fish held like a posy, was slowly approaching him . . .

At the boarding house (he had hoped that finding it again would be difficult, might even be impossible) he went up the bare steps to the room, then paused at the door, five, six seconds, listening to sounds he could make no sense of. Going in he saw that Calley had shifted the table from its place under the slope of the roof to a new position, directly under the window. He was leaning over it.

'Thought you'd fucked off back to Spain,' said Calley, without looking round.

'I considered it,' said Medina. He edged closer until he could see what Calley was up to. In one hand he had a small saw; the other hand held down a gun, a carbine, pressing it to the table. He was cutting through the shoulder stock.

'You're in my light,' said Calley, though the light, what there was of it, came from the other side of the table.

Medina sat on the bed. He took off his boots, his coat. He thought of telling Calley about the man with the boards on his feet, the mud-skimmer, thought he would probably like the story. Instead, he stretched out on the bed and pulled his coat over himself. Within a minute, he was asleep, dropping through the trapdoor of himself and falling, falling, until he came to with a gasp, a shudder. How long had he slept? Half an hour? Longer? Long enough to feel that something had shifted, that in sleep (it had been like a fever sleep, the last of a fever) he had put away resentment and discovered a quality of unhappiness he could, for now, endure.

When he sat up he saw that Calley had finished his work. The gun – one of those English cavalry carbines with a barrel no longer than the distance between a man's fingertips and his elbow – was lying on the table. The room was scented with the oil he had rubbed into the cut wood.

'You would be fortunate to hit the door with such a gun,' said Medina.

Calley nodded. He too seemed to have found a new mood, purposeful but calm. 'I would,' he said. 'If I was standing next to it.'

'Point-blank,' said Medina, pleased to have recalled the expression, one he had learned from English dragoons.

'I will load it,' said Calley, 'with rat-shot. You know what that is?' He held out his hand, a dozen of lead-shot cupped in his palm. 'These,' he said, 'will tear a man like canvas.'

Later he showed Medina the slings he had sewn so he could carry the gun inside his coat. Showed him the gun hidden. Showed him how it came out again.

5

He was seasick from Penarth to St David's Head. Expecting it did not make it any easier. In his sleep, the *Jenny* became the transport to Lisbon. He heard horses whinnying in terror though there were no horses on the ship, and as far as he knew no animals at all other than some hens in a coop on deck. Also, presumably, an untellable number of rats and mice.

He lay in what they had called his cabin, the space between two bulkheads, a curtain separating him from the passageway. He lay on the cot-bed, vomiting into a jug. No one came to visit him, or once – though this too he may have dreamed – the master pushed his head past the curtain in such a manner as to make it seem his head was floating . . .

When the worst of it was over he fell into a deeper sleep, and on waking, pulled on his boots, groped his way along the passage, climbed a ladder to the open hatchway and emerged on to the deck like the devil in a stage play.

The wind was brisk but the sea – grey, scalloped – was calm enough. To the north, a mile or two in the distance, the Welsh coast showed itself in patches of green and grey. It looked, he thought, as if it might be raining there.

He could not see many of the crew; he was not sure how many there were to be seen. The master was standing at the stern rail, staring back along the boat's wake. Same black jacket he had worn at their first meeting, same solid posture. There was a man at the wheel, another sitting at the foot of the great mast, plaiting strands of hemp. The boy who had fetched him from the Star was holding a hen in his arms. He came down the deck with it, speaking to the bird as though to a pet. Then a man with a leather hat – a hat like a horse's nosebag, something medieval about it – appeared up to his waist in the hatchway and took the bird from the boy. He held it by its feet and when he saw Lacroix lifted it up and called something. Lacroix, not quite hearing the words but guessing the sense, called back, 'Yes!' The man grinned and disappeared.

He stayed on deck for what was left of the day, standing just beyond the dark line where the spray landed. Clouds hurried past but the ship herself seemed to get nowhere. He grew cold, cold enough to shiver, though could not quite be bothered to go below and dig out his cloak. He did not mind being uncomfortable. It kept him aimed at the dull miracle of sea and air, of time slipping like honey through muslin.

In the last full hour of daylight, the man with the leather hat thrust his head above the hatch again and beat a saucepan with a metal spoon. He waved the spoon at Lacroix, flourished it like a sabre. Lacroix followed him down into the ship's underworld, past his own cabin, past the entrance to the galley, and into a low room (much wider than it was high) where a table was laid between benches. Here he was left alone, standing behind one of the benches and peering into the room's restless zones of light and shadow. A small cat observed him from the seat of a grand but much battered easy chair, the chair itself lashed to the timber behind it.

'You know you do not know me,' said Lacroix quietly. The cat shut its eyes, withdrew to the edge of the visible.

The master arrived, entering by the door opposite the one Lacroix had come in by. He was followed by the boy, and a few moments later, by the sailor who had been plaiting rope. The master sat on a stool at the head of the table. The sailor and the boy sat on one side of him, Lacroix on the other. The cook, still in his curious hat, brought in a covered dish, set it on the table and swept off the lid. The chicken had been jointed and stewed and laid on a great bed of rice and cabbage. The master examined the food through its steam, nodded his approval, and after a short grace began to spoon it on to the plates in front of him. Lacroix had not eaten since the breakfast at his sister's house. How long ago was that? A day? A day and a half? He was, suddenly, frantic with hunger, and he followed the others' example of beginning his food the moment his plate was passed to him.

'The crew,' said the master, 'will have their usual refreshment. You, sir, might prefer wine or brandy. I cannot answer for the wine. I would suggest the brandy. It found its way on to a Devon beach not long ago. Washed up, I suppose.'

'Brandy then,' said Lacroix.

The master pointed to the cook with his fork. 'Erikson here will keep your score.'

'My . . . ?'

'Of bottles. Your score of bottles.'

The cook left them and returned a moment later, wiping a bottle with his sleeve.

'Will you have some with me, Captain?' asked Lacroix.

'Well,' said the master, chewing his meat, 'just enough to calm a tooth.'

They drank from tin mugs – mugs untellable, thought Lacroix, from the one he had carried with him through Portugal and Spain. Once they had settled their first hunger, the master spoke again.

'Erikson is our cook and purser. By the book he is also a seaman, but we do not let him near the ropes. The boy is Wee Davey. And this here is Crawley.' He gestured to the sailor beside Wee Davey, and such was the room's dimness it was only now, as Lacroix nodded to him by way of greeting, that he noticed the tattoo on his neck. It was a bird, though what type of bird he could not have said. Not an English bird.

'The mate, Mr Berryman, is on watch with Suliman and Fritz. They will be down after us.'

'Are we making good progress?' asked Lacroix. He had anticipated being able to dine alone in his cabin. He had imagined his cabin would be a proper space, perhaps with a small table and some sort of window. But the food and the brandy had greatly revived him and he was not sorry to find himself in company – company that knew next to nothing about him and seemed content to leave it that way.

'We will be in sight of Bardsey Island by the morning,' said the master, 'if we keep this wind. Is that good progress, Wee Davey?'

The boy looked up from his plate. His expression was vacant, the gaze of a halfwit. Then he smiled, and for a second or two his face took on an entirely unexpected beauty, some light-of-God settling on him, and Lacroix was still looking at him when he became aware again of the master's voice. He turned, shook his head, touched one of his ears.

'I was saying,' said the master, raising his voice, 'that Crawley has sailed as far as Greenland. He saw bergs big as Lundy. Every manner of whale.'

'You were on a whaling ship?' asked Lacroix.

Crawley shook his head.

'We might see a whale on our way north,' said the master. 'You would like to see a whale, eh, Wee Davey?'

'So long,' said the boy, 'as he don't see me.' It was unclear if he meant it as a witticism but the master laughed and Crawley grinned at his cleared plate.

With no warning, the ship broke its rhythm, juddered, rolled more deeply. It was not alarming, just enough to slide the dishes a few inches towards Lacroix. He caught his own plate as it teetered at the edge of the table.

The master stood up from his stool. 'The mate will come down now with the others. You can try their company.'

For two minutes Lacroix had sole possession of a gently pitching room that smelled of stewed chicken and caulking tar. Thoughts seeped in; he hardly bothered to attend to them. The usual phrases, a recitation like the reading of General Orders, punctuated by a voice that seemed to cry for help and sometimes did so, unambiguously.

Then a noise of boots – or at least of feet. Three sailors came in, nodded shyly to Lacroix and sat in a line on the other side of the table. One – Suliman? – was as black as the man with the ship on his head in Bristol. Erikson returned with the serving dish. It was heavy again with food, like a magic pot in a fairy tale.

'Mr Berryman,' said Erikson, pointing to the tallest of the sailors. 'Mr Suliman and Mr Fritz.' He served the men, then, with a wink, put another ladleful of the food on to Lacroix's plate.

Now that the master was on deck it was not clear to Lacroix

what the correct etiquette might be. Was he the senior person at the table, or was that Berryman, the mate? He would have offered them brandy but he had been instructed not to. They ate with their heads down, forks in one hand, the other arm curled around their plates. He asked the mate what manner of night it was and the mate said it was fair and likely to stay so. After that he let them be. He finished his food, swilled down the last mouthful with the brandy left in his mug, put the bottle in his pocket, excused himself, and made his way cautiously over the uncertain floor to the tied-back door and the passage beyond it.

At the opening to the galley – a room like a large wardrobe, a space Nell would have scoffed at, found useless – he stopped to ask Erikson for some light. Erikson fetched out a candle from the pocket of his apron. The candle had perhaps half its life left to it. The cook trimmed the wick and lit it from the stove with a paper spill. He set it inside a lamp of curved glass, where it faded for a moment then revived. 'No putting us on fire,' he said, holding the light beside the sharpness of his face. 'Ships burn lovely.'

Lacroix carried the lamp to his cabin. He wedged it by the top of the cot-bed and went up on deck hoping for stars, but the night was black and the only meaningful light came from the lantern hanging at the stern. Fifteen feet below him the sea hissed by in darkness, though by leaning over the rail he could see the now-and-then flash or glimmer of spume. He shut his eyes, breathed deeply. One way – the idea coming to him quite clearly though not entirely in his own voice – one way would be to lean a little further over the rail until there was more of him hanging above the water than there was standing on the deck. Then let himself drop. Would they hear? And what if they did? Would they turn about? Start to search for him? Unlikely. Very. And soon the ship and her stern light would be far away. His clothes would grow heavy. He was a poor swimmer at the best of times but in top boots and clothes in a cold sea, the land invisible, and too distant even if he could see it, there would be no chance for second thoughts. The thing would be certain. He thought of what the master would say to William, or what he would write to him from Glasgow. *With deep regret . . . unexplained . . . a most unfortunate accident . . .*

Do drowned men have headstones? Those whose bodies are never recovered? But they might screw a brass plaque to the wall beside the family pew. *Captain John Lacroix of the — Hussars, lost at sea May 1809.* The book of his life would be closed. Nothing to answer, nothing to explain. No more thinking or wishing. No more staring inwards at what shifted like shadows on a wall. He clutched at the rail. He was faint again, might have toppled one way or the other, might have howled (he had heard men howl), but a whip of spray broke over his cheek and the brief salt sting of it returned him to the passing moment, its innocence, its indifference. He tottered back to the hatch, clambered down and went to his cabin. He took the cork from the brandy and drank a deep mouthful straight from the neck. It was nonsense to suppose that drink didn't help. It was how the army functioned. The navy too, no doubt. Strong drink. Copious quantities.

He tugged off his boots, took off his coat and jacket and waistcoat. From the larger of his two bags he pulled out his oiled cloak. He wrapped himself in it, loosely, and lay on the little bed, drawing over himself the blanket he had been issued by way of bedding. It took him an age to warm up. He made a study of the shadows on the wood above him. His nose was damp, his mouth dry. He played songs in his head. 'Soldier's Joy', 'Harvest Home'. He heard a man's feet on the deck, then the sound of the hatch being secured. Behind its smut-grey glass the flame, responding to the change in the atmosphere, the movement of the air, bent at the waist then straightened. The candle would not last much longer. He watched it, the feathered edges of its light, waiting for it to gutter.

When he woke, Erikson was there, or Erikson's ghost. A grey shade with ribbons of daylight on his back. He had a message.

Lacroix listened, grimaced. 'Again,' he said.

Erikson pointed upwards. 'The captain. Wants words in your ears.'

'About?'

'That you will know when you are on the deck. But coffee first.' He held out a bowl.

Lacroix took it and the cook slipped away, the curtain falling behind him. To cool the coffee he added a splash of brandy, emptied the bowl in four gulps, then, finding himself ravenous for light, he dressed, pulled on his boots and fumbled his way to the ladder. The hatch was open, a square like the mouth of a furnace, and he climbed out into a May morning that was cloudless, almost warm, the sea in a dazzle.

He was, to begin with, looking the wrong way – nothing but sea and sky. Then he turned and saw, less than two hundred yards away, a ship, a naval frigate, several times the size of the *Jenny*. Both ships appeared to be sailing, very slowly, in parallel. Perhaps they just drifted with the tide, it was hard to tell. Some canvas up but not much. As he watched, a small boat appeared from around the back of the frigate and started to pull towards the *Jenny*. Four oarsmen, a man at the tiller, another standing, quite securely it seemed, at the bows.

'Something for you to know,' said the master, who had come up quietly and stood just behind Lacroix, close enough for him to feel his breath against the whorls of his ears as he spoke.

'They are looking for men. Most of all they are looking for any who were with them before. So I would ask you, for all our sakes, to forget the existence of Crawley.'

'The sailor with the bird on his neck?'

'He was five years with them and five was long enough. When he had the chance he made himself free. If they find him they'll take him, and we're short-handed as it is.'

'He's a deserter?'

'You might call him a man who has played his part,' said the master, still speaking like a familiar into the lug of Lacroix's left ear. 'One who has done more than most.'

'And is that all they want?'

'If the mood is on them they may take everyone but you, me and wee Davey. They may take wee Davey.'

'There's nothing you can do?'

'We cannot outrun a frigate. Not in this.'

'I mean, nothing you can say?'

'Very little,' said the master. 'Or it might be *you* will think of something.'

The gig had come within hailing distance. The man at the bows shouted for them to put down a boarding ladder. The mate, Berryman, already had one in his arms, a roll of rope and wooden rungs. At a nod from the master he made it fast and tumbled it over the side. They could not see the gig now, it was directly below them. Lacroix looked across to the frigate, her flags shifting idly in the softness of the breeze. She had the look of a vessel that had been at sea a long time. Her black and yellow paint was streaked with greens and browns. All the gun ports but one were shut. From her quarter-deck came the glinting of a spyglass.

The crew of the *Jenny* – everyone but Crawley – stood in a huddle behind the master. Almost too late, Lacroix realised that his own position, a stride ahead of the rest, might cause confusion, and he stepped back, stepped again to the side.

A hat appeared, a head, a face, scowling, flushed from the climb. The blue coat and white waistcoat of a naval lieutenant. He surveyed them a moment, then swung himself over the rail. Three ratings came after him then a midshipman, older than Wee Davey but not by very much. They were all armed with the short swords favoured by the press gangs. Two of the sailors had belaying pins in their belts. The lieutenant had a pistol. He looked the length of the deck, then strode towards them, a man rich with purpose. 'Who is in charge here?'

Captain Browne stepped forward.

'Is this your whole company?'

'Other than the man on the helm.'

'We saw more when we looked at you earlier.'

'No,' said the master, glancing round as if to be sure, 'this is all there is.'

'Where are you bound for?'

'Dumbarton.'

'Dumbarton by Glasgow.'

'The same.'

'And your cargo?'

'Window glass, flint glass, loaf sugar. Some linen. Ten boxes of brass buttons.'

The lieutenant nodded. His face was seamed, the skin of his cheeks mottled with shallow scars. Smallpox.

'And you,' he said, turning to Lacroix, 'you do not look like a sailor to me.'

'I am a passenger,' said Lacroix.

'On a pleasure cruise?'

'I have business in Glasgow.'

'You are in business?'

'Yes.'

'And what sort of business is that?'

'Land,' said Lacroix. 'Rents.'

Briefly, the lieutenant looked unsure of himself. 'You own land?'

'I do.'

'And your name, sir?'

'My . . .?'

'Your name.'

'Lovall.'

'Lovall?'

'Yes.'

'Very good.'

He turned back to the master. 'You will not object, I suppose, if we look below. You and your crew will remain where you stand. Are any of you armed?'

'None of us,' said the master.

'Mr Parks!' called the lieutenant. The young midshipman stepped forward. 'You will keep these gentlemen company. The rest of you with me.'

They walked aft, paused to interrogate Suliman at the wheel, then one by one disappeared through the companionway behind him. The crew of the *Jenny* stood in silence. At the flap of a sail the master and Berryman looked up and frowned. The midshipman glanced at Wee Davey, who grinned back at him, shyly, as if they might now start a game together. The day was utterly benign. The hens clucked in their coop. A gull, more silver than white, circled overhead with barely a flick of its wings. Lacroix studied the frigate (he could not see her name), then, sensing himself being observed and unable to keep himself from knowing if it was so, he glanced round and met the master's gaze.

'I hope, Mr Lovall, you passed a pleasant night.'

'I did,' said Lacroix. 'Thank you.'

He had, until that moment, been unsure whether the master knew his name, his true name. He had not given it himself, he was confident of that, could not remember hearing the master use it, and if William had mentioned it, it might easily have been forgotten. Now, from the master's remark, from the watchful, amused light in his eyes, it was obvious he did know – *had* known – and that at some point it would be necessary to offer an explanation. But what sort of explanation? He could not explain it to himself, was astonished at how easily the fabrication had come to him, as though, in some deep fold of his being, he had been rehearsing it for days.

They waited on the deck the best part of half an hour. The cat, disturbed by the searching, strolled along the scuppers, paused a moment to observe them, then made a nest for itself inside a coil of rope beside the capstan. They waited. There were no sudden shouts or alarms from below. Was it really possible to hide a man on a ship like the *Jenny*? Was there some place they kept ready for just such a moment?

The lieutenant pushed his head above the forward hatchway. 'Mr Lovall?' he said. 'Yes, you sir. If you would be good enough to come with me a moment.'

He went. He did not look back at the others. As he climbed down the ladder he half expected to feel himself seized round the waist, bundled, pinioned. He also knew this was an absurd idea. They were here to find Crawley and he had nothing to do with Crawley. He was a bystander, albeit one who had just stood in the sunshine telling lies about himself.

The curtain to his cabin had been hooked back. There was light from a lamp – not the one Erikson had given him but a larger one they had brought from somewhere else in the ship. The lieutenant, cocked hat under his arm, stood by the cot-bed. On the blanket, laid out neatly, were the contents of Lacroix's bags.

'We do only what the times require of us,' said the lieutenant.

Lacroix nodded. He was looking at his things, wondering which of them might have betrayed him, but of what he could see on the blanket the only object that carried a name was the writing case.

'You are on your way to Glasgow?' asked the lieutenant.

'I am,' said Lacroix.

'To collect rents.'

'Yes. That is part of it.'

'And the rest?'

'The . . .?'

'The rest. In Glasgow. Besides your collecting.'

'I may visit relations. Friends.' The man was forcing him to tell these lies! He was indignant, he resented it. At the same time felt a kind of latitude, childish no doubt, immoral, but not without its own strange appeal. Having mentioned his Scottish relatives, none of whom had existed the moment before he spoke, he instantly saw, in his mind's eye, faint pictures of their homes.

'You play the fiddle, Mr Lovall?'

'So you have seen.'

'In different circumstances we might invite you on board. Our captain is very fond of music.'

'Yes,' said Lacroix. 'Another occasion.'

'And you are well armed.' The pistol was lying on its wrapper of oilskin. It had been placed like an exhibit at the centre of the piled belongings on the blanket. 'It looks like a military piece. Swivel ramrod. Looks like a cavalry pistol.'

'It is.'

The lieutenant waited.

'I was, for a time, with the volunteers,' said Lacroix. 'It was a very local affair.'

'Parades in the market place and such?'

'Exactly.'

'You have fired it though?'

'Fired it? Of course.'

'And you thought to bring it with you? You are going the wrong way, Mr Lovall, if you hoped to meet with the French.'

'Does your frigate hope to meet the French? Up here?'

'We are keeping an eye on the Irish, Mr Lovall. The French come and go but the Irish are always with us.'

Lacroix said nothing. Both men looked at the things on the blanket as if considering making a purchase.

'What can you tell me,' asked the lieutenant, 'about the sailor who is hiding?' He had dropped his voice to ask the question but when he saw Lacroix had not heard him well he spoke up again. He was a man used to pushing his words through weather.

'If we find him we could press the whole crew and tow you into Milford Haven. But if you were to oblige us, Mr Lovall, we'll take just the man himself and leave you to go on your way.'

'You'll not find anyone,' said Lacroix. 'I have seen them all. None is missing.'

'He is known to sail on this vessel. We have knowledge of it. We would have stopped her last time if we had been at leisure to.'

'I suppose,' said Lacroix, 'the crewing of a ship like this must be a casual affair.'

'He's a deserter.'

'A what?'

'A deserter. A runaway.'

'I am sorry to hear it,' said Lacroix.

By the entrance to the cabin one of the boarding party appeared. He was the biggest of them and had to stoop in the passageway. Must spend his life stooping on the frigate.

'Well?' said the lieutenant.

'Nothing.'

'Nothing?'

'No, sir.'

The lieutenant turned back to Lacroix. 'I have your word as a gentleman, Mr Lovall?'

'You do.'

The lieutenant sniffed. 'How's this,' he said. 'We take you all off, sink this ship and see who swims?'

From the deck of the *Jenny* they watched the gig row back. Almost before it arrived, the frigate began to shake out her sails. She steered a few points to the west, gathered speed, eased away from the *Jenny*. The master watched her until there was a good mile between them. Only then did life on board resume. He studied the skies, gave instructions to Berryman, sent Erikson below to make coffee. The men – without Crawley – worked the ropes. Sails were loosed, trimmed, trimmed again. The day freshened. The *Jenny* became a living thing once more, her bows butting a sea dark with cold. For a long while the frigate remained in sight, but she drew steadily away until, between one glance and the next, she was gone entirely.

Several times throughout the afternoon Lacroix readied himself to speak to the master. He would tell him, plainly, why he had given the lieutenant a false name. He would say, for example, that he had found the man impertinent. That, surely, one was not required to give one's *actual* name every time some jackass in a blue coat asked for it. It was a question of one's dignity, one's liberty as an Englishman. Was that not what the war was about? Not trade or national advantage but liberty, which the French pretended to champion but in truth extinguished wherever they went? His lie therefore, was a type of assertion. It was patriotic. Or some such. Something of that. You may call me Lovall or Lacroix, sir, whichever takes your fancy. Then laughing together. Perhaps a handshake? Remarks about the weather, the ship, poor Crawley who must be hiding in the bilges or in the hold with the glass.

How does a man hide behind glass?

In the end he approached the master, found himself treated to that same droll gaze, knew immediately the folly of any attempt at explaining himself, and asked if he might try his pistol at the sea. It had been unused a long time now and he wished to test its action.

'As you like,' said the master.

Lacroix thanked him. He went forward, descended through the hatch, then along the passageway to the galley. He found Erikson there and asked him for a fresh candle. Behind Erikson, peeling a potato over a wooden tub, was Crawley. Erikson pulled another candle from his apron, lit it as before with a spill touched to the flames of the stove. Crawley glanced over. The smallest of nods, then back to his work.

In his cabin, curtain drawn, Lacroix repacked his bags, put them out of the way, and laid the fiddle case on the cot-bed. He took out the fiddle and tilted it in the light of the lamp. There were grey finger smudges on the varnish and these, he decided, belonged to the lieutenant. He wiped the wood with a square of green velvet from the case. The back of the fiddle was sycamore, the grain of the wood like ribbed sand under clear water. He polished until there were no more traces of the lieutenant, then settled the instrument back in its case and took up the pistol.

The fiddle, full of air, had floated in his hands; the pistol was all heft and drag, a dead weight. He raised it, lowered it. With its brass heel it was as much a club as a gun and would, swung hard, fell a man just as surely as a ball would. He squinted into the barrel, felt in it with his fingers, then placed the gun on the blanket and took up the gunsmith's parcel. The parcel had a slit in it through which the lieutenant or one of his men had peeped at the contents. They were lucky they struck no sparks or the day would have ended very differently for them. He drew the string, picked open the knots, smoothed down the paper. As he did so he caught a whiff of powder. His face stiffened, his fingers were still. Then he set to work making cartridges.

He had watched practised men knock up as many as five inside a minute. He was not as quick, nor had there been any need of it. A cavalry officer's principal weapon was his sword. In the case of light cavalry, a sabre, the Le Marchant model, with its leather grip and iron knuckle bow. The pistol, in an action, you might fire once and reload once. It was not like standing in an infantry line firing and reloading until your face was black. In Spain he had discharged the gun perhaps half a dozen times. The first – the only occasion he might actually have hit someone – was after they charged the chasseurs through the snow and morning mist the week before Christmas. After that, two or three shots at enemy patrols to make them wary. The last time was in the mountains, a long way north, a rabbit or hare at thirty yards it would have taken a miracle to hit. There was no miracle.

He folded the cartridge paper, cut it with his clasp knife until he had eight rectangles laid like playing cards on the blanket. He glanced at the lamp, the flame, then opened the bag of powder and the larger bag of lead balls. The first cartridge fell apart in his fingers but the next was a passable success and the third – a neat tube of ball and powder, a loop of thread wound beneath the ball – was one he might have shown to the colonel and won a nod of approval for. When he had finished, he gathered the cartridges together, put one aside, and after looking round for somewhere to keep the remainder, lifted the fiddle from its case again, opened the little lined box that lay under its neck, and stowed the cartridges there. It turned out to be perfectly sized for them.

He half-cocked the pistol and loaded it with the set-aside cartridge. Powder, ball, wadding. Everything pressed home with the swivel rod. When he had primed the pan he went on deck.

It was the first of the dusk, the sky mostly clear, the wind steady from the west. To starboard, the land, though miles off, was picked out with strange precision by the low sun. He knew roughly where they were and that the distance held mills, foundries, towns, whole cities darkening with human population, yet he could see no smoke haze or glint of fire. Only bays and headlands, pristine and fret-like under a sky the colour of irises.

He drew back the hammer to cock the pistol fully, held it at arm's length, then, after a second, brought it back to his chest, barrel to the sky. It seemed wrong somehow to shoot towards the land, even if the ball would only travel a fraction of the distance, and he crossed to the other rail where there was nothing but sea, the flaring sun, an infinite play of shadow on the water. He held the pistol out again. The gun had no sights – it was not that type of gun – and there was, anyway, nothing to aim at but the sun itself. He breathed in, breathed out, slowly squeezing the trigger. Squeezed it a little harder. Felt it start.

6

Tom had just left. He had smelled of the fields, the animals. He had smelled as close as a man can to a May morning. She had made no mention of it, of course, it was too whimsical, but she served him his coffee in one of the cups reserved for the family, one of a set with gilded lips, the porcelain painted with wild flowers. She had not done that before. The cups were old and beautiful and very fragile.

She washed it now, washed away the grounds (that she might have studied to tell her fortune), dried it on her apron and set it back among the others in the dresser.

And what did it matter if they used such things? There was no one else to use them. If she had been a dishonest servant she could sell the place off, cup by cup, plate by plate, the china stuff, the pewter, the silver. Then start on the furniture – the old settle, the tall clock (moon and all). The pictures on the stairs? She did not know who would want them. The women looked worse than the men and the men looked bad enough. As if their wealth had brought them no joy at all.

She could sell the books. The brewing tubs. The clothes! Of

the girls, only Lucy had taken any of her mother's gowns and petticoats. The older girl might only be a farmer's wife but she would wear nothing but what was new. Catch her in the fashions of 1770!

There was one gown – she knew exactly where it was, could go and lay her hand on it now – made of red damask that had faded to the colour of berries stirred through cream. *That* one she would have for herself. She would sit in it – you certainly could not work in such a dress – drinking coffee and chocolate with Tom until they were dizzy. And Tom could wear one of old Lacroix's long waistcoats that had so much gold thread in the front they stood up on their own. And they would keep some of the good glasses to drink some of the good port. And they would keep (the thought a hushed thought even in her privacy) the bed from the great bedroom, its columns carved from some black wood she could only guess at, a tree that had grown in no English forest.

She laughed at herself. The dog observed her, then came closer and pressed his head against her knees.

'You are a mournful creature,' she said. 'You should have gone with your master. He should have taken you with him.'

She went to the meat-safe in the pantry. There was a beef bone in there she had been meaning to make a jelly with but it had been there a while and she wanted to give pleasure to something, if only to a dog. She took the bone from the safe, went out through the kitchen door into the courtyard garden where they grew herbs and where the well was. She held the bone out to the dog. He accepted it very gently and carried it to a corner of the courtyard, a flagstone sheltered by the bough of an apple tree growing on the other side of the wall.

She watched him for a minute then came in, closed the kitchen door and opened the door to the scullery. On the brick floor and leaning against the whitewashed walls were all her brushes and pails, including the chimney brushes. But the chimneys did not need cleaning because there were no fires to fill them with soot. The beds were all stripped, the linen clean, folded, put away in the dark of the cupboards. She lifted the carpet beater from the wall. Dust fell even in an empty house; sunlight excited it. She would carry cushions and rugs outside, some spot that caught the breeze, and she would thrash them. She held up the beater, swished it through the air, much as she had seen John Lacroix swish his sword (a book of drill in his other hand), then she quit the scullery, passed through the kitchen and had stepped into the hall when she saw, through the narrow window beside the front door, a man's narrow face, very close to the glass, staring in at her. She stopped dead. Stood under the clock with the beater in her hand.

The face disappeared. There was a knock at the door, quite soft. It was a knock intended only for her and she suffered a moment of confusion, as if some outrageous knowledge had moved through her, but so swiftly she could not recognise it or say what it had been. She leaned the beater beside the clock, smoothed her apron and went to the door. When she opened it she saw that there were two of them, both in coats and hats, coats too long and heavy for a day like this. The one at the front was shorter, paler. The other hung back.

'Hello, Auntie,' said the shorter man. He stepped past her into the hall.

She did not think to say anything, not even when, with the three of them inside, he glanced towards the lane then shut the door. For a moment they all stood in silence. She had the impression the men were listening. Then the shorter one asked her where the kitchen was.

'Why?' she said.

'Why not?' he said, and though his answer answered nothing she led them there. She might have refused but she didn't. It was like a game in which only they made moves.

In the kitchen the shorter man told her to sit down by the fire. Then he asked the other man to leave them alone and have a wander about the house. She didn't want the other man to go. She fixed her eyes on him, concentrated on him, and at first it seemed he might not go. But the shorter man repeated himself – 'Have a wander about' – and after a shrug, the taller one left.

Perhaps he wasn't taller. Just different. If the shorter man's legs were straighter would he be as tall as the other? She wasted whole seconds on this.

'I didn't want him along,' said the man. 'And he didn't want it either. You can see that. But we do as we're told, eh?'

She started to get up but he waggled a finger and she sat back.

'Your master,' he said. 'I know he's not here because I've been watching the house.' He paused, as if waiting for her to deny it. '*He's* free to come and go. He's got money, horses. All this. What have you got? You haven't even got a husband, have you? I can see you don't.'

He sniffed, dabbed his nose with the back of his hand. 'Slept out last night,' he said. 'Saw a fox. A big one.'

It was warm in the kitchen and he unbuttoned his coat. When he saw she had noticed what he had there he opened that side of his coat like a wing to show it more plainly. 'Don't worry about that, Auntie,' he said. 'We're not using that today.'

She nodded. She touched her knees. She had a story cooked up about somebody coming to mend the roof – coming very soon. She would say that when she heard the knocking she had thought it was them, the workmen. But it was like her tongue had gone to sleep in her mouth. Like she was suddenly a hundred years old. She watched him move about the kitchen, picking things up and putting them down, looking for the thing that was in his mind. She turned away to the window. She pictured the dog in the yard happy with his bone in the shade of the tree. Then she thought of Tom, and imagined him crossing a field, the taste of coffee still in his mouth.

Later, when they could move freely in the house, they studied a painting near the top of the stairs. A cavalry officer with a fox-coloured moustache. He had a scroll in his hand. God knows.

'It is him?' asked Medina.

'It's him all right,' said Calley.

'You are sure?'

'Of course I'm sure.'

'Yet you saw him only once. In the dark. And not close.'

'It's him,' said Calley. 'Can't you see murder in those eyes?'

'There is nothing in his eyes,' said Medina. 'It is not even a good painting.'

'What the fuck do you know about painting?'

'And now he is in Bristol?'

'At his sister's place.'

'And you know how we find it? The sister's house?'

'I do.'

'Then we should leave,' said Medina.

Calley nodded. 'In your España,' he said, 'a house like this would belong to a duke. Here it's nothing special.'

'Where is the woman?' asked Medina. 'The servant?'

'She's all right.'

'Yes?'

'She's having a lie down.'

'Have you taken anything?'

'You what?'

'Have you taken anything?'

'What's it to you?'

'We are not . . .' For a second, in the strangeness of it all, the effortless way he had stepped into a circumstance he could not really grasp, Medina's English deserted him. 'Not *ladrones*.'

Calley started on the stairs. '*Ladrones*,' he said. 'I actually know what that means.'

At the bottom of the stairs he paused to look at the carpet beater beside the clock. It bothered him; it was out of place. He carried it to the kitchen door, opened the door a little, and tossed it inside. Then he buttoned his coat.

7

On the morning of the tenth day they could see the mountains of Arran and in light winds ran towards the mouth of the Clyde. There were more ships now, headed both ways. Many of them the master seemed to know, and though they were often at a distance and far beyond hailing, he nodded to them, as you might to an acquaintance in the street.

At supper that night he came below with a mood of satisfaction on him and drank more of Lacroix's brandy than his usual mouthful. He said, 'Unless we meet with something untoward you will have solid ground under your boots tomorrow. I dare say that will please you.'

Lacroix agreed; he thought it would, but after dinner, alone in his usual place under the shadow of the staysail, looking ahead across a not-quite-perfectly dark sea, he was less sure. He had become used to the *Jenny*, her incurious crew, his bed barely big enough for a child. Life on board was orderly, slightly boring, like life in a barracks. He had become a student of weather, watching rain arrive from miles off. He had played chess with Erikson, had spent entire hours gazing down at the skirt of weed at the water line, noting how soon the movement of the sea escaped the language he had to describe it with.

So the days had propped him up – and even the nights had been tolerable, had not opened beneath him like a trapdoor, as he had been afraid they would. One dream in which he hid like Crawley among the glass in the hold, hearing (a series of shatterings) the lieutenant from the frigate closing in on him; one dream of the Polish lancers – snow, birds, silence. But these were dreams he could bear. Those things he most feared to find himself in the presence of, they had not found him and he was grateful. It was a respite. A chance to gather strength.

Their tenth night was their last. In the early morning, going on deck to empty his pot he saw they were in the river and near enough to the right bank to see the windows of lime-washed cottages, to see washing on a line. Other vessels were closer now and a wave was answered with a wave. Up river, the sky was smudged with smoke but behind them, in the west, the air shone like spring water.

At two in the afternoon, towed behind a pair of tenders, they came into the harbour at Dumbarton. They threw mooring ropes to men on the shore, men known by name and who bantered with the crew as they drew the *Jenny* tight to the splintered wooden lip of the wharf. Sails were rolled, lashed. For an hour the master became a tyrant. Nothing could be done well enough or quickly enough. Then it was over; the master rubbed his face, pressed it hard as though to squeeze from it all fatigue, all care, then turned down the collar of his jacket and went ashore.

Lacroix descended through the forward hatch. He fetched hot water from the galley and shaved in his cabin. He felt unsteady in this new stillness and nicked the skin on his upper lip, bled a little. He thought of his old moustache and whiskers that someone had shaved off in Portsmouth when he was too sick to complain or care. Had they ever suited him? He had been pleased enough when they were first grown, though his moustache was never as bushy as Broadhurst's nor as glossy as Vane's. The colonel, of course, had the best of all. It was, conceivably, why he was appointed colonel – that and the reputed thousand guineas he paid to the Duke of York's mistress. Poor Lagan couldn't grow one at all and transferred to the artillery. Lovall's, as he remembered it, had been very blond, white blond and patchy.

He wiped his face then packed his things, the larger bag, the smaller. He brushed his hat with his sleeve, put on his green coat, took a last look around the cabin, that damp, snug space whose air would carry some faint print of him for a while, an hour or two.

On deck it seemed he had the ship to himself, then noticed Wee Davey and the cat sitting side by side on a gaff, the boy's feet dangling in the air. When the boy saw Lacroix he pointed to one of the houses on the shore, made the drinking gesture. Lacroix nodded, smiled, lifted an arm in farewell. He had settled his accounts, he was free to go, and though sorry not to part more formally from people he had come to have a regard for, he did not wish to make an appearance in the tavern, the conspicuous stranger, the man about whom – it may already have been said – there was some doubt as to his true identity. He walked to the rail. There was no gangway in place and he was looking for where he might best swing himself over when he saw the master crossing the quay back towards the ship. He came aboard at the ratlines and crossed the deck to Lacroix. He had a high colour but seemed sober. Sober enough.

'You want to get on to the city, I suppose.'

'If I can. Might I walk the distance?'

The master frowned. 'You are still not thinking like a seaman. No, no. We will find someone to take you up the water. There is a cousin of my late wife's who will do it for a shilling or two.'

'You are married?'

'My *late* wife.'

'Ah. I am sorry.'

'And you?'

'A wife? No.'

The master nodded. It was already more than they had disclosed to each other throughout the entire journey. 'Well,' he said, 'if you do not have a wife you cannot lose one. Will you stay long in Glasgow?'

'My hope is to get out to the islands,' said Lacroix.

'You know the islands?'

'Only what I have read.'

'It would seem the English have a taste for them now.'

'I want to hear the music. Songs.'

'You have your fiddle with you.'

'I have . . .?'

'The fiddle.'

'Yes. It was my father's once.'

'Then I don't doubt you will take good care of it.' The master was looking past Lacroix to where Wee Davey and the cat were sitting on the gaff. 'Have you ever noticed,' he said, 'how like owls they are?'

'Boys?'

'Cats.'

'Yes,' said Lacroix, who hadn't. Even the most sensible people, he thought, have an edge of lunacy to them, like fat on a cutlet. They shook hands.

'There are plenty of boats out to the islands from Glasgow,' said the master. 'Go down to the Broomielaw. You may mention my name. Some will know me.'

The cousin of the dead wife was as lean and silent as a pin. Once he had been paid and Lacroix was sitting on a thwart by the bows, bags at his feet, the man said nothing until the waterway had entered the city and they were almost in the shadow of the Broomielaw bridge. He spoke then, asking a question which, repeated, turned out to be an enquiry as to where Lacroix wished to be set ashore. As they were closer to one bank than the other – the south – Lacroix pointed to some steps there and the man put the tiller over.

From Dumbarton they had sailed the narrowing river through the fading light of late afternoon. Now, on the bridge, the lamp-lighters were at work – half the bridge already lit, half to go. The tide was on the ebb. They slipped past the stern of a larger boat whose keel was already wedged in the mud, and came, gently, alongside the steps. Lacroix clambered out, a little nervous of upending himself on the weed and slick stone. The man passed over his bags, his fiddle, then – wordlessly – pushed the boat back with the blade of an oar and let it glide out into the channel.

At the top of the steps, beside a heaped pyramid of coal, a watchman was busy lighting his stove (he would not want for fuel). No one, it seemed, had noticed the arrival of a stranger, a figure in green, bags in hand, walking up from the stink and complications of the river, though for Lacroix himself the change was everything. For ten days he had been carried. Now he must carry himself. He had been at sea and hidden, like Crawley. Now he was among people again, out in the open.

He walked to the bridge, reaching the roadway just as a troop of cavalry approached, thirty men or so in blue jackets, the horses coming on at a smart walk. He stepped back, watching them from beside the coal. They were dragoons – militia, not regulars – but well turned out, on good mounts. A gang of boys ran beside them and he felt some envy of the men, guessed at the pleasure they took in crossing the bridge, the lamplight rippling off buttons and scabbards. At the same time it was unsettling to come across them so short a time after stepping ashore, as though the whole of Britain had become a barracks. It would be difficult soon to be of serviceable age and walk about out of uniform without being challenged.

He waited until the woollen comb of the last trooper's helmet was over the brow of the bridge, then slowly followed them. The city ahead was as unknown to him as Lisbon had been. He saw the masts of shipping, the silhouettes of spires, industrial chimneys. Beside the last lamp on the bridge he stopped to look at the houses along the northern quays for a place he might stay. He did not want to find himself in some sailors' rest home or the sort of lodgings where the rooms were had by the hour. The better places, the more genteel, would, he decided, be tucked away, withdrawn a little from the bustle of the waterside. A clean room in a quiet house! Clean bedding, a view of the sky, a bed he could stretch out in. That would do. And when he found such a place he might stay for a week – why not? – come to know the city, write sane and comforting letters to Lucy. (*My Dearest Sister, I have found Lodgings very much to my taste, not at all expensive, and spend my mornings in leisurely strolls during which I discover much that is both charming and instructive . . .*)

He turned into the street immediately behind the quay, walked a hundred yards one way, a hundred the other, tried the next street, then a third. He began to remember how cities can be: places both open and completely shut; places you can move about in freely but cannot always enter. He tried a fourth street. He was growing tired of carrying his bags; he was also very hungry. He paused at a junction thinking he should pick out one of his fellow pedestrians and ask advice, directions, then saw, near the corner of the street diagonally opposite him, an open door between a pair of well-lit windows. A man came out, put on his hat, adjusted it with a vast amount of care, then tottered away, smiling. Lacroix crossed the street behind a nightman's wagon (careful to hold his breath as he did so) and peered in through one of the windows. A smoky room. People sitting companionably at tables. Bottles, dominoes, pipes. There was even the drift of music, though the singer was not in view.

He went in, moving through a maze of jutting knees and drowsing dogs, until he found a place for himself at the end of a bench at the back of the room. He nodded to his neighbour, a man with a pitted, gingery face who, glancing at the fiddle case, made movements with his fingers as if plying a tiny bow across a tiny instrument.

A girl came. She had a squint eye or she was blind in one eye. Lacroix asked for brandy but she returned with something else which, after tasting it and liking it, he decided was whisky. He looked round to see if anyone was eating. No one was. They were drinking and smoking and talking and sometimes they paused to look at the singer, a boy more than a man, who sang pleasantly, songs Lacroix imagined the others all knew.

He held his empty glass up to the girl. When she filled it he asked her about food but she just looked at him blankly and when he repeated the question he could make no sense of her reply, though he thought he had heard it clearly enough. It amused him more than frustrated him. Perhaps he should try speaking to her in Spanish. He had learned a little while they were waiting to go out, the officers passing round a dog-eared copy of Mordente's

Spanish Grammar. Algo para comer, señorita? Tengo mucho hambre. Su pais es muy interesante. Anyway, the whisky seemed to be a type of food and later, at his lodgings, he would send out for something. Oats. A fish. More whisky.

His neighbour, he realised, was speaking to him. He was, at least, leaning forward and working his mouth. Lacroix nodded, said the first things that came into his head. 'A ship! From the south!'

The man grinned. It was a pity, thought Lacroix, that no one was wearing a kilt, that there was not, in fact, any tartan to be seen at all. Even the singer was dressed as he might have been in Bath or Wincanton.

He ordered a last glass of whisky. This time when she served him he asked about a room. Did she know a good place? Somewhere respectable? The questions seemed to irritate her.

'There's nae room here.'

'Somewhere near?'

'Wha?'

'Near here?'

'Aye,' she said. 'Somewhere.'

He paid her, wondering if she would take English coins, if there would be some trouble, but she swept them off the table with barely a glance and tucked them into a pocket beneath her apron.

Outside, he breathed in the chill of the spring air; breathed in too the whiff of a nearby piss alley. Had he seen his way to open country he might have gone there, walked clear of the city and found some sheltered place to lie down under his cloak, sleep out like a hare in its form. But there was only the street, and beyond it the view of another. Nor could he quite remember the way he had arrived. Well, it hardly mattered. He did not know the city well enough to be lost in it. He set off, turned left, left again, traversed a square, walked past the black bulk of a church, past a statue of a warrior on horseback, sword to the sky. A knot of staggering men beckoned to him and he turned into a side street to leave them behind. He had hoped to come to the river again, had expected to. Now, he lost faith in his sense of direction and started to retrace his steps – if the river was not one way it must be the other – but what he began to pass did not seem to be what he had passed by earlier. Where was the statue? Where was the church? Where were the drunken men?

From a narrow street he stepped into a broader one. This new street was lit along one side with a line of lamps, ten or so, their globe heads shedding a blue light like the blue of a spark . . .

'But this is gas!' he said, out loud. In London, on leave, he had seen gas lamps in Pall Mall. Not many. Not many anywhere. None, to his knowledge, in Bath or Bristol. But here, in Glasgow, a little row of them, perhaps experimental!

He went to them and walked beneath them. You could close your eyes and still the blue was there, seeping through the skin or caught under the skin in a blue dissolve. The future, he decided, would be well lit. Light would be a moral force. Gas would do more good in the world than Jesus Christ or Mohammed. Imagine if there had been lights like these that night in Spain . . .

When he opened his eyes there was a woman standing in front of him holding out an orange. Even the orange was blue.

'Do ye want it?' she said.

'How much?'

He did not hear her answer, or he heard it but didn't understand. She had a small, neat face. Freckles. She wasn't smiling but he liked her.

'I'll give you something,' he said. He put down his bags. He had never gone with a woman from the street before though he knew several from the regiment who had, or claimed they had. Wood, for example. Was it wrong? All he really wanted was a bed for the night. He decided he would let the change in his pockets decide. If it was only enough for an orange then the orange would be his supper. If it was more, enough for her, then the decision would be made for him. He was giddy, or suddenly overfull of a sort of vertiginous air. It was the whisky, of course, but also being at the edge of something, a thinning-out at the brink of what he understood or knew. And might it not be exactly what he needed? The breath and skin of another? That. Might there not be immense comfort in it? He reached into his pockets. As he did so he saw her glance over his shoulder and he started to turn, but too slowly. A kick to the back of his right knee and he was dragged down to the ground. The moment he was there he was kicked again, hard, this time in the ribs. He twisted about, he squirmed. He could see a man's legs, his stockings, blue in the blue light, and was stretching for them with some idea of tackling him, getting him on to the ground too, when he was struck from the other side by an assailant he had not even been aware of . . .

They must, while he was senseless, have dragged him away to the unlit side of the street. He had a short dream in which he was lying in the cot-bed on the *Jenny*, rising and falling with the movement of the sea, quite at ease. When he opened his eyes he was on his back with one of his legs in the air, a man tugging off his boot. He kicked out at the man and was immediately kicked himself, though the kicker's aim was poor and rather than the toe of his foot connecting with Lacroix's temple, the sole of the shoe rasped across the skin of his brow. Somehow – rage, fear – he got to his feet, rising up under a heavy rain of blows. He swung at the nearest shadow, connected with the man's neck, saw him stagger backwards. Then the girl was there and he paused. Was she with them, or was she also under attack? He tried to speak to her but she ran at him and tripped him and the kicking began again, kicks from her too, lifting her petticoats to kick more freely, her feet as sharp as pins.

Then they fled, in one movement, like birds.

He stood again, set off in pursuit, running on stockinged feet until he came on them, all three, crouching behind railings. He knocked down the first man to rise and immediately straddled him. What he wanted above all was to hurt him; the whole night had narrowed itself to that, the desire to hurt, to repay the injustice of their actions by striking a face until it was pulp. The man writhed beneath him like a great fish but the others had not abandoned him and now the second man – it might even have been the woman – struck Lacroix with the fiddle case, crashed it into the back of his skull, and sent him reeling.

Hard to know how long he was out for this time. When he came back to himself he was spread-eagled on the cobbles as if they had tumbled him out of an upstairs window. He lay like that a while, not daring to move, then reached for the railings, pulled himself closer and propped his back against them. His mouth was full of blood. He gagged, turned his head and spat it out. Ahead of him, pale ghosts, were his own bootless feet. His money had been in his boots, most of it. Notes from the bank in Bath. Two fives, a ten.

He spat again. That last crack on the head with the fiddle was the one that really hurt. He touched the place gingerly, half afraid to put his fingers into the combs of his own brain. He tried to find it funny that he had survived the war but come to grief in Glasgow, cut down by an orange seller and her paramours. He tried.

The street was deserted. Other than himself, the only visible living entity was a small dog that had settled nearby. He found its presence comforting, and though they were strangers to each other he knew (for he knew dogs) that it had settled there out of some instinct to serve him. He muttered to it, reached out a hand to it, then, troubled by its stillness, looked harder and saw that it was one of his bags. He crawled to it. It was the smaller bag, and beyond it, a yard or two, lying on its lid, was the fiddle case. Had they been disturbed? A window thrust up on its sash, the approach of a carriage? He looked for the larger bag, looked hopefully, but there was no sign of it. So, goodbye to the boat cloak, his buckskin breeches, his shirts, his only pair of spare boots. He could not quite remember what was in the smaller bag – he had repacked everything on the *Jenny* – but he feared it was the less useful part of what he had carried.

I am being punished, he thought. Then, after a dozen seconds during which he considered the wisdom of being sick, he thought, no, but this is how I learn.

Learn *what*?

He made himself as comfortable as he could against the railings. It was hard to tell how much damage they had done, what might be broken. It was hard to attend to anything at all other than the ringing in the air, a sound like a wetted finger around the rim of a glass. And he was drifting into a type of sleep, into blankness, when a voice spoke from a column of night somewhere above and to the right of him. A measured voice. A voice you might imagine belonging not so much to the Good Samaritan as to the Good Samaritan's lawyer.

'Is the man muntered, or is he hurt?'

Lacroix raised his head, looked up. Silhouetted against the line of gas lamps (they burned more feebly now; the pressure was dropping), two men were standing over him. He tensed himself for more kicks but they did not come. Instead, one of the men leaned down with a dark lantern. When he opened the shutter the light shoved at Lacroix's eyes and he turned his head away.

'Can you stand?' asked the man.

'What?'

'Can you stand?'

But before he could answer, before he could make the attempt, he felt hands slide under his shoulders and he was raised up.

'Are you the watch?' asked Lacroix.

'We're the new police,' said the man who had lifted him. 'We patrol about the place. We help if we can.'

'I have been . . . attacked,' said Lacroix. His voice was thick and to his own ears not entirely familiar. 'They took my boots. And my bag.'

'You had another bag?'

'My money was in my boots.'

'People do that,' said the one with the lantern. 'It's why they take the boots.'

'Also,' said the other, 'they want the boots.'

'There was a woman,' said Lacroix. He could not get past the knowledge he had been kicked on the ground by a woman.

'Small one or a big one?'

'She had freckles, I think.'

'Well, we will look for her. You never know.'

They stood a while in silence, as if they had forgotten whose turn it was to speak. 'I need to lie down,' said Lacroix. 'I am hurt.'

'Are you a visitor?'

'A what?'

'A visitor?'

'Yes.'

'You won't think much of the place now.'

'Can you take me somewhere?' asked Lacroix. 'Please. I need to lie down.'

144

'It would be best to go somewhere close,' said the man who had lifted him, and who now picked up the bag and the fiddle. 'For the sake of your feet.'

It did not feel close. They walked the length of the street, then the length of the next. They turned down an alley, came out on to a third street, and finally up a dozen stone steps to a door. Beyond the door was a passage. It was lit at the end by a single cruisie lamp on a table.

They sat Lacroix on a stool. After much calling a woman appeared. She was, thought Lacroix, what the police must call a big woman. Between her and the men – who Lacroix now saw were dressed neatly in blue coats to their knees – there was a conversation he did not try to follow, though at some point he became aware they were asking him his name.

'My name?'

'For our records.'

'You keep records?'

'Oh yes. The records are very important. Everything in writing. Now then . . .' His pen, dipped, was poised over the paper.

'Lovall,' said Lacroix.

'Once more?'

'Lovall. Lov-all.'

The policeman wrote it carefully. He had a kind face, a little like the choirmaster's at Wells. When he had finished he showed it to Lacroix. 'Have I got it?'

Lacroix nodded.

The woman led him up the stairs. He was carrying his own things now. He lagged behind her. It was clear she did not want him there, that she had only agreed because the police had asked her. She let him into a room. There was a candle stub on the wooden bed-head, fixed there in its own wax. She lit it for him and left him. He sat on the bed feeling his skull. He started to shake and gripped his own arms, willing it to stop. When it did, or when it was less, he put the fiddle case on the blanket beside him and opened it. The instrument appeared whole, though he would need daylight to tell if the wood was cracked. He opened his bag, rummaged. The writing case was there, and the pistol, though the gunsmith's parcel was not. He closed it, pushed it under the bed. He thought he should take off his boots, then remembered. He got beneath the blanket. The room was cold, as if the building had a season all its own, untouched by May.

He put the candle out with the flat of his palm. The room folded around him, darkness like the heaping of cinders, grey ash. He started to whisper the Lord's Prayer but broke off at 'forgive us our trespasses' to listen to the sounds from the room next door. A rhythmic tapping against the partition wall, a woman's sighs, a man's sighs, a woman's cries, a man's goading. The rhythm built, became a crazy drumming on the wall. The wet slap of flesh on flesh. The woman's cries were delirious, comical, a kind of false singing. In the dark, he filled his chest with air, swelled his lungs, ignoring the pain, and let out a roar, a sound bigger than himself: '*ENOUGH!*'

After a moment of utter silence the house roared back at him.

———◆———

When he woke it was raining. The sound of it, arriving in gusts against the window glass, was like a cool hand on a wound. He listened to it, closely, then he slept again, woke definitively and tried to sit up. He couldn't – certainly not in a single movement. He shifted, tested, negotiated with those parts of himself that were most raw, most intolerant of any disturbance. Eventually he got his legs out of the bed. That was something. He wiped the gum from his eyes, peered at the room, its collection of facts. The night before began to reassemble itself. The girl with the freckles, the blue orange, the feel of his fist against a man's neck, the new police. He looked round for some water. There was none. He looked for a mirror but there was no mirror either. He looked for his boots and cursed himself.

To begin with he needed to get out of the house. Once he was out of the house he could think of what came next. There would be momentum. He pulled the fiddle case from under the bed, picked up his remaining bag, made it to the door. It would not have amazed him to find it was locked and that he was a prisoner. There had, in the night, been some miraculous communication with his colonel, with others too, news from Spain. But the door was open, there was no one outside it, and he shuffled towards the top of the stairs, went down them like a man of eighty crippled with the ague.

The hall at the bottom had shallows of silvery light on bare grey stone. He had no idea whether or not he had paid for his room.

'Hello?' he said.

There was a door hidden behind a piece of faded tapestry. A woman pushed past it, stared at Lacroix, disappeared, then came back with a cloth in her hand.

'You need to wipe yiself,' she said.

The cloth was damp. He pressed it against his face then worked it around the back of his head, his neck.

He gave her back the cloth. She frowned at it. He asked for a drink.

'Wha?'

He mimed drinking. She nodded, returned behind the tapestry, and reappeared with a tumbler. He assumed she would bring him water but it was whisky, and after struggling to get down the first sip, the liquor finding out all the broken places of his mouth, he was grateful for it and showed with a slow blink, a tilt of his head, that he was.

It was the same woman as the night before, he recognised her now, but her displeasure at him, his existence, seemed to have passed.

'You've nae boots,' she said. She pointed. He grimaced. It was a moment when either one of them might have laughed but neither did. She fetched her shawl, a thing like a fishing net, black and loosely knotted. 'Follow me,' she said.

They went out into the morning. The rain was over but it was hard to avoid puddles and after a while he gave up trying. Several times people stopped the woman to ask what she was doing and who he was, this poor wee man with his swollen face and wet feet. And each time (arms crossed over her bosom) the woman patiently explained while the strangers observed him, shaking their heads, as if sudden misfortune, the mad descent of the wheel, was a truth they understood perfectly well. Then he was off again, the captain of hussars in trust to a woman who led him as she might a child or a dancing bear. Had the circumstances been described to him twenty-four hours earlier they would have sounded absurd, insupportable, yet they turned out to be not quite either.

They came to a shop. In a niche above the door was a plaster head, mouth open, eyes screwed shut. A silent howl. They went in. It was an apothecary's, a druggist's. Strange stinks, glass-fronted cupboards, big brass scales, small brass scales. The woman began a conversation with a much smaller woman whose shop it was or who was minding it. After a few minutes, Lacroix was waved forward.

'You can understand me if I speak English?' asked the small woman. She had an accent. German, Dutch.

He nodded. She sat him on a chair under a window and probed his head. She had him open his mouth and pull up his shirt. She was very thorough.

'You will heal,' she said, when she had finished.

'Yes,' he said. 'Thank you.'

'I will give you something for the pain. Then you must go home and rest. One week in bed.'

'Are you German?' he asked.

'Polish,' she said. 'You know Polish people?'

He shook his head, blinked away the images.

'I will make you something,' she said. 'You have had laudanum before?'

'Lord . . .?'

'Laudanum.' She went to the counter, ducked down behind it and stood again with a large stoppered jar of ruby liquor in her hands. 'I use only Turkish opium,' she said. 'Very pure.'

He watched her decant some of the liquor into a bottle of ribbed glass about the size of his index finger.

'And I add licorice root so it is not so bitter.' She corked the bottle. 'Here you have enough for two weeks.' She brought it to him. He had found in the slit pocket of his coat one of the pound notes he had kept there so as not to have all his money in his boots. The gang had either not searched him or had not found the pocket. He was glad he had done something right. He held out the note to her.

The druggist looked at it. 'She said you had nothing.'

149

'Not nothing,' he said.

She went to look for change. She did not have enough change so made up another bottle of laudanum. 'Now you have a month,' she said.

Some of the change he gave to the woman to pay for his room. He thought she had preferred him when he was destitute. A man with a pound note was perhaps less interesting. She whistled to a boy, one of those who stood about in the street waiting for an errand. She gave him instructions. The boy looked at Lacroix, his face, his feet. 'He will take you to where you can buy some boots,' said the woman.

He thanked her. He did not want her to go. 'You have been kind,' he said. She nodded to him; it was the conclusion of their business together and he watched her walk away, the hunch of her prizefighter's shoulders under the net of the shawl. The boy tugged at his sleeve. 'Yes,' said Lacroix. 'Yes.'

They walked until they came to a square, or not a square but a field with buildings on three sides, and on the open side the masts of shipping. There was a market in progress. Black cattle wandered around quite freely. There were horses, ponies, sheep. Among the animals, among and between the knots of men in deep discussion about the animals, there were stalls selling hats and blankets, tin kettles, knives with carved handles. Also food. He found himself in front of a stall (two planks over two trestles) that sold smoked fish. The fish were split, looked like leather and had a rich savoury reek to them. They were not big. He bought two, gave one to the boy and began immediately to eat the other, scraping with his teeth at the bones, eating the small bones, making his mouth bleed again, swallowing blood and fish and ash. A dozen yards from the fish stall was a whisky tent and he hurried into it. He was in pain; the pain had no novelty now; he wanted it to stop. Inside the tent the ground was churned. No one seemed to mind or notice his bare feet. They served the drink in cups of horn. He shook some drops from the druggist's bottle into the whisky, red swirls uncoiling, dispersing. He drank it and went into the market again. The boy was waiting for him, his fish in his hand. He had not forgotten his errand. He guided Lacroix through a flock of sheep to a structure of canvas and boxes, the sketch of a shop. On top of the boxes were displays of footwear. They were all seconds, thirds, fifths. Farmer's boots, soldier's boots. Some looked as though they had no more than a week of walking left in them.

He was not the only barefoot man among the customers. Another, older, winked at him as though to acknowledge a shared ambition. Lacroix blinked back. The drug was spreading through him like a venom. He was not entirely new to opium, had taken Dover's Powders several times and thought Nell had given him something when he was first back at the house. But this was more complete. Turkish opium. It had its own throb. He stood stock-still, breathed the market in, breathed it out. If he clapped his hands he thought everyone would take to the air like flies from carrion.

He tried on a pair of clogs. He tried on a pair of sheepskin boots he thought Caractacus might have worn. In the middle of the stall he had a vision of his own boots. They were standing, somewhat proudly displayed, on an upturned tea-chest. He reached out for them, touched the leather, the creases. They were his boots. The thieves had not even bothered to brush off the dust from the struggle. He sank an arm inside them but the money was gone. Of course it was gone.

'These are mine,' he said, to anyone who cared to hear. He sat on the box, pulled on the right boot and was about to pull on the other when the stallholder arrived. After speaking at each other for a minute it became clear that the man wanted two pounds for the boots.

'I paid twelve guineas for them in Bath,' said Lacroix.

The stallholder seemed unsure what to do with this information. A surprising move in a familiar game. Another man came up. He was perhaps the stallholder's brother, his twin. They conferred. 'Two pounds,' said the second man. 'Or yi can feck off.'

Lacroix considered mentioning the new police but thought better of it. He was in no position to defend himself, would not survive a second thrashing. He did not even feel indignant. He could see their point of view. He found, deep in the slit pocket, another of the pound notes, added to it some of the apothecary's silver. It was several shillings short of what they wanted but they stood out of his way. He walked. Walking was quite different with boots on. He had been walking *in* the earth, now he walked *on* it. He looked for the boy. He could not find him but found the fish seller again, bought four more of the smoked fish and put them in his pockets. He bought a bottle of whisky in the whisky tent, laid it next to the wrapped pistol in his bag, then set off towards the masts. Groups of animals were being driven in the same direction so that he was often walking in their midst.

Like this he came to the shore where an open boat half the size of the *Jenny* was taking on some of the cattle. A figure in a collarless shirt was overseeing it all. Lacroix approached him and explained what he wanted. The man ignored him; no doubt he hoped he would go away. When he did not go away, when he repeated his request more boldly, more insistently, the man looked round at him, glanced at the fiddle case.

'I can pay you a little,' said Lacroix. 'Though I have had to buy back my own boots.'

The man spoke to another on the deck of the boat. At first Lacroix imagined he was mishearing English, or mishearing Scots, then realised it was what he had heard the Highland soldiers singing on the march into Spain. Erse. Gaelic. He smiled at the man. Though the drug had not made the pain go away it had made him cease to care about it much.

'I will try to learn your language,' he said. 'And I have brought my own food.'

The man tipped his head. It was not clear what had been agreed between them, if anything, but Lacroix followed the last tail, the last shitty backside down the planks, was not shouted at or ordered back, and so took his place among the gentle shoving of the creatures.

8

He had worked for hours – it was, among other things, a way of testing himself – and he had not gone down to lunch with Lucy. There was an apple on the desk, its flesh pared to a slender, discolouring core, and a last mouthful of cold tea in a dish decorated with a Chinaman lounging in his garden, birds, swallows perhaps, flitting in the air around him . . .

Though it was not yet late the room was growing dark. On the wall, next to the chart of the coast – Bristol Channel to the North Passage – the lithographic face of John Wesley was being slowly buried in shadow. On a May evening he should not need to light a candle until after seven but this afternoon the weather had set in. Rain, the threat of rain, more rain. There had even been a growl of thunder that had made him look up and wonder if the children would be frightened. But he knew that Lucy would tell them a story to soothe them. And anyway, they were probably too big now to be frightened by thunder. If he did not attend to them for a week, if he did not speak with them, if his mind was elsewhere, he found they had changed. The old fears, the old appetites, replaced by new.

He rubbed his temples, renewed his focus on the ledger in front of him. Neat columns. Figures written like scripture, like stitches in a sampler. What he had, what he might get, what was owed, what he owed to others. Also the names of ships, their tonnage, the names of their masters. And at the back of the book, in the secrecy of Byrom shorthand, a collection of intelligences, things seen on the wharfsides at Liverpool, Gothenburg, Memel, Dublin. Rumours about timber or flax or Swedish iron. Who knew his way around the White Sea.

He turned to a fresh page, smoothed it and wrote, upper left, the number of the page and then, across the top, his own name, William Swann. He dipped his pen – then hesitated. In the middle air of the office, suspended there like a web or a picture drawn in rain, he seemed to see his wife's back as he had seen it on the previous night when, standing in the doorway of the dressing room, he had watched her get free of her corset and drag her shift over her head. On the floor by her feet was a basin of water for her to wash herself with and she had sat on the bed and leaned down to it. She had thought herself alone and he had spied on her, his own wife, by the light of the two candles they had carried up from the floor below (a third candle left in glass by the window for her brother's sake). And on the skin of her back – it had taken him a good half-minute to realise what it was – he noticed the marks her corset had left, a print of the lacing eyelets running like two columns of zeroes either side of her spine. He had not seen such marks before. In their marriage now – now and for a long while – he met his wife dressed or in darkness; he was not familiar with her nakedness, certainly not since the twins were born. The marks, a strange tattoo, had startled him. In truth they had troubled him, as though they were a sign he was supposed to read and understand, and he had felt the urge to go to her, to reach across the bed and erase them, perhaps with his mouth. Yet he did not. He could not have said why. It may have been the chasteness of her washing, the way she touched herself with the water. Or else it was worrying about that candle downstairs, burning unattended . . .

He was lost in this, his vision (and how he longed to have a truly *spiritual* vision, something he might share with the minister), when he heard the scrape of the street door being opened and he looked over, angry at the intrusion, and troubled to have it come in the midst of what now felt like a species of idleness.

The door was behind a curtain. The curtain rippled. He heard the door shut. And then a strange thing. He could not be certain of it but he thought he heard the bolt being pushed home.

He stood behind his desk. 'Who is it?'

A man came round the curtain. He seemed to slide round it. A man in a long coat, the coat dark with rain.

'Cats and dogs out there,' said the man, wiping the water from his face. He walked to the desk and stood facing William across its surface.

'Are you come on business?' asked William. The anger of a moment ago had become something else, more guarded.

'I'm looking for someone,' said the man. 'Someone you know.'

What was that accent? London? Something of the north country too. A crossing sweeper's voice.

'Lacroix,' said the man. 'John Lacroix.'

'And who are you?'

'Me?'

'Yes.'

'Henderson.'

'Henderson?'

'That's right,' said Calley. 'I'm Henderson.'

'I do not think I have heard of you.'

'You don't need to have heard of me. What's it matter if you've heard of me? You just need to have heard of Lacroix. Which you have. Because you're married to his sister.'

A pause.

'Are you a friend of his?'

'We were in the army together. We still are.'

'You're a soldier?'

'That's right.'

'You served with him?'

'That's right.'

'In Spain?'

'You ask a lot of questions.'

'It's simply that I have not heard of you.'

'You have now.'

'And you have . . . a message for him? For John Lacroix?'

'I do.'

'Well, then. If you care to give it to me I will see he receives it.'

'Obliging of you. But I need to give him the message myself.'

'Why?'

'It's that kind of message.'

'It is personal?'

Calley nodded. He was looking round the room. He seemed to have lost interest in the conversation.

'That is no obstacle,' said William. 'If you write the message I have wax here you may seal it with. Or if you . . . prefer not to write it . . .'

'You're getting in a muddle,' said Calley.

'There is no muddle.'

'I have to see him.'

'Yes, but why? I don't understand.'

'No,' said Calley. 'I don't think you do.' He was fingering the Moor's head on the desk, a paperweight in brass, a slave's head in truth, the kind of trinket Bristol was full of.

William watched him. As a boy he had once witnessed his father beat a man unconscious for some offence that was never made clear to him, never explained. It was down by the Horse Fair. His father knocked the man down then kicked him until he was still. For two months afterwards, William suffered a great many baffling symptoms – boils, nosebleeds – and when he recovered he began the habit, unbroken to this day, of thinking of his father with active disgust. And yet there was something else, a thing not admitted to, never admitted to – pride. He *liked* that look his father inspired, the way men took care not to vex him, not to hold his gaze too long. He should step around his desk now and show this jacksnape he had no fear of him. He would say something like, I will tell him you came here. I am sure he will know how to find you. Now I have matters to attend to, as no doubt have you. I bid you good day, Mr Henderson. Or just Henderson? He would look at him, stare him down. He was comfortably the taller of the two, nor did he think there was much brawn under that coat. He waited, weighing the moment. The room was full of the sound of rain. No boots in the alley, no voices, nothing of the world.

He sniffed, then stepped around the desk. The instant he came clear, Calley brought the brass head down on the spur of his left hip. Brought it down like a hammer. William dropped to his knees and Calley caught him, pressing a hand over his mouth, waiting for the first wave of pain to pass. Then he spoke into his eyes.

'You want to know who I am? I'll tell you who I am. I am the war. Yes? And today the war has come to you. It has come right into your house and struck you down. Now, it's like I said. I have pressing business with Captain Lacroix and you will tell me where he is. I know who is downstairs. If you don't give me what I want I will make you so as you are no use to her. Then I will go down and be snug with her and she will tell me what I want. She will. You know she will. Are you hearing me?'

William nodded. Tears of pain, tears of outrage, were curling over the skin of his assailant's fingers. Over the skin of a worthless, godless man. Then the hand was taken from his mouth. He dragged in a breath, not deep enough, dragged in another, and began to speak. He gave up everything – or gave up what there was. The ship, the destination, the date of sailing, the likely arrival. He offered to write it down. Anything to get him out of the house.

'I don't need things *written*,' said Calley. He asked about the master of the *Jenny*.

'Browne,' said William.

'Speak up.'

'*Browne.*'

'He has a house or he lives on his ship?'

'A house. In Dumbarton. A town close to Glasgow.'

'Address?'

'He comes to me. But the town is small. He will be known there.'

'You're expecting him back?'

'Not for another month. Longer perhaps.'

'And he'll be in this Dumbarton until he sets off back here?'

'I think so. Yes.'

'Well this is all very tiresome,' said Calley. He bent down to help William stand, walked him round to his desk chair. He looked down at him. He still had the brass head. He turned it in his hands. Seconds passed. Softly, as if intended only for these two men in the privacy of the room, the cathedral bells rang the hour. 'All right,' said Calley. 'This is how it is. I am going to leave a man watching this house. Watching night and day. If I find you have spoken to anybody about my visit this man will come into the house and he will see to you. Then he will see to your wife. Then he will see to your children. Are you following me? I need to know you understand me.'

'I understand,' said William. 'No one will know you were here. I swear it.'

'We have a special liberty, William Swann. The law has waved us through. We cannot be touched.'

He placed the brass head on the desk, stepped backwards and opened his coat so William could see what he had there. Then he buttoned it again, took another stride back, paused by the curtain as if listening for any movement in the outer world, turned, slid behind the curtain, and was gone.

For a long while William stared at the curtain, then he lowered his forehead on to the open page of the ledger. He was sweating; his sweat smudged the ink. When he raised his head there was a smear of it on his forehead, possibly an S. He cursed Lacroix under his breath. The adored brother. The *idle* brother. And no wonder he had looked as he did, a creature like Henderson running him to ground. But to have said nothing! To have given them no warning! Nothing!

He shuddered. He had a killing rage in him, as though his father had woken in him at last, his father's blood. But all too late.

On the steps from the house to the quay the water moved in a living skin and carried what it found: a mussel shell dropped by a gull; the button from a lady's coat; petals the rain had knocked from a cherry tree, one of whose boughs, pink and extravagant, overhung the steps.

Because it was spring rain, there was, behind the premature twilight, the sense of something warmer and brighter, and as Calley reached the last steps and came out on to the quay, a low yellow light broke from between the buildings to his right, and where it settled on things they acquired a curious fragility, as if buildings, ship's masts, a dray loaded with shining barrels, were only leaning into existence for a moment and would, shortly, lean out again, back into what was formless, into chaos.

He looked for Medina. He did not want to stand around on the quay while everyone got a good squint at him. Then his eye was drawn to a patch of colour by the wall of the pub, a yellow umbrella, a black man beneath it wearing a curious sort of hat, and next to him, sharing the shelter of the umbrella, was the Spaniard. Calley tilted his head and Medina crossed to him.

'He was there?'

'No.'

'No?'

'He's fucked off.'

'In English, please.'

'He's gone. North.'

'He knew we were coming.'

'He knew nothing. Knows nothing.'

'Then why has he gone?'

'He's running. But not from us.'

'Someone has warned him.'

'No one has warned him. Who the fuck could warn him?'

'The same who sent us?'

'And why would they do that? Eh?'

Medina shrugged.

'Who's your new boyfriend?' asked Calley.

'My . . .?'

'The cunt with the boat on his head.'

'An actor. A storyteller.'

'Yeah?' Calley looked more closely at the man. He liked stories. Up on Saffron Hill, at the spike, stories were scraps of coloured cotton you pieced together in the dark. If you pieced together enough the world whispered to you.

'So now,' said Medina, 'we have to go to the north. Where I suppose there will be snow.'

'Snow, icebergs. All sorts,' said Calley. 'End of the fucking world.'

By one in the morning, the rain gone, the clouds gone, a cold sky rippling with stars, they reached the old ferry crossing on the Severn at Aust. Their quarry had taken ship but Calley, who did not much like horses, cared for boats even less. A ferry he could manage, and yes, a ship when he had no choice. But a ship, over-hauled, was a trap. Where could you go? He could not swim and would rather hang than drown. So they would travel overland, keep clear of great roads, enter towns and cities only when they had to. They would lose a day or two but they could trust to their own strength rather than the vagaries of wind and tide. It was the way of the stalker, the beater. It was the hidden way. It was the correct way for infantry to advance.

They sat on the hull of an upturned skiff listening to the secret life of the river at night. The first ferry would not come until daybreak. (It would harden out of river mist, water-glare, the boatman, scull-ing, grey as a heron.) A drover arrived; they heard his song long before they saw him. When he noticed them, their silhouettes against the river, he stopped his singing and kept his distance, squat-ting among his cattle. Over on the far bank, by Swansea, smudges of dirty orange fire showed in the throats of furnaces.

9

The Polish woman had said thirty drops or thirty to start with but it was hard on a rolling boat among beasts who skittered in their dung, who danced on their blunt hooves when the boat went about, to measure the drug in any exact way. He put it directly on his tongue, a private rain, bitter despite the licorice. Then a swallow of whisky, mouthfuls of northern air, the public rain, the salt and rot of the sea.

The boat was low in the water; that was her type. You did not look down at the sea, you looked across at it, and with every second roll the foam broke in through the scuppers. To be on the boat was to be without any meaningful shelter. He was up by the bows. The crew – there were three of them – kept mostly to the stern, one on the tiller, the others doing little obvious besides sitting. They knew where to be dry. They sat. They watched whatever they watched, the weather, the birds, an island on the beam, an island ahead . . .

To Lacroix the islands were a surprise – how soon they came on them, how many there were, how close to each other, how varied. He wanted to call back to the sailors – 'Which is this?' – but they seemed unsure still as to whether they had agreed among themselves he was there at all, an Englishman with a torn face eating fish from his pocket. To have called to them would have forced them to acknowledge him. It would, he thought, be indecorous.

And did he really care about the names of the islands? This was the tall one, this the sleek, this the bare, this like something made entirely from light and water. They were beautiful – more so than he had prepared himself for, and it comforted him a little that he had had the sense to find them, the world's scattered edge, that there was in him, perhaps, some trace of a wisdom that could guide his actions.

It stayed light until very late, the dusk a thread pulled taut, blue then silver. Sitting in his place, a lashed barrel on the boat's port side, he took out his fiddle and searched the wood with his fingertips. It had, he decided, survived its night in Glasgow better than he had. He did not even think it was much out of tune. He rubbed the hair of the bow with a nub of rosin and began a prelude by Purcell, but his fingers were cold and he stopped and slid his left hand under the long hair on the flank of the nearest cow. It was snug in there and the animal seemed not to object to his touch. When his fingers were warmed he started to play again. He could only remember the first thirty bars or so, and he played them twice, with a tempo suggested more by the sea than by Purcell. The men at the stern were figures in stone but he felt them attending to him, and for the minutes he was playing there was an enchantment he had hardly known before with music. Perhaps it was only the drug. He didn't care. Let it be so. If so, then good. He played, he finished, he stowed the fiddle in its case, rested the case across his lap. He thought of his old music master at Wells, the room in the cathedral where history slept like a dog. (It was always wintry in there and they had started each lesson with a song to bring the blood to their cheeks, to get them breathing. 'Ah, Silly Soul', that was a favourite. So too 'Awake, Sweet Love', though pitched too high for them.) Then his thoughts moved to his father, to the songs in the books, the wild flowers, and he seemed to see him, a tiny figure, toylike, very distant, coming down the stairs of the house, not to the hall but to the sea . . .

His father had loved him! He had no reason to doubt it. But could that love still touch him? Was love, once given, always possessed? A gift, a quality, you could scatter over your head like sacred ashes when you had need of it?

He had not wept at the funeral. He had sat in the family pew, dry-eyed, while Lucy's nose turned red with blowing and Sarah, on the other side, dabbed with a handkerchief and sighed. Nell had cried. Even *Tom* for Christ's sake (he had seen him quite plainly across the nave in the common pews). Tom who worked the fields, who was paid – what? – one and six a day at harvest, less in other seasons. He had wondered at it during the prayers, had been self-perplexed, made angry even by these displays of grief. Was it vulgar? Was it false? Might it be false? Or was it simply that he lacked something the others had? Some common response, a sense of pity? Was *that* what had happened in Spain? He did not know, he did not know. In his effort to understand he had worn language thin but made it no sharper. He was bitterly tired of thinking about it, thinking and a minute later beginning again with the same bare and terrible facts. That was almost the worst of it, not being able to stop the *thinking*. Or not until the world broke in with hunger, a fist, stars above the sea. Then, for a breath or two, he went free.

In the morning he saw they were closing on an island. Were they going to land? On the shore a small fire showed a meeting place, a welcome party. The sailors worked the boat to within parleying distance, then, in a minute of swift activity, the sails were dropped and an anchor thrown clear. The boat swung and was still. The party on the shore – men and women – walked down to the sea. There were no houses in view, no nearby village. One of the sailors climbed on to the bows and called across in their own language. When he was answered he came down again, took Lacroix by the arm, picked up the fiddle and led him back along the boat, out of the way. He said nothing to him but there was no unkindness in his actions. Then he went among the cattle with the other sailors. They drew one of the animals to the shore side of the boat, and with a sudden movement – a thing they must have done together countless times – they launched it into the sea. Its panic was comical. Whatever it had expected of life it had not expected this. It bellowed. Its eyes were wild. Then, having floundered a while, it discovered itself to be a creature that could survive in this new element and began to swim for the beach. A second animal soon followed, until there were five of them, swimming like dogs, necks straining, heads held clear of the water. At the surf they were met, and, even at a distance, there was something beyond the merely practical in the way they were surrounded and touched, then led towards the dunes.

Another delivery took place towards evening, a neighbouring island. Four animals this time. The people on the shore shouted out to them. The animals struggled through, stumbling out of the sea, hides glistening, streaming. Lacroix thought they might shake themselves as dogs do but they simply stood, patient, good-natured, perhaps already forgetting the sea.

They did not sleep at anchor but spent another night in open water. Lacroix, on his barrel, thought he saw all of it, for the laudanum brought him repose rather than sleep. At some hour, very late or very early, when even the western sky was dark, he fancied himself on picquet duty – the outlying picquet, that uneasy station, tensed between armies, listening for alarms. Later, he saw things etched on the sea. A woman in a white dress turning like a star, then a whale, immense and silent, its black skin slack as a coat. A whale imagined by a man who had never seen one . . .

But he must have slept eventually, for he was woken – or startled into some new sense of himself – by one of the sailors offering him a bannock. He was grateful for it; there was no more fish in his pockets. He washed it down with whisky then studied the land ahead of them, a long island faint as a cloud, or else several islands, like stepping stones, north to south. They sailed towards them for hours. They lost the sun then had it back again. The boat nosed her way through the swell, the prow sometimes shattering a slab of green water so that the spray flew back almost to the feet of the helmsman. The cows ate damp hay. When they looked up, chewing, they were the most resigned creatures on earth.

Late in the day the boat crossed an invisible line and the land at last showed itself for what it was. There was no harbour, no bay, no beach, nothing but walls of streaked rock with white birds rising and drifting like chaff. They were closing on it fast now. Lacroix waited for a change of course but it didn't come. Soon, even he could hear the birds, their incessant calling, could see, with perfect clarity, the sea in a smother around the base of the walls. He looked back at the man on the tiller, at the crew, all of whom gazed ahead as though there were miles of empty ocean before them. Had they gone blind in the night? Mad? Should he warn them? Or were these quiet men, who perhaps he had come upon all too conveniently, not what they seemed at all, but servants of the Furies carrying him to where he could settle his debts in the surf? Then a fold in the wall became a gap in the wall and they were carried through on a surge of current, the way so narrow he could have spun coins from his pockets and bounced them from the rocks on either side.

It was a river, a loch, and no wider at first than its entrance. Then, as they passed a boulder on which a seal was basking, the creature's grey and the rock's almost identical, the banks fell back and they were in a body of water calmer than the sea, the land on both sides low and bare.

The boat glided forward, trailing the faint silk of her shadow. The animals, the few that were left, scented the new air. Lacroix began to see houses, all of them small, all built of the same stone they stood on, some with a scrap of worked ground beside them. The sailors dropped the canvas and swung the anchor over. The boat was lying off a shelf of foreshore, a place strewn with smooth stones and weed. Some score of the island's inhabitants stood there, dun-brown figures, silently waiting. There was a cart and a pony. Also a collie dog that seemed to watch the boat with the same rapt attention as the people.

The sailors gathered at the stern, talking, and though Lacroix could hear only the stone-tap and stray music of their voices (and would not have known their words had he heard them perfectly) he understood they were speaking about him and that his journey was over. One of them came forward, the same he had spoken with at the waterside in Glasgow. Lacroix stood up. 'I'll go ashore here,' he said, 'if you will show me how.'

'You must take off your boots,' said the sailor. He spoke softly. If he had just given an order it had been given in a way that was hard to object to.

Lacroix sat and took them off. The big toes of both feet poked through the filthy wool of his stockings. The man took the boots from him. He made loops of rope about them both, then threaded the rope through the handle of the bag and the handle of the fiddle case. The other sailors came forward now. There were only four of the cattle remaining in the boat. Three of these they put in the water, watched them begin their swim to the shore.

'And this is for you,' said the sailor who had roped Lacroix's things. He tapped the back of the last animal.

'For me?' said Lacroix. He had misheard; or no, he had not misheard. He shook his head, began his protest, but the men were about their business and not interested in what he had to say.

They put a tether round the animal's neck, tied the end to a cleat and heaved the animal over the side. 'Quick now,' said the man.

They lifted him – he must have been light enough after the cows – swept him clear of the gunwales and settled him on the cow's back, his legs in the water to the tops of his thighs. It was cold! The shock of it almost sobered him, it certainly silenced him. Someone hung his gear around his neck, then the tether was freed, the end given to Lacroix as a type of rein, and the cow prodded away from the boat with the point of a boathook. He had, out hunting or on manoeuvres, forded half a dozen English rivers. In Spain he had crossed the Esla on Boxing Day, the French vanguard an hour's ride behind him. But that was on a cavalry mount, on Ruffian, and the horse's hooves had never left the river bed. This was a cow! This was swimming! He gripped the rope, gripped the wide back with his thighs. The possibility of simply sliding off and being dragged down by his own possessions seemed very real and for the first half-minute he was

169

frightened. He urged her on as he would a horse. Behind him, the skirts of his green coat drifted like weed. He heard the rattle of the bottles in his pockets.

On the shore the people were calling encouragement, though more, he thought, to the cow than to him. When she touched the ground she lost her footing a moment, staggered, and seemed she would tip him between her horns, but she recovered herself and step by step lifted them both clear of the water. The collie was delirious. A group of men came down to meet them. Shy, stern, leather-faced men dressed in homespun. They would not look at him directly. He slithered from the animal's back and stood on trembling legs while they led her away. He waited for instructions, for someone to tell him where he should go, where he *could* go, but no one did. He was too strange perhaps, too unexpected. He thought they might not be able to see him in the way they could see the cows, that they would have to go away for a while and imagine him.

He trudged up the landing place on to the track at the top of the bank, turned to wave to the boat (had he paid them anything? He did not think he had), then sat on a patch of yellowish grass looking at his wet legs, his bare toes. He wrung out the tails of his coat, examined the bottles and found them undamaged. He shook some laudanum on to his tongue, took a swallow of whisky. Everything tasted of salt.

The party on the shore were dispersing now. He opened his bag. The leather was damp but the contents dry enough. He wanted something dry for his legs and after a little digging found, rolled tight like a loaf of bread, his nankeen trousers. This was good; he had not been quite sure they were there. He held them, thinking of home, of Nell, the comforts of home, then stood, stiffly, and carried the trousers away looking for somewhere private to change, somewhere out of view of the cottages. One thing to come ashore on the back of a cow, another entirely to make a show of his bruised legs to people he suspected did not, for reasons both moral and practical, do much undressing.

He followed the track. No trees, no convenient rock, the low places all boggy. He kept going. The track handed him forward, curved sinuously to follow the line of the water. The sun was sometimes in his face, sometimes at his left shoulder. He saw no one, no solitary reaper, and the only house he came across was a ruin, its stones scattered, and marks of burning on the timber above the empty doorway. The sight of it disturbed him. He picked up his pace to leave it behind, was relieved when a turning of the track hid it from him.

Now the water narrowed again – gradually, then abruptly – until it was only a stream that he crossed with the help of a stepping stone that lay between two twists of clear water. On the other side he lay down on his belly to taste the water. It was fresh, or mostly so, and he scooped up handful after handful. When had he last drunk anything but whisky and laudanum?

Once he had taken his fill he looked up again – water dripping from his chin, his three-day beard – and saw a hill of russet and purple, a thing on its own rising out of the flat country, conical, steep-sided. He made for it; the old human instinct to be above. The track took him close to the lower slopes, then he set off through young bracken and past the bracken on to brown heather that crackled under his boots. Quick little birds broke from cover. High in the east, something much bigger made lazy, inward-leaning circuits of the cloudless sky. He climbed, listening to the rasp of his breathing. Here and there, standing in the heather, were stones as tall as he was, shaped, he thought, placed there with some intent, their faces blue with the blue of evening.

At the top he found the wind. At first it refreshed him, then it began to burrow into his head. He crossed over and found a place under the brow of the hill, a dent, a ledge, where he could sit and have some shelter. Below him was a view made up as much of water as of land. To the north was another hill, isolated like the one he was on, though much higher. The rest was like a shattered plate with shards of land connected by narrow isthmuses, land that struck him as being more frail than the water, as if it stood only by the water's consent and would, at a time of the water's choosing, be covered again.

He touched his legs, the damp cloth, the cold cloth, then looked, like a lunatic, at his own bare hands. *Where were his nankeen trousers?* He felt about himself, looked back at the hill above him, hurried up there hoping for something pale lying on the dark of the heather. There was nothing. He had dropped them. Or he had put them down when he drank from the stream and had forgotten to pick them up again. He went back to the ledge, sat and held his head. He passionately wanted his nankeen trousers and their loss seemed the loss of his ability to maintain purpose, to act purposefully in the world. He pressed the skin of his face, ground at it with the heels of his palms. For three or four seconds he did not know what he was, and when things returned to him – his true name, his assumed name, his rank, his family, his crime – they came without their old solidity as if, one by one, they were being offered to him in the form of questions. He groaned – though it seemed already the moment for such an expression had passed. He let his hands drop. Below him, the moon was rising, the moon at its first quarter, still very low, one horn resting on the earth, then, as he watched, lifting free. He hoped for poetry, something noble and remembered, but managed only to repeat 'moon', wonderingly, until the word lay on his tongue like a silver penny. But he was calm now, packed away by the drug, by fatigue. Even the realisation that he had left the bag and the fiddle down by the landing place did not enter deeply. The fiddle he had been holding on to like his father's hand; he would do better without it. As for the rest, the pistol, the writing case, somebody would want them.

He rolled on to his side and threw up. Water, whisky. The tincture too, presumably. He waited, trembling, then shoved himself away from the ground, first to his knees, finally to his feet. He was suddenly quite certain that if he tried to spend the night on the hill he would die on it. He would be found up there with a crow on his chest, be buried in an unmarked grave. Or with the name Lovall above him.

He started down. There were people on this island somewhere. He would not ask them for much. Some shelter, a bite of bread. And if they would not open their doors to him (oh, the savages!) he would find a byre and sleep with the cows again . . .

He was halfway down when he saw a point of light, fragile in a fold of dark just beyond the base of the hill. He stared at it, fixed his gaze like a compass needle, then went on more swiftly, more carelessly, sprawling several times full-length in the heather, getting up, finding the light again and keeping going. He stumbled through the ring of bracken, through the roots of things, through shallow water. He smelled smoke, and a minute later he came to a house, the light spilling from a window imperfectly shuttered, and at either end of the thatched roof a chimney, one of them sending its smoke across the face of the moon. And there was . . . yes! . . . singing! He went close, pressed himself against the wall. A voice, unaccompanied. Their own language of course. A wavering voice, husky, wonderfully foreign . . .

He felt his way to the door, groped for a latch, found one, raised it, and walked into the low confusing light of the interior.

There were six or seven of them, sitting in a semicircle by the fire. On stools, on chairs; two, side by side, on a chest. The song broke off. An old dog, blind, white-snouted, growled at him out of its belly. Someone called it back. They looked at him. They were watchful but not, it seemed, much startled. He made a bow to them, which ended unsteadily. For a man who had been out in the air for hours, he felt surprisingly drunk. A chair was fetched. The others shifted back a little to accommodate him. He sat. He did not know if he was in a private house or a tavern of some kind. Certain objects made their presence felt. A great black kettle, a spinning wheel, a storm lantern. In the fire the peat had furred itself in grey and the smell of the house was the smell of the fire.

He took the whisky bottle from his pocket. There was only a mouthful left. He offered the bottle to the man on his left. The man gravely took it, and after pausing a moment, touched the neck to his lips, drank nothing, and passed it back. A square of black bread was put into Lacroix's hand. He dropped it, picked it up. The singing returned or it had never stopped.

He tried to mark time with the bread but only succeeded in dropping it again. The blind dog, he thought, will come for it eventually. It will swim out like an eel.

Did they know who he was? He felt sure that they did, that even if they had not seen for themselves his arrival on the cow they had heard of it. So be it. He was in no condition to pretend, to present himself as anything other than what they saw. Show up like this in an English village and they'd take you to the lock-up, or better still, march you to the parish boundary and put a boot in your arse. Here, presumably, the parish boundary was the sea.

They took it in turns to sing. He wondered if he would have to sing too, if he should, if that would be the correct thing to do. What could he remember? 'As I Walked Forth'? 'Black-eyed Susan'? He was hunting about for words when there was a shifting on the stool beside him and looking over he saw there was a new man there, a man in a red jacket. Lacroix sat up. The man nodded to him. Sandy hair, pale eyes. Twenty-five – no, thirty-five, at least, the skin around his eyes pinched with crow's feet. The jacket had a tartan patch on the elbow (tartan at last!). Yellow collar and yellow cuffs. At the ends of the cuffs there were no hands. The man turned away to the fire. Still looking there he said something, but too softly.

'I cannot hear you,' said Lacroix. 'My ears . . .'

The man spoke again, this time with his face to Lacroix and leaning towards him a little.

'Have you come far?'

Such a simple question yet he did not know how to answer it. He did not answer.

'My name is Ranald,' said the man. 'I live on the island. I am from the island. Do you have a place to sleep?'

'You were a soldier,' said Lacroix.

'I was. From a boy.'

'And your hands?'

'In Egypt.'

A new song began. The singer was one of the women on the meal chest. She appeared elderly, someone's grandmother, but her voice piped like a girl's.

'I have lost my fiddle,' said Lacroix. 'My bag. My trousers . . .'

175

'They are all safe,' said Ranald. 'Can you walk a little?' He stood and moved to the door. Lacroix followed him. After the light in the house he felt blind outside. He took the other's arm and let himself be guided. They walked a mile. Perhaps it only felt like a mile. Other than their own footsteps it was just the night birds and the now-and-then sound of running water, like the playing of small glass bells. They came to a house. It was on its own and loomed out of nowhere. Ranald tapped at the door with his elbow but went in without waiting for an answer. The door was very low. Even men of modest stature – and neither Highland infantry nor light cavalry were tall – could brain themselves going in in a hurry in the dark. Lacroix thought of the grave barrows he had explored as a boy with his father on the Wiltshire Downs. His father's bent back, the dance of the candlelight. It was well known that wild men sometimes slept out in the barrows. Fugitives, curled in the burial chambers . . .

'Through here!'

A passage, a second door. Ranald was kneeling by the side of a fire that burned dully in the middle of the room. He put his face near the ground and blew on the embers until two or three small blue flames appeared.

'The house belongs to an old man you will see in the morning,' he said. 'He is called Jesse. You can stay here. He will not trouble you.'

'In Lisbon,' said Lacroix, 'I slept in an onion loft.'

Ranald nodded. He was spreading straw on the ground. He seemed to manage well enough without hands. He made a bed beside the smouldering peat. The smoke-hole was not directly above the fire-pit and the smoke gathered in lazy wreaths under the roof.

'Here,' said Ranald. 'It is good to rest now.'

Lacroix sat on the straw. Ranald held out a tin cup to him that Lacroix assumed would have whisky in it but it turned out to be water. He drank then lay on the straw. Ranald draped a blanket over him. Like a mother, like a sister. Lacroix spoke for a while though he did not know if Ranald was still there, if anyone was. He shifted himself, writhed worm-like, until he had his face under the smoke-hole and could see through to the sky, a single blue star. The music of the old woman's song went through him like the blood-memory of the sea. He was being handed down, deeper and deeper. For a while he did not dare to shut his eyes, to lose sight of the star. Then he could not fight it any longer and he let himself go.

10

They headed north on tracks, greenways, hollow ways. The river was never far away. If they could not see it they could hear it, or see between the trees the light it carried.

Sometimes they rode side by side; sometimes the way was too narrow and Medina would fall behind a little. The trees were in their first true green. Birds darted to and fro across the track, dark against the green-shine of the new leaves.

The noise of rain on the leaves, an hour in the darkness of a passing storm. Then the light pouring in through a thousand openings, the men's coats steaming, the horses spooked by the flicker of a shadow, by things the men could neither see nor hear.

They bought bread and cheese and cider from isolated farms. They did not steal, did not enter into conversation beyond what was necessary. Now and then they passed others on the road, skilled men with tools over their shoulders, labourers with nothing but a rolled blanket, a stick to walk with. They passed a camp of gypsies – men, women and animals lolling under the trees. A cautious nodding of heads. Some of the gypsies looked closely at Medina, looked as if they might address him.

At a place near nowhere, the woods thick and the track itself seeming to hesitate, they saw the figures of men and boys, slender as deer and as watchful. Calley unbuttoned his coat. They kept the horses going, picked their way through to where the track was plain again, glanced behind themselves.

'Runaways,' said Calley.

'Runaways?'

''Prentice boys. Mill hands. Soldiers. All sorts.'

They slept that night in a dell by the edge of the woods. The night was mild. They slept on their backs, both men mostly silent in sleep, both gently flooded by the air they breathed. When they woke they found themselves observed by cattle. One of these they milked, swallowed down the blood-warm milk then walked the horses back into the woods, two men advancing, the war spooling from their backs like silk.

On the third day, coming out of the woods on to open ground and crossing towards the river – the river broad and brown and lined with reeds and bulrushes – they came upon a body, stripped and spread-eagled in the long grass. They looked down from their saddles, could see no wounds, and though the sound and shadow of their horses did not disturb the man it was clear that he was sleeping rather than dead.

Closer to the bank they found others. Pale men, peeled men, sprawled, delighted by sleep. Soft bodies softly breathing. Not the bodies of farm boys or runaways. Then, from the water beyond the reeds, came laughter, scraps of song. They climbed down from their horses and went to look. Four, five men, swimming and splashing.

After a while one of the men noticed them. He was about their own age but bigger than either of them, shoulders like a grenadier's. He raised an arm in greeting, shouted something neither could make sense of but which made the others laugh. He swam to the bank and waded out on to the curve of river-gravel that served them as a beach. He was as naked as the sleepers in the grass. He stood there, unashamed, as the water poured off him. He welcomed them, called himself Phyrro (though later, Calley would say he had called himself Boy-o like a Welshman). He was, he said, a pilgrim, a traveller, an apostle. He invited them to take off their clothes and come into the water. 'All men are brothers,' he said. 'And the women' – waving his hand towards a group of females who, dressed and red-faced from the heat, were busy tramping the long grass and preparing a camp – 'they are our brothers too.' He grinned endearingly, then turned away and walked his heavy arse back into the water.

For another minute Calley and Medina watched them. Then Medina sat on the grass and began tugging at a boot. 'Even on campaign,' he said, 'there is some resting. Some pleasure.'

Calley made a sound, a little reflex of contempt, but raised no objection. Medina dropped his clothes around him, stepped down on to the gravel. The touch of the river against his bare feet excited him. He laughed and, to the cheering of the other swimmers, threw himself into the deeper water, surfacing again in their midst, his black hair flattened against his cheeks.

Some of the women came to the bank. They were of different ages, though most seemed young. They wore walking boots and dusty-hemmed dresses. They had the practical appearance of camp followers, looked fitter than the men, wore on their faces the cheerful, unfocused smiles of the devoted. They bobbed their heads to Medina, but soon returned their gaze to the large man, to Phyrro.

In the water the men splashed about, swam in circles, said whatever the water suggested to them. The day was warm but the river was cold. One by one they came out and settled themselves in the grass. Medina dried himself with his shirt then spread his shirt over the points of grass. He did not know where Calley was and didn't care. He made a pillow of his coat, slept. When he woke it was cooler and he dressed and joined the others by the fire. The women had made a soup, a broth. They gave him some in a mug. It tasted of herbs, of things picked from the hedgerows and wayside. Later, the brandy bottle came round. Some of the men smoked. There were songs, recitations. The day drained slowly into the river. Phyrro was lying with his head in a woman's lap. His eyes were shut but he was speaking, his life spilling through him as a chain of words. People told Medina their names but they were like stage names – Diodorus, Zeno. None of them, he thought, was real. He gave his own name as Sancho.

Lounging at the edge of the circle, a fullness of ease he had not enjoyed since rooftop *tertulias* at home before the war, he looked across to the river in time to see the flash of a kingfisher, and following the line of its flight, the green ghost of it, he saw Calley standing in the shallows with his trousers rolled. It was hard to say exactly what he was doing other than staring at the water's surface, its skim of golden insects. Then he stepped away from the bank, was still again, and after a pause took another step so that the water was well above his knees. Medina sat up, wondering if he would launch himself out into the river, begin to swim, to float, to sink. But if there was a moment when he considered it, it passed, and he turned and came back clumsily to the bank, clambered out.

Medina refilled his mug with the broth from the kettle. He took it down to Calley, who accepted it.

'All wankers,' said Calley mildly. 'Every one of them.'

'Yes,' said Medina, who did not know the word and thought perhaps Calley had said 'walkers'. Then he saw the bird again, darting from the far bank, as green as a scarab. He pointed but found himself pointing to nothing.

Calley nodded. 'I could drop the big cunt with one punch,' he said.

'Yes,' said Medina.

'Fuck it. Even *you* could.'

Medina thanked him.

'I mean it,' said Calley. 'I think you could.'

They grinned at each other. Calley sipped the soup. 'Why can't they make tea,' he said, 'like normal cunts?'

In the first of the morning, while the others slept on under a veil of river mist, Calley shook Medina awake and the two of them, with no conversation, saddled their horses, mounted them and rode away. Looking back, Medina saw Phyrro standing with his head and shoulders above the mist watching them go. They followed the river bank. The day progressed, grew warm again. As the mist dissolved they saw they were riding through a mile of poppies. Later, as if to restore the world's balance, Calley stole a hen from the yard of a farm they were passing. They cooked it in the dusk, somewhere between Hereford and Ludlow, then spent the night with their backs against trees. As the embers of the fire died down so the light fell from their faces. Owl hoot, fox scream. A smear of stars. Calley with the gun across his knees. Medina remembering the touch of water.

THREE

11

So began his days with the old man. The house was a house but also just the land heaped up – the walls scraped together by giant hands, the roof something birds might have built, the floor a small field of packed earth.

Various dogs that were perhaps the same dog. Various cats likewise.

As for the old man he was a song that came and went. He had his bed in a kind of cupboard, its open side a heavy curtain that at night, drawn, muffled the singing, and in the morning, drawn back, released it into the room again.

All night and all day the fire smouldered. Kneeling, the old man broke the squares of peat into smaller pieces, placed them carefully in the embers, leaned his face down, his skin like sacking, to blow the embers into brightness.

He brought oatmeal, black bread and pieces of fish. He brought once an egg that Lacroix woke to find settled in his right hand, the shell a perfect fit for the curve of his palm. It was like the evidence of something, a proof out of theology. Also just an egg that he cracked on his front teeth, letting the yolk roll on to his tongue.

When he needed to go outside it was a long stagger. The outer world dissolved him. He did his business (wondering if he had the flux again) then hurried back to the dark of the house, lay down on the straw, dragged the blanket over himself. Somewhere down there, ten thousand miles below, a drum was beating. He could feel it through the bones of his back. The drum of the world.

He blabbed to the old man things he had not spoken of to anyone. The lancers in the snow. The man who crawled out of the forest with most of his face slashed off and who lay by their fire with his shirt over his head and was dead by morning. He told him about the killing of the horses at Corunna, the troopers ordered to execute their own mounts. A first order to shoot them, a second order to cut their throats. Both botched.

Did he listen? Could he make any sense of it? Ravings in a foreign tongue? About the rest of it he said nothing. He had no story yet with which to speak about that.

On the fourth or fifth day – the sixth? – he was woken by rain falling through the smoke-hole. It was not heavy and he lay still, letting it put its fingers through his hair. A cold rain with a clear marine smell. When he opened his eyes he saw first the marbled grey of the sky above the thatch, then, turning his head, he saw, close beside him, a pair of narrow boots – laces, eyelets and hooks, the black leather spotted with mud. Above the boots the hem of a dress, a coat. He looked up. A blonde face with ringlets of blonde or even golden hair, was hanging over him. She watched him a while, without much expression. Then her face lifted, the boots turned, and there was nothing but the suggestion of a scent that had not been there before and did not belong to the old man or the fire or the dogs or the rain. He was puzzling over it when another pair of feet came into view, a pair of metal pattens, buckled around shoes. He rolled his head. A darker, plainer face looked down at him, a pinched gaze, a frown. She spoke. He shook his head and she spoke more loudly.

'My sister thought you might be Thorpe,' she said. 'But you're not.'

She moved away from him. He saw Ranald in conversation with the old man. The old man had stopped his singing and seemed suddenly quite ordinary. Then Ranald came and squatted on the ground beside Lacroix.

'Are you fit to ride?' he asked.

There was a pony outside. It looked wily and bad-tempered. With Ranald's help, his stumped wrists, his hooks, Lacroix climbed into the saddle. The two women were there, the blonde one in a blue cloak, the other in a brown coat like a man's coat. It may, indeed, have been a man's coat. Ranald had said they were the Misses something, sisters who lived on the west side of the island. The one who had spoken to him had certainly not sounded local. A southern voice. A city voice? Not, he thought, a gentleman's daughter. Not quite. Even in a reduced condition one recognised such things. Could not avoid recognising them.

They set off. He twisted in the saddle hoping to see the old man, to bow to him, but only a dog remained by the door to watch him leave. He turned back and gave himself up to the journey. Ranald walked by the pony's head. The women, both brisk walkers, stayed several paces to the fore. There was nothing so obvious as a road or even a track but to the women, to Ranald, to the pony itself, no doubt, the way was clear enough.

It was the same bare land he had seen from the hilltop the day he arrived, a heathland of coarse grass and heather, though less broken, less riddled by water. The rain stopped. The wet grass shone. No one spoke to Lacroix and he was grateful for it. He dozed on the pony's back, woke, dozed, and waking a second time saw, through a haze like a heat-haze, the dark blue line of the sea.

As they came closer he caught on the breezes the smell of smoke. It grew stronger and more bitter.

'It's the weed,' said Ranald. 'They are burning the weed.'

He nodded. He remembered William saying something about it, the ash, the residue, sent south and used for industry. Glassmaking. Other things too, he thought. A high value on it.

At a hundred yards it began to make his eyes itch. They mounted the grassed back of the dunes and near the top moved between two trenches where the kelp was burning. On either side of the trenches men and women poked the fires with iron poles. Ranald called a greeting to one who, standing in the bitter smoke, answered him briefly through the cloth over his mouth and nose.

The party descended to the beach. The sand was firm and the onshore wind kept the smoke from their faces. They moved by the edge of the sea, northwards, the pony sometimes choosing to walk in the surf, Ranald, slipping off his brogues, barefoot in the water beside it. The women watched him, then glanced at the sea as if alone or in different company they might have stripped off shoes and stockings and gone in themselves, worn the Atlantic round their ankles like bracelets.

Once or twice Lacroix thought to ask where they were headed but knew he would see it soon enough and that once they were there they would be back in the social world, asking questions, answering them. He supposed he would tell more lies, or more half-truths. He found himself hoping – or not hoping, imagining – they would catch him out, or that on this empty strand they would pass some man who would come close, peer up, and say, are you not Captain Lacroix of the — Hussars? Do you not know your regiment is even now preparing to embark for the Peninsula? That you are looked for at every hour?

And he would reply? I *was* Lacroix of the Hussars. I cannot say, sir, with any certainty, what I am now . . .

'I heard wolves in Spain,' he said to Ranald.

'In Egypt,' said Ranald, 'I saw the Sphinx.'

They passed from beach to beach, climbing the spurs of land between them and descending past boulders and rock-pools, the dark-haired woman taking her sister's arm where the path was steepest. The loudest noises were from the birds. They all sounded angry. And beneath this screeching, the growl of the sea, an old lion licking its paws.

Then it was heathland again, green, brown and yellow. Sheep observed them mildly. Stout lambs butted at their mother's teats. There was no sign of the shepherd, and now they had left the weed burners behind the landscape's only human mark was a white house half a mile off, close to the sea. The pony became purposeful, picked up its pace. The house grew bigger, showed green shutters, a green front door. It was not like the other houses he had seen on the island. It had, for a start, an upper floor and did not have a roof weighted down with stones or a curved end-wall to lean into the wind. It stood almost casually on the bare land, unsheltered from the sea and what it might bring. A place waiting for some once-in-a-century storm to erase all sign of it.

He rode to the green door. Ranald helped him to dismount. As soon as his feet were on the ground he had a violent cramp in his bowels. He gasped, gripped hold of the stirrup. He was afraid he would foul himself, shoot hot crap down his legs, shoot it over the women, over the house, the entire island. He gritted his teeth, swallowed, waited for it to pass, then drew himself up. The women were watching him. He made a remark about the view. How pleasant it was. He had noticed before how men can say quite mild things, even while dying.

But I am not dying, he thought. I have not earned that yet.

Beyond the green door was a small hall, just big enough for coats and boots and hats. Through a second door they entered a larger room. It appeared to run most of the length of the house, had a door at either end, a flight of steep, narrow stairs by the right-hand wall.

Sitting at a table by the window was a man with a thin moustache. He was wearing a bed gown decorated with hieroglyphics, the sleeves rolled back to the elbows. He had a bowl of water and was washing something in it. He looked up and smiled. A pale, intelligent face.

'Not Thorpe then,' he said.

'No,' said the dark-haired sister.

'Cornelius Frend,' said the man. 'At your service.'

'Friend?' said Lacroix.

'Our brother,' said the woman.

'Ah,' said Lacroix. 'Lovall. John Lovall. My apologies for this . . . intrusion.'

'But this is excellent,' said the man. 'We are Frends and you are Lovall!' A look of childish excitement came over his face. He held up what he had been washing. 'Do you want to see what I've got here? Amber beads. We found them yesterday. Ranald and I. Where do you think they come from? Eh? Amber is derived from the resin of trees. There are no trees on the island. None to speak of.'

The woman said, 'Mr Lovall is not well, Cornelius. He needs rest.'

Cornelius wrinkled his nose. 'Emily will look after you,' he said. 'It was your coming ashore on a cow that made us think you might be Thorpe. It's the sort of thing he would have done.'

Lacroix nodded. He looked to the woman, the dark-haired sister. (Where had the other gone?) He expected her to lead him through one of the doors at either end of the room, or perhaps up the stairs. Instead, she went to the tongue-and-groove wall at the back of the room, pushed at it and swung open a piece of the wall the width of five or six planks. There had been nothing to suggest the presence of a door. No handle, no visible hinges. Cornelius laughed. 'It was what decided us on the place. Who does not wish for a secret room?'

Inside, it was ordinary enough. No grotto, no workshop of filthy creation. It was narrow, ran parallel to the large room, had a window looking over the land at the back of the house.

He sat on a chair. The woman came and went. Linen, cushions. A chamber pot! There was a couch under the window that was changed, with some small effort of dismantling, into a truckle bed. She made it up. He watched her, her briskness, her slight clumsiness. Then he pointed to the instrument hanging from a peg at the far end of the room. 'Who plays that?' he asked.

'I do,' she said, tucking in the blanket at the bottom of the bed.

It was not quite a lute or a cittern, not a Spanish guitar, but something like them all. There had been one, all unstrung and in poor repair, in the corner of his music master's room at Wells.

'It's an English guittar,' he said. 'Or is it a Scottish guittar up here?'

She answered him but spoke to the bed. He could not make out the words. When she was finished she stood back from the bed, pushed a lock of hair behind one ear, turned to him. He noticed again the redness of her eyes. It was the smoke from the weed-burning perhaps.

'There are no curtains or shutters,' she said. 'Can you sleep in the light?'

He nodded. For the first time he felt conscious of how he must look. And God knows how he must stink. He wanted to apologise. He would shave, he would wash. Which bag had the soap been in, the Windsor soap?

'We will not disturb you,' she said.

He thanked her. He could not remember her name, then it came to him. 'Emily,' he said.

'Yes,' she said. And for the first time she smiled at him.

———◆———

He slept for a long time and woke to the uncertain light of an hour he could only guess at. He knelt up on the bed, elbows on the window sill. Evening or dawn? He tried to work out which way the window faced, could work out nothing, but slowly the light deepened and he knew it was morning. He felt hollow, bare as the hills. But also rested, easy, without any sharp complaint from the body. He had taken none of the tincture the day before; not much the day before that. He was sober, factual, inescapably present. He was not sure how much he liked it.

He scratched at himself then got off the bed and went to where the instrument hung from its peg on the narrow end wall. An English guittar, a Scottish guittar, the body shaped like an almond, an intricate brass rose over the sound-hole. Ten wire strings. What was the wood? He wasn't sure, though there was tortoiseshell and ivory on the neck. Curious tuning mechanism at the top: no pegs but a brass box with a key like the key to a secret drawer in a desk. Softly, he ran his fingers over the strings, then, his ear almost against the sound-hole, he brushed them again and smiled. The guittar was tuned to play an open chord of C major. Just to touch it was to make something sweet with it.

He had slept in his shirt. Now he pulled on his trousers – the same he had lain in on the old man's straw, that he had come ashore in – pulled on the rags of his stockings, his boots. The door, hidden on the far side, was plain enough on this, the planks painted with a scene of two men on horseback riding on a lane under the shade of trees. The style was loose, amateurish, but also vivid and pleasing, and with a sort of charm to it. He imagined the artist was one of the sisters though he could not decide which of them was the more likely.

He went out into the larger room. It was chilly, cluttered, somewhat shabbier than he recalled it. He saw things he had failed to notice the day before: an old ottoman against the wall, blue silk, frayed in places, worn through; three Turkey rugs on the wooden floor; a branch of antlers nailed above the fireplace. On the table were dishes from a meal the family must have taken while he was sleeping. He chewed on a corner of dry bread then took the stopper from the decanter, sniffed the contents, replaced the stopper.

Which way now? Which door should he choose? He went to the one by the stairs, opened it quietly. On the other side was a small room with a piece of thin cloth tacked over the window. A muddle of boxes, books, clothes. On the bed, most of him buried under blankets, was Cornelius. He was deeply asleep, his mouth slightly open beneath the not-quite-successful moustache. Something like grief in that face. A child in need of comforting.

Lacroix stepped back, drew the door shut, crossed to the opposite door and walked into the kitchen. Here too was the disorder that seemed to characterise these people. Did they have no servants? The table was piled with unwashed pots, and on the brick floor there was enough flour for a cat to have left a trail of paw prints. The cat was still there, drinking the milk that lay in a generous splash beside one of the table legs. It traded glances with him then went on with its lapping.

The door to the outside was open. He stood on the stone step and looked down to the water. A hen appeared, stopped, turned its head a little to study him, now one eye, now the other. Then Emily came, walking from around the side of the house, a clutch of fresh eggs in the curve of her apron.

'It's you,' she said, breaking her step, getting him in focus, much as the hen had done.

'Yes,' he said.

He moved out of her way and she came into the house.

'You have slept a long while,' she said. 'I hope it has done you good.'

He stood, somewhat awkwardly, watching her unload the eggs from her apron on to the tabletop. When she had taken out all but one she let her apron drop, then looked down with a pursed mouth at the broken egg on the floor. The cat shifted from the milk to the egg, floated its face over the mess of it, then dipped its tongue into the yolk.

Emily asked if he was hungry. He said he was.

'There is no need to stand,' she said.

He sat on one of the ladder-back chairs at the table. He watched her take oatmeal from a metal bin, watched her add water to the pot, carry the pot to the range. Then he watched her back, her narrow waist, the flatness of the upper back, the movements of

194

her shoulder blades as she stirred the porridge. Her hair was lifted off her neck and held in place by a painted comb.

He became aware that she was speaking to him, though the only word he heard from her was 'dream'. He said it back to her.

'We talk of our dreams,' she said, turning to look at him over her shoulder. 'Thorpe always insists on it. I dreamed of you. You were dead and then somehow you were alive again.'

'I did not dream,' he said, though even as he spoke he remembered a dream of a frankly amorous character involving . . . who? The squint-eyed girl from the drinking house in Glasgow? Something to do with the way she had tucked his money under her apron . . .

When the porridge was ready, she carried over two bowls, set one down in front of him, kept the other for herself. 'Jane and Cornelius sleep in,' she said. 'Jane needs to and Cornelius chooses to.'

'Who is Thorpe?' he asked.

'Thorpe,' she said, blowing on a spoonful of porridge, 'is a man and no more.'

He ate some of his own porridge. Perhaps he didn't care who Thorpe was.

'There is a community,' she said. 'We are a part of it. The vanguard. Thorpe and the others are on their way to join us. We believe they are. We had intended to go to America but there wasn't enough money so we have come here. Thorpe thinks it is better than America and perhaps it is. Are you staring at me?'

'I am watching your mouth,' he said.

'Why?'

'It helps me to understand you.'

She paused then nodded. 'This is our second summer here. The winter was difficult. Cornelius had a cold from December until March.'

'I suppose the community has rules?'

'We do not eat meat,' she said. 'We do not attend church or chapel. We try to love people, though Cornelius and Jane do that better than I.'

'How is that?' asked Lacroix.

'They know less about people,' she said.

He finished his porridge. He was deeply grateful for it and looked hopefully towards the pot on its tile beside the fire.

'Your bag,' she said, 'and your fiddle. They are in the hall here. Ranald brought them.'

'It was kind of him,' said Lacroix.

'He says you were a soldier.'

'I do not remember telling him so. I am not sure that I did.'

'But is it true?'

'Yes.'

'And now?'

'Now? I don't know.'

'A traveller,' she said. 'A rider of cows.'

'Yes,' he said, smiling.

'Mr John Lovall,' she said.

'I would prefer to be called just John.'

'John then.'

'Yes.'

'You are welcome to stay with us,' she said. 'Cornelius is delighted to have another man in the house. He will take you to his excavation. He will want your views on the origins of the world. He cannot take seriously the thoughts of his sisters on such matters.'

The rest of the morning was given up to correcting his appearance. He took his bag with him down to the water. There was a boathouse there, and by positioning himself at the far side of it he was hidden from the main house, though in such a landscape – all light, open ground and water – any sense of hiding was relative, unconvincing.

He shaved, made his face raw with the blade, then cooled it with the water. He took off his boots, stockings, shirt, glanced over his shoulders and peeled off his trousers. He walked into the water, gasped as it reached his belly, then squatted down, rubbing at himself vigorously. He plunged his head under the water and kept it there until it throbbed. Each man his own baptist. But you couldn't stay long in such water, or he couldn't. He came out and dried himself with his shirt then carried out a cautious audit of his bruises. In places his skin was spoiled paper. Odd streaks and flarings of brown and yellow and green. Amazing no bones had been broken, though he wondered if one or more of his ribs might be cracked. If so, there was nothing to be done about it. He pressed the water out of his hair, tilted his head to clear his ears of the sea.

When he opened his bag he saw that his nankeen trousers had been carefully rolled up and put back in. He dug deeper hoping for a clean shirt, touched the writing case, a waistcoat, a pair of woollen stockings, a neck-stock, the bundled pistol, but no shirt. His shirts were being worn by footpads in Glasgow. The soft linen. The careful stitching. Somehow the thought didn't trouble him much. God knows they were wretched men, a wretched woman with them, but make a jury out of those he had met on the island – the singers in the house, Ranald, these curious Frends – then see who they thought most fit to wear good linen.

He dressed in the nankeen trousers, put on fresh stockings (they felt wonderful), his boots, and finally the old stinking shirt,

197

damp now. He started back for the house but paused to lean an eye against the gap between two boards in the boathouse wall. Inside, like some patient creature in its stall, was a rowing boat twelve or fifteen feet in length, a pair of slender oars resting across the beams above. He could not imagine the Frends in such a vessel, could not at all picture Cornelius pulling at the oars. It had, presumably, come with the house and would stay in there, afloat on shadow, until they left.

He went in through the kitchen door. Emily, on hands and knees, was cleaning the floor. No servants then. She looked up at him. He wondered if he should offer to help her stand but she got to her feet without difficulty. He said he had been down to the sea, hoped he had made himself more presentable.

'You will miss your wild self,' she said. She stepped closer. It was evident to him now that there was something amiss with her eyes. She must, he thought, come close to see me well, as I must have her close to hear her. She lifted a hand as if to touch him, but stopped short. 'Is that shirt wet?' she asked.

He said it was and that he did not have another. He told her, briefly, the reason for it.

'Cornelius's shirts will be too small,' she said. 'But ask Jane if she will allow you one of Thorpe's. She keeps them like relics but you must make her give you one.'

He nodded, bit back the question as to why Jane would have Thorpe's shirts, why she would treat them like relics. 'And where might I find her?'

'She will be in her room upstairs,' said Emily. 'It is the door painted with the dove and the owl.'

He went up. The stairs were almost as steep as the steps up to the hatch on the *Jenny*. At the top was a corridor lit by a window overlooking a patch of garden, the garden enclosed by a stone wall that did not look high enough to keep much out, not even hens.

The first door he came to was a plain white door but on the next he found the owl and the dove. They were, undoubtedly, the work of the same artist who had painted the horsemen in the room below. The dove, he thought, was particularly well done, though there was something farcical in the pairing, the owl too large for the bough, the dove somewhat in love with itself.

He knocked. A voice invited him to enter (he was fairly sure it did), but going in he found the window curtained and the room in twilight. The air was warm, scented, slightly stale. Clothes, some glimmering like flowers at dusk, were heaped over the back of a chair. The bed, twice the size of the one Cornelius had been sleeping in, took up nearly half the room. He could see her head clearly enough, her hair spread over the pillow, one plump arm curled on the covers.

'Your sister,' he began, 'thought you might be kind enough to give me the loan of one of Mr Thorpe's shirts. Just until this one of mine is washed and dried. I was careless enough to be robbed of my bag in Glasgow. The one with the shirts in. But I will return at a more convenient time.'

Her eyes. And the somehow rosy glow of her.

'The bottom drawer,' she said, moving her hand a little to indicate the chest behind the door.

'The bottom drawer?' He went down on one knee, opened the drawer. He reached in, touched gauze, silk, silky things that seemed to cling to his skin. He squeezed the ribs of a corset, got his fingers tangled in small-clothes, in ties, lappets, hooked whatnots. His rummaging released a scent, a more intimate version of what hung in the air of the room.

'Not in here, I think,' he said.

'Try the middle one,' she said.

He tried it, found unpinned sleeves, mob caps, pockets. Finally, thank God, an item that might be a man's shirt. Unless it was one of her shifts. What if it was and he put it on?

He closed the drawer and stood up. 'You have been very kind,' he said. 'And it is only for a day or two, I hope. If there is a shop on the island I might buy some shirts.'

'There is no shop,' she said. 'A pedlar comes up sometimes but there are no shops.'

'I suppose not.'

'Will you ask Emily,' she said, 'to bring up my coffee?'

'To . . .?'

'Bring up my coffee.'

'I will,' he said.

'Are you going to be staying here?' she asked.

'If I may,' he said. 'For a while.'

He left her, took the shirt down to the room where he had slept. The music room, the secret room. He stripped off the damp shirt and pulled on Thorpe's. It was too big – too big by several sizes. He tucked in the tail, rolled up the sleeves. He had thought it might smell faintly of Jane's things, but it smelled of something else, and after sniffing at the arms, the armpits, he realised it must be Thorpe. It was not offensive, though his skin did not feel wholly his own.

He put on his waistcoat (the moleskin) and went back to the kitchen. Cornelius was sitting at the table, shoulders hunched under the hieroglyphic gown. He was sipping something from a bowl. He moved a hand in greeting but did not speak.

'He is a martyr to his teeth,' said Emily. She did not sound particularly sympathetic.

'Your sister,' said Lacroix, 'wondered if she might have her coffee.'

He went out to ramble. He learned that the house was quite as isolated as it had seemed on his arrival. From the top of the nearest hill – not a particularly high one – he could see no other houses, no other human figure in the landscape, though to the south he could see the smoke of the weed-burning and knew there must be people there.

He watched birds, seabirds, some of them big, wheeling on the long grey span of themselves, suddenly swooping. He walked through grasses studded with clover. Down on the strand he found the corpse of a young seal, part devoured. He hurried away from it. He tried to think clearly about his new circumstances, to have a view of himself, a man in another man's shirt stalking about an island he did not, he realised, even know the name of yet. But what *was* there to think? He spoke in a hushed voice to his sister. He told her about the Frends, about the community, the mysterious Thorpe. Later – further on – he woke himself out of deep reverie crying, 'Damn you, Wood!'

It did not take him long to weary himself, and when it came it came suddenly, as if he had been walking hard all day. He hauled himself back to the house, went in unnoticed, pushed at the wrong part of the tongue-and-groove wall and had to work his way down until he found the door. He hurried to his bed, sat on it to take off his boots, thought he would take them off in a while and woke, bewildered and briefly frightened, in a light that slanted into the room from the west. He sat up, felt wild with thirst, and went out to the larger room to find the family sitting at their supper. They looked at him in a way that mixed kindness with something like appetite. These people, he thought, are starved of company. He might not be Thorpe (even in Thorpe's shirt) but he was *someone*.

He sat in the remaining chair, Jane on his left, Emily to his right, Cornelius opposite him. There was a lot of drink on the table – a bottle of whisky or brandy, two bottles of wine. Also a chipped blue jug of water. He filled a glass with water and emptied it, twice.

'We are eating cockles,' said Emily. 'And sea carrot and bread. And this cheese, which does not look pretty, is, we think, almost the nicest we have known. It was made by Jesse Campbell, whose house you were staying at.'

'Then I honour it,' said Lacroix. He served himself, took something of everything. Of the others, only Jane seemed to have much interest in the food. He smiled at her, nodded. She was wearing a spencer jacket over a muslin dress, the jacket red as a soldier's but worn loose, undone.

Cornelius preferred to speak rather than eat. He had put on a waistcoat of green silk with two rows of metal buttons and a high collar. He was excited, slightly drunk. Lacroix, picking out the little bodies of the cockles with a pin, heard clearly about half of what he said but enough to piece together a sort of family history, and one that might have been made no truer by his hearing the other half of the tale. The Frends were Londoners, the children of a man in trade, though one whose true vocation had been teaching some personal and bramble-wild version of the Gospels. They spoke of their father – the sisters adding occasional asides when Cornelius paused to refresh his glass – with a wry, elliptical humour, that seemed to have at its roots more fear than love. The impression was of a great high-coloured puppet, a Mr Punch, spouting Revelation and using his tools more for the disciplining of his children than the earning of their bread. There were followers (tailors, printers, carpenters). Sunday meetings in the parlour, hours of prayer. Visions, trances. Jane was the angel lifted on to a stool to sing the psalms. Emily was valued for her prophetic dreams – 'She made them up,' said Jane; 'I made up *some*,' said Emily – though valued even more for her ability to make two and six feed them all for a week.

'Of course,' said Cornelius, 'they were not called Jane and Emily then.'

Lacroix raised an eyebrow.

'I was Basemath,' said Emily. 'Jane was Tapeth.'

'Tapeth?'

'And Basemath. The daughters of Solomon.'

'You chose new names for yourselves?'

'Not I,' said Cornelius. 'I am unaltered. Original.'

'Thorpe chose our names,' said Jane. 'He said our new names should be like empty boxes. For us to fill as we liked.'

'So you are no longer the daughters of Solomon,' said Lacroix.

'We are Thorpists!' cried Cornelius. 'Phyrronists! Free livers!'

Lacroix tried the ugly cheese. It fizzled on his tongue, tasted briny, rotten, creamy, unaccountably good. He drank a glass of wine. He didn't want anything stronger. He was experimenting with clarity, with time in its ordinary clothes. And he liked these people, liked their company, felt no urge to blur their faces with strong drink.

Through the windows, the day seemed powerless to put itself away.

Cornelius set out in a new direction. He spoke of his excavations, the things he had found in the hill – not the hill behind the house, another, further down the coast. Beads, pottery. He had even found bones, though Emily insisted they were merely the bones of a cow. 'But tell me, Lovall. How is she qualified to tell a man's bones from a cow's?'

'I am as qualified as you are, brother.'

'Thus speaks Basemath!' said Cornelius, raising his arms above his head as perhaps the congregation had once done at their father's prayer meetings. Then he winced and touched, tenderly, the sides of his face.

'Your teeth,' said Lacroix. 'Is there not a surgeon on the island?'

'He will come with me to Glasgow,' said Emily, 'when I go to see Mr Rizzo.'

'How will an eye surgeon assist me?' asked Cornelius.

'He is afraid,' said Jane.

'I am busy,' said Cornelius. 'I am *très occupé*!' He grinned desperately. His teeth looked terrible, even for teeth.

Lacroix turned to Emily. He was trying to follow this. He hoped he was. 'You are to see an eye surgeon?'

'I am to be the patient of Mr Rizzo. At the new hospital in Glasgow.'

'Rizzo was recommended to you?'

'We saw his name in the *Review*. He had penned an article on the poetic eye. I wrote to him.'

'But he is a surgeon?'

'He is eminent.'

'She hopes he is eminent,' said Jane.

'And are you to go soon?' asked Lacroix.

'I shall go,' said Emily, 'while I can still see my way.'

Lacroix nodded. He tried to think of something comforting to say. When nothing came to him he said, 'I am half deaf.'

'I know,' she said. 'It is why you watch my mouth.'

'Enough of this!' cried Cornelius. 'I refuse to be miserable! We shall have music. You be Dionysus, Lovall. My sisters can be two of your maenads. I will be Apollo or some such.'

'What if he does not wish to play?' asked Emily.

Cornelius shrugged. 'Then he has carried his fiddle an awfully long way for nothing.'

Instruments were fetched. A lamp was lit, though it was still not entirely needed. The three musicians – Emily, Jane and Lacroix – moved away from the table, Jane to the ottoman, Emily and Lacroix on their chairs at either side of her. Cornelius, alone at the table, made himself a smoke with tobacco, dried hemp and a quartered sheet of writing paper. The hemp he called 'bang'. They had managed to grow a tolerable good crop of it in the garden last summer.

Lacroix's fiddle was held and admired. When he looked for his rosin in the little box inside the case, he found the cartridges he had made on the *Jenny*. He had forgotten them, and wondered now exactly what he had made them for.

He and Emily tried to tune their instruments to a common pitch. Jane sang notes to help them. After several minutes of turning keys and pegs they declared themselves close enough. Emily played first, something decorative and Italian. Music for a garden, music that might best be accompanied by the scent of jasmine. She played with her eyes closed, her right hand, thumb and forefinger, touching the strings between the brass rose and the bridge. It lasted three or four minutes. When she stopped they applauded her. Fat sparks fell from the end of Cornelius's smoke. He extinguished them with his fingers. He looked happy.

Then it was Jane's turn. She sang with perfect confidence, a voice rising out of her throat with no more sign of effort than an ordinary breath might take, an exhalation. There was no trickery, or trilling or false notes. Something to do with gypsy boys and gypsy girls, their lives under the trees. You could not listen to it without smiling.

Lacroix watched her closely. It is permitted, of course, to watch the singer – nor did he think she was one who would object to being looked at. Was she not used to it from childhood? The girl on the stool, the angel. At some point near the end of the song it suddenly occurred to him – the unbuttoned spencer, the curve of her dress, her full breasts – that she was not merely luxurious of form, but pregnant.

When it came to his own turn he chose the prelude he had played in the boat to the islands, and though it did not sound – would never sound – quite as it had that night at sea, it sounded well enough and they were full of compliments for him.

They tried to find music they all knew, swapped titles, hummed snatches of a tune, settled on 'Greensleeves'. Lacroix carried the melody, Jane sang, Emily played the four, five chords the piece required. Cornelius joined in. He too could sing a little, and for several minutes, as the song spooled out in the dimness of the room, the summer grey, they were self-forgetful and unopposed to the world. Their private histories, the private suffering of their bodies, released them. They escaped their names. Religion and its shamings might never have been thought of. Even their own fates, separate and shared, appeared to them with subtle alterations that altered everything. One more round, one more verse. Pleasure crept up their limbs like hemlock.

Lacroix lifted his bow from the strings. Everyone looked at everyone at once. It seemed possible. And in the silence that followed, the two or three seconds before the weight of 'what next' came in, the music's echo ebbed away towards the whispered beating of the sea, as if for safe keeping.

Cornelius filled his glass and raised it to the musicians. 'The Frends and Lovall,' he said. 'Lovall and the Frends! Is it not perfect?'

12

They crossed the River Mercy and arrived at Liverpool in the rain. The horses needed new shoes and something more to eat than wayside grass. The men were in similar wise – saddle-sore, creak-kneed, in want of stillness, settled air. They worked their way into the quarters of the poor, found a stable in Comus Street and, in the street adjoining, a public house called the Lamb and Fox. They rented a room above the bar, two beds (narrow as those the dead are laid on), a stand with a basin on it, a piss pot under the bed by the door. Hanging from a nail on the wall between the beds was a print in a frame. Medina studied it and after a while decided that it showed Christ's entry into Jerusalem.

Though it was the first night in many they had a roof and a bed, neither man could sleep. Perhaps they missed the speech of trees, the scent of damp earth. Medina lay on his back listening to dogs fight in the street, to the drinkers in the bar below, their attempts at singing. He heard Calley go out. When he came back he brought with him the sour air of the bar, tripped over the end of Medina's bed, cursed. Tempting to ask if they served tea in the bar – tempting but unwise. Medina opened his eyes a little, just enough to peep at the ceiling where points of light coming up between the floorboards made a kind of constellation. He could not see Calley but heard him lie down, and then – the sounds almost lost amid the tireless raging of the dogs – heard him mutter and sigh. Half-words, gasps, hisses. Was Calley starting to feel as he did? That they were fools on a fool's errand? Men who, far from being engaged upon an urgent mission, had been cut loose? He could ask him, whisper across in the dark, invite a confidence. But that too would be unwise. And more likely Calley was simply rehearsing some complaint Medina would hear in the morning, or finishing an argument begun in the bar or some quarrel started years before, the antagonist forgotten but the theme remembered. One of those endless rebuttals that become a man's protest at what he has been given . . .

In some sliver of the night – too late and too early to be easily explained – they heard horses on the street and sharpened at the sound of them, suspended breath. But the horses did not stop and the men settled again, scratched at their skin, picked at their blankets, each man a small wave that broke on the other's shore, each the other's burden, perhaps his comfort. Below them, the last of the drinkers had perfected himself and swum away into the summer night. One by one, the landlady's breath put out the stars.

In the morning they moved on as soon as there was light. The city gave way to brickfields and then to farms, but they could not leave it behind entirely. In every valley they rode through they found the chimneys of mills, or if not a chimney then some building, big as a barracks, where work was going on, the new work that was the labour of crowds.

At one place – a day's ride north – they looked down from their camp in the early morning to see men and women hurrying

through the gates of a mill, five storeys of raw brick that straddled the shining wire of a stream in the crease of the valley.
Behind the adults came the children, and behind these, one on
his own, a boy. Calley pointed to him, followed his progress with
a finger as though with the barrel of a gun.

'That one is me,' he said.

'You were here?' asked Medina, amazed.

'Not here,' said Calley. 'Not this one.'

He said nothing else but when they rode on, picking their way
along a sheep track over the ridge of the valley, he began to speak
of it. At eight he had been sent out of London in a haulier's
wagon loaded with boys and girls much like himself. High
summer on the Old North Road. They saw what they had not
seen before – open fields and great woods, haycocks and hedgerows mad with birds. They saw rabbits under the briars, and at
dusk the soundless running of deer. They saw distance, the haze
of far hills, the sun setting right to the flat of the earth. Country
folk stood up from their work to watch the wagon pass. They
knew where it was headed. It was not the first they had seen come
up that road loaded with pale children. After a week they arrived
at the mill. By moonlight it looked like Newgate prison, and
though the children were all familiar with buildings that pinch
the soul, they were frightened. They followed a man with a lamp
to the apprentice hall, a stone house behind a stone wall, one
door in and out, kept locked. They followed him up the stairs and
at the top the boys were sent to the right, the girls to the left,
filing into dormitories to find space for themselves by touching
strangers, other children so dead asleep they could have been
tumbled on to the floor without fear of waking them. In the
morning – or was it night still? – the man came back with a bell
and took them into the mill.

'Fourteen hours a day we laboured there. Sixteen when business was brisk. Well, we thought we knew what work was, had all of us been picking oakum for years, but this was different. Cotton yarn will snap in the cold so they keep the machine room hot enough to grow lemons. And the air is thick with fly, little bits of cotton that get up your nose, get in your throat, wad up your lungs. As for the noise in there, I did not hear the equal of it until I stood in my first battle.'

Medina listened closely, in part because he was interested, in part because he knew Calley wished him to, that he was saying more perhaps than he had said before to anyone. Many of the words were new to him – the strange language of the work – but he let them go, not wanting to interrupt. The creeler, the gaffer, the carding room. The winding stroke. Doffing and piecing. As they rode under the broken green roof of a larch coppice, Calley stopped his horse to sketch in the air the wheels and pulleys of the frames. He was angry when Medina said he understood. He began again. '*Here* are the bobbins, *here* are the spindles. When it does *this* it's called drawing out. When it does *this* it's called putting up.'

They went on, bare hills now, and to the left of them, the distant crystal bloom of sea light.

'My first employment,' said Calley, 'was as a piecer. I would mend broken threads . . .' He raised a hand to show Medina how it was done, the quick twist between thumb and finger. 'A piecer must also serve the machine by cleaning it and this is the most dangerous work. You run in low under the yarn, never letting it touch your back. Miss your timing you lose your fingers, or worse. There was a girl called Lizzie Bentley from the spike in Southwark. It pleased her to call me her brother though I was no more her brother than I am yours. She had ginger hair for a start.

Anyway, the dozy cow slipped when she was under the machine and the belt caught her hand and took off her arm at the shoulder. She was nine. The blood was like water spun from a twirl mop . . .'

'But she lived?' asked Medina.

'She lived. They gave her a job running messages, one arm being enough to carry a piece of paper with.'

He was quiet then. Medina dozed in the saddle, was roused by rain on his cheek. Ahead of them the road ran down into another valley – a church, a bridge and five tall chimneys, their smoke slightly paler than the sky. Calley started to talk again – or perhaps he had been talking all the while. His theme now was discipline.

'In the last hours of the day the overlookers beat us without pause. They beat us to keep us awake for we would, in truth, have slept on the floor, in the grease there. Sometimes they used a bobbin, sometimes a strap like those that drove the machines. One, name of Ramsden, had a knob-stick he called "father". Thy lids are drooping, lad. Shall I fetch out fadder? I will tell you this, I have known mill boys in the army, a good number of them. They think it *cushy* to get ten licks of the cat for coming on parade with dirty boots. What others boast of they don't even fucking mention.'

The rain, in the stealthy way of dusk rain, had grown heavier. It shone like thread against air the colour of gritstone. They turned up the collars of their coats. Medina asked about the girls, if they were also beaten. Calley shook his head. 'They had other things for the girls.'

'And what were those things?' asked Medina, though it seemed to him suddenly that he already knew.

'They were made to stand on a chair,' said Calley, 'where all could see them. Then the overlooker took a knife or shears and he cut off their hair. Their hair was what they were proud of. It was what they had.'

He glanced back at Medina. It was hard to say what his expression was. Did he think he had been careless? That he had said too much, this most deliberate of men? For ten yards of fading road they held each other's gaze, the rain dripping from the brims of their hats. Then Calley straightened himself in the saddle, and with a twitch of the reins, steered his horse into a lane that led them away from the houses.

13

They were on a hill above the sea. The hill was shaped like a sugar-loaf and had a trench, fifteen feet long, cut into the sea-facing slope. It was mid-morning and the day was already hot, the sun beating a scent out of the land. Pine? But it could not be pine. There were no pine trees, few trees of any kind, none at all on the hill. Lacroix wondered if he was remembering Portugal, that month after they landed, when he began to understand what the south and southern heat might mean. He had not expected to meet it again on the islands.

'Now tell me squarely,' said Cornelius, rising, trowel in hand, from the bottom of the trench, 'are you with Buffon? On the age of the world, I mean. And putting aside for the time being the whole question of his being French.'

The wind on the hill was a muddle. Warm gusts blew one way and then the other. It made hearing difficult, though Lacroix believed his hat helped him a little, a broad-brimmed hat, a reaper's hat, dog-coloured and borrowed from among the collection in the hallway. Those words that found their way under the brim stayed with him. As for the rest.

'Remind me,' he asked. 'What *does* Buffon say?'

'Seventy-five thousand years,' said Cornelius. 'Thorpe says it might be even more. He believes it is. Intuitively. Ranald won't venture an opinion, on religious grounds, I think. My sisters just make up numbers. The bigger the number the better they like it.'

'Well,' said Lacroix, 'I will go with Buffon. If we have set aside the question of his nationality.'

'I would ask your opinion of Hutton,' said Cornelius, 'but I am afraid you will not have heard of him. He is too new!'

The two of them ducked down into the trench again and began to scrape and probe with their trowels. It was peat mostly, a few stones. They worked one behind the other, turning the ground and stooping to investigate anything that made the trowel blade chime. The next time they surfaced, Jane and Emily were walking over the brow of the hill. They were carrying a bag between them, one handle each. Jane wore her white muslin (was it the same or were there several?). Emily had on something cool with green stripes. Both had hats of straw tied with ribbon.

'Have you found anything?' asked Emily.

'A crown?' asked Jane. 'Or a chariot?'

'Ha ha,' said Cornelius. '*Très amusant*. I hope you have brought something nice for us and have not just come to talk nonsense.'

Emily unpacked the bag. It had bottles in it – old wine bottles stoppered with paper and filled with water stirred through with oatmeal, the water still mostly cold from the spring behind the house. Lacroix and Cornelius had been at the trench two hours. They had not done much work, not real work, but enough for a sharp thirst. Lacroix drank most of a bottle, apologising if he had taken more than his share.

'Where's Ranald?' asked Emily.

'Ranald?' said Lacroix. 'He is with that party below.' He pointed to where, some fifty yards further down, a group of men and women were digging for peat.

Emily nodded, though he was not sure she could see them.

'The peat will dry well in this weather,' she said. 'It is the hottest day we ever had here.'

'Yesterday was hotter,' said Jane.

'It only seemed so to you,' said Emily, 'because you did not leave your room.'

'It has been hot since Lovall arrived,' said Cornelius. 'The flames lick at his feet.'

'It is summer,' said Jane. 'It is June. We should not be astonished if the sun shines.'

Lacroix grinned and kept his peace. He was, after nine days, becoming familiar with the way the Frends spoke to each other. Sometimes they drew him in; sometimes they seemed to perform for him. As always, with other people's family, there was a deep story he had not the slightest hope of untangling. He did not doubt they loved each other yet he wondered if each to the other represented that which they longed to distance themselves from. The old life, the old tyrant. Their freakish days in Shoreditch. Without Thorpe and the community, would they have gone their separate ways long since? He knew he liked them though. Cornelius's chatter, the spirited company of the sisters, the music at night in the untidy, comfortable house. His secret room at the back. And he had grown stronger – real progress at last – so that he was now a very long way from the man who lay on old Jesse Campbell's floor staring at the sky through a smoke-hole. He should, he supposed, be more pleased about it. To be healthy, to be strong again. Wasn't that what he had strived for ever since opening his eyes to find Nell spooning brandy and milk into his mouth? But what when it was done? When he no longer had the luxury of considering himself an invalid? The world would sidle up to him again. There would be demands he could not simply faint away from. Sometimes, his face pressed against the onrush of time (as against a film, something ectoplasmic and lucent, like the skin of an egg), he thought he could almost see it, a moment, a reckoning, a decisive moment, when everything would depend on some virtue of character he no longer believed himself to possess. One clean cut, one sweep of the blade, as in those sword drills out of Le Marchant's *Rules and Regs* he never really mastered . . .

The women had settled on the grass below the trench. They had taken off their hats. Emily, kneeling behind Jane, had both her hands in her sister's hair as though buried in sand. She was drawing the hair out, squeezing it, holding it in a fist while the other hand shuttled back to collect, to smooth. Then she lifted it all and wound around the blonde stem a fine chain the colour of red coral. When it was done, the hair sleek and orderly, Jane reached up and pulled strands free, corn-coloured helixes to hang down the sides of her face, finishing the work by undoing it a little, a careful spoiling. Then each took the other's place and it was Jane's turn, opening the wings of her sister's hair – shorter, darker hair – collecting it with drowsy rollings of her wrists, with sudden sharp tugs that made Emily wince. Then the lifting, the piling up, the cunning one-handed tying of a ribbon. She was quicker than her sister, more careless, more skilful.

'I would sell you one of them,' said Cornelius, emerging almost under Lacroix's arm, 'if I thought you had any money. Though I suppose Jane is not really in a condition to be sold.'

'No,' said Lacroix, 'that would not do.'

The question of Jane's condition, the facts of it, had been settled some days earlier, a supper-time conversation, an aside from Jane herself, no blushing or awkwardness. She was five months with child and the father was Thorpe. The other two had nodded and smiled as though between them was an agreement that the facts were pleasing ones, or certainly not troubling ones. Lacroix hoped his own expression had been something similar. He did not think she was disgraced, not at all, but the word had been in his head. That, and other words that belonged to the world of the barracks.

He climbed out of the trench (it would make a fine defensive position, a line of muskets, artillery on the hill behind, cavalry waiting on the far side) and stretched himself out on the heather, tipped the hat over his eyes and carried the blonde and the dark hair into sleep with him.

He woke, stifled by the hat. He brushed it from his face and sat up, slightly giddy. He was looking seawards, and though there had been nothing out there when he lay down, now, at the centre of his view, less than a mile from the shore, was a ship. She looked, he thought, like a military vessel. She looked, in fact, exactly like the ship that had stopped the *Jenny* and boarded her. Was it? *You are going the wrong way, Mr Lovall, if you hope to meet with the French.* He had not, of course – the pockmarked lieutenant believed a word of his story. Collecting rents! And now they were here, and he, Lacroix/Lovall, was perched on a hill on a treeless island, his face floating in the eyepieces of their telescopes.

Launch a boat, row a boat. They could be on the beach in twenty minutes.

'It is the emigration ship,' said Ranald. 'For Canada.' He was standing up to his chest in the trench and must have come up while Lacroix was sleeping. On each stumped wrist he wore his false hands, two sheaths of buckled leather ending in blocks of wood and a pair of right-angled hooks, iron. There was no sign of the Frends.

'A navy ship?' asked Lacroix.

Ranald shook his head. 'It is a private man who owns her though she was a navy ship once. She is called the *Nessus*.'

'The what?'

'The *Nessus*.'

'Ah, like the centaur?'

'I do not know the centaur.'

'A sort of Sphinx, but Greek. Will she stop here?'

'Here? No. Here the chiefs do not want the people to leave. They are wanted for the burning. The kelp.'

'But she is headed south, I think.'

'South to Ireland. She will take on more there. Then to Cape Breton.'

'Perhaps they will have a better life in Canada.'

'That may be,' said Ranald. 'But they would stay if they knew how.'

For several minutes they watched the ship in silence, the white specks of seabirds hovering over her wake. No naval frigate, then, but an emigration ship. Lacroix was relieved – deeply – but when he glanced at Ranald and watched him watching, he thought he saw in that face the dry-eyed grief of an entire race. They might, the two of them, both be soldiers – ex-soldiers – but they were not the same. *He* came from among the victors, the owners. If he was not collecting rents in Scotland, rents were being collected in his name elsewhere. Things were due to him and backed by law. And it was Ranald and countless like him who were put into the line to defend it. And did so. Gave their hands to a class of men who would later see them ruined and packed off to Canada . . .

He had these thoughts then let them go. It was hot and they did not lead anywhere, or nowhere he felt able to follow them. It was like Christ's teaching of living the life of the spirit. You heard it at the service then went home for your dinner. You weren't changed.

'Have you found anything?' he asked.

'Only this,' said Ranald, touching with one of his hooks a small curved shape in the grass above the trench. Lacroix picked it up and wiped it with a thumb. It was clay. A two-inch-wide section of something shattered perhaps a thousand years ago. It had a pattern of lines, a slanting design grooved into the clay, lines that brought to mind a tool, a hand.

'You have done better than the rest of us,' he said, settling the pottery on to the grass again. 'Cornelius will think it a prize.'

'It is what is left,' said Ranald.

'Yes,' said Lacroix. 'It is what is left.'

Hard to know if they were speaking of the same thing.

All day they kept the sun and the heat. When they sat for their evening meal the windows of the long room were as wide as they would go. The inside world and the outside world were smudged a little. They watched the sky work through its tints. A few clouds in the west floating like toys. It was a little mysterious.

They ate fish – saithe – and gritty bread and the first leaves from Emily's garden (Emily's as she was the only one who worked in it). Lacroix found he did not miss eating meat. Occasionally he thought of the meat pies and collops of beef Nell used to cook for him but he was content to eat simply, reckoned a light regimen did him good. It also made him feel less awkward about accepting their hospitality.

When the meal was over they pushed back their chairs. They talked. The poetry of John Clare. The paws of otters. Napoleon's wife. The heat. Cornelius consulted his watch. It was ten already, or it was probably ten. It was a long time since he had been able to set his watch by anything larger and more reliable. There had been many small adjustments, some guesswork when he forgot to wind it.

'It might be midnight,' he said, and laughed excitedly.

'I want to sleep outside tonight,' said Jane. 'My room will be unbearable.'

'And what if it rains?' asked Emily. 'We are all outside with our bedding and it starts to rain? You know very well how the weather can change here.'

Jane shrugged. 'There will be air. I will be able to breathe. It is not the same for you.'

'It is an *exquisite* idea,' said Cornelius. 'And I believe Lovall knows all about sleeping in the open. He will build a type of igloo. Or something like an owl's nest. Anyway, it will be lined with moss. Don't you wish to see that, dear Basemath? Don't you? Lovall's ingenious nest?'

They carried their bedding outside, walking through the shadowy house with armfuls of sheets and blankets. Jane's mattress was the largest and it was not thought practical to bring it down. She would have Cornelius's mattress and he would have a bed made up from the cushions of the ottoman.

They built their camp on the level ground at the front of the house. Lacroix, unsure of the etiquette, placed his own bed at a distance from the others that he thought replicated the distance he slept from them inside the house.

'Why are you *there*?' asked Emily.

He dragged his bed closer. Now it lay at the outer edge of the camp, slightly nearer to Cornelius's bed than to that of either sister. The whole camp was confusing. It was not even clear which end of the mattresses people intended to have their heads.

Jane went into the house and came out in her night clothes. They were not very different to what she had been wearing in the day but her hair was down and she had a dark-coloured shawl around her shoulders. Emily went next. When she reappeared, also with a shawl, there was a softness to her movements, a fluidity, that may have been a trick of the moon-light or else the absence of those garments that disciplined a woman's body and could not, even on a hot day, be set aside. Certainly neither of his own sisters did. Or Nell. Or any of the women he knew.

For himself, he had got no further than taking off his boots. He did not have a nightshirt and hoped no one suggested he borrow one of Thorpe's.

Cornelius, in the hieroglyphic robe, busied himself fetching what they might want, or what he might want. His bag of bang, a whisky bottle, a candle, two books. He held the books up. '*King Lear* or *Gulliver's Travels?*'

They chose Gulliver, unanimously, and Cornelius, holding up the candle, began to read to them. (*My father had a small estate in Nottinghamshire; I was the third of five sons . . .*)

When he had read two or three pages he passed the book and candle to Jane, who passed them to Emily, who passed them to Lacroix.

'As you don't appear to be going to bed,' she said.

He took the book and read to them. They were all lying down now, all but him. Cornelius smoked on his back, flicking embers, curls of fiery bang, from his cushions. The sisters lay on their sides. He noticed that they held hands for a while, held each other's fingertips, as perhaps they had done as children. He noticed Jane pull a pillow under the covers and wedge it between her knees or thighs.

I am reading to the baby too, thought Lacroix. To Thorpe's homunculus.

He read. The wax thickened on his fingertips. When the moon had sunk below the boathouse gable he shut the book, paused, then blew out the candle. He fancied they were all asleep now. They lay very still, dark forms sunk in lighter air. It made him uneasy that he could not hear their breathing, though he knew it was just his deafness.

He took off his waistcoat, got beneath the covers and lay on his back staring up at the faintness of stars. The novelty of it! Not the novelty of sleeping out – Cornelius was right of course, he knew all about that, had bivouacked across the Peninsula in tents that kept out neither rain nor cold, had slept many nights in the open with nothing but his greatcoat (his legs thrust through the sleeves). But to lie out as a kind of game, with all their bedding. Men and women muddled together! Was this how the community behaved? The Thorpians, the Phyrronists? It would be something to tell Lucy about. Something to scandalise her husband with. Or did Wesleyans not trouble themselves with such things? He was not entirely sure what they believed, other than they were more likely to pass through the eye of a needle than Unitarians or Anabaptists.

It was deep night when he woke and for a moment or two he was utterly lost. Then he realised he must have turned in his sleep. He had been facing outwards but now could see the uncertain coastline of another sleeper. The rumpled blanket, a pillow, a head. Cornelius? No, not Cornelius. Emily. He tried to get her into focus. The moon was gone but there was a residue of light in the air, enough to establish a nose, a hand up by her chin, her brow. She was closer to him than he could easily explain, as if the mattresses were moored like boats in a pool and had swung on their lines. Her face was like folded cloth; then, a moment later, it was a mask in which, free from detail, from all animation, he could plainly recognise the family face: spare, handsome, inward. The father's face? The mad saint of Shoreditch? He gazed at her, his regard, he thought, that of a philosopher more than anything . . . warmer. He gazed, was lost in gazing, seemed hardly to know any more *who* was gazing, when it occurred to him that the gleam at the centre of her face was, in fact, the gleam of her eyes.

She was looking at him. She must be. Or else she was sleeping with her eyes open. And who does that?

He shut his own eyes, opened them again. He wanted to be sure. He looked, pushed the dark aside with his looking. He was sure. His heart thudded. He was close to laughter. He had done, quite innocently, what he would never have dared do knowingly. And what did she think of it? This man, this newcomer, lying within reaching distance, staring at her? And because it was night, deep night, and everything had softened, all shapes and truths on the cusp of being other shapes and other truths, he began, with no effort of conscious invention, to imagine things that pleased him. It began with a vision of touching – his ghost arm stretching out, his ghost hand, the feel of her face, the shock of her breath on his fingertips. Then outwards, onwards, rushing ahead (it was the work of seconds) to a tableau in which he stood with her in the drawing room of the house in Somerset receiving callers. May I introduce Miss Emily Frend of Shoreditch? In his picture of them they looked young, unmarked by life. Themselves, but themselves made good. There was nothing wrong with her eyes, nothing amiss with his hearing. Then being served at table by Nell. And Tom fitted out as a kind of footman. Tom in a powdered wig and buckled shoes! The dining room would need redecorating of course. Fifty years since anything was done there. The bedroom too? Something from Bath, something modern. Plain? Stripes? Was green a good colour for a bedroom wall?

Then all of it was rubbed out. He shut his eyes and turned, as if in pain, first on to his back and from there on to his other shoulder. What was he thinking of? Had he forgotten *everything*? He might make love to a Glasgow orange girl – and no doubt he had been justly served there – but to Emily Frend? He had a moment of rage so sharp and sudden he thought he would shout out, wake them all like one in a fit. No. Not this. Not ever. Tomorrow he must leave them. He would make his excuses (anything would do), ask Ranald to guide him to a ferry crossing. There were islands to the north of this one – he knew that from Captain Browne's charts. He would get clear. He would keep moving. Or he would go back? Take the *Jenny* or some other ship back to Bristol, then the London mail. Walk across the parade ground to the colonel's office and present him with a history of the retreat. His history.

He mouthed to the dark. 'They could shoot me.' And he almost revelled in it, the rightness and bitterness of such an ending, the quick slide of last thoughts as he waited for someone (Wood?) to give the command. There was a wall behind the guardhouse in Croydon that had been used for such things in the past. A brick wall splashed with whitewash . . .

In the morning they all seemed to wake at once, sitting up in their beds, a gloss of dew on their faces, their expressions sombre from the strangeness and beauty of the night. They exchanged their dreams. Cornelius had been riding a crocodile. 'Was it Father?' asked Jane. Cornelius said it had been, undoubtedly.

Jane's own dream was of Thorpe striding in a river, though whether an English river or a Scottish one she couldn't say. Emily had dreamed her bed was on the sea and that she had looked back at the island and seen the house.

'Were you alone?' asked Cornelius.

After the briefest pause she said she had been.

'Liar,' said Jane. She looked at Lacroix.

'I didn't dream,' he said. 'I often don't.'

Cornelius begged for coffee. Emily swung her legs out of bed, stood carefully, and went into the house. After a minute Lacroix also got up, pulled on his boots, buttoned his waistcoat and followed her inside. He went to his room, closed the door and crouched on the floor by his bag. He still had his resolve from the night before, though in daylight it did not feel quite the same, as if it had been made in a language exclusive to the night that now, translated, was less emphatic.

He took out the writing case, freed the brass hook that kept it shut and examined the green solar glasses. He fiddled with the lens that had come out of its frame, finally got it to snap back in. He polished both lenses on his sleeve, straightened one of the wire wings. Then he went to where his coat was hanging on a peg by the door. He searched in the pockets for the remaining tincture bottle, drew it out, shook it, and held it to the light. It was still two-thirds full and the sight of it, the pink tint, tempted him for a moment. But what would it be to take his leave of them under the influence of laudanum? He would end up slack in front of a window, muttering to himself. He would see whales, dead fathers. He owed them something better than that.

It bothered him he had nothing for Jane. He considered giving her the writing case but could not picture her with it and, anyway, wanted it himself. His copy of *Pilgrim's Progress*? Absurd. How about a part-used bar of Windsor soap? A cavalry pistol? He would, he decided, if it was possible, send her something later, a gift for the new child, a christening bracelet perhaps, though christening might well be something the community frowned upon.

He went to the kitchen. Emily was pouring boiling water from a pan into a coffee pot. Some of the water was already pooled around the base of the pot. 'Put it down,' he said. 'Emily. I will pour it.'

'You are very masterful this morning,' she said. She set the pan down and looked at him. He could not read her expression.

'You spoke in your sleep,' she said.

He cocked his head. 'I did what?'

'You spoke in your sleep, John. Unhappily.'

'Ah. I am sorry for it.'

'Why? You were asleep. It was your true self that spoke.'

He nodded, then held out the solar glasses. 'I have a present for you.'

She came closer. It was odd, like tempting a cat with a titbit. She took the glasses from him, turned them in her hands.

'Against the sun,' he said. 'Do you think they will help?'

'Yes,' she said. 'Thank you. I think they will.'

'Good.'

'Is green best against the sun?'

'I believe it is.'

'It will be like looking from the inside of a bottle,' she said, laughing. 'Perhaps you should give them to Cornelius.'

'No,' he said, suddenly laughing too. 'They are for you. I have something else for Cornelius.'

She thanked him again. She looked so pleased, as though the gift were much greater than it was. He wanted to ask her if she had been looking at him in the night, if she had seen him look at her, but he had no idea of the tone or phrasing of such a question. He walked to the stove, lifted the pan and began to fill the coffee pot. By the time the pot was full he knew he was not going anywhere. Not today.

They carried the bedding inside. The morning was already warm and promising to be much warmer. The big hats were out again. Ranald came up. He had put on his old regimental kilt, the first kilt Lacroix had seen since crossing into Scotland. Had he gone ashore at Aboukir in it? Had he been wearing it when he saw the Sphinx? He told them that the mainland boat would be in tomorrow. Emily sat with him at the table in the big room to write out a list of provisions. Coffee, wine, rice, sugar. Six yards of undyed linen for sewing sheets. Wheat flour, oats, salt. Turpentine, candles. A box of assorted buttons. Writing paper. Newspapers, any. The list was long. She wrote with a slate pencil, her nose three inches above the paper.

The money to pay for it all – the community's economic basis, certainly the economic basis of the Frends – came from a man with half a dozen copperworks near Swansea, a man who, as a child, had enjoyed visions of Christ and Socrates, had larked with them on the banks of the Tawe, but now had eight hundred souls labouring under him and needed others to do the dream work. The money was routed through Thorpe, though it seemed the benefactor might be having doubts, had perhaps found dreamers more convenient to Swansea. There wasn't much money in the house. There had not – according to Cornelius, who had complained of it to Lacroix more than once – been any fresh funds since Thorpe's last visit in the winter, and little enough then. Lacroix watched Emily pick the necessary out of a purse of crumpled blue satin then

227

went to his coat, teased a water-stained – a sea-stained – pound note from the slit pocket (there was one more inside, perhaps two) and tried to make her take it. She wouldn't. She was polite but firm. 'You are our guest,' she said. 'We *invited* you here.'

He was still trying to talk her round when Cornelius came out of his room. He had already taken some of the tincture, had swallowed it with his coffee immediately Lacroix had given him the bottle, and minutes afterwards had stripped off his clothes and gone to bathe in the water beyond the boathouse, talking incessantly – in and out of the water – and boasting that today he would simply bite his way through the earth and pick treasures like raspberry pips from between his teeth. Now, however, as the three men set off for the excavation, the drug shifted its mood and Cornelius walked in silence under the shade of a tasselled umbrella. On the hill he sat staring at the empty sea (the islanders would rather grow potatoes than catch fish), then climbed into the trench, stretched himself out on the earth and fell asleep. Ranald and Lacroix looked down at him. The likeness to a corpse in a grave was strong but neither man mentioned it.

'It may have been wiser not to have given it to him,' said Lacroix. He had told Ranald about the drug, had told him too how he came by it. Glasgow. Blue orange. The new police.

The two of them sat on the grass. The kilt had a nice way of settling around Ranald's knees. Lacroix wondered if an Englishman might ever be allowed to wear one. He thought not. 'May I ask,' he said, 'if your hands ever hurt you now? Or your wrists, I mean. Of course.'

'It is ten years,' said Ranald. His hooks were crossed in his lap like cutlery. 'In the winter the cold goes into the bone. But I am used to it now.'

'You were with General Abercrombie?'

'I was. And you with General Moore, I think.'

'Yes. Though we might have preferred Abercrombie.'

Ranald nodded. They sat in silence. They had compared their generals. Would they now compare regiments? If he asks me, thought Lacroix, I will tell him plainly. Regiment, squadron. I do not know this man but I trust him as I would trust him in a battle.

He waited but nothing came.

Below them the peat diggers were at their work again. Lacroix had learned the name of the spade they used – a *troighsgear*. He asked Ranald who the people were.

'It is Donald Mackinnon and his sons Donald and Duncan. And the woman is Peggy Mackinnon and the other man is Robert Flynn. The child is Wee Annie.'

The child moved in loops around the adults, small arms whirling. She had nothing on her head and the light shone off her black hair.

'I had better go down to help them,' said Ranald, getting to his feet. 'If he wakes and wishes to start the work I can come up again.'

He set off, descending the hill at the kind of steady pace good infantry advanced at in the line. After Egypt the Highland regiments had become famous. When they paraded through London people leaned from their windows to see them pass, though there was some surprise at their not being larger men.

When the child saw Ranald she ran up the slope to meet him. She spoke with him, then looked past him to where Lacroix was still sitting by the trench. She waved; he waved back, delighted to be saluted by a child who did not need to wave to anyone, certainly not to him. And how intrigued she must be, Wee Annie, with Ranald's hooks! She would remember them all her life, tell her children, her grandchildren. Say she was six or seven now (he knew he was not very good at guessing children's ages) then she might, conceivably, live to see the year 1870! See a world he would not see. See what? Gas, steam ships. Electrical this and that. A sky full of air balloons. Balloons driven by steam? Why not? Sightseers would fly to the islands from London, drop anchor in a spot like this, swarm around with their sketch books, then up the ladder again and off to God knows. Iceland. Greenland. America? What if one day wee Annie emigrated in a balloon?

He was deep in this – the imagined departure for the New World by air balloon – when he heard himself addressed. He thought Cornelius must have woken but when he turned he saw it was Emily. She was wearing the solar glasses. She laughed self-consciously as he took her in.

'I look like an insect,' she said. 'Do I?'

'No,' he said. 'Not at all.'

'I don't mind,' she said. 'Jane takes care of beauty. I am here for other things.'

He nearly asked, what things? But corrected himself to say, 'She does not have it all.'

He could not see her eyes clearly behind the glass, nor could he decide if she coloured a little or if it was just the sun on her cheeks, the heat. She looked down, took the glasses off and peered into the trench.

'Is that Cornelius?'

'It is. He is sleeping. The laudanum, I suppose. I hope I did right to give it to him.'

'I am glad you did,' she said. 'It will help him until we go to Glasgow.'

He nodded at this. He was getting into the bad habit of pretending to have heard what he had not, but she guessed it and repeated herself.

'So you have settled on a time, then,' he said.

'I have written to Mr Rizzo this morning. I do not know what inspired me but I am glad. I have told him he must expect me within the month. And I have asked him to assist in finding a reputable tooth surgeon for Cornelius. We need something better than a mere puller. Such people must exist.'

He saw now that she had a square of paper in her hand, a little package.

'Is Ranald not with you?' she asked.

'He went down to the peat diggers.'

'The Mackinnons.'

'Yes,' he said. 'And here is the child coming up to us.'

Half a minute later and she was there, wee Annie. A tangle of black hair, eyes as black as a gypsy child. She had carried something up with her. She glanced at Lacroix but held it out to Emily. Emily took it, spoke to the girl, and gave her the letter. The child ran down the hill with it. She tumbled twice – perhaps for the joy of it – then reached Ranald, held up the letter and put it in the bag he carried over his shoulder.

'Safely delivered,' said Lacroix. 'What was it she gave to you?'

Emily was holding it up to her face. She shrugged and passed it over the trench to Lacroix.

'Flint,' he said. 'And definitely shaped. You can see where the edge has been worked. A tool of some kind . . . A dagger? It could be. Your brother will be cock-a-hoop. Or will he be piqued that others found it?'

She reached out a hand for it and he gave it back to her. For a few seconds she explored it with her fingertips – the chipped and rippled edge – then dropped it into the trench half a yard from Cornelius's sleeping head.

'We will let him find it,' she said. 'When he wakes.'

Lacroix laughed quietly. He was looking up at her from under the brim of his hat. She had arranged her face into an expression he had not seen there before. What was it? It seemed to challenge him, or challenge her brother, or challenge them all. 'Were you speaking to the child in Gaelic?' he asked.

'I was,' she said. 'Ranald has taught me some and we have a grammar at the house. One must find something to do on winter evenings. You cannot forever be playing spillikins.'

'Or music,' he said.

'In the winter,' she said, 'my fingers were raw with the cold. They bled.'

He grimaced to show his sympathy – a fellow string player – though it was impossible to imagine the cold on such a day, to imagine it feelingly. What came instead was a scene from last winter, the high passes around Nogales, men like scarecrows huddled over smouldering fires of green wood. When she spoke again he missed it entirely. He raised his chin and she repeated it.

'*A bheil thu 'g iarraidh a dhanns?*'

'Ah,' he said. 'You are trying it out on me.'

'I am asking if you would like to walk.'

'With you?'

'I do not think it would cause a scandal.'

'And how,' he asked, 'do I accept?'

'*Tha,*' she said.

'*Tha?*'

'*Tha.*'

He accepted.

They walked down the hill towards the sea. As they passed the diggers, Ranald raised a hand, a hook.

'He will take your letter to the boat?' asked Lacroix.

232

'It will be in Glasgow in two days. If anything can sail in this weather. I suppose they must row when there is no wind.'

As they reached the marram grass above the beach, they turned to walk parallel with the coast. The sun was overhead. Emily wore her hat of Italian straw (it was not in perfect condition but had survived from before the embargo and was Italian in truth rather than merely in style). She wore the green glasses and a dress with sleeves that ended in little frills or flounces above her elbows. They walked between two fields of green oats and came out on to the untilled machair. Moon daisies, buttercups, purple vetch. There were black cattle grazing here, lashing their tails and moving heavily over pools of flowers.

'Do you recognise your old mount?' asked Emily.

'My what?'

'The cow you rode ashore on.'

'Oh no. She was much grander. Horns set with topaz. Emeralds.'

She laughed, then said, 'She should not be hard to find again. If you wished to leave.'

The ground was flat or almost flat yet she walked beside him as if picking her way across a marsh. Was fear of blindness her constant thought? And would this Rizzo be able to help her? A surgeon! A sawbones! It was bad enough to have them do your hands like poor Ranald, but to have them come at your eyes!

They walked a quarter-mile in silence. Two boys sitting up on the blackland waved to them and Lacroix waved back.

'Who is it?' she asked.

He told her. 'Do you think they will know you?'

'I am sure they do,' she said. 'And you also.'

'And when Thorpe arrives,' he said. 'What will they make of him?'

'Of Thorpe? They will sit on his hand like sparrows.'

'He has no enemies, then? This marvellous Thorpe.'

'I did not say that.'

'And will there be a happy day with your sister?'

'You mean a wedding?'

'I suppose they must wish it.'

'Why? Because she is carrying his child? We are here, in part, to escape such conventions.'

Lacroix frowned at the flowers. He approved. He disapproved. He had not come across it before, not among polite people.

'Are you such a great believer in marriage, John?'

'Some people must find it pleasant. And society must depend on it in some way.'

'We are born into a world not of our own making,' she said. 'We are told we must accept it. But why *should* we?'

'Would there not be anarchy?' he asked, hoping he had heard her correctly through the noise of the birds. 'Look at what happened in France. First revolution, then chaos, then dictatorship.'

'The revolution was run by lawyers. Lawyers and journalists. Yes, and bad actors like Collot. We shall avoid them all. And we renounce violence. We despise it. Nothing good ever came of it.' She stopped by a break in the dunes, peered around herself. 'Is this the way?' she asked. 'I believe it is.'

They turned on to a soft path between the dunes and stepped out on to an expanse of painfully white sand.

'No weed-burning here,' said Lacroix.

'Not yet,' she said. 'And there are other places more profitable. They cut the best weed from the rocks offshore. Here there are no rocks.'

It was true. The beach gave on to the sea and the sea to the horizon. An unbroken flow. They walked down and stood at the edge of the water. Here at last was a fluttering of air. They shut their eyes. It was what such distances demanded – to be taken in over the tongue, to have the intimacy of breath.

'You said,' she began, still looking or not looking at the sea, 'left shoulders forward.'

'I did? When?'

'In your sleep. Last night.'

'It is a cavalry command. Left shoulders forward. We wheel to the right.'

'I thought it was,' she said. 'I think that I have read it in a news-paper. Or a novel.'

'You like novels?'

'Not as much as Jane. And now if I want more than a page I have to ask them to read to me.'

'What else did I say?' he asked.

'You spoke of your sweetheart.'

They turned to look at each other.

'Sweetheart?'

'Lucy.'

'Lucy is my sister! She lives in Bristol. She is married to a man called William Swann. She has two children, twins, who I cannot tell apart from each other.'

'Then your sweetheart must have another name.'

'I suppose she must,' he said. He smiled at her. 'You have not told me the name of your beau. If Jane has Thorpe, who do you have?'

'Perhaps I have Thorpe too,' she said. Or that is what he thought she said. He could not have heard it, of course. Thorpe too? What could that mean?

He said, 'In the community presumably spiritual love counts for more. More than the other.'

'You may presume it,' she said, 'but it was not spiritual love that got my sister with child last winter.'

'He came to the island?'

'Thorpe?' She shook her head.

'Where then?'

'What a strange question! And how interested you are in Thorpe and Jane.'

He denied it. She grinned at him.

'Jane took the boat to Oban. They were in a hotel there. I cannot tell you the number of the room.'

They turned and began to walk along the sand. The tide was coming in. At each smooth wash of the surf it crept forward the breadth of a finger. She asked him if he could hear the peeping of the oystercatchers. He said he could, that he found it easier to hear birds than people.

'You must have been very dashing in your uniform,' she said.

'Dashing?' He saw himself – or rather he saw the portrait in the house. Had it been in reach he would immediately have lifted it down and turned it to the wall. 'I fear I thought myself so.'

'As a rule I do not like soldiers,' she said. 'Though I like Ranald. Ranald has saved us more than once.'

'I like him too,' said Lacroix.

'Why did you join?' she asked.

'Why . . .?'

'The army. Why did you join?'

'We are at war, Emily.'

'I know lots of men who are not in the army. Or the navy.'

'Like Thorpe?'

'Thorpe, for one. And Cornelius.'

'My father had died,' he said. 'I did not know what to do with myself. And I was used to horses and riding.'

'And that was enough?'

'Yes. It must have been.'

'Did you think about killing men?'

The question startled him. He shook his head vigorously. 'I thought of uniforms and riding and getting away from rooms where I used to sit with my father.'

'I do not mean to taunt you,' she said. She asked him to tell her about his father and he did so. His character, his love of village music. The tall books written out with songs, pressed flowers between the pages. She listened carefully, despite the heat. He felt her listening as a gift to him. He thanked her.

'You have no need to thank me, John.'

They had come near the end of the beach. They turned about and regarded their own footprints.

'If you were to look away,' she said, 'I think I would take off my shoes and stockings. Or in truth I don't care if you look away or not as you have certainly seen a woman's feet before.'

She had spoken rapidly; he caught about half of it, but as soon as she bent down he understood what she was about. He stared for a moment then looked away to the dunes. When he turned back she was standing in the sea. She had her stockings and shoes in one hand. The other hand held up her dress.

'Will you not come in too?' she said.

He sat on the sand and began to push at a heel of a boot. She laughed. 'Do you always grit your teeth so when you take off your boots?'

He laughed too. 'My ribs are still sore,' he said. 'My friends in Glasgow.'

Now he was sitting he saw that there were tiny skeletons on the sand. He had not noticed them when he was walking. This, for example, the shell and claws of a crab, perfectly dry, perfectly white, the whole carapace smaller than his thumbnail. Was the sand made of such things? Were they walking on a million bones? A million million ground small by the sea?

He got the boots off and rolled up his trousers. Emily had already set off and was three, four yards ahead of him. He followed her, wading through shallow water that breathed and sucked between his toes. He was walking in her wake and sometimes felt the print of her feet beneath the soles of his own. She was talking; her words flew past her shoulders like scraps of paper in a paper chase. Something about hatboxes? Then her words came differently and he realised she had started to sing. He was not close enough to pick up the tune so he started his own song: 'Blow the wind southerly, southerly southerly! Blow the wind southerly . . .'

He wished the beach was miles long, wished he could sing and walk behind her until the moon rose like a petal and he was cured by something as simple as beauty, but when she came again to the spot where they had first arrived at the edge of the sea she stopped and waited for him.

'We shall have to dry our feet,' she said, stepping out of the water on to the sand. 'Do you suppose the sand itself might dry them?'

'If we ran about?' he asked. But it was too hot for running. He considered offering her the use of his stockings but she sat on the sand and began to dab away with her own. He sat nearby, took off his hat and wiped his brow.

'You are very free,' he said.

'Free?' She stopped wiping the sand from her toes. She stared at him through the green glass that now, through some trick of the light, had become entirely opaque.

'I mean . . . this . . . your manner . . .'

'*Free?*' It was as though there were no word he could have used that would have stung her more. 'I shall tell you,' she said, 'how I am free. I am an unmarried woman no longer in her first youth. I am what some people call a spinster. I have in savings something less than seven pounds. I live under the protection of my brother, which is to say – though I love him as a sister should – that I live with no effective protection whatsoever. As for the community, for all I know they will never arrive. We have not heard from them in weeks. I have not the slightest idea how we shall survive another winter here. And if that was not enough I am, day by day, losing what remains of my sight and so must, in a short time, lose whatever small independence I still enjoy. So, you will tell me please where, in all of this, you find me to be free. Is it because I take off my stockings to paddle in the sea? That I have let you see me do it? Is *that* my freedom?'

She held his gaze then looked away. She was shaken by her own anger. He thought she might weep but if there were tears the green glass hid them from him. He felt as he had when he and Ranald watched the emigration ship. Side-struck. Implicated. He poked a finger into the sand, drew a shape there, then smoothed it away.

'I was thoughtless,' he said.

She shook her head.

'I have offended you, Emily.'

'No,' she said. 'Though I might have offended you.'

'Mr Rizzo,' he said. 'I feel certain he will be able to help. Did you not say he was eminent?'

'I know almost nothing about him,' she said, though her tone now was matter-of-fact. She smiled a sad smile. 'Let us not spoil the day, John. All these things. They are an old story and one I am tired of. Now, if you will give me your back I will put on my stockings. I can assure you I am very particular when it comes to questions of modesty. Thorpe calls me an old vestal. A prude.'

He gave her his back, looked down the glittering white length of the beach. 'It may be,' he said, 'I will not like this Thorpe after all.'

They did not walk back to the excavation but went directly to the house. There was no sign of the others. They went to the kitchen. A half-dozen wine bottles filled from the spring were standing on the floor in the shade under the window. They drank a bottle between them, dabbed their lips.

'I will do some work in the garden,' she said.

'Why not rest?' he said. 'Sit somewhere cool for a while.'

'Like an invalid? No. I will do things while I can. And you can help me later. I will need to water the vegetables.'

He promised he would. They parted. Lacroix went to his room (once again pressing the wall rather than the door and having to stand back and guess again). He sat on the unmade bed, got out the writing case and settled it on his lap. The ink in the silver pot had dried to a gum. He spat into it, spat again and mixed it with the steel nib of one of the patent pens. He had the urge to write poetry. Lines Composed in the Western Isles by Capt . . . whoever he was. The walk on the beach would be at the centre of it. Emily as a Nereid, himself a shipwrecked sailor. Or the spirit of one? And if he liked the piece why not set it to music? Something slow but not mournful. An air to the air! He dipped the pen, paused with the glistening nib above the paper, then began a letter to his bank in Bath. He requested that they send, as a matter of urgency, a draft for twenty-five pounds to the Ship Bank in Glasgow and that the draft might be collected and cashed by Miss Emily Frend (he did not want Cornelius getting hold of such an amount). He had not seen the Ship Bank himself when in Glasgow – what had he seen? – but William had mentioned it and the name was not difficult to remember. Emily would bring the money back with her and they would, for a time, not have to depend on the satin purse or Thorpe or the whim of a visionary turned factory master.

The ink – powder and spit – dried to an uncertain purple, as if he had written the letter with wine lees. It would do. He folded the paper, wrote the address. He didn't have anything to melt wax for a seal but he could do that later. He would give the letter to Ranald this evening. It would go to Glasgow with the list of provisions and Emily's letter for Rizzo.

He cleaned the nib, closed the case, pushed off his boots and lay down. Poor Lovall. The face came to him more clearly than it had in many weeks. How quickly they had put him aside! A little grave in Castelo Branco, then the auction of his effects – a jacket, a pair of overalls, a saddle, spurs, the writing case . . .

He shut his eyes. He would have a short sleep now. He needed one; the heat had drained him. And when he woke he would see if it was time to carry water to the garden, a job he was already relishing the prospect of (light slopping in the mouth of a pail). But when he did wake – the usual confusion following upon a sleep in the day – he heard Cornelius, his voice shrill, angry it seemed, and he sat up on the bed, braced, uneasy. He strained to hear but the only word he could be sure of was 'How?' – spoken twice, the second at a higher pitch than the first. Clearly all soporific effects of the drug had worn off. Then he remembered the piece of flint the child had brought up and that Emily had tossed into the trench. It had been found of course! Cornelius was not angry but excited. And if it was Emily he was speaking to she must be struggling to keep a straight face.

He peeled off his stockings, shook out the sand, put them on again, pulled on his boots. He was tugging on the second boot when he paused once more to listen. Another voice now, a woman's. Words close-packed, words in flurries. Then Cornelius again, as if trying to bat the words away. Then silence.

Was it silence?

He did not want to intrude on a family spat but he was curious. Why should the finding of the flint occasion a row? He went to the door. If he was in the way, if his presence was awkward, he would nod to them, cross the room and leave the house, make himself scarce for an hour.

He opened the door and went in. They were all there: Cornelius, Jane, Emily, Ranald. Cornelius was standing at one side of the table. He had the appearance of a man falsely accused, a raggedy, half-size Danton. On the other side of the table was Emily, her cheeks shining with tears (no green glasses to hide them now). Jane was in the shadows by the bottom of the stairs, arms folded beneath her breasts. Ranald was beside the hall door, his gaze on the floor, the old rugs. On the table, and somehow the centre of everything, was a parcel of black earth, of freshly cut peat, about the size of a family Bible.

Then several things happened at once. Jane began to speak; Emily turned and made for the kitchen door; Cornelius slumped on to a chair by the table. Only Ranald kept his former pose.

'Cornelius,' said Jane, 'has found something, or the Mackinnons have, and now he will not go to Glasgow with Emily and Emily is in a rage with him.'

'I appeal to you,' said Cornelius. 'A fellow man. A rational being. How can I go now? It is . . .'

'What have you found?' asked Lacroix.

Cornelius looked at the table, the slab of peat there. 'They dug it up where they were digging their peat,' said Cornelius. 'They sent the child to fetch me. At least they had that much sense.'

Lacroix leaned over it. The peat was moist, dense, sticky black. And bedded into its surface was something else. Fibrous, whorled. He would have touched it but Cornelius stayed his hand.

'It seems to be an ear,' said Lacroix. 'Is it an ear?'

'It is!' said Cornelius. 'The ear of a Caledonian Achilles.'

'Achilles?'

'I mean it is ancient, Lovall. It is an ancient human ear. It heard the sea when the sea was new!'

Lacroix bent lower. Now he knew it was there it was unmistakable. An ear! For love of Christ. Black. Black leather. Black exactly as the peat but unmistakably human.

'And the rest?' he asked. 'The head? The body?'

'Nothing,' said Cornelius. 'It is an ear on its own. But the rest must be there, somewhere. I have persuaded the Mackinnons to suspend their digging. They are horribly reluctant but you can imagine the damage they could do with their spades. Damn it, Lovall, there is some man or woman in the ground and I must find them. I feel they are depending on me.'

'It is certainly a remarkable thing,' said Lacroix.

'Of course! Of course! And now you understand why I cannot go on a jaunt to Glasgow. The moment I'm gone the Mackinnons will dig again.'

'But your teeth?'

'I have the tincture. I do not need a surgeon now. Perhaps next year.'

'And what of Emily?'

'Yes,' said Cornelius. 'That is unfortunate. I would ask Ranald to go but he will have duties here.'

'Then I will take her,' said Lacroix. He thought he heard Jane laugh. He looked at her; she wasn't laughing. 'I will take her,' he said, 'if I have the family's consent to it.'

'And if he operates?' said Cornelius. 'This . . .'

'Rizzo,' said Jane.

'You will stay with her until she can travel?'

'I will,' said Lacroix. He did not know how any of this sounded. He had been acquainted with the Frends less than a fortnight. A man who arrives on the back of a cow, who does not speak about his past. But Cornelius reached forward and seized his hands. He gabbled, was dewy-eyed, though it struck Lacroix that his offer was exactly what they had expected of him, that he had walked in on a piece of theatre and known his line.

'You had best go and tell her,' said Jane, cutting in above her brother.

'Do what?'

'Emily,' she said, and pointed with her chin to the kitchen door.

He nodded, freed himself from Cornelius's grasp and went through to the kitchen. The cat was on the table lapping at a dish of melted butter. There was no sign of Emily. He went to touch the cat's head, to stroke it, but the instant it saw his raised hand it twisted about and fled.

14

South of Carlisle they rounded a bend at the edge of a stand of pine trees to find, two hundred yards ahead of them, a line of cavalry drawn up across the road. They kept going.

'Are they waiting for us?' asked Medina.

'Why would they wait for us?' said Calley. They spoke without looking at each other.

'Two men,' said Medina, 'travelling north. One a Spaniard. To be stopped.'

'Bollocks.'

'They are looking for someone.'

'Not for us.'

Nature was at its most benign, or benign for Cumberland. A small shower of rain in the early morning had given way to sunshine and clean blue shadows. Trees shone. The hills looked comfortable.

'Twenty,' said Medina.

'Twenty-two,' said Calley. 'No. Twenty-three.' He had picked out the officer, a man on a grey horse riding slowly just to the rear of his men. There was no one else on the road. No farm cart, no pedlars or packhorses. Nor were there any turnings, left or right.

Fifty yards now. It was a game! Twenty-three pairs of eyes were staring them down. Medina's horse tossed its head and he reached down to smooth the heat of its neck.

At thirty yards the four troopers in the centre of the line started their horses forward and peeled away, two to one side and two to the other, facing across the road. Had they rehearsed this? Drilled it? There was now a gap on the road about the width of a field gate. Ten yards to go. Five. They were entering the range men fight at. Length of a man's arm plus the length of his blade. Close enough now to see the braiding on a collar, the creases in a boot. Medina nodded. He did not aim it at anyone, just nodded. No one spoke. The silence was inhuman. They entered the line; they passed through. It was like passing under the shadow of a bridge. The road ahead was empty, its surface spotted with the glossy dung of the cavalry horses.

'Don't look back,' said Calley.

'I do not intend it,' said Medina.

'Don't even look at me.'

'I do not intend it.'

They were both grinning, both light as air.

The last part of the journey was the most tedious. They felt they were close but they weren't, not yet. They crossed the border, crossed a line of hills, crossed another. They learned the name of the river they were following, the Annan. Several times they stood their horses off the road to let drovers pass. On one occasion more than three hundred cattle were herded past them, heading south. There was something military about it. The numbers. The smell and churn of the road.

To Medina the land seemed wild as Spain, as old Castile. In the high country he saw eagles – small bent sticks turning in the currents of the sky, the sky itself a type of blue like the lining of something, like the source material of distance. *Madre perla. Madre de Dios* . . .

Two nights they slept in the hills, waking shivering, hugging themselves, foul-tempered, though by noon the sun was hot enough to suck the damp from their coats so that each man rode inside his own cloud. On the third night they stayed at an inn, solemnly eating everything that was brought to them, then sleeping in a windowless room on two straw pallets, sprawled, silent, dead to everything.

In the morning they followed a new river. ('Fuck the Annan,' said Calley, and Medina had said, 'Yes, fuck the old Annan.') The sense was of having climbed the country river by river. The Severn, the Wye, the Eden, the Annan. Now they had the Clyde.

One more night in the open, then, early afternoon the next day, Medina stood in the stirrups of his horse and pointed to the smoke that hung in a brown cloud over the river. An hour later they could pick out spires, the stacks of industry, and later still – pushing their horses on – the sun setting in window glass, all Glasgow for half an hour like the embers of a fire.

The city built itself around them. A zone of scrubland, a midden ghosted by dogs. Then shanty, brickfields, the first formal streets newly built or still unfinished (tons of dressed stone with a watchman camped at the top). Further on they saw the bones of an older city, streets in a curl, houses piled like broken crockery, human faces white as bindweed . . .

They had lost the river; now they discovered it again, its channels running through mud beneath a handsome bridge. There were globe-headed lamps on the bridge and the lighters were at work, one of them, a boy, holding a length of smouldering cord of the kind gunners use.

On the far bank they found a lodging house so close to the quayside you could, without much risk, leap from an upstairs window and catch hold of the yardarm of a ship. The place was Calley's choice – all were Calley's choice – though it seemed to Medina he had simply walked up the steps on impulse. Beside the house was a shop selling wines and spirits, a light in an alcove above its door like a wayside shrine. Medina decided he would go there later and buy enough wine to get drunk. He thought he still had the money for that, just. Two bottles of northern wine. Drink one fast, then find somewhere private to lean, drink the other slowly.

They stabled the horses and went up the stairs of the house behind a man carrying a fish-oil lantern, its orange glow creeping up the walls with them as they climbed. On the fourth floor he opened a door and led them into a room. He said they had a view of the river though when Medina went to the window there was no river in sight, only what appeared to be a garden or perhaps a small burying ground that had come adrift from its chapel.

'You know a place called Dumbarton?' said Calley. He repeated the question four times before the man understood him.

Dumbarton! Of course he knew Dumbarton.

'Far, is it?'

'Far? No.'

'So how do you get there?'

The man pointed to the window. 'You go doon the water.'

'And what about a man called Browne. Lives there. A sea captain.'

'Browne?' said the man. 'Browne of Dumbarton?' He bared his teeth; he was thinking, perhaps passing the residents of

Dumbarton, one by one, before his inner gaze. He shook his head. 'Someone will know him.'

'All right,' said Calley.

The man looked at them both. 'Are you two Swedish?' he asked.

'No,' said Calley.

'Yes,' said Medina.

The man seemed satisfied with this. He left them the lamp and went out.

15

As they crossed the water he told her stories from his journey on the cattle boat. He left out the full extent of his intoxication, his despair. He recast the whole as a comedy, much as he had hoped to recast the war for Lucy. This time, however – the material being more promising – he was successful. Emily laughed, open-mouthed, and his stories and her laughter gave to the journey the character of a pleasure-trip, a cruise, weightless.

There was just enough wind to fill a sail and more of it as they moved further into the channel. After the heat on the island it felt fresh. Now and then licks of cold water broke on to the deck and startled them.

They had brought a parcel of food, and bottles of water from the spring behind the house. They ate with the bench between them for a table, threw crumbs for the gulls. Slowly, the light shifted. The day settled into endless afternoon. Emily put on the green glasses; Lacroix gave up his describing. They had spent the night in a township on the south-east coast of the island and boarded the boat before first light when all the water of the loch had a carpet of mist over it, perfectly smooth and about the depth of a man's arm. They were tired now and moved in and out of cautious sleep, not quite leaning against each other but sitting close enough on the bench for her shawl, in stronger breezes, to lift against the green of his coat.

By the time they entered the harbour at Oban the night was already well advanced. They tied up at the side of another vessel and with Emily's hand on a sailor's shoulder they clambered over hatchways and coiled rope and finally up an iron ladder on to the harbour wall. The sailor passed up their bags. They had brought just one apiece: for Lacroix the remaining leather bag, for Emily, a thing sewn from heavy fustian, the material worn to a shine by time and the world's grease.

Among the matters they had not discussed – a great deal had not been discussed, almost everything – was where they would spend the night in Oban before taking the morning flyer to Glasgow. Now, with Lacroix carrying the bags, they walked along the front towards a large building with a lamp outside and the word HOTEL written in tall, Gothic letters between the first- and second-floor windows. The street was empty, and to Lacroix's ears, the whole town was silent. On the door of the hotel a poster had been nailed up and he stopped to read it. Under the heading *General Information for Emigrants*, was news of the *Chiron*, a first-rate ship bound for Cape Breton, coming down from Scalloway and taking on passengers at Oban at the end of the first week in July. There was a picture of the ship – of *a* ship – all sails hoisted, her pennants streaming.

'Another emigrant ship,' he said. 'For Canada.'

'I would like to see it,' said Emily.

'I saw the last one,' he said, 'when it sailed by the island. I was with Ranald. A sad sight.'

'I meant Canada,' she said.

'Mmm?'

'I should like to see Canada.'

'Nothing there but snow and bears,' he said.

They went through an unlit hall into the parlour. Empty glasses on uncleared tables, a fire burned down to the bones of a big log, a lamp on the serving hatch barely bright enough to do more than show itself.

'Hello?'

They waited, bags at their feet, slightly dazed from being suddenly inside after so many hours in the open air.

Lacroix called again, louder. A door opened where they had not seen a door and a man came through, patting into place a wig of the kind Lacroix remembered his grandfather sometimes wearing. Remembered the smell of it. Singed.

'Yes?' said the man, who had clearly been asleep, who was not yet, perhaps, quite awake. He had on buttoned breeches, white stockings, a black coat. He looked like someone's footman but it turned out he was the manager of the place.

Introductions, arrangements. Some confusion as to whether they were asking for one room or two.

'Two,' said Lacroix. 'We need two.'

'Of course,' said the manager, moving his hands as if everything had been clear to him from the first. 'Two very comfortable rooms on the second floor.' He laughed. He had an accent that was neither English nor Scottish. A German of some sort? What was he doing in Oban?

A girl was summoned, yawning so hard her jaw creaked. She led them up the stairs, a candle in either hand, flames streaming. On the second floor she nodded to a door. 'Tha's one,' she said, 'and tha's the other.' She nodded to the door opposite. She gave them their candles. Lacroix asked for some supper to be brought up.

'It will have to be bread and cheese,' said the girl. 'The cook's gone hame.'

'Very well,' said Lacroix. 'And whisky. And two glasses.'

The girl nodded and at the same time shrugged. She had understood or she had not. She would do it or she wouldn't. She left them. Lacroix and Emily went into their respective rooms. Lacroix's looked over the back of the sleeping town. He stood at the window listening for the girl's return but heard nothing until there was a sharp rap at his door and Emily was there to say the tray was in her room. He went through. He brought his candle with him, dripped wax on to the mantelpiece and fixed it there, where it could throw back its light from the mirror. The tray was on the table by the foot of the bed. He poured them both a generous glass of whisky, drank off his own in two mouthfuls.

'It will be day again in a few hours,' he said.

She didn't answer or he didn't hear her. He asked if she felt well. She nodded and smiled a weary smile.

'The manager,' he said. 'What is he? A German?'

'I think that is probably Spinkey,' she said. 'A Russian.'

'A Russian!'

'One who has lived here twenty years or more. Insulted the tsar's wife. Or one of his wives. I don't know how many they have.'

'You didn't say you had been here before.'

'I haven't,' she said. 'But Jane has.'

'Jane? Here?'

'I cannot think there are two Russians running hotels in Oban.'

Then he understood. 'With Thorpe you mean?'

She nodded.

He glanced at the bed, looked hurriedly away. He poured himself more whisky and carried his glass to the window, looked out, looking at nothing. Jane and Thorpe! Here! Perhaps in this very room! The place of union! The bower of bliss! The . . .

He could not get the word 'fucking' out of his head. He was afraid he would say it – that Emily would ask some perfectly innocent question and he would say it. *Fucking*. Would it be funny? He was sure it would not.

'Is it raining?' she asked.

'Mmm?'

'Is it raining?'

'No,' he said.

'I thought I could hear rain.'

'No. But no stars now so perhaps it is on its way.'

They sat at the table to eat. They were too tired to eat much but wanted something. They chewed the hard bread, cut thin slices from the questionable cheese. In the lamplight their movements were feathered, smoothed in air, delayed, golden. He asked her about Spinkey. It was, he knew, a way of asking about her sister and Thorpe, but she could not tell him anything else, though she thought the girl who showed them up might be Spinkey's daughter.

'It's strange though, isn't it?' he said.

'What is?'

He shook his head. He didn't really know. Something to do with how unlikely it was, the two them being together in a room in Oban. All the things that had led to it. Her father, his. The war. Her eyes. Endless decisions and coincidences. The thought excited him briefly, felt important, then commonplace.

'Do you think,' he said, 'Cornelius has found the other ear yet?'

'Or a nose?'

'A . . .?'

'Dug up a nose.'

'Ah, a nose would be excellent. Even better than an ear.'

'He will have to stitch the poor man together again,' she said.

'That will give us occupation for the winter,' said Lacroix. 'I will sew on the feet, you may do the hands. Cornelius himself must have the honour of reattaching the head. When Thorpe comes you can make him a present of it.'

She laughed, then said, 'So you think you might spend a winter with us, John?'

With the Russian manager's help they secured the last two places inside the Glasgow coach. It was seven in the morning, the sky overcast. The coachman wore a cape of thick blue canvas. Only his head, hands and boots protruded, so that he appeared like an actor playing the part of the sea in a pantomime. Emily and Lacroix were the last to board. They had places opposite each other, one shoulder against the leather wall of the coach, the other against the warmth and restlessness of a stranger. The rain started before they had finished their slow climb out of the town. It washed the dust from the windows. It had the look of rain that did not intend to let up. Inside the coach people breakfasted from parcels of food in their laps. Food smells, human smells, then all indistinguishable. They spent an hour held up by cattle on the road. Some of the animals, climbing a bank, peered in through the window. One, with a purple tongue the size of a man's handkerchief, licked the glass. Lacroix had hoped to find a newspaper in Oban but there had been nothing at the hotel, not even an old one. He studied the scenery, peeked down to fast rivers, looked at the walls of bare hills. He swayed against his neighbour, exchanged smiles with Emily, exchanged smiles with the wifely woman beside her who was, he thought, trying to decide who he might be and what he was to Emily. At least there were no military men in the coach. No one to make guesses about him in *that* way.

They stopped for lunch; stopped several times for the men to stand behind trees or for the women to shelter in a cottage, the cotters making a kind of living from the coins that were offered in exchange for a private place and a pot. The horses were changed, the old horses led away steaming, their heads low. On the roof, the outside passengers clung to their places; it was better not to think about them. Inside, the water dripped through a dozen split seams, seeped in past the ill-fitting windows, came up somehow through the floor. This wetness was discussed, then not, and they sat in the near-darkness of each other's presences, asleep, awake, dull, silent.

They arrived in Glasgow hours after they had ceased even to long for it. Lacroix found his chin against his chest, his chin damp with drool or rain, his neck so stiff he winced when he moved it. They were in the lit courtyard of an inn. The doors were opened and they spilled out on to the stone and straw. The coachman struggled out of his cape. A heroic figure! Of the outside passengers, one, a schoolboy or young apprentice, had to be lifted down and was for a time unsteady on his feet, like a fledgling flown against a window. Emily and Lacroix took rooms at the inn, each of them sharing a bed with one of their fellow travellers. Lacroix woke at dawn, half held by a man who, in conversation before sleep, had tried to explain the interior workings of a new steam pump – plug rods, steam jackets – he was selling into Scottish mills. Lacroix rolled away from him a little, slept again, waking a second time to discover his bed-mate gone and the room full of light.

Downstairs, he found Emily alone on a window seat, sipping tea and looking out at the street, or what she could guess of it through antique glass. She was wearing the blue summer coat she had borrowed from Jane. On the table was a blue bonnet, a pair of grey feathers in the ribbon, the feathers picked up on the island. He sat beside her. He was hungry, felt hollow with it, and when the girl came he ordered himself a beefsteak.

'You don't disapprove, I hope?'

'If you are happy to have the poor beast's blood on your hands.'

'You forget,' he said, 'that I am not yet a member of your community.'

'Did I say you were?' she asked. 'And one cannot simply *choose* to be a member.'

'You mean you might not have me? Or Thorpe might not?'

She shrugged.

'You are welcome to your community,' he said. 'I wish for no part of it.'

He did not know where this sudden disagreeableness between them had come from. He sat, scratching the tabletop with his thumbnail. Then his steak arrived, huge and smoking, on a blue-and-white Dutch plate, but he could not enjoy it properly.

He finished – made a point of finishing it all – and pushed the plate away. He saw her glance at it.

'John,' she said. 'You would not fit well with the community but I do not think less of you for that. We are not a company of saints. We are not your betters or anybody else's.'

His anger vanished. 'Thank you,' he said. 'And I promise I will not think less of you for being *in* it.' He hoped she would smile at this but she took it differently and he wished he had found something else to say. They were silent again, a little lost.

'You must tell me,' he said, after some minutes had passed and the inn's old clock had wheezed out a long chiming, 'what you wish to do today.'

This too, perhaps, was a mistake. She frowned at him. 'Do? I wish to do what we came here to do. What else?'

'You want to find Rizzo today?'

'Yes,' she said. 'Of course!' She looked away from him, stared into her empty cup.

Whatever she had been before, whatever her mood – the laughter of the crossing, the laughter at the hotel – she was scared now, openly so. He should have known it the moment he came down and saw her. It should have been obvious to him. He felt ashamed. His meat-lust, his testiness. He put an eye to the bubbled glass of the window and looked out at the transport of shadows.

'I do not know exactly where we are,' he said.

'The Trongate,' she said.

'The what?'

'The Trongate. Or somewhere near it. The woman I shared with last night knew the city. She drew a map for me.'

'And you have it?'

'She drew it on the mirror with her finger. But the infirmary is only a short walk away. That is where we will ask for Rizzo.'

They left their bags at the inn. Yesterday's rain, last night's rain, lay in broad puddles whose surfaces glittered and darkened in fitful sunlight. The road was full of business, men and animals breasting the cool air, shoving through. Everywhere you looked a face looked back, absorbed you without expression. Emily and Lacroix were out of practice. The island had softened them, attuned them differently.

As the road turned and climbed it became quieter. They saw the cathedral. It was no beauty. It sat there like a man bowed under the weight of his own pack. It did not soar. Then, beyond it, they caught sight of something in a different idiom entirely, with pillars and balconies of pale, unweathered stone. On top was a dome roofed with glass, like an observatory.

'You think that's it?' asked Lacroix.

They skirted the walls of the cathedral and came to a halt beside the gates of the new building. No question now of what it was. Under a fanlight, the double doors of the entrance stood wide. A man came out, a woman, two nuns. Then a young man with one leg, swinging himself between crutches, and another man with both hands heavily bandaged, an expression of deep perplexity on his face. Others passed on their way in. A woman, her face sunk on to the bones of her skull, her hands shaking in a palsy, and behind her, two men in top hats and good coats, doctors perhaps, or undertakers. In the gardens between the railings and the door, a person, hidden by a bush, was being comforted by a woman Lacroix thought was probably drunk.

'I doubt even in London,' he said, 'we would find anywhere as impressive as this. In the way of a hospital.'

'Think of the suffering in there,' she said.

'Think of what . . .?'

The building should have had a grand vestibule – deserved one – but instead they entered a corridor – brown below, green above – that smelled of carbolic and kitchen steam. In the right-hand wall was a hatch, curiously low down. Lacroix had to bend his knees and stoop in order to poke his head through. On the other side was a room lined with shelves, record books of some description, ledgers, tall like his father's music books. At a table in the centre of the room two men played dominoes. A third man was sleeping precariously on a narrow bench.

'Mr Rizzo,' called Lacroix. 'The surgeon, Mr Rizzo. Can you tell me where I might find him?'

The players did not know. They had not heard of any Rizzo, and they had been at the hospital since the day it opened its doors. There was a Mr Rice. There was a Dr Rollo. Might it be Dr Rollo that he wanted? They could tell him where Dr Rollo was.

'Rizzo,' said Lacroix. 'An eye surgeon.'

'What does he look like?'

'I've never seen him.'

'Third floor,' sang the man on the bench, who had perhaps been awake all along. 'Far end of the ward . . .'

Neither Lacroix nor Emily had been inside a hospital before. They went up a swoop of stairs to a large room lined on both sides with beds, all of them occupied. They went up more stairs to a room identical to the first, though here it seemed there were more serious cases. One man, seeing Lacroix, called out, 'Doctor! For sweet Christ's sake!' Lacroix smiled at him, made a gesture that might be mistaken for an intention to return.

Another flight, a third room with its uneasy smells, its mood of lassitude and restlessness, as if the patients had all been assigned a problem out of *Euclid's Elements* they must solve before they could leave. They stopped a woman on her way between the beds. She looked at them from over the top of a bundle of used sheets in her arms.

'Rizzo?' she said. 'Does he work with the unfortunates in the basement?'

'He is a surgeon,' said Emily. 'An eye surgeon.'

'Does he have a beard?'

'We have never seen him.'

'Spectacles?'

'We don't know.'

From behind her, the great swell of her hips, a boy in a night-shirt appeared. Skin like watered milk, enormous brown eyes. 'I will take you to him,' he said.

They followed him to the end of the ward. There was a swelling on the side of his neck the size of a hen's egg. It did not look angry but lay under the same milk-white skin as the rest. He led them into a corridor, past one door, past the next. At the third he stopped and knocked. After a moment the door was opened. A man stood there, broad shoulders in a dark grey coat. Late thirties, perhaps early forties. He *did* have a beard. It was black and well tended. In this house of sickness he shone with health.

'More patients for you, Mr Rizzo,' said the boy.

'Thank you, Robert,' said Rizzo. 'I will come and say hello to you later.'

The boy left them. They watched him go.

'He has been with us a month,' said Rizzo, once the boy was out of sight. 'He is not my patient but I am trying to keep him away from my more eager colleagues. Where there can be no benefit . . .' He tailed off. He smiled at Emily. He was noticing her eyes, was already, perhaps, some way on with his diagnosis.

'I am Emily Frend,' she said. 'I am hoping you received my letter.'

'But of course. It is on my desk.' He turned to Lacroix. 'And you are the brother who has come for his teeth.'

'This is Mr Lovall,' said Emily. 'He has been kind enough to accompany me. I believe his teeth are perfectly well.'

'A great pity,' said Rizzo. 'I had someone excellent in mind.'

He invited them into his room. He apologised for its smallness. There was a desk, and behind that a chair by the window, the window propped open with books. He asked Emily to sit on the chair and make herself comfortable.

'Should I stay?' said Lacroix. The question was addressed to both or either. Emily looked at Rizzo, Rizzo at Emily, then at Lacroix.

'Of course,' he said. 'It is good to have the company of a friend. Miss Frend and her friend! Ach, I am sorry. You must have suffered such witticisms before. The Swiss, I fear, are not so celebrated for their humour.'

'You are Swiss?' asked Lacroix.

'From Grindelwald,' said Rizzo, 'where we speak German. But my grandfather came from Turin and his grandfather from Naples. So I confuse people with an Italian name. They expect me to sing more.' He shrugged. To Emily he said, 'Perhaps you would like to take off your hat?'

The room was not the kind of room given to eminent men. Its smallness, its lack of a fireplace, sconces, furniture of any standard beyond the disposable. He had other rooms, perhaps, grander, somewhere else in the city. On the walls were closely pinned charts of eyes. Eyes in faces, eyes alone, eyes in cross-section. Fig. 1, Fig. 2, Fig. 3. One chart depicted an eye the size of a soup plate, a cyclop's eye that stared back at Lacroix until it stared him down and he turned away from it towards the window.

Rizzo was leaning over Emily in the posture of a man inviting a woman to dance. She had her bonnet in her lap. He raised her chin, tilted her face to the light, then tilted it away. He asked her to look out of the window and describe what she could see. She did so. It was not what Lacroix could see or it was some poor fraction of it.

He asked her to close her eyes.

'Close them?'

'If you would be so kind.'

She closed them, her face still angled upwards, still flush with light from the window.

'You will feel me touching your eyelids,' said Rizzo. 'There . . . But please, you must not forget to breathe.'

After a few moments he glanced over at Lacroix.

'Perhaps Mr . . . ?'

'Lovall.'

'Perhaps Mr Lovall could do as I am doing. Touching the eyelids. You will not object, Miss Frend?'

'No,' she said. She spoke as in a trance. (Who was that man in Paris who placed women in a kind of stupor? What became of him?) Lacroix walked past the desk to the window, stood in front of the chair, Rizzo at his shoulder.

'Very lightly,' said Rizzo. 'Your hands here, and here. Your fingers . . . Yes. That is excellent.'

The instant Lacroix touched her he felt her response. The barest movement – a flinch, though he did not think she flinched *away* from him. He stroked his thumbs across the lids of her eyes, the living fragility of the skin with its shadowings, its tiny deltas of blood vessels. He touched an eyelash. He felt her breath on the inside of one of his wrists. Her own hands still gripped her bonnet. Knees together, boots together. Her back in the blue coat slightly arched.

'Now,' said Rizzo. 'Please do the same with your own eyes . . . Yes? And now' – he took hold of Lacroix's hands – 'feel mine . . .'

The surgeon's face. His skin warmer than Emily's. The soft scrape of his whiskers. He smelled of something. Lacroix thought it might be Windsor soap. Emily looked up at them, blinking.

'There,' said Rizzo, removing Lacroix's hands.

'Yes,' said Lacroix.

'You feel a difference? Miss Frend's eyes are more stiff, yes? They do not . . . yield.'

'Yes,' said Lacroix. 'I could feel that.'

'You could, of course.' The surgeon returned his attention to Emily. 'You have headaches, Miss Frend?'

'On occasions.'

'You vomit?'

'No.'

'But each week you see a little less.'

'Yes.'

'Your father's eyes?'

'Green,' she said, after a short pause.

Rizzo looked pleased with this. 'I was thinking if he had a problem like your own.'

'No,' she said. 'His eyes were always clear.'

'And your mother's?'

'She died young. I was seven. I don't remember her eyes.'

'Sisters, brothers . . .?'

'They are both well,' she said.

'Except the teeth,' said Rizzo. He went to the desk, opened the drawer and took out a magnifying glass. It did not look particularly medical. More like an heirloom. He stared through the lens into Emily's left eye, then the right. He muttered to himself. He scratched the bridge of his nose. Minutes passed. A slant of sunlight crossed the room. It lit the blue of Emily's shoulder, the grey of Rizzo's coat cuff, one of the knees of Lacroix's trousers, then broke on the skirting board behind him in an eye-wide patch of light containing the rippling of tiny shadows, fern-like and hard to explain.

The cathedral bells sounded the half-hour. Rizzo seemed to wake from a dream of looking. He stood, returned his glass to the drawer, closed the drawer and took hold of his own elbows.

'The first thing I must tell you,' he said, 'is that I do not know if I can be of assistance to you. Help you.' He waited.

Emily nodded. 'And what is the next thing?' she asked.

'Next?'

'That was the first thing,' she said. 'So there must be another. A second thing.'

'There is,' said Rizzo. 'I can give you drops for your eyes. Belladonna. Or a tincture of aconite. I can give you a little bottle and three times each day you lean back your head and put the drops in your eyes. It is very simple.'

'It will cure me?'

'No,' said Rizzo. 'It will not cure you.'

'Will it help me?'

'It may do. It may.'

She dropped her gaze to her lap, the blue bonnet, then looked up at Rizzo again. 'I was hoping for more,' she said.

'Of course,' said Rizzo.

'I think I will be blind before the year is out,' she said.

'You wish me to operate on you,' said Rizzo.

'Can you?' asked Lacroix, who had been watching them intently, determined to miss nothing of the exchange.

'There is a procedure,' said Rizzo. 'It has existed for many years, though in a very imperfect form. Recently, in Vienna and in Paris, there have been great advances. A colleague of mine at the Salpêtrière has performed it several times.'

'And you?' asked Emily. 'Have you performed it?'

'He has sent me his drawings,' said Rizzo. He gestured to his desk. 'Despite the war, Paris still speaks to Glasgow. The drawing are very exact. Rather beautiful. I have studied them. I have seen their . . . logic.'

'And what does it involve?' asked Lacroix. 'The procedure?'

'It does not matter what it involves,' said Emily. 'The question is whether Mr Rizzo can do it and whether it will help.'

'Dear Miss Frend,' said Rizzo, 'if I thought I could not do it I would never have mentioned it. Never. As to whether it will help you . . .' He paused, then held his hands in front of his chest in an attitude of prayer. Slowly, he moved them apart. 'Between yes and no,' he said, 'we may imagine a line. The answer to your question is on that line, and closer, I believe, to yes than to no.'

'Much closer?'

'Closer.'

For a moment both Emily and Lacroix studied the air between Rizzo's hands. Then Emily nodded.

'It is what I came for,' she said.

'You should consider it most carefully,' said Rizzo. 'You should discuss it with your family. With your friends.'

'Mr Rizzo,' said Emily. 'I have thought of little else for several months. I do not want to think about it any more. Nor is it anyone's decision but mine. If you can do it, if you will do it, if I am . . . suitable, then I wish it to be done. I wish that very much.'

Rizzo nodded. 'You wish it to be done,' he said. He smiled. It was a kindly smile but seemed also to reflect some private thoughts on the character of human wishing. 'As for your suitability,' he said, 'how would you describe your general health?'

'Excellent,' she said. 'I can walk all day without fatigue.'

'I might struggle to keep up with you,' said Rizzo.

'You might,' she said.

'And your appetite?'

'I do not eat meat but as you can see I manage perfectly well without it.'

'You eat fish?'

'I will eat whatever you tell me to eat.'

'If all my patients were so agreeable!' He turned to Lacroix, raised his glossy eyebrows then looked again at Emily. 'So you wish me to operate?'

'I do.'

'What we are discussing will not restore to you the vision you had five years ago. Or even one. It cannot repair the damage already done. It is to stop further damage. To stop a deterioration.'

'To stop me from going blind.'

'Just so.'

'I understand.'

'And you understand also that I cannot offer you a guarantee of success?'

'I am not a child,' she said.

'No,' he said. 'You are not a child and I do not wish to treat you as one.'

'Thank you,' she said.

'You wish to know something more about my training?'

'Would they let you be here,' asked Emily, 'if you were not suitably qualified?'

'I prefer to think not,' said Rizzo. He stared at Emily, fixed her with an intensity of regard that was, perhaps, part of his training. 'Very well. I will do it. I will. Though first I must explain to you what the procedure . . . requires.'

Emily stood up. 'I have confidence in you,' she said. 'I do not need, do not *want* to be told, the particulars. I think then I might lose what courage I have.' She smiled. 'Perhaps you would be kind enough to explain it to Mr Lovall? He will tell me what he thinks I should know. In the meantime I will go and sit with the boy who brought us to you. Robert, is it not?'

She walked between the two men but did not quite manage to leave the room before she wept. Two, three big shudders, her face to the door.

'Emily,' said Lacroix quietly.

She did not turn around but raised a hand as if to keep either man from approaching. She said something, speaking to the door. Lacroix only heard the word 'excess'. Then she touched her face, opened the door and left them.

'So . . .' said Rizzo, after the men had spent some seconds staring into separate corners of the room.

'Yes,' said Lacroix. Then, 'I am somewhat deaf. Or I hear very imperfectly. If you would speak as clearly as you can.'

'You have always been so?'

'It is a recent . . . affliction.'

'Following on an illness?'

'Yes.'

'Then perhaps it will improve. You may hope for that.'

Lacroix nodded. 'Miss Frend's eyes?'

'The eye,' said Rizzo, 'is a bulb of living glass. Within this bulb are many things. Lens, sclera, cornea, nerves and so forth. There is also a fluid, an aqueous humour, that serves the eye in ways we may readily imagine. This fluid has its springs and channels, but if the channels are blocked and the spring continues to be productive, then the pressure inside the eye must be greater. That is the hardness you felt in Miss Frend's eyes. As the pressure grows so it acts on the optic nerve. Over time the nerve is damaged. The result is loss of sight. In the operation I will seek to release the pressure and to allow the channels to flow again. As I have explained, the damage she has already suffered will remain. I cannot restore it. But if I am successful there will be no deterioration. She will keep the sight she has.'

'She will not be blind.'

'She will not.'

He stepped over to where the charts were pinned to the wall. He selected one and tapped it with a finger. 'I will make a cut here, very small, and with a blade no larger than a needle and so sharp it parts the matter it touches as lightly as a thought. Through the incision I will draw out a part of her iris and I will remove it. For this I will employ another blade as precise as the first. All my instruments are made for me by Mr Norie of Hutcheson Street, who is no village blacksmith, I may assure you. The entire operation will take less than half an hour. I will operate on the left eye first. It is the more damaged. Then the right eye when we are confident she has recovered her strength.'

'I suppose there will be pain,' said Lacroix.

'There will. But I believe she will bear it.'

'She must keep very still?'

'I will give her a soporific. I will calm her. And my assistant, Crisp, will hold her head.'

'For the cutting?'

'Yes.'

'And afterwards?'

'Her eyes will be bandaged. The dressings will be changed every day. This for a week or so. I cannot be more exact. Then, for another week, during daylight or in the presence of any strong light, her eyes should be covered. A simple silk scarf will suffice.'

'You make it sound straightforward enough,' said Lacroix, staring at the drawn eye on the chart. 'What is the danger?'

'Bleeding. Excessive bleeding. Shock. Scarring. Above all the wound becoming morbid. But we are learning many new things in our new hospital. We are learning, for example, to wash our hands.'

'Yes? How can that help?' asked Lacroix. He was starting to turn against the whole business.

'It is a great debate among us,' said Rizzo. 'The senior men still hold to the theory of night air, miasmas. But all the younger men, or most of us, are with Spallanzani. Soap and boiling water!' He walked the few steps to the door. 'Come,' he said. 'I will show you our theatre. It will reassure you. Or so I hope.'

Out of the room they turned away from the ward, following the corridor until they reached a short flight of steep stairs with a white-painted door at the top. They went up. Rizzo took a key from his coat pocket. 'This is the surgeon's entrance,' he said. 'The patient enters on the other side.'

He unlocked the door and swung it open. Inside was a chamber, perfectly round, and perhaps three times the size of Rizzo's consulting room. At the centre was a wooden table like a carpenter's workbench, and on the floor beside it a woman was on her knees scrubbing the boards. Seeing the men she stopped her work and sat back on her heels.

'There's nae supposed to be another until four o'clock,' she said. 'Mr Boyle is doing that poor wee man's legs.'

'We are just visitors, Maggie,' said Rizzo. 'We do not wish to disturb you.' To Lacroix he said, 'In here we never need to operate by lamplight.' He pointed upwards to the curved roof of glass and iron, the luminous grey midday sky.

'This is the dome on the roof,' said Lacroix. 'We are inside the dome?'

'We are!' said Rizzo. He picked up two chairs from where half a dozen were huddled by the patient's door. He placed the chairs under the glass, stood on one while Lacroix climbed up on the other. Now their heads and shoulders rose above the bolted metal collar of the dome and they looked down on the roof of the cathedral, on smoking chimneys, the broken curves of the river, and out – out to heathland, woodland, the far hills of the western edge.

'We have been struck by lightning,' said Rizzo. 'We have had to melt snow from the glass with pans of hot coals. Sometimes we are in a cloud. In general, however, I find the effect on patients to be excellent. In particular they like to see the birds. They take comfort from the sight of them.'

Lacroix nodded. He wondered how much comfort the poor wee man having his legs done that afternoon would find in the sight of seagulls overhead.

They climbed down from their chairs. The woman scrubbed still at the floor, dipping her brush then working it with both hands. The boards under the table were noticeably paler than those further out.

'When will you do it?' asked Lacroix as they descended the stairs.

'Now it has been decided,' said Rizzo, 'it should be done as soon as possible. I will spend tonight studying my colleague's notes. Can you be ready tomorrow? For noon? If you wait in the cathedral I will send someone to fetch you.'

They had reached the bottom of the stairs. They turned to each other.

'Tomorrow?' said Lacroix. 'Surely you do not mean the operation?'

'First of all I will conduct another examination. Then, if I am satisfied and if Miss Frend is of the same mind as today, we will proceed. I intend to book the theatre for three. I have already seen there is a space then, a clear hour. Quite long enough.'

'But she cannot possibly be ready tomorrow!'

'No? Why not?'

'She must . . . prepare.'

'In what way?'

'I don't know. She must . . . think about it.'

'You feel she has not done so? Not sufficiently?'

'You have only met her once!'

'This is true. Which is why tomorrow there will be a second examination. A very thorough one. That before anything.'

'Even so . . . Tomorrow!'

The surgeon smiled. He touched, very gently, Lacroix's arm. 'It is you perhaps, Mr Lovall, who is not ready. And please, I mean no criticism. You do not wish to see her place herself in any danger. But your Miss Frend sees it quite differently. The door you are afraid to watch her enter is the very same she longs to pass through. Of course, if she wishes for more time, then we delay. If she wishes to give up the whole affair, we give it up. If not, then tomorrow you wait in the choir of the cathedral and I will send someone to collect you. To collect Miss Frend.'

'At noon?'

'Noon precisely.'

As soon as he was outside with her, he led her into the hospital garden and told her Rizzo's plan.

'And what did you say?' she asked.

'I said it was too soon. Of course.'

She nodded. She was silent. The city circled around them. From somewhere came the inexplicable sound of clanking chains.

'What time tomorrow?'

'Noon. In the cathedral.'

'The cathedral! Why there?'

'He did not say. I suppose he thinks it a more . . . peaceful place to wait.'

'He thinks I might want to pray,' she said.

'To what?'

'To pray. And you too.' She smiled. 'This is *vastly* better,' she said.

'Is it? *How?*'

'He might have kept us waiting a week, a fortnight, a month. Think of it, John. Each morning rising to spend yet another day contemplating what is to come. I don't think either of us could have stood it for very long. Or he might have thought me unsuitable. Or I might have thought him unsuitable. A thousand things.'

'You trust him?'

'Don't you?'

'Yes, I suppose . . . But tomorrow!'

'It is you, I think, who is not ready,' she said.

'Me?'

'Yes.'

'That I am not ready?'

She nodded.

'That at least,' he said, passing a hand across his eyes, 'seems agreed upon.'

They spent the afternoon taking in the sights, the alternative being to sit in a room at the inn endlessly picking over the interview with Rizzo. Lacroix instructed himself to accept. He was there as a companion of sorts, a friend. He was not a brother or husband. His role was to ensure she did not fall into someone's cellar, that she was not accosted. Beyond that? Nothing, perhaps. Nothing but to be obliging. Kind.

They went to see Hamilton's new playhouse on Queen Street. The summer season still had two weeks to run and in the foyer, in a gloom of unilluminated plush and dull gilt cherubs, Lacroix read out the playbill, a Caledonian adaption of *Don Quixote*, with

Mr Hamish Brewse as the Knight of the Sorrowful Countenance and Mrs Adelaide McMartin as Sancho Panza. It sounded charming and foolish, and they pretended to each other that they might go and see it. Not tonight, of course, or tomorrow night or the next, but before the end of the run. 'We could take a box,' said Lacroix. 'Cornelius and Jane could join us.'

'And Ranald,' she said.

He nodded. He thought they both might feel the comfort of Ranald's presence.

On Queen Street again they walked up to the square, counted the sheep grazing in the middle – big, black-faced Cheviots – then came down Miller Street and along the Trongate to the coffee house. Here, in an oval room – a space the members paid twenty-five shillings a year for but which strangers, for a limited period, were permitted to enjoy free of charge – they sat near the doors at one of the few tables still unoccupied. It took ten minutes to catch the waiter's eye and it was another ten before he stood beside them. They ordered coffee and hot chocolate and a bowl of sweet cream. Over a wooden rail along the wall newspapers hung like laundry. Lacroix asked Emily if she would object to his fetching a couple, seeing what the larger world had been up to without them. She did not object. She asked if he would read to her what was of interest. He said he would, gladly. He went and came back with a Glasgow paper and a copy of *The Times*. He started with the local paper, shook it out, smoothed it.

'They have built a new lighthouse,' he said.

'In Glasgow?'

'No, no. Somewhere off the east coast. They say you'll be able to see its light from thirty-five miles away.'

She nodded. He tried to find something more interesting than a lighthouse, and came on an article – a puff – for a proposed lunatic asylum to be constructed in the form of a saltire in one of the city's parks. The design was intended to allow a single warden to stand at the centre of the building and see into all its wings, the wings themselves to be divided according to sex, social class and degree of insanity. He read the piece out in a mildly satirical voice, though gave it up when the waiter returned, not wishing to appear to be slighting the city's ambitions for itself. He moved on to the London paper, started with a letter about the king's jubilee in October, then some news about Captain Barclay's walking challenge (he seemed likely to win his bet), and finally, an editorial concerning the Duke of York's former mistress, Mrs Clarke, who was threatening fresh revelations about the sale of army commissions.

'Did you buy yours?' asked Emily.

'Hmm?'

'Your commission. Did you buy it?'

'Of course.'

'How much did it cost you?'

He could see, over her shoulders, a table of young officers, infantry men in high spirits, their coats still as they had come from the tailors, a red undimmed.

'It cost me the value of four good fields. That and some ready money from my inheritance.'

She nodded. She seemed satisfied with this. He hoped she would let the matter drop. The last thing he wanted was to catch the attention of the young men, to have them pull up their chairs, find himself in the role of 'one who knows', fending off good-natured enquiries with evasions, lies.

'I have something written down,' she said, 'about military men. About the military. I will read it to you later.'

'As you wish,' he said. He could not tell if this was a return to her mood of the early morning, the spikiness of it, or if her question about his commission was simple curiosity. Where was she now? Was her excitement in the hospital garden all gone? Was she about to tell him she could not go through with it, not, at least, tomorrow? He studied her; she studied him back. He took up the paper again but did not read out any more from it. He turned the page, turned another and stopped at a map of Portugal. Beneath the map was an account of some fighting at Oporto (*On landing we took up our position on a height where we had an uninterrupted view of the town. We could see for several miles in any direction, and distinctly observe the whole of the enemy's cavalry retreating* . . .). He glanced to the bottom of the column and saw that the correspondent was from the 14th Light Dragoons. A Captain Hawker. Hawker? He didn't know him, and the 14th had not been on the retreat. He read through the account carefully for any mention of his own regiment but there was none.

'Perhaps we might leave now,' said Emily. 'It is very loud in here.'

'Is it?' He folded the paper and passed her her hat. The larger world be damned. His work, his interest, were here. As they left the table, one of the officers, barely old enough for the moustache he wore, inclined his head to them. A courtesy – absurd, touching.

They walked again. She could, as she had told Rizzo, walk all day without fatigue. They visited dull churches. They looked in the windows of shops and he noted how, nose to the glass, she peered in with real desire at dresses and hats, at shoes that would not last more than a day or two on the island. They went down to the river, crossed and recrossed the bridge by the Broomielaw. He pointed out the steps, almost hidden now under high water, where he had come ashore from the silent cousin's boat. She knew the story of that visit, though there were pages of it he had removed, mostly to do with the orange seller (his thoughts, her kicks). He wondered what he would do if he saw her again. Would he know her? Would he be sure? And what would *she* do? Run? Laugh? Or fetch her friends and this time strip the shirt off his back, a trick he imagined them having a special, rapid method of performing. But more than the orange seller, he hoped to avoid coming upon the men who had helped him that night, the new police. He was grateful to them, of course, but thought of them as the type who would deliver you to the scaffold without rancour or any ill-will, regretfully even, because that was where their enquiries, their written records, had directed them. They were the type who remembered things. The slow, methodical men of the future.

At six they went back to the inn. They spoke to the landlord about rooms. Emily was given her room of the night before, though this time she would not need to share it.

'I cannae do so well for you, sir,' said the landlord. 'We're packed like a herring barrel on account of it being a club night. I can only offer ye a bed wi' a foreign gentleman.'

'Foreign?'

'I'm no expert but I have him down as a gentleman of Spain. Came in wi' an Englishman I took to be his manservant, but then the way he spoke to him I'm no sure I could say any more who is servant and who master. Anyway, seems they prefer to be apart for the night so I put the Englishman in the attic.'

'Then the Spaniard is the master,' said Lacroix. 'If the other is in the attic.'

'Not necessarily. For the Spanish gentleman had the room on the understanding he would gi' up one half of the bed. If there was a need for it.'

'Yes,' said Lacroix, perplexed, irritated. 'Whatever is most convenient.'

He and Emily took a table in the dining room and ordered supper. They had the room to themselves for a while, then the members of the club began to arrive and the place grew rowdy. He hoped she would eat but was not surprised to see her leave most of her food on the plate. He ate little enough himself, and after they had drunk a glass each of wine and had whatever entertainment was to be found in watching the club empty their punch bowls and begin on speeches, they went up to her room. The room overlooked the stable yard and the noise from the dining room was no louder than the sound of the sea heard from the house on the island. She took off her shawl and sat on the end of the bed. He thought of how she must long for her sister, or even for Cornelius. Of how, instead of family, she had him.

'You said there was something you wanted to read to me, Emily. About military men.'

'Did I?'

'In the coffee house. When I was reading that piece on Mrs Clarke and the Duke of York. Do you remember?'

'It does not matter any more, John.'

'Does not . . .?'

'I was petulant. It does not matter now.'

'Even so, I am curious. What would Emily Frend write down about military men?'

She shrugged, went to her bag, lifted it on to the bed, unfastened the buckles and sank her hands inside. After a few moments she drew out a book bound with green cloth.

'Your diary?' he asked.

'More like a drawer,' she said, 'where I keep the things that interest me. Or did so when I saw them first.' She carried the book to the window. There was still an hour of light left in the sky. In the yard the groom held a horse's leg between his knees and was picking the hoof.

'The military,' she began, 'the military is ... is but a ... dastardly carcass ... of ... of ...'

She held the book out to him. He reached across the bed to take it from her. The writing slanted down the page. Letters were missing, no t was crossed. The sort of writing that would earn a schoolboy a thrashing. He moved his finger, line to line, until he found the place.

'Of corruption, full of sottishness and selfishness, preying upon the hard labour of honest men.'

'I copied it from a pamphlet,' she said.

He smiled, hoping to show he had taken no offence. 'I think there is some truth in it. A dastardly carcass of corruption. I wonder if the writer was a military man himself.'

As he held the book a dozen pages fanned across his thumb and when he glanced down he immediately saw his own name. *Today John and I* . . . He closed the book and placed it on the end of the bed.

'I know,' she said, 'what I am going to wear tomorrow. I decided on it before we left the island.'

He nodded and looked down at the floor, at the knots in the boards that were, he thought, the tree's hidden flowers. He had, during the last hours, been marshalling a short but compelling argument against the coming day, what was proposed, what had been accepted, almost flippantly it seemed. He had been waiting for the right moment to deliver it, but now the moment had come he felt no conviction.

'Emily,' he began. 'Emily ...'

'No,' she answered. 'You mean it well but it does not help me. Do you remember what I spoke to you of when we sat beside the sea that day? I am going tomorrow because I mean to keep hold of whatever independence I still possess. I intend to fight for it, my liberty. For that I will do anything at all. I will undergo anything. Can you understand that?'

He could. He thought he could.

'John?' she said.

'Yes?'

'Do you think I will bleed much?'

'No,' he said. He turned from her, found himself in the mirror, the not-entirely-plausible reflection. Then saw the smudges on the glass – the city drawn by a woman's finger in the morning.

His own room was on the floor above and for the moment at least he had it to himself. The foreigner, the Spanish gentleman, had not yet retired, though there was a pack on the chair, and spread on one side of the bed, a horse-coat that looked to have seen a good deal of hard use.

On the near side, the door side of the bed, was his own bag, carried up by the landlord or one of the servants. There was not much in it. He had brought only what was essential – no writing case or pistol. Once his draft arrived at the Ship Bank – and please God it would, and soon, for he did not know how else they would manage – he intended to fill the bag with new things. Shirts, a new waistcoat, perhaps a pair of walking boots like the ones Cornelius had, with oil-silk cuffs above the ankles and sturdy back-straps for pulling them on.

He took out his toothbrush (it was one he had found in the house in Somerset and that he thought had probably belonged to one of his sisters; his own, tortoiseshell and badger bristle, was somewhere in old Castile). He poured water from the pitcher into the basin, splashed his face, rubbed away at his teeth, then carried the basin to the window, opened it, and emptied its contents over the roof tiles below.

In the bed he lay gazing at the outline of a beam above his head. He had no candle with him and the beam gradually lost its edges, dissolving into an obscurity from which it seemed, occasionally, to reappear before sinking again, more completely. Now that he was motionless he realised he was exhausted. It was like an echo of his fever days at Jesse Campbell's house. He drifted, his thoughts moving over the remembered day in a series of touchings that seemed both predictable and random, like a bee's progress across a garden. He saw the cherubs in the theatre, the moustache of the young officer in the coffee house. From there it was Rizzo, the feel of his face, his shut eyes, the feel of Emily's, her breath on his wrist . . .

He slept, uneasily, some residual sense of self hanging like dross in an expanse that was neither entirely silent nor entirely dark. He began a dream in which the cleaning woman in the glass dome was his sister Lucy, and that she knelt in a black slick of blood, scrubbing brush in hand, talking calmly to him about her Comforter. Then something cut across it all and he came awake in a series of swoops, confused, frightened, some primal fear on him.

'What?' he said. 'What?'

'*Tran-quillo*,' came a voice, a mouth that could not be more than a few inches from his ear.

'Ah . . . The Spanish gentleman . . .'

'Yes,' said the voice. 'The Spanish gentleman.'

Lacroix shifted towards his own side of the bed. He felt the other settling. He was not sorry to have company, someone to dispel the vile, senseless dream. 'Madrid?' he asked.

'Cordoba.'

'Cordoba. The south.'

'You know Spain?' asked the voice. *'Usted habla español?'*

'Habla? Pequeño. Su pais . . . es muy interesante.'

'Gracias. Muy amable.'

'You are going home now? To Cordoba?'

'Not yet,' said the voice. 'But one day . . .'

'Mmm,' said Lacroix, circling towards sleep again. 'For me also. Home, but not yet . . .'

He turned away. They slept back to back through the depths of the night, on each face a frown of concentration sleep softened but could not erase. In the morning, when Lacroix woke, the man had already gone. The man, his pack, his heavy coat.

They ran the last yards to the cathedral, hurrying in from a rainburst, Emily clutching Lacroix's elbow as they came through the door into a space of high, even light. It was a few minutes past eleven thirty. They stood by the door catching their breath and brushing raindrops from their faces. Ten or twelve men and women were strolling quietly about the walls, pausing to squint at the faded Latin of memorials, at empty niches that must once have held images. On the western wall, hanging from a pole above a tablet of freshly worked stone, was a flag, the cloth tattered as though by shot or fire. Despite the damage it did not look particularly old and Lacroix would have liked to examine it. It was, conceivably, the colours Ranald followed ashore on to the beaches at Aboukir, but these next minutes – now to the striking of midday – belonged to Emily and he would not break in on them, certainly not for something connected to the 'dastardly carcass of corruption'.

They walked to the choir screen, passed through and sat at the back, a pew close to a window, somewhere they could see from and be seen.

They had talked in practical terms on the way up from the inn. When he would come to the hospital, what of her things he should bring with him. She had asked if he had given Rizzo any money. He said he had not. In truth he had none to give until the draft came. 'I'll pay for my own eyes,' she had said, 'though I trust it will not be more than seven pounds.'

Now they rested in the hush of the place. There had, presumably, been a matins, and there would, presumably, be something later, but for the moment the place was an unlit theatre and the few figures who came down from the nave were casual and hardly bothered to glance at them.

On the ceiling, the wooden ribs were studded with carved stone bosses. Lacroix described them for her, what he could see of them under their veilings of shadow. Bishops, saints, a white hart, a white rose. A thistle. She said she liked thistles.

'Better than roses?' he asked.

She didn't reply. She had shut her eyes and appeared to have withdrawn completely, though when the window beside them suddenly brightened – the end of the rain shower – she was aware of it, the swell of coloured light, and she smiled.

'I don't object to religion,' she said, 'when it's human.'

'Yes,' he said, unsure if he had heard her rightly but sufficiently used to her flights to suspect that he had. He looked at her, the settled profile of her face, and thought of the inn where now all rooms were surely free, all beds. It was not too late – and Rizzo might be relieved. Next to the horror of having a knife in your eye must be the horror of being the one who wielded it. They would walk back to the Trongate, they would take a room, they would lie down together. After all, you did not need eyes for any of that. And when they were done they would rise up like the king and queen of the day. He called to her, silently, told himself that if his calling woke her, if she were suddenly to look at him . . .

Then he saw, beyond her, standing in the side aisle just at the edge of the wash of window light, the figure of a man. It was Rizzo. He had come in person. He was holding a furled umbrella to his chest, the umbrella black like his coat. Each man made a small gesture of recognition. Lacroix touched Emily's hand. She opened her eyes, read in his own what she needed to, and turned towards Rizzo. The surgeon made a bow. She stood, shuffled sideways along the pew. Lacroix was still sitting. He watched them exchange a few whispered words. He felt entirely unable to move. As in Morales. As in Morales. Then both of them glanced at him, smiled, and set off for the choir screen. He twisted round in time to see her take the surgeon's arm. Then they passed through the door to the nave – sank through it, it seemed – and he was alone.

FOUR

16

The plan was to pose as engineers though it seemed they must be close to the time they would not need to pose as anyone but themselves. Calley asked Medina to draw up a list of the islands. Asked him, told him. Medina wrote the list by candlelight in the room he shared with the stranger in Glasgow, the inn a place he himself had chosen when they came back from Dumbarton, for if he was still taking the corporal's orders he was also, of late, experimenting with insistence and finding it sometimes worked.

On the list – ink, pen and paper supplied by the management (that's what you get in a decent place) – he wrote down, as best he could, the names of islands as he had learned them from the various men and women he had entered into conversation with. He included, of course, the names Calley had been given by the sea captain, or that he reported being given, for he had gone alone into the house while he, Medina, stood watch in the street, the moon flickering behind clouds, a black cat observing him from a wall and seeming to hear from inside the house things he could not hear. *Gracias a Dios.*

Then, the list being somewhat short still, or simply because he had the pen in his hand and had not written anything for weeks, he added the names of his parents, the name of a girl from Cerro Muriano he had once been insanely in love with, and the name of his horse, from that time when Spanish cavalry still enjoyed the use of horses.

In the morning he showed the list to Calley.

'We'll be busy,' said Calley, who could count if he could not read.

'Unless he is on the first,' said Medina.

'First what?'

'First island.'

'Some fucking chance of that,' said Calley.

Medina shrugged. He had not enjoyed the moment as much as he had hoped and was, anyway, distracted by the woman sitting near the window, brown dress, blue shawl, a hat with a feather, her dish of tea untouched. Her face was away from him. She had her hair pinned up and the light lay silver on her neck. Her stillness. What was the meaning of such stillness? Then the noise of a door shouldered open – the butcher's boy on his way through, half a pig in his arms – and she turned, startled, scanning the room. She saw Medina, or she looked at him, at where he was sitting, the air he occupied. He inclined his head to her but she made no gesture in return. She turned away again, resumed her stillness.

On the Broomielaw they called down to the decks of boats being readied for sea and a short while before ten boarded a vessel bound for the Isle of Arran. Arran, explained the man who had waved them on board, who wrote out each of them a little ticket, fanning the paper in the air to dry the ink, was an excellent place to start a tour. They should go for a tramp up Goat Fell. Views to inspire! Take your sketch books, gentlemen! Your watercolour boxes!

It was early evening by the time they reached the island. They walked from the quay to a hotel, leaned at the bar, stood drinks and brought the talk around to a friend of theirs, a man travelling ahead of them, English, an army officer, perhaps with a fiddle among his things and wanting to hear music. Name of Lacroix, though sometimes, for whimsical reasons, introducing himself as Mr Lovall.

It was a risk of course, after the business with Captain Browne. One thing to make a man swear on his life, to fill him with the fear, another to be confident your work will last. What news from Dumbarton might have been carried on the boat ahead of them? But no one had heard of any English officer travelling alone with a fiddle, though some took half a bottle to be sure of it.

In the morning they sailed for Islay, and later the same day paid a man to row them over to Jura. In Jura, in a boarding house, they sat out two days of storm, the weather dementing against the windows so that they dared not sit too close for fear the glass would come in. Medina took lessons in Gaelic from the landlord, a large man who appeared always to be dithering at the edge of some hilarity and who, above the crashing of the storm, recited phrases about old battles between people with almost identical names. Medina, swaddled in a tartan blanket, called the phrases back to him, was gently corrected and called again. Calley was sitting in a chair on the other side of the room. He wore his coat and turned the pages of a picture book about the lives of Scottish saints, brawny types who put men's severed heads back on their shoulders, who befriended lions.

'What's this?' said Calley, breaking in on the lesson. 'What lions? There are no lions in Scotland.'

But the landlord detected the uncertainty in his voice and with a smile, a mild blinking of his eyes, told how his grandfather had once seen a whole nest of them up on the Paps, and that they had turned and turned as though they were *boiling*.

'Yeah, right,' said Calley, but he looked pleased and went back to slowly turning the pages of the book.

The afternoon of the third day they went over to Mull. The wind had dropped but a big sea was still running. Both men vomited on the journey and on reaching harbour staggered among crab pots, shuddered, felt for stone and could not speak. Once they had recovered themselves a little by sitting an hour, boots dangling over the harbour wall ('the sea,' said Calley, 'is a fucking disgrace'), they set off walking between the houses and the boats and came soon enough to a narrow way, a half-open door, the glimmering of human forms, the clink of bottles. They went in. Faces turned towards them like stone flowers turning towards the sun. Medina addressed them with a word of Gaelic. Perhaps it was a greeting; perhaps it was the name of a type of outhouse. 'We're engineers,' said Calley. 'We're having a scout about.'

They sat on a bench. The smell of fish was as strong in the bar as it had been on the front by the pots. It leaked from the men's clothes, their homespun, their shoes made of bark or sealskin. One man seemed to be wearing birds on his feet and it was hard not to comment on it. A bottle was asked for, a bottle was brought, and though there must have been complicated rules pertaining to hospitality, the offering of gifts, rules stretching back to the time of the brawny saints, the islanders seemed glad enough to forget them in another's ignorance. Medina topped up tumblers, tin mugs, vessels of horn. He made encouraging remarks to them, sometimes in Spanish.

'Anyway,' said Calley, raising his glass. 'We've been wanting to hear about a friend of ours. Someone you might have seen . . .'

The men listened and when Calley had finished those who had understood translated for those who had not. There were glances and nods, then one of the English speakers, a sonorous voice, his English full of strange inversions, unexpected stresses, said there *had* been an Englishman, though whether he had arrived recently or perhaps during the War of the Three Kingdoms dressed in the armour of Cromwell's New Model Army, was unclear. There was a long teasing-out of details. Calley could be patient when he needed to, when there was some advantage. Slowly, the Englishman took shape. He had come alone, in the summer, a week or two before the feast of Almus. The fiddle could not be confirmed but the man with the birds on his feet thought there was one, yes, and that the Englishman had played it at the landing place and the bairns had danced to it.

And now?

He has gone to Cola, said another. He pointed to a corner of the bar. Calley and Medina looked there. A wall.

'It is an island,' said the man. 'You may go there tomorrow I think.'

'And why did he go to this other island?' asked Calley. 'Why did he leave here?'

The question, translated, produced an answer they all seemed agreed upon. One word, a single word, not English. Calley and Medina waited. The word was passed about, flew from mouth to mouth until the most confident of the English speakers, his face in an ecstasy of concentration, suddenly opened his eyes wide, nodded emphatically and said, 'Grief.'

They reached Cola the next afternoon. The sea was calmer and they were not sick this time.

On Cola the story of the Englishman thinned out. What on Mull had been plural and feathered became, on the new island, a single voice, thin as a bootlace, the speaker not from the island at all but an official of some sort, dressed like a lawyer and there to collect rents. It was true, he said, there had been a stranger but he had stayed on the island no more than three days.

'He's gone?' said Calley.

'To Mingulay. If you climb the hill there and look west or somewhat north of west you should see it. On a clear day.' He said it was a hard place to get to and when you got there the effort could not be justified.

'So why would he go,' asked Calley, 'when there's nothing there?'

'I did not say there was nothing there,' said the man. 'And the people here did not want to keep him. They are given to superstition. They considered the man unlucky.'

He looked at them, the cool gaze of an appointed man, then, with a final taking-in of the long coats, the packs, the travelled faces, he turned to leave them.

'But someone,' said Medina, 'must have taken him.'

'Aye,' said the man. 'Neil MacCuish and his cousin. I would not go in a boat with them myself but . . .'

He walked away along the street they had been speaking on. It was, perhaps, the only street on the island. A cow stood at one end, the other end debouched into the air.

They spent the afternoon hunting down MacCuish. They were pointed towards farms, towards cottages, towards sprawls of open ground where the birds flew up under their feet. They stood on a rock and looked west. There was something out there, a hazy complication of islands, stretching northwards. Then a cloud of insects found them and drove them, beating at their faces, back to the shore. Here they came upon a man lifting a pair of ugly fish out of a lugger drawn up on the beach. On enquiry, the man turned out to be MacCuish himself. He was missing three fingers from his left hand, had an odd dent in his forehead. On one forearm he had a mermaid with a tipsy grin and on the other, in uncertain black letters from the elbow, CALEDONIA.

He had served four years in the Royal Navy – he and two brothers lifted out of their boat by a passing frigate, the boat sent back in the care of an old man, who then had the pleasure of breaking the news to their mother. 'We never saw her living again,' said MacCuish. He lit his pipe, worked at it a while. 'That might be something you know about,' he said.

'What's that?' said Calley. When he thought of his mother, of the word 'mother', he pictured a gate. High. Locked.

'The king's shilling,' said MacCuish.

'We're engineers,' said Calley.

'You'll be building us a bridge to the mainland perhaps?'

'We might,' said Calley.

The other nodded. He remembered the Englishman of course. The man was drunk when they set out. By the time they landed at Mingulay he had to be carried ashore. But he had paid them what he promised, had been courteous in the way a man three sheets to the wind may still be if he has sufficient breeding. He had a bag with him, his dunnage, but no fiddle unless it was a very small one and inside the bag. Which he doubted.

'He mention Spain or anything?' asked Calley.

'Spain?' MacCuish shook his head. There had been no mention of Spain. 'He spoke,' said MacCuish, 'of the world's beauty. And as we carried him up the beach he begged us to remember a woman's name.'

'What name?' asked Medina.

MacCuish could not remember but then his cousin arrived, coming down the face of a sand dune in three long glides like a skater. He looked much like MacCuish though without the dent, the missing fingers, the tattoos. They talked in their own tongue a while.

'Lucy,' said the cousin.

'That was it,' said MacCuish. 'Lucy.'

Calley looked at Medina. In a voice not much above a whisper he said, 'That's the sister's name.'

An arrangement was made. If the weather held they would go in the morning, first light. Calley and MacCuish walked down the beach to do the money business. The former rating's rolling gait, the soldier's bandy legs.

'*Fada, fada, fada bho thir,*' said Medina to the cousin. It was from a song the old man on Jura had chanted to him, something about the sea (he thought their language, in general, was an endless address to the sea). The cousin listened politely, looked for a moment as if he might offer a response, then went on plaiting strands of marram grass into a slender rope.

They spent the night at a house belonging to one of MacCuish's relatives. Dark inside and smoky, and with a sweet dungy smell.

'In England—' said Calley.

'I know,' said Medina. 'You would not keep your dogs in such a place.'

'Dogs? We wouldn't keep fucking *badgers* in here.' But he was in an excellent mood, almost at ease, almost affable. He drank his smoky milk from the bowl, ate his food squatting on a low stool by the fire.

'A week from now,' he said to Medina – there was only an old woman with her head in a scarf to overhear him – 'we'll be on a

boat back to Lisbon. And when we get there that cunt Henderson will have something nice for us. I'm going to put in a word for you. Yeah? I'm going to say you did all right. There might even be a medal in it. Imagine someone like you with a medal. A proper one.' He laughed. 'Then they can start the war again.'

They slept side by side in their coats on the straw, were woken by MacCuish, his voice in the darkness. On the beach the cousin was waiting by the bows of the lugger. They pushed the boat over the sand until she lay half in and half out of the water. Calley and Medina climbed in with their packs, then MacCuish and his cousin shouldered the boat into the shallows, pulling themselves aboard with little flicks of water from their bare feet. They rowed out until they found the wind, shipped the oars and hoisted their single sail. The lugger, noisy before with the rowing, now fitted herself to the quiet of the morning. At first she hardly seemed to be moving at all, then she heeled, very slightly, there was the whisper of water over clinkered wood, and they were under way, the beach, the bay, the island, withdrawing from them in a kind of smoothing.

It was a long crossing – the longest yet for Calley and Medina, who sat on their packs by the bows feeling beneath them the restlessness and infinite tonnage of green water. MacCuish watched everything. The sense was of making the crossing while the weather's back was turned. No cloud showed itself at the horizon without MacCuish noting its presence. Medina even saw him pick weed from the sea as if that too carried some message for him. In the early afternoon he pointed casually to the south. 'A whale,' he said.

Medina looked. He thought he saw something, a black something in the sea's glitter but could not be sure. How can you miss a whale? Calley preferred not to look but made a face, a whale-hating face, that lasted several minutes.

The moon rose, a waning crescent in a sky the colour of pearls. As night came on the wind picked up and the boat became jittery, the bows skipping from sea-hold to sea-hold. Calley drooped his head over the sea and conversed with it in a series of groans. Medina was in Spain, al Andaluz, a grove of almond trees in spring, the wind running down slender avenues of trees, the air a whirl of white blossom . . .

He was broken from the dream by the cousin coming forward to crouch at the bows. What now? More whales? MacCuish called out, the cousin called back; MacCuish adjusted their course. Medina, though straining his eyes, could not see what they saw. Or was it what they were *hearing*? For there was a new sound, a rushing, like the air in a shell. It had not been there before and it frightened him a little. The cousin called again; another shifting of the course. Then, a hundred yards ahead, Medina saw that what he had taken for grey moonlight on the sea was, in fact, the shore. Another call, another response. MacCuish, the shade of him, loosed the sail. An oar tested the water's depth – then the cousin was gone, sliding into the sea and appearing again, standing beside them in the water. He walked the boat in as you would walk a horse. MacCuish joined him and they dragged the lugger's nose up on to the beach. Calley and Medina climbed out, tottered on stiff legs over the sand. In the air above them a dog let out a single bark.

'We'll stay tonight with MacCusk,' said MacCuish. 'We were on the *Achille* together.'

They climbed the dunes then went in single file up a steep path cut into the rock. The dog must have woken someone. A voice hissed at them out of the invisible. MacCuish answered and the voice became the sound of greeting. A minute later there was a patch of yellow light and another voice drew them all to a door

and then to a room, small, wood-lined, full of little cupboards and remarkably like a ship's cabin. A woman was leaning over the fire and blowing sparks out of the dull heart of it. She straightened up as the men came in. Her face was the colour of the copper pan hanging from the beam above the fire, her hair a darker tint of the same, thick curls that had needed no curling iron.

'This is MacCusk,' said MacCuish. 'His wife Sara.' To MacCusk he said, 'These two men are interested in the Englishman I brought.'

MacCusk looked at them, then he and MacCuish spoke in their own language. Whatever it was they were saying to each other, the details, the finer points, it was clear from the tone that the interest was not welcome.

The woman brought a bottle and glasses. She put out a loaf of flat bread, unwrapped the muslin from a joint of cold meat. Her gown at the back was not properly fastened. She must have pulled it on at the sound of voices.

'*Lo siento por llegar tan tarde*,' said Medina, speaking to her under the noise of the other's talking.

She glanced at him, went on setting the table. He was sure, however, she had understood him.

Calley was watching the to and fro between the old shipmates. Then it broke off and they all sat at the table.

'Well,' said Calley, once he had eaten his bread, 'we're still wondering where our friend might be. As he doesn't seem to be in the house.'

MacCuish glanced at MacCusk. On MacCusk's hands two rust-red fish and an angel. Letters across his knuckles. *Hold. Fast.*

'He went away,' said MacCusk.

'Away where?'

'To the north.'

'North where?'

'He did not say.'

'So you didn't take him?'

'I did not.'

'Who did?'

'A boat came in. I did not see it.'

'And whisked him off to the north.'

'That is it.'

'Well, that's not very convenient,' said Calley. 'Given we've come a long way.'

'You can come back with us in the morning,' said MacCuish.

'Back to where we came from?'

MacCuish nodded.

'That's no use to us,' said Calley.

'You want to go north?' asked MacCuish.

'We want to go where our friend has gone. Unless you know some other way to find him?'

It ended there. The men did not meet each other's eyes. MacCusk splashed drink in the glasses for a last time, then beds were made up near the fire, the visitors lay down, the lamp was extinguished.

Four, five hours later, MacCuish and his cousin got up from the floor. An unshuttered window showed the first greys of morning.

'You are staying?' asked MacCuish.

'Unless you want to take us north,' said Calley.

'No,' said MacCuish.

'Then we're staying.'

The men left. There was the sound of the wooden latch, a moment of colder air, and half a minute afterwards the bark of the dog again, sharp and single.

The woman rose next. She slid down from the cubby where

the bed was and sat lacing her boots. When she saw Medina and Calley she paused as though surprised to find them still at the house. They sat out of her way while she went about her morning chores. When MacCusk came down from the bed he stood at a distance from Calley and Medina and weighed them up. Medina, without looking at Calley, knew he would have his coat unbuttoned, knew he would be returning MacCusk's regard with perfect steadiness.

'We will eat,' said MacCusk, not looking at the others now, 'then you must find somewhere else to go. Ask in the village. Someone will go across with you.'

'To the north,' said Calley.

MacCusk nodded, began to tie back his hair with a piece of leather cord that dangled between his fingers. Medina stood up. Though he knew it was not entirely safe to leave Calley with MacCusk, he needed to piss. He found his way outside, scraping his head on the lintel as he went. Cold, clear air; the usual frenzy of birds. Full day was still an hour off, but could he see the beach where they had landed and half a dozen thatched houses on the heights above.

He walked behind the house looking for somewhere he could use as a latrine. He saw the woman, a dripping bucket in one hand, coming towards him.

'*Buenos dias,*' he said. She stopped. He did not think she was afraid of him. He stepped closer. '*Hablas español?*'

She shrugged, or she moved the shoulder on the side that was not weighed with the bucket.

'*De donde eres?*'

'*Brasilia.*'

'*Una brasileña?*'

She nodded. He tried to guess how old she was. Younger, he

thought, than she looked. Had she sailed from Brazil on the warship? The *Achille*?

'*Has cruzado el mundo*,' he said.

'*Sí*,' she said. '*Hecho*,'

He asked her if she had seen the Englishman.

She nodded again.

He wanted to ask her why her husband was angry. Instead he asked simply, '*Qué ha pasado aquí?*'

'*Pasado?*' she said.

'*Sí*.' Then a moment of certainty. A thought that had not, until that instant, occurred to him at all. '*Está aquí, no? Todavía aquí.*' He's still here.

Her gaze dropped to his chest then lifted to his face again. He wondered if she had ever been a slave.

'*Sí*,' she said. '*Ele está aquí.*' He is here.

She walked past him, carrying the water to the house. Medina went to piss. Another treeless island. He found a rock and watched the heat of himself steam off its surface.

When he went back into the house he heard, then saw, the woman and MacCusk in a hushed wrangling with each other. They used three languages, three at least, while Calley watched them from his chair, looking now at the husband, now at the wife. MacCusk was insisting on something, on silence perhaps, but Sara was holding her ground. They argued either side of the fire and its light lit them strangely. The copper of her face, the blue and grey of MacCusk's; the sailor's body like a tool worked from wood, from the roots of something, the woman in her old gown, stout and short but supple and upright. It was MacCusk who backed away. He unslung his jacket from a hook on the door and left the house.

Calley looked at Medina.

Medina said, 'He's here. On the island.'

'Our man?' asked Calley.

'Yes.'

'Is he close?'

'I think she knows,' said Medina.

Calley turned to her. 'Go on then,' he said.

'This night,' she said. And to Medina, '*Esta noche.*'

Calley shook his head. 'By *esta noche* he might have flown away. He does that.' He moved one hand. A wing.

'No,' she said.

'No?'

'*Vocês são seus amigos?*' she said.

Medina nodded.

She paused. '*Ele está morto,*' she said.

'*Morto?*' said Medina. '*Muerte?*'

'*Sí, muerte.*'

'What's this?' said Calley. 'Is she saying what I think she's saying?'

'She says he's dead,' says Medina. He laughed. The woman gaped at him. 'No,' he said. '*Es . . . triste.*' But he almost laughed a second time. It was over. This lunatic crawling after a man who vanished before them like a trick of the light.

'Where?' said Calley. 'How?'

'Dead,' she said.

'I'm asking how,' said Calley. 'How dead? How?'

She raised a hand to her neck, then drew the tips of her fingers across her skin. The meaning was plain though it looked more like a caress.

'His throat?' said Calley. 'Someone kill him? Your husband?'

'No,' she answered, 'no one.'

'*Se mato?*' asked Medina.

'*Sí*,' she said.

'In English if you please,' said Calley.

'He killed himself,' said Medina.

'Done it himself?' said Calley. 'Stuck himself?'

For several seconds they were silent. Out of sight somewhere, a clock ticked erratically.

'Well, I didn't see that coming,' said Calley. 'Did you?'

'No,' said Medina.

'Course you fucking didn't,' said Calley.

'His guilt,' said Medina. 'His . . . shame.'

'We'll need to see him of course,' said Calley.

'See him?'

'I assume that's where she was taking us tonight. His grave. I mean I assume they didn't just leave him for the birds.'

The woman was following this, or trying to. '*Seu túmulo?*' she asked.

Medina nodded.

'Tonight,' she said.

'What's wrong with now?' asked Calley. '*Porque no ahora?*'

'A suicide,' said Medina. 'In such a place. You . . . hide it. You never speak of it.'

Calley looked at him and for a moment he seemed to be thinking about it. A community of thirty, forty souls, life's fabric rent by a stranger. The need to forget, to look away. Then he stood up and buttoned his coat. 'Bollocks,' he said, 'we'll go now. And we'll need a spade.' He looked at the woman. 'To dig?' he said, and lifting one boot he mimed for her the driving of a blade into the earth.

The grave of the Englishman was as far from the cove, the house, the settlement, as such a small island would allow. They walked, the three of them, less than a mile across the place's humped stone back. The woman, head covered, her jacket a sailor's jacket, walked at the front. Then came Medina, then Calley carrying a peat spade on his shoulder like a musket. They walked from sea to sea, then out on to a promontory, the island's last extension. A short-legged horse – a thing still as the land it stood on – watched them come. The mind of an animal up here. The mind of a person. How much sky can one life bear?

'Here,' said the woman, pointing to what they were all already looking at, the shallow heaping of stones between her boot caps and the cliff-edge.

'You'd think,' said Calley, 'they would just have heaved him over the edge. Still, lucky for us I suppose.'

The woman lingered long enough to see him lifting away the first stones, to see him stare at Medina until Medina joined him. Take a stone, lift it, set it down. Take another. Then she left them.

'*Adios,*' said Calley. '*Hasta la vista!*'

Under the stones were squares of peat, then smaller pieces the size of your fist, then smaller still, a black rubble mixed with roots and pebbles. It was not a deep grave, nor did they need the spade. Calley knelt one side, Medina the other. The wind tousled their hair, played with the hems of their coats. They came to a layer of stone again and underneath it a sheet of canvas, something spared from a sail, brown with tallow. Calley took off his coat, lay on his belly and stretched down. When he tugged free a corner of the canvas they saw a man's black hair. He tugged again and they had the whole head. The weight of the stones had done something to the shape of his face, and the peat or the tallow or both had begun to colour his skin, but he was not, it seemed, much altered by his stay in the ground and would, presumably, be recognised by those who had known him in life. The wound to the neck had been bandaged with the man's stock, the linen still white in places though most of it brown-red like iron in a rock.

'It's him,' said Medina.

Calley looked across the grave. 'You what?'

'It's him. The man I saw in the painting at the house. The man responsible for the massacre. In the ground. Finished.'

'It doesn't look anything like him,' said Calley.

'No. It's him. I will swear it.'

'Fuck off,' said Calley. 'Look at him.'

'I have looked.'

'Look at him again. I've *seen* the man. Remember? I've seen him. This is not even close.'

Medina shrugged. 'I disagree.'

'You can disagree all you like. This is not the cunt we're looking for. And you know it. So stop pissing around.'

He dragged the canvas lower. The man's hands had been arranged on his belly. One hand open, one closed. Calley turned the closed hand over and peeled back the fingers. Something bright slid from the palm and lodged itself between the man's body and his arm. Calley, lowering himself a little further into the grave, rummaged in the folds of the man's coat and came up holding a circle of bright metal, a polished brass case like the case of a small watch.

'What is it?' asked Medina.

Calley shook his head. He was working at the catch. Was there a lock? Then it opened and he stared at it, baffled at first, then grinning. He held it up for Medina though did not let him touch it. Medina squatted, one hand on the earth to steady himself. Inside the case, on what might be a piece of ivory, was a painting of an eye. It was clearly a woman's eye, a single blue eye with a curl of blonde hair above it. At the eye's inner crease, painted perhaps by a different hand, perhaps later, were two grey tears.

'His Lucy,' said Medina.

Calley nodded. 'How do they make it so small?'

'A brush with two hairs,' said Medina. 'One hair . . .'

For almost a minute, under the raving of the birds who rode the currents at the cliff's edge, they studied it, the woman's eye staring back at them as though through a keyhole. Then Calley snapped the case shut, a small sound that somehow, in all that emptiness, held its own.

'You must give it back to him,' said Medina. 'We are not tomb thieves.'

'Don't you worry about that,' said Calley. 'Tomb thieves! What the fuck!' He laughed, though not unkindly, and getting on to his belly again, he reached back down to the man's hands. Closed one, left one open. Pulled up the canvas.

17

To reach the women's ward you passed through the room where the boy with the tumorous neck had his bed, then through the corridor, past Rizzo's consulting room, the steps to the theatre, and on to where a curtained doorway was guarded by a female doorkeeper, a type of nun perhaps, sitting on a stool. Lacroix said who he had come for. The woman stood, drew back the curtain and pointed.

It was the first bed on the left-hand side. Beyond it were ten or twelve more, the same on the other side where the morning light was slightly stronger. All the beds were occupied. Some of the women were sitting up in their gowns. One, whose bed was opposite Emily's, dragged a brush through long red hair.

What is gallantry on a women's ward? He smiled, bowed. Some of the women smiled back. The woman with the red hair went on with her brushing.

There was no chair by Emily's bed so he stood at its side looking down at her. She was sleeping, lying on her back, deeply absent. They would have given her something, of course. He hoped they had. A draught, a calmative. Grains of opium. Her left eye was covered with a dressing held in place by a bandage that wound diagonally around her head. She looked neither better nor worse than he had imagined her. She looked . . . different, as if the shock of what had taken place the previous day was in her still. As though, stretched out on the table under the glass roof (someone stepping forward, apologetically, purposefully, to keep her head from moving), she had clenched around her fear and not yet let go.

He bent to her. He wanted to whisper her name but was afraid of waking her to pain. He wanted to touch her shoulder or her hand but was aware he was still being watched. So he stood there, a messenger from the outer world who had, apparently, forgotten his message. He looked round. The red-haired woman was speaking to him. He thought she said 'peaceful', or 'piece meal'. He thanked her (for what?) and was preparing to leave when Rizzo swept aside the curtain and entered the ward with a cry of 'Good morning, ladies!' He smiled at Lacroix, came to stand next to him.

'Well, you have seen for yourself,' he said.

'Seen?'

'Miss Frend.'

'I have. Yes.'

The procedure, explained Rizzo, speaking in a clear though confidential voice close to Lacroix's right ear, had been without any alarming incident. True, it had lasted somewhat longer than he had hoped – longer, certainly, than Miss Frend would have hoped. But at the end she had been able to stand and come down the ward with no assistance but his own arm. The dressing had been changed this morning. The eye looked as he would wish it to. There was some fever in the night but that had passed off. He was, in conclusion, very pleased.

'This is excellent news,' said Lacroix. He felt slightly nauseous. He had drunk a lot of brandy the night before and going up the stairs to his room had tripped on the top step, gone down on the boards like one struck. A servant, a girl with a club foot, had seen him and grinned. He thought she might have said something saucy to him.

'I am glad she is sleeping,' he said.

'Yes,' said Rizzo. 'Yes. We will let her sleep. Then a little nourishment. Then more sleep. Come back this afternoon. It may be she will be ready for a short conversation.'

'You will tell her I was here?'

'I will.'

'And that I am coming back?'

'Also that.'

'Good. Thank you. I cannot say how . . . relieved I am.'

'Ah, but you have,' said the surgeon.

Lacroix left the hospital – or he set out to leave but having descended two rather than three flights of stairs he turned at the volute, was led by it, its wooden flourish, and walked some twenty paces before waking to the fact he was not where he had expected to be. He was in a gallery at the rear of the building, a part of the hospital he had not seen before. There were large windows with long views, and on the opposite wall life-sized portraits of men who looked like hanging judges but who were no doubt donors or hospital governors – tobacco merchants making a lunge for heaven. Halfway down the gallery a collection of armchairs and a pair of leathery aspidistras made a kind of public drawing room. Two of the chairs were occupied by men dressed in the hospital uniform of brown woollen robes, those for the men indistinguishable from those worn by the women. They were playing chess, were engrossed, and did not look up at Lacroix. He settled himself in the chair nearest the window, stared out a while then let his eyes close. He felt subtly poisoned by the brandy, perhaps more unwell than the chess players. Would he object if someone came and wrapped him in a brown robe? He thought he would not. Yet he also felt perfectly at ease, languorous, cheerful. Tempting to call it happiness.

On the way up from the inn – though he had not allowed the words to sound in his head – he had come close to convincing himself that Emily Frend was dead. He would meet a grim-faced Rizzo, be given a parcel of her clothes and be taken to a room to view her corpse. But she was alive still! They had cut her and she had stood on her own feet, had descended a flight of stairs with no more help than the surgeon's arm! O Shoreditch! What daughters you have!

He slept for an hour – deep rest, deep contentment – and on waking (the chess players both gone) he went down the last flight of stairs and out into the day just as the cathedral bells were sounding midday. Already he felt a familiarity with the town, or at least with the streets and buildings between the inn and the hospital. That shop, that stall, that nailed door, that beggar. The Ship Bank was on the Trongate. He had spotted it the previous afternoon, though it had already closed for the day. Now its doors stood open and a man in livery tipped his hat as Lacroix passed inside. It was, after the hospital, a reassuring place to be. Mirrors, marble heads, large, polished tables. It smelled, he thought, of the slight bitterness of ink, but there was nothing in the air to remind him of bodies and the troubles of bodies. Ahead of him, behind a high counter, sat a row of clerks, their faces seen through wooden rails. Shorter men, approaching the counter, made use of one of the scuffed wooden boxes provided for the purpose. Lacroix did not need a box, but only just. He stretched up; the clerk heard him out, answered, saw his answer went unheard and pointed to the stairs. 'Drummond!' he said. 'Mr Drummond . . .'

Upstairs had its own atmosphere. Less polish, less show, fewer people. All along the corridor shelves ran floor to ceiling. A boy on a ladder was handing down papers to two others, documents that might be older than the boys themselves.

'Mr Drummond?'

'In there, sir,' said the boy up the ladder.

The door was open. Lacroix tapped and went in. Drummond was eating something. Seeing he had a visitor he opened a drawer in his desk and placed the food inside. He listened to Lacroix, tapped the tips of his fingers together.

'Lacroix, you say?'

'That's right,' said Lacroix, who had been within a heartbeat of naming himself as Lovall.

A book was consulted. Lists of names, some with figures against them, others without.

'No,' said Drummond. 'Nothing. Not today.'

'I'll come tomorrow then,' said Lacroix.

'Aye,' said Drummond. He closed the ledger. Lacroix could see now what he had put in the drawer. A slab of cheese with the ragged half-moon indent of a man's bite.

He walked back to the hospital, half his thoughts on Emily, half on the need for ready cash. If it came to it, he could pawn the few clothes he had brought with him. Pawn the bag itself, why not? But would it raise much? He had no idea. He had never been inside a pawnshop, though he had seen their signs in several of the streets he had walked through in Glasgow and knew some of the men in the regiment resorted to them when they had need.

When he reached the ward she was still sleeping. He fetched a chair from the other end of the room and sat beside her. The woman with the red hair offered him something to read. It was a religious tract, Calvinist, an essay on the Fall, innate sinfulness, hell. He read the first two pages for the sake of politeness (he thought she might be watching him) and marvelled at how unattractive it was, how sad a branch to clutch at as you were swept down the river, how little there was in it of love or even kindness. When he glanced up, the woman was indeed watching him. She smiled encouragement; he read another page, knowing it for the despair it was. He had had such voices in his own head for months. They were as familiar to him as the folds and creases of a sick-bed. He was listening for something else now. A different voice, a different message. Or just the silence that might precede such a message. He would settle for that. A cessation, a hush.

Other visitors came to see other women. Each arrival was a moment of interest and the curtain lent a certain theatricality. Hawkers came up. A milkmaid, a woman selling thread and yarn, then a girl with a tray of prawns and periwinkles.

Lacroix decided he would leave again – an hour by the bed of someone sleeping is a long hour. He would take a turn in the town, make enquiries about the mail coach from the south, its schedule, but as he stood she woke, her right eye flickering open, her hands travelling up to the covered eye, the dressing, the bandage.

'No, no,' he said, taking her hands and settling them back on the blanket. 'You must not touch.'

'John?' she said. She rolled her head on the pillow. He sat down, shifted the chair to make it easier for her to see him.

'John? I was afraid you would not come.'

'Not come?' He was grinning at her, leaning in to hear her. 'Why should I not come?'

She did not answer him. She looked past him into the ward, then shut her eye, lay back, sighed, opened the eye again to look at him. In some curious way one eye seemed more expressive than two.

'Rizzo is pleased,' he said.

'Pleased with himself,' she said.

'That's true,' said Lacroix.

'When he did it,' she said, 'he was as white as paper. I was afraid his hand would tremble. Do you know how he prepares? By threading needles. He told me so. He threads a needle ten times. And John, there is a glass roof and before I lay down we all looked out. Rizzo and Mr Crisp, his assistant. I could see very little of course but I imagined a great deal. I thought I could see Jane and Cornelius and even Ranald.'

'On the island? What were they doing?'

'Oh, just standing. But with encouraging looks on their faces.'

'You must be their constant thought,' he said.

'No,' she said. 'There are ears and babies. And I do not want to be in anyone's thoughts *constantly*.'

She shut her eye, was quiet a moment, then said, 'The imagined is not the contrary of the real, John.' And after a longer pause, 'I can smell the sea.'

He started to tell her about the prawn seller, who had indeed left both the scent and somehow the image of the sea behind her, but Emily was asleep before he had finished. He crossed the ward and returned the tract to the woman with the red hair.

'I have been among the worst,' she said, accepting the book from him.

'I too,' he said, and for three or four seconds they stood regarding each other as if the secret marks of the fire were on them.

There was one more visit before the day was out. Rizzo was changing Emily's dressing. Lacroix waited for them just inside the ward. At the end of Emily's bed was a screen of wood and white linen and through the linen he saw Rizzo's outline, leaning and rising like a living watermark. After a few minutes the surgeon appeared around the side of the screen carrying a tin dish with the old dressing in it. They greeted each other. Lacroix kept his eyes off the dish, the pinkish linen. Rizzo said he would order tea and toast for them all. In the meantime Miss Frend was now in a condition to receive visitors.

She was pushing herself up into a sitting position. She did not need his help, thank you, though she allowed him to rearrange her pillows, then focused on his face, frowned and said, 'I do not care how I look,' which made him laugh.

Rizzo rejoined them (smells of soap), and when the tea tray arrived in the arms of a man who looked winded by his climb from the kitchens, the surgeon poured for them all. The screen gave them privacy. Emily drank her tea, had a second cup and finished that also. They spoke about the hospital, about Glasgow, about the islands, the white house by the sea.

'Mr Lovall,' she said, 'arrived on a cow.'

Rizzo nodded. Perhaps he thought her mind was straying, touched still by whatever he had given her from his pharmacopoeia. But the conversation – polite, aimless – was evidence of something. At the very least there was nothing to evoke the room above them, what had taken place there, would take place there again. When the pot was empty and they had eaten the last of the cold toast, a bell was swung somewhere down in the belly of the hospital.

Rizzo took out his watch. 'Visiting time,' he said, 'has come to an end. You must forgive us but we were in our early days much used by those who had nowhere to go at night. Many times on my morning rounds I saw a man's feet beneath a patient's bed. Well, it is not a way to run a hospital. Not that I suspect you, Mr Lovall, of having such . . . designs.'

Lacroix rose. There was a moment of awkwardness with Emily, a sudden lapse into strangerhood. He did not know where to put his hands. He undid then refastened the bottom button of his waistcoat. He wished her a peaceful night. Someone, not Rizzo, folded the screen and took it away.

He had his supper at a chop house. It was cheaper than eating at the inn – a shilling for a plate of brawn and cabbage, a glass of something called claret – his fellow diners mostly men alone, men without the convenience of wives or, like Lacroix, moment-arily or chronically without funds. It was not brotherly but it was easy and the man who presided, who came and went from a back kitchen, empty plates one way, plates loaded the other, calmed them, their solitary condition, like a sergeant moving among recruits (the enemy not at hand but not distant either).

When he had eaten he climbed to the street again, saw the evening star in the gap between two tenements, greeted it, and walked back to the inn. There he made a point of showing himself to the landlord, of treating him to the kind of nod a gentleman whose pocket book is well stocked with large, painterly bank-notes, bestows on an innkeeper. He took a small glass of brandy standing by the fire, then went up to his room hoping to find no one there but finding the club-footed maid who had seen him stumble on the stairs the night before. He did not think she was stealing anything. She had, perhaps, just made up the bed. The room was dim, and as she came towards him, her face shadowed but her eyes carrying points of light, he wondered if she would hold out an orange and ask if he wished to buy it. Instead she asked him if he wanted a candle brought up. He said he didn't.

At the Ship Bank, half an hour after he had seen the mail coach come down the Trongate through morning air and morning dust, he went up the stairs to see Drummond. Drummond wasn't there. Lacroix sat on a bench outside the door, its wood polished almost to blackness by the backsides of those who had waited before him. He watched the coming and going of the boys, the youngest of them children dressed as men, wrists and necks raw from the rub of their clothes. In Spain the child soldiers died alongside veterans, boys of ten or eleven with men who wore their hair in a grey queue. Bury one, bury the other. Harder of course to ride past a boy who is crying for help. He hoped he had not done that. He could not remember. He hoped he had not. Had he?

Drummond arrived. He saw Lacroix and waved him into the office.

'It was with us yesterday,' he said, 'but not with me or you should have had it then. There is a progression. So many hands, so many eyes. We are entirely at the mercy of the floor below. Their systems are not ours. But there it is. We are an animal made up of its various parts. A horse with the trunk of an elephant, the feet of . . .'

It seemed he could not think what the feet might be. 'A sort of Sphinx,' said Lacroix.

'Aye,' said the man. He was looking along a slotted wall of docket boxes. He plucked out a folded sheet, examined it at arm's length and passed it to Lacroix. 'Captain John Lacroix,' he said. 'From your bankers in Bath.'

'I thank you.'

'There has been a murder there,' said Drummond.

'A what?'

'A murder.'

'In Bath?'

'There or somewhere in the county. Or it was an assault perhaps. Someone's cook. Our Mr Montcrieff spoke of it. I believe he saw it in the Bristol paper at the coffee house across the way.'

'I will look,' said Lacroix, checking the document in his hand, immensely cheered to have it, delighted almost to the point of laughter.

'It is what you were expecting, I hope,' said Drummond.

'It is. Exactly.'

From the thoroughfare below came the beat and clatter of horses. Both men stepped to the window, gazed down. Uniforms, the morning sun on helmets and spurs.

'Now what are they?' asked the banker. 'Dragoons?'

'I believe they are artillery men,' said Lacroix.

'Are they? They look like dragoons. Same hats. But you would know of course.'

Downstairs, at the high counter, the document was turned into money. Notes with blue lettering and the engraving of a ship, also blue, a picture that reminded Lacroix of the flyer at the hotel in Oban, the emigration ship. He folded his money and left the bank, determined to guard it better than the last, to keep not a single note in his boots.

He set off for the hospital, then crossed the street with the intention of going into the coffee house for ten minutes and seeing the Bristol paper but found himself drawn to the window of a jeweller's in the arcade by the coffee-house doors. He leaned into the glass, hands either side of his face, and peered in at the rucked velvet sheet on which the precious things lolled in a kind of nudity. Inside, the shop was no more than a small room, much of it taken up by a man in a close-fitting coat, a brass-barrelled musketoon propped against the wall behind him. In a race, thought Lacroix, might I get to it first? Cock it, fire, fill my pockets, run? He wished the man a good morning. The man returned his salutation with the barest movement of a cropped and nubbled head.

From further off, a part of the room hidden by the guard's shoulders, a woman's voice said, 'Did you have something particular in mind, sir?'

She came into view, dressed in grey silk and wearing – neck, hands, ears – a good scattering of what she sold.

'Something,' said Lacroix, 'for a friend. She is in the hospital.'

The woman came closer. She smiled at him. A respectful but confident smile. 'And what does your friend like?' she asked.

'Like? Well . . . She is thin. Or slender rather. Hair about your colour. A strong walker.' He paused. The woman's smile had broadened a little but she continued to look up at him, the tilted head of a patient listener, her hands clasped softly in front of her dress. 'She has,' he continued, 'not much in the way of family. A brother who is almost no use at all. A sister who has her own affairs to think of.'

'A woman of independent spirit?'

'She's pregnant,' said Lacroix.

'Your friend?'

'Heavens no. Her sister.'

He realised he was talking strangely, unguardedly, and that the woman was somehow making him do it. He did not mind. It did not feel wrong. It also amused him to think of the work she was having to do, trying to guess what he had, what he would spend, what he might mean by the word 'friend'.

She had keys in a hidden pocket. She opened cabinets, fetched pieces from the window display, laid rings out on a square of plush spread on the counter, turned a bracelet under the lamp. She watched what he touched and how he touched it. She was not afraid to look into his face, to show how she was leading him. With a flick from the side of her hand she tidied the rings away by covering them with a fold of the cloth then set down three brooches in a line. He liked the brooches. He picked up the middle one. It was formed like a little shield, had two silver thistles at the centre, a small crown on top.

'A luckenbooth,' said the woman. 'And here' – touching the edge of the brooch with her little finger – 'are two types of Scottish granite, cut thin as skin.'

He weighed the brooch in his palm. 'Her eyes are bad,' he said, 'but I think she would feel it out. The thistles. I think she would guess them.'

'I am sure of it,' said the woman.

There was a long moment of silence between them, the silence itself like something laid out on the plush, offered.

'I am . . .' he began.

'Yes?'

'You called it a luckenbooth.'

'A luckenbooth. Exactly.'

'I think it will do very well,' he said. 'Do you think so?'

'I do,' she said. She paused, then gently, with cool fingertips, took the brooch from his palm and went behind the counter with it.

Lacroix slid notes from his fold, blue ships. She could, they both knew, have sold him a more expensive piece, but she had sold him the right one and they were content. He glanced at the guard. Surely he was an old soldier, and one who had found something better than a street corner for himself and a hat set out for coppers. Tempting, in this mood of spending, to ask him where he'd served. Tempting to do and say more than was wise.

On his way up to the hospital he chided himself – five minutes with money in his pocket and he was inside a jeweller's shop! – but before he reached the cathedral he had lost interest in such arguments and swept through the doors of the hospital, a man with silver thistles in his pocket on his way to a woman who would be glad to have them.

On the third floor, walking between the beds (he had already greeted several patients on his way up), he stopped by the foot of the boy's bed. He had forgotten his name, then remembered it. 'Robert! How are you today?'

'I am very well, thank you,' said the boy. He held Lacroix's gaze with a steadiness that soon became difficult to match. The perfect brown of his eyes, the hint of a smile. The egg in his neck.

'I have come to see Miss Frend,' said Lacroix, wondering if he might show the boy the brooch. 'Emily.'

'Oh, she's gone,' said the boy.

'What's that?'

'She's gone.' He pointed to the ceiling.

'What are you talking about? Gone where?'

He did not wait for an answer. He hurried through the corridor, ignored whatever the doorkeeper was trying to say, swept aside the curtain and stared in at Emily's empty bed. From across the ward the red-haired woman, immediately on seeing him, also pointed to the ceiling. Three or four of the others joined her.

'She has gone to theatre,' said the doorkeeper, tugging him around and speaking to his face.

'Theatre? The operating theatre?'

'Half an hour ago.'

'With Rizzo?'

'Of course. With Mr Rizzo. The other eye.'

'But she had barely recovered from the first!'

'Mr Rizzo believed she was ready. She believed so herself. I heard her say it.'

That again! Her readiness, Rizzo's. His utter lack of the same. He was silent a moment. He wondered how he must have looked coming in like that, bursting past the curtain like the cuckolded husband in a farce. 'I should have come earlier,' he said. 'I had meant to. I only . . .'

The doorkeeper held up a hand. She was listening, but not to him. She busied him away from the door, went into the corridor, came back and held the curtain clear. Out of the corridor's throat came a huddle of human forms, Emily at the centre, dressed in one of the brown robes, Rizzo on her right, and on her left an older man in shirtsleeves, presumably the assistant, Crisp.

Both her eyes were covered now, a single bandage, so that she had the appearance of a poor queen led to the scaffold by her confessors. They came very slowly. When they reached the bed the doorkeeper helped remove the gown, then all three eased her backwards to the pillows. She let out a sigh – loud enough for Lacroix to hear it. Then she lay, soundless and still, or still but for her hands that moved, it seemed, in a blindness of their own.

Rizzo leaned down to speak in her ear. When he was done he stood back from the bed, conferred in a low voice with his assistant, saw Lacroix, crossed to him, led him to a quiet place by the curtain and said, 'You are unhappy. You think it was too soon.'

'Another few days,' said Lacroix, less sure now of exactly what he did think. 'A week perhaps.'

'Then you will allow me please to explain my reasoning.' He joined his hands, raised both his large, glossy eyebrows. He is, thought Lacroix, still high from the work.

'Half of those who are admitted to this hospital, more than half, more all the time, are fever patients. A healthy man or woman, if they are careful, may hope to continue well, but a patient who has undergone an operation is less strong, less able to resist. And so I try to do all things quickly. Safely but quickly. First the operation. Then, as soon as is practical, I send the patient away, send her home where, I hope, there is no contagion. Miss Frend this morning was rested. Her left eye was, and is, healing to my satisfaction. Had you been here no doubt she would have discussed it with you. But now it is done. *Pflück die Rose wenn sie blüht, Schmiede, wenn das Eisen glüht.*'

'May I speak with her?'

'Of course. But briefly please. Even a short operation is hard. A few words of reassurance. No more.'

Lacroix went over to the bed, looked down at her, sat on the chair, reached over and stilled her hands with one of his own.

'John?' she whispered. He saw it more than heard it.

'It is over,' he said. 'It is finished.'

'John?'

'You are safe, Emily. And Rizzo wants us gone as soon as possible. Think on that. We shall go back to the island. Soon. Both of us.'

She smiled. There was a streak of dried blood in her hair, just at the side where her hair had been pulled back tightly across her temple.

'And the money came,' he said, thinking at once of how crass it was to speak of money at such a time. He watched her mouth. There were no eyes to distract him. What was she saying? He turned his head, brought it closer.

'The baby,' she said. 'Jane's. Can you imagine it?'

'The baby?' He sat back. 'I can imagine a baby. I am not certain I can imagine *that* baby.'

Her smile broadened – then something, something going on under the bandage, the dressings, made her face suddenly stiffen. He glanced round for Rizzo, saw him, standing at a respectful distance. The surgeon raised a hand, palm out. It meant, perhaps, do not be alarmed. And when he looked back he saw that the pain had passed.

He stayed another minute. He was deep in concentration. Some animal resource for holding another's suffering, for surrounding it. Then, at a nod from Rizzo, he stood and went out to the corridor. There were tears on his cheeks. He hoped the doorkeeper, this woman whose name he had failed to learn, might notice them.

He came back in the early afternoon and again a little before six. Both times he stood at the end of the bed watching her shallow, uneasy sleep. She was, beneath the bandages, in the well of those hurt eyes, contending with things. With pain, of course, but not just with pain. Was her father present, railing at her child self, demanding dreams of her?

He went back to the inn, supped alone, went up to his room. He thought he might read something or write something. He thought he might go back down to the parlour and drink brandy until his chest burned. And while he thought these things he lay fully dressed on the bed, turning the silver thistles through his fingers.

The next morning she looked worse, the skin flushed at her neck, all the bones of her face showing their edges. Around her right eye, what he could see of it, she looked as if she had been struck. The red-haired woman said she had called in the night for Jane. Was Jane her sister? And there had been a second name. A name she had not been able to clearly hear.

'Thorpe,' said another woman, two beds down, her sewing gear in her lap. 'It was Thorpe.'

'Are you Thorpe?' asked the red-haired woman.

He shook his head. He asked if Rizzo had seen her. The woman said he had, that he had been behind the screen with her.

'I like an old-fashioned doctor,' said the woman with the sewing. 'I like them to have white whiskers.'

Lacroix went in search of Rizzo. He was not in his room, not in the male ward. He looked in the wards below, enquired of the men the other side of the hatch, gave up, came back and found the surgeon standing, arms crossed, head down, at the end of Emily's bed.

'She is having to fight,' said Rizzo.

'To what?' asked Lacroix.

'She has a reaction,' said Rizzo. 'It is troublesome but not, I think, severe.'

'You will treat her for it? You will need to bleed her perhaps.'

'I assure you,' said Rizzo, a sudden testiness in his voice, 'bleeding is the last thing she needs. The very last.'

'Then what do you intend?' asked Lacroix. His own voice was sharp now.

'I will support her.'

'How?'

'By letting her rest. By keeping the wound clean. By giving her nourishment when she can take it. By leaving her alone.'

'Alone?'

'The patient must cure herself. The physician must know his limits.'

They turned to each other, confronted each other.

'She is fighting,' said Rizzo. 'But she is strong. I mean her wish for life. She will not give up. And neither will we.'

Lacroix spent the day coming and going. He could not bear simply to sit there. Twice, when he was present, she turned her head, sensing him. He wanted to say, 'You asked for Thorpe!' It had pricked him. It still stung. Instead, he whispered her name, and had she asked him to he would have gone in search of Thorpe – hard to believe such a man would be difficult to uncover – and brought him to her. Perhaps Thorpe *could* heal her. He would lay on hands, would kiss her unchastely, sing psalms or recite the *Odyssey* in thumping Greek, his shirt blowing around his shoulders in a holy wind . . .

She asked for water. He held the cup to her lips, his right hand under her head. Her head, at least, was reassuringly weighty. At the evening bell Rizzo came through and said he was free to stay if he wished and that, before he left, he might like to join him in his room for a simple supper. So he stayed – another hour, most of the next. The women on the ward settled; the light thinned. A man – Lacroix had not seen him before, the night-attendant presumably – placed a lamp on the shelf above the door. A cat came in, slunk past the curtain and began its silent patrolling of the ward. Was its presence official? Did it wash its paws in soap and water? But he was glad to see it and hoped it might settle on Emily's bed, place a purring head by her feet.

Someone – he thought it was the new woman at the far end – let out a cry that sounded closer to grief than pain. He had been starting to drowse and it startled him. The attendant leaned in but the place was quiet again and he did not enter.

He listened for the cathedral bells. He thought of his old watch, the DuBois and Wheeler, stolen out of his trunk, thought of Wood waiting for him in the drawing room (*They've been sending me all over the country to find people*), thought of Nell ghosting the corridors of the house, the dog at her heels. In the window beside the bed he saw a piece of the lamplight and his own head, a blot of ink on the vague blue vastness of the night beyond. He yawned, shuddered with it, hovered his fingers above Emily's mouth to catch the curl of her breath, decided she was easy enough, drew a quick cross in the air above her head and crept out of the ward.

In Rizzo's room two candles burned on the desk either side of the book he was reading. Also on the desk was a parcel wrapped in brown paper, the paper spotted with grease. The surgeon gave Lacroix the room's only chair, the chair Emily had sat on for her examination. (Why could there not be another chair? Could the hospital governors not afford a second chair? Would chairs encourage people to stay? Slow down the machine?) He asked Lacroix how Emily was. Lacroix said he thought she was easier, that she was sleeping deeply.

'It is as I hoped,' said Rizzo. He unwrapped the parcel. Bread, cheese, meat of some kind.

'When we have eaten, you will go to your inn. I will remain here, in this room. The night-attendant has most strict instructions to fetch me the instant there is any cause for concern.'

'He is reliable?'

'He would not be here otherwise.'

There was a knife. Rizzo, with a quick brush of his thumb across the blade's grain, began to slice the meat. Lacroix looked away and found himself confronted again by the wall of eyes. Candlelight did not make them easier to bear.

For their meal together Rizzo perched on the edge of the desk. They took the food they wanted out of the brown paper. They talked. Rizzo knew about Cornelius's digging on the island, the blackened ear that had kept him from coming to have his teeth pulled.

'Will he find the rest?' he asked.

'If there is any more,' said Lacroix. 'And if finding it does not involve too much effort.'

He had also learned something about their music. Emily's guittar, Lacroix's fiddle.

'At least she does not need to see in order to play,' said Rizzo.

'But she will see?' asked Lacroix. 'You are still hopeful of that?'

'Of course,' said the surgeon. 'I did not mean . . .' He smiled. The tension between them of the afternoon – Lacroix's doubt about Rizzo's judgement, Rizzo's own doubts, perhaps – was gone entirely. In two small glasses that did not match at all, Rizzo poured them each two mouthfuls of wine. It was ruby red – a thin, light wine you could see the candle flame through. Rizzo said he liked Haydn. *Il Mondo della Luna* had enchanted him. Lacroix said he thought he had heard some Haydn, a concert in Bath, years ago.

'You knew he had died?' asked Rizzo.

'Haydn?'

'In May, I think. In Vienna.'

They did not ask questions about each other's family. They did not ask about the past at all, or if they did they did so glancingly. This was tact, or weariness, or the pleasant way two men can find to treat each other's history with indifference, to meet in what is public and impersonal, as though passing between them certain interesting artefacts from the museum that is the world: a dead composer, French wine, coffee houses, newspapers. Somehow they came to the war, or they came to it inevitably – it was the conclusion of so many conversations – but after general remarks about the blockade, about the military use of balloons and the army's insatiable need for horses, Rizzo steered them away. Had he heard something in the other's voice? A reluctance, a restlessness? Then a gun went off in the streets or gardens below. The men grinned uneasily.

'The end of a fox,' said Lacroix.

'Or I will have a new patient in the morning,' said Rizzo.

Lacroix turned his glass in his hands then set it down on the table next to the brown paper and stood. 'You know where I am on the Trongate,' he said 'I could be here in a quarter of an hour.'

They took their leave of each other. They shook hands. Lacroix moved through the hospital, descended the stairs with their rivers of shadow, nodded to various watchmen, waited for one to draw the bars on the front door, then stepped out into the hospital garden where night had released the scent of some flower he could not see. He turned towards the cathedral. There was a man standing by the west door with a lantern and as Lacroix crossed the close he saw it was one of the new police, though he could not see enough of him to tell if he was one of the pair who had found him, sprawled and bootless, on the cobbles. He was up there, presumably, on account of the gunshot. Lacroix muttered a goodnight to him and went on down the moon-splashed street, a dozen bars of music in his head, conceivably by Haydn.

In the morning he walked back through the day's first spread of light and arrived at the hospital before the doors were unlocked. He knocked, and the man who had let him out the night before let him back in. Lacroix gave him a sixpence, which he looked surprised at, amused by. On the ward most of the women were still asleep. Certainly Emily was. He stood over her, watched for several minutes the rhythms of her breathing. If she was not obviously better than the night before then she appeared no worse. He tapped on Rizzo's door, found him with a pair of scissors in one hand, in the other a mirror that looked too small to be really useful. He was bright-eyed for a man who must have slept . . . where? Had he slept at all?

'I have seen her,' said Lacroix.

'And she was resting?'

'She was.'

'She woke twice in the night. I was called both times. The first time I was frightened. I confess it. The second time less so. This morning . . .' – he frowned into the mirror, snipped a fine black curl just under his nose – 'I am looking forward to my coffee.'

Lacroix went out for his own coffee, sat in the coffee house on the Trongate where the waiters were still sweeping the floor, scattering water, scattering sawdust. He looked for the Bristol paper, found papers from London, Dundee, Dublin, Berlin, Halifax Nova Scotia, but not from Bristol. He finished his coffee and bought warm rolls from a street seller, bit into one and put the other in his pocket for Emily or Rizzo. Then, at a bookstall outside Old College (he could not resist a bookstall) he purchased Volume One of Hutton's *Principles of Knowledge*, carried the book to the hospital and sat at the side of Emily's bed working his way through a chapter on erosion. Several times throughout the day she came towards the surface of herself but never seemed fully awake, fully present. On one occasion, late afternoon, she spoke some jumbled sentences about her mother. Neither of them had spoken much about their mothers before, perhaps because the store of what they had to say was so small. Later she seemed to speak *to* her mother. 'Mama?' she said, as you might, standing at the door of a darkened room, call out. As a child might.

At the inn that evening, his room, at the table by the window (on which, among the initials, the hearts and dates, someone had scratched the word *Nada*) he wrote to Cornelius and Jane. He said things plainly and left the letter open for further news. Then he lay down on the bed with Hutton, read three paragraphs, read them again. Sweet Christ, it was impenetrable stuff! Yet he admired it, the way it came up honestly against the difficulty of knowing, the difficulty of saying, the difficulty of being clear.

In the night he thought he heard hailstones on the window but the morning was a beauty. He dressed, wedged the book in his pocket, discovered in the other pocket one of the rolls he'd bought the day before, breakfasted on it, washed it down with a mug of small beer in the parlour of the inn, and walked up to the hospital, filling his lungs to the brim with sun-ripened Glasgow air.

On the ward the windows had been opened. Emily was sitting up in her bed listening to the conversation of the red-haired woman who, as she talked, laid out crumbs on the window ledge and already had a pair of sparrows feeding there (another coming down even as Lacroix looked, and another).

'Now here is your visitor,' said the woman, standing at the second attempt and shuffling out from between the beds. 'I shall take myself off and visit Mrs Cameron.'

Lacroix thanked her, wished her a good morning. The chair was facing the window. He set it to face the bed and sat down. 'This is a damned good sight,' he said.

'Is it?' asked Emily, sitting pert as a blade of grass. 'I must look strange.'

'No. You look well. I cannot tell you how much better. We have been . . . uneasy.'

'I am sorry for it.' She was turned to him though her aim was inexact. She smiled, confidently, at a vacancy several inches to his left.

'How do *you* look?' she asked.

'What's that?'

'You told me the money had come. I remember that, I think. Have you bought yourself a splendid new coat?'

'I have bought nothing.'

'You could tell me you were sitting there wearing a bearskin and I should have to believe you.'

'You would touch me,' he said. 'To find out.'

'Yes,' she said, smiling, 'I would.'

'Though in truth,' he said, 'I have bought something. Two things.'

He teased her with a long pause, noting as he waited the line of small grey bruises stippling both her cheeks. They were, quite plainly, the marks of someone's fingers.

'A hat,' she said. 'Or . . . a red velvet waistcoat. Or new boots. No. I think it is a hat. Two hats.'

'I have bought a copy of Hutton's *Principles of Knowledge*. It is to impress your brother. It includes a chapter entitled "Theory of Rain".'

'Especially for the Scottish edition,' she said.

He laughed.

'And what else did you buy? I am very interested.'

He drew it from his pocket, unwrapped it from its cloth.

'Here,' he said. 'Some work for your fingers.' He touched the granite rim of the brooch against her left hand. Her hand – a creature woken to curiosity – opened to take it. A smile of pleasure, a smile of concentration.

'A shield,' she said. 'And in the centre . . . a stem, a flower . . . Two flowers. Not roses. These have a burr. Have you brought me *thistles*?'

'I have,' he said. 'And you have clever fingers. In the shop the woman called it a luckenbooth. I suppose that's the Scot's word for a brooch.'

'A luckenbooth? I shall ask one of the ladies here what it means. Thank you, John. It is your second gift to me. You will keep it safe until I leave?'

She held it out. He took it back. He asked about her eyes. She said they felt as though someone had blown sand into them. 'The right eye especially,' she said. 'But neither hurts me as it did at first.'

'And when Rizzo changes the dressings,' he said, 'are you able to see anything?'

'Something. But through a glass, very darkly. My hearing however is uncommonly sharp. I hear every drunkard in Glasgow singing his way home at night.'

'They might not all be drunk,' he said.

There was no relapse, though Lacroix was braced for it. She found her appetite. He bought her shrimps from the shrimp girl, bought her cinnamon bread, bought her an orange and watched her break its skin with untrimmed nails. Catching Rizzo on the stairs – 'I'm writing it all up,' said Rizzo. 'I will send *my* drawings to Paris!' – he asked how much longer Emily would need to stay in the hospital. Rizzo shrugged, touched his beard. 'Three days. Three or four.'

'So soon?'

'Why not? You already know my thinking on this.'

'And her dressings?'

'No, we will have finished with them. You must buy a fine silk scarf for her. She will wear it for a week, then wear it only when the light is most brilliant. Then it is over, and we will know. I expect a letter from you. This is very important. How she is, what she sees. What she sees exactly.'

'I will do it, of course,' said Lacroix. 'And I may include drawings of my own.'

'Wie Sie wollen, mein Freund!' called Rizzo, running up the stairs, taking the steps two at a go. Lacroix followed more cautiously but thought that he would, back on the island, do some running himself. Go down to the beach, take off his boots, drop his coat in the sand . . .

The red-haired woman left the hospital. She was better or she could not be helped. She made her farewells around the ward. She had a stick Lacroix had not seen her use before and her street clothes looked too large for her. He did not ask if anyone was coming for her, did not ask what she was going on to. He was afraid of her answers.

On the following day they went for a walk. Emily wanted to be outside. She said she needed to be outside. Lacroix, as nervous as though he had charge of a new-born, was over-solicitous.

'It does not help me,' she said. 'All I need is your arm and that you should warn me if I am about to step over a precipice.'

All the same, they went slowly. To reach the front door was the work of half an hour but the effect on her of being outside – immediate, unmistakable – rewarded all effort. He led her about the garden. It was a place the season was making untidy in lovely ways. He lifted her hand to the honeysuckle, to the silk edges of tulips, to cornflowers whose colour she would not allow to be simply 'blue'.

'Like the sky,' he said, though the sky overhead was white and grey.

But this too she sent back. The morning sky? The sky at midday? The sky at sea?

'Blue like your coat,' he said, unsure if air and movement were making her excitable or if she were merely recovering her old intensity. 'Like Jane's coat.'

This she accepted and they moved on to small white roses and the not-quite-open spikes of foxgloves, to poppies he thought no gardener had sown, and a great thriving bush of rosemary where they stood a while, crushing the needles and smelling their fingertips.

When he got her back to the third floor she climbed into her bed, a blind, awkward creature too long out of its element. He asked her whether she had enjoyed her walk. He did not hear her answer and inside ten minutes she was asleep. When Rizzo came through Lacroix confessed to the outing and wondered aloud if they had been reckless. Rizzo looked at the sleeping woman – a regard that seemed both rigorous and tender – then turned back to Lacroix.

'Very soon,' he said, 'I will give her into your care, Lovall. I have no uneasiness.'

The next morning the city was caught in the skirts of a storm. The islands out west were taking a battering, or you could guess

333

it so. It was weather to lose your hat in but Lacroix had not brought a hat to Glasgow – a hat was on the list of items he hoped to purchase (though he wanted something particular, probably of straw, straw and green silk, the kind of article no military man would ever wear) – and he arrived at the hospital with his hair dripping, his face slick, the taste of the rain in his mouth. He sat by Emily's bed drying himself with his handkerchief. Emily was eating toast. There were a great many crumbs, not all of which could be collected with propriety. Three beds along a new patient had been admitted, a new woman. Her hair on one side had been shaved away and there was a remarkable scar, red as lips along the white of her scalp. Like a sword-blow. He was glad Emily could not see it.

She asked if they were walking again today. He told her about the weather. She said she had listened to it, had listened as you might listen to music, should listen.

'Rizzo likes Haydn,' he said.

'We need not go outside,' she said. 'We could go to the basement and look at the people they call the unfortunates. Or you could look at them. There's a man down there teaching them to sing.'

'I know a place we can go,' he said. 'Though it may not be as exciting as the basement.'

He waited in the corridor while the doorkeeper helped Emily put on stockings and shoes and one of the brown woollen robes, then they went through the heavier air of the male ward, down a flight of stairs, down the next, and turned towards the gallery and the armchairs where he had slept off the brandy. He tried to recall if he'd been happy that day. He thought he had, but his emotions of the last week seemed to have altered by the hour, to be packed like strata in rock, like one of Hutton's 'angular unconformities', and he was thinking he might try that out on Emily, the geology of feeling, of sentiment, and what she might say of it, if she would think it clever, when a voice called out his name – barked it – and the world he had been walking in was a world no more.

'You! Lacroix! Aye, sir. Lacroix, Lovall, or whatever you call yourself now.'

A figure had risen, shot-like, from one of the armchairs. A man in a seaman's short black coat, his head and shoulders framed by a window, a rolled cap in his hand. His right eye was covered with a patch strung on black ribbon. The other eye was trained on Lacroix like a weapon.

'It is you. I know it is. I can still see well enough for that.'

'John?' said Emily. 'Who is it? He has mistaken you, I think.'

'No mistake, madam. I brought him up with me from Bristol, sat with him at my table—'

'Captain Browne?' Lacroix stepped closer. He drew Emily with him, though he hardly knew she was there.

'You did not think to come across me again, eh?' said the master. 'Had washed your hands of me.'

'But . . . why are you here? You have been hurt?'

'Hurt? Oh I'd say I had been hurt. Yes. I'd say that much. Is this lady in your care?'

'She is.'

'Then I hope you were not the cause of her troubles.'

'Far from it,' said Emily. 'Very far. Who is this person, John?'

Lacroix would have told her, had opened his mouth to do so, but the master reached out for him, caught hold of his free arm between elbow and wrist. Forty years of pulling rope in that grip.

'You *knew*?'

'Knew?'

'That he was after you, damn you! That he would come for me!'

'Who? Who are you speaking of?'

'Your friend from Spain, Lacroix. The one who calls himself Henderson.'

Lacroix shook his head.

The master went on. 'Bandy legs. London voice. Face like a choirboy who's sold himself to the devil.'

'Called Henderson?'

'Well, we know how easily a man makes up a new name for himself. Said he was in the army with you. In Spain.'

Lacroix shook his head again. 'There were many of us in Spain.'

'*That* is not an answer.' The grip tightened.

'I do not know any Henderson, sir. In Spain or anywhere else.'

'No?'

'No.'

'You'll swear to it?'

'On my life.'

For three, four seconds more, the master's single eye continued to search Lacroix's face. Then the grip softened and broke. The blood crept back into Lacroix's fingers. The master let out a long sigh.

'Well, he knew you. And seemed most anxious to renew the acquaintance.'

'John,' said Emily, 'what is going on? Why does he call you Lacroix?'

'Oh ho,' said the master softly.

'I will take you back to the ward,' said Lacroix.

'Why? I do not wish to go back to the ward.'

'I need to speak with Captain Browne. It would be best if—'

'Best if I do not hear your business? No, John. No. I have respected your privacy. I have not pried. But if there are things to be said now, if there are truths to come out, then I wish to hear them. We have come too far for it to be otherwise.'

'Emily . . .'

'If you take me back to the ward it will be the last you see of me. Do you understand? If you will not trust me then I cannot trust you. We will have nothing.'

It was the master who spoke first. He had been looking at Emily; now he looked at Lacroix. 'I'd say you were run to ground,' he said.

'I am what?'

'We can talk over there,' said the master. 'The lady . . .'

'My name is Emily Frend.'

'Miss Frend may sit between us and hear what there is to hear. Though I should warn her my part of the story has nothing pleasant in it.'

They moved to the wall, to the window, a chair facing the window. Lacroix lowered Emily on to the seat, then he and the master took their places either side of her at the chair's wings. In the gallery a pair of old men, turtles stripped of their shells, made their way, arm in arm, towards the stairs. The master glanced at them, then turned back to Lacroix.

'Nine days ago, ten if I count today, I was at my house in Dumbarton making ready to retire for the night. I have lived there alone since my wife died. I have no children. Anyway, I did as I always do. I carried the cat out into the street and stood a minute to view the sky. It was a quiet night with a piece moon. I saw no one and heard no one, but as I walked back inside a man walked with me and so tight to me and so silent I swear I took him at first for my own shadow. As I have said, he was not a large man. A runtish, bandy-legged devil. But he carried a gun with him, a carbine of some type, and though everything was strange to me at that moment, I did not doubt that he would use it. He shut the door, bolted it, never took his eyes off me. We went into the parlour. There was a lamp in there. He stood me by the lamp, stood himself in the shadows. He said he had urgent business with John Lacroix, an officer of hussars, with whom he had lately been in Spain. Well, I knew Lacroix was your name. William Swann had told me that much. Your giving a false name to our visitor from the frigate was, I assumed, some matter I did not need to enquire into. And when you kept your mouth shut about my sailor I was grateful to you. Grateful enough to let the pretence continue.'

'And this man,' said Lacroix, afraid his hearing would deepen the confusion, that this story, wild enough already, would grow wilder through his failing to hear it. 'He gave his name as Henderson?'

'He did.'

'And he had some business with me? What business?'

'Is that not for you to tell me? He had followed you from Spain to Scotland, man! You ask me to believe you have no notion of the reason for it?'

'I *was* in Spain,' said Lacroix. 'I was on the campaign with General Moore, was evacuated from Corunna with what remained of the army. All that is true. Then, when I reached home . . . I was . . .'

'Are you still in the army?' asked the master.

'What?'

'In the army. Are you still one of theirs?'

'I have not . . . formally . . .'

338

'So that is why you did not give Crawley up. You are in the same scrape! But I'd say this Henderson has other things on his mind. Unless they send such creatures after all who jump ship, in which case they would need a great many.'

'He knew,' asked Lacroix, 'that I had come with you on the *Jenny*?'

'He did.'

'How would he know that?'

'How did the navy know we had Crawley on board? Every dockside in the world is full of men who make a living selling what they see there. I'd say you were noticed.'

'Might he have spoken to William Swann?'

'He might. Though he did not say so. Nor do I believe he would have done in a fine house in Bristol what he felt safe doing with me. I don't think he would have risked it.'

'And with you?'

'Eh?'

'With you . . . what?'

The master nodded. His eye, the living eye, turned its light inwards. 'Well, we stood in the parlour together. It's a damned odd thing to be in a place you know like your own face and have a man, a stranger, aim a gun at your belly. He wanted me to tell him where you'd gone when you left the *Jenny*. I told him Glasgow, for I remembered you had not intended to stay in the city long so there could be no harm in his knowing. But he was ahead of me. He spoke of the islands. I said you had not mentioned any islands to me. Well, that was my first lie and he did not like it. He struck me with the gun and put me down as easily as I might throw Wee Davey down, had I a mind to it. He stood over me and asked again. I said you had not known yourself what island you might visit, that we had spoken of the islands only in a general way and you had not mentioned any in particular. But he had caught me out once and now I suppose everything I said had for him the savour of a deceit. He did not warn me, did not offer me the chance to change my story. He was, I imagine, in a hurry to be gone. He caught me with the barrel of the gun, a most careful and deliberate blow, and I knew immediately the damage it had done. There was a minute after that I don't much care to recall. Once I was able to speak again I told him everything about you I could bring to mind. Every conversation, our last in particular, word for word or near enough. Had I known where you were, had you been hiding in my cellar, I would have given you up to him then. Men will sail with a one-eyed captain. They will not sail with a blind one.'

'He is insane,' said Lacroix. 'Some lunatic got into your house.'

'A lunatic? He may have been. But a purposeful one and in perfect command of himself. He told me he was the war. He said the law could not touch him. And something else, something I did not consider much at the time, I had not the leisure to, but have thought of a great deal since. He told me he had been sent by one whose word could not be gainsaid. I don't know what you make of that. One whose word could not be gainsaid. It was strange language for such a man.'

'He meant Christ perhaps,' said Emily.

'With respect,' said the master, 'I think he spoke of a living man. Living as you and I do. And could even a lunatic conjure up a Christ who would have him do as he did to me?'

'Men have done worse,' she said, 'with that name on their lips.'

'It was some fantasy,' said Lacroix. 'It was to justify his violence to you.'

'Not that either,' said the master. 'No. *Someone* had impressed him. Had put ideas in his head.'

'He left then?'

'He did. He knew I had no more to tell him. He even tidied me up a little, handed me my own neckcloth to hold over my eye. Then he explained, very patiently and thoroughly, what would become of me if I blabbed of him. I gave him my word I would not, and I have not, until now. He hung about a while longer, studying me from beside the door. I believe he was debating with himself the wisdom of leaving me with breath in my body. Then he was gone, lit out swift and quiet as he'd come. Well, I sat there a good half-hour on the floorboards before making my way to the house of my late wife's cousin. You'll remember him. He asks no questions. The next day he brought me up the water. Brought me here.'

'Your eye?' asked Lacroix.

The master shook his head.

'But surely . . .'

'Nothing.'

Lacroix nodded. His thoughts were full of oddments, glimpses. A tune ran through his head, something a pair of beggar children had been singing outside the inn, yesterday or the day before. This was not how he had imagined it, the truth-telling time. It was as if his secrets had altered in the keeping, had grown like living things, so that he did not quite know them any more. Or that they were not entirely his, not the private stash or black treasure he had imagined. And once more it came to him, the thought that had touched him several times since coming back from Spain, that we are not private beings and cannot hide things inside ourselves. Everything is present, everything in view for those who know how to look.

'Captain Browne,' said Emily. 'Where is he now?'

'Henderson? If he is still searching for Lacroix here I'd say he was out in the islands.'

'The islands?'

'Unless he has given it up. Which I doubt.'

'John,' said Emily. 'John?'

He touched her shoulder and she twisted round to him.

'John. You heard him? You heard what he said?'

'I did.'

'Then we must go. Today. We must leave. Immediately.'

'She is right enough there,' said the master. 'Run south. Put as many miles as you can between yourselves and this man.'

'She does not mean that,' said Lacroix. 'Her brother and sister are out there.'

'Where? The islands? Well do not, in God's name, tell me which one. I want to know nothing of where you are headed. Go for them if you must, but you would be wise not to spend a single night in any house where he might have good reason to look for you. Not till you hear they've strung him up in the Grassmarket.'

'He has already had ten days,' said Emily.

The master heard the catch in her voice; he moved to comfort her. 'He would need to find a boat first,' he said. 'And this weather will slow him down. And there are many islands to search.'

'He does not need to search them all,' she said. She stood, her hands in front of her, open, steadying herself. 'Take me upstairs, John. I will dress while you find Mr Rizzo.' She turned to where she thought the master was but missing him addressed the window, the world in its mist of rain. 'I am sorry for what you have suffered,' she said.

'Likewise,' said the master.

'And I,' said Lacroix, who knew he must now make an offer, that the offer would be futile, would be refused. 'Is there some way, any way, I might assist you?'

'You mean money, I think, but unless you have an eye in your pocket you are of no use to me. I do not know what kind of man you are. Nor do I know what else there is to this story. In truth I do not feel I understand much more than I did. But for this lady's sake I'll give you some counsel. Should you meet with Henderson, here, on the islands, anywhere at all, you must not hesitate. I remember what you carried with you on the *Jenny* and I do not mean the fiddle. I suggest you keep it with you and keep it ready. You will have one chance. If you fail to take it . . .'

'I understand,' said Lacroix.

'Yes,' said the master, who seemed suddenly to have lost his powers, to have fallen in on himself and some sharp dream of trouble, 'but I wonder if you do.'

FIVE

18

The weather had come up on them. The air had thickened, the sea and sky were colourless reflections of each other, the wind small, the afternoon sun a lustreless silver. The sailors – two men of savage appearance, distinguishable only by one being slightly shorter, slightly more savage-looking than the other – no longer sang or spoke as they had at setting out. They were silent. They nosed the air like hounds.

Before leaving Mingulay, Calley had made clear to Medina, several times, how little he liked these men (were they brothers?), how little he trusted them. But he had grown weary of sitting on the shore watching an empty sea, and the sailors, having brought their boat from somewhere else, having crossed open water and made landfall, must be assumed to know their business. They spoke only a few words of English and Medina's Gaelic, scraps and feathers of language, served only to deepen the confusion. It was money, the grubby King Georges in Calley's palm, that kept the sailors from walking away entirely, but they had withdrawn to a sand dune of their own and conferred there, smoking their pipes, nodding their heads like beam engines, occasionally drawing in the sand.

No specific island was mentioned – or if it was, not in a shared tongue. Calley and Medina pointed north along the beach, repeating the word – north! north! – while the sailors looked on like men addressed by gannets, moon-fish. But away from Mingulay, rocking in a slow green swell, they did indeed seem to be headed north. That was good enough, that would do, and there was at least one island at no great distance from them, and beyond that the suggestion of others, perhaps a chain of them stretching up to latitudes belonging more to the imagination than any sensible geography. An hour passed, a second hour. Then came the smoke, coiling over the water from the west and making everything into the shadow of a shadow.

The sailors altered course. A third hour began in which they passed the spectre of land, passed one island and, conceivably, a second. Or was it the same one? It was hard to be sure. It was impossible. Calley and Medina exchanged meaningful glances, then gave that up and looked past each other at the mercury-coloured sea that now and then slopped over the gunwales to swirl, bubbling, around their boots.

Another change of course and the boat slid round a point of land – low, treeless – and entered a bay where the beach was a silver line that shone brighter than the smoke-coloured sea or the smoke-coloured air above it. One of the sailors, the short one, made gestures, briefly spoke. This, it seemed, was arrival. A minute later the boat snubbed her keel on the sand and the brown sail shivered. The sailors were in a hurry now and their language needed no translation. Calley and Medina took off their coats, rolled them tight then slithered over the sides of the boat, standing up to their thighs in the water as the sailors dug their oars into the sand and pushed the boat away from them. At sea, everything is slow until, without much warning, it's quick as a wing-beat. The brown sail became a grey sail then just an uncertain line, like a flaw in the lens of the eye.

The soldiers turned in the water and waded ashore. They were relieved to find it real enough, the sand steady under the sodden leather of their boots. They put on their coats, they faced the land, looked, listened.

'Where have those cunts brought us?' said Calley, and at the sound of his voice something thirty yards to their left dragged itself from the beach into the sea. A heavy thing in a panic. The men stared (at nothing) then started searching for a path. On their journey together they had developed a deep faith in the ubiquity of paths, that places seemingly untouched, as emptied of life as an upturned box, were always on the way to *somewhere*. They walked, paused, walked the whole length of the shining beach in their sopping clothes, found no paths, grew weary of the search, and set off over rocks and heather, stumbling, seeing things in the weird bled whiteness of the air, their ears full of the sound of their own breathing. In a hollow they came across a tree, a wind stunted pine. It cast no shadow, was not much taller than Medina. Should they feel encouraged by it? They moved on, followed the twistings of a gully, Calley in the lead, Medina six strides behind him. Then Medina veered off – some small rebellion against having for his view the back of another man. He started climbing one of the sides of the gully, scrabbled up over loose stones, went on all fours for the last yards, and stood up in clearer air (air like water in which the sediment has settled). On the brow of the neighbouring hill he could see two houses, side by side, both of them ruins.

He peered down into the gully where Calley was peering up at him. He did not have to see the corporal's face clearly to know the expression on it. He beckoned to him, and watched as he toiled upwards, a mad and dangerous beetle he would one day tell his friends in the south about, and while they laughed at the thought of such a small, ferocious man, he would explain how this Englishman was exactly as he had been made, a blank sheet formed of rags on which the world had printed some outrageous truth, something like – *You will not be loved.* Something like that. And then, of course, the laughter would have to stop.

In both houses the roofs had tumbled in but one had kept a little of its thatch – the straw more garden now than roof – and this they choose for their camp. They looked out through an empty doorway, crossed over to look from a shutterless window. Perhaps they were at the tip of a large island and further on there would be villages, towns even. But that wasn't the sense. That wasn't what they felt.

They gathered the materials for a fire and built it under the shelter of the thatch.

'You see anything to eat?' asked Calley.

Medina shrugged. 'There will be something. There is always something.'

'We'll have to eat that tree,' said Calley.

Medina worked his way back to the beach. The fog was breaking up, drifting through. At the end of the beach he began to clamber over likely, sea-touched rocks until he found what he was looking for, a tilted block, slippery and cluttered with black shells. He began to pick them off, leaning over the sea and filling both of the large side pockets of his coat. He was singing, '*La Gallina Que se Perdió*', and wondered who was the last who had sung on the island and if anyone had ever sung there in Spanish. (Hadn't the armada of Rey Felipe's time come down this coast? Might they have stopped here? Taken on water? He thought of the portrait he had seen in the *ayuntamiento* in Cordoba of the armada's general, the Duque de Medina Sidonia, whose sallow face had seemed so well fitted to defeat. As Spain herself, perhaps, was well fitted to defeat.)

On his way back he was guided by the firelight above the walls of the house and when he reached the house Calley was crouched by the flames, tidying and poking. Without looking round he asked Medina what he had found.

'*Mejillones*,' said Medina.

'You what?' said Calley. He stood and turned. Medina took one of the shells from his pocket, held it up.

'One oyster,' said Calley. 'That's fucking brilliant. What are we then? Voles?'

'Not an oyster,' said Medina. '*Mejillones*. And many of them. You will not sleep hungry.'

He tried to tempt Calley with eating them raw but the Englishman shook his head and Medina fetched water from the hollow of a stone, rainwater in which he glimpsed the rising moon and his own dark face. They cooked the mussels in their mess tins, threw the shells into the shadows.

While they ate, Calley explained what he would do to the savage sailors should he ever find them again. It involved fire and rocks, firearms, a rope. 'And they wouldn't even complain,' he said, 'because they know what they've done. Sticking us here like Robin what-the-fuck.'

On the fire they burned the house's own roof beams. As the end of a beam charred and fell away they pushed it along and gave fresh wood to the flames. Medina searched his pockets for more mussels. The moon had climbed above the walls of the house. Other than the smoke from their fire the air was perfectly clear now. Stars opened like flowers.

'When you were small,' said Medina. 'A boy. Who was your friend?'

Calley made a noise, something connected to laughter but not laughter. Medina was familiar with the sound, knew it was intended to express astonishment that such a frivolous question should be asked, the kind of question that marked you out as a fool. He also knew that Calley liked to hear such questions, that he found a pleasure in them he would never admit to.

'There were other boys,' he said, 'in the yard. I can't remember our games. It was the time before we were fit for work. When our hands were not yet strong enough for the picking.'

'The yard?'

'The spike. The grubber. The workhouse on Saffron Hill.'

'*Azafrán!*' said Medina, into whose mind had come an image of the child Calley at play in fields of crocuses. 'They grew saffron there?'

'They grew thieves there,' said Calley. 'Did they grow saffron! Where do you think it is? Eh? Saffron Hill? It's the middle of fucking London.'

'But once,' said Medina. 'A long time ago.'

'There was a Vine Street too,' said Calley. 'And a Field Lane. But there weren't any vines or fields.'

Medina nodded. There was a long pause. Calley prodded the fire with his boot. Medina was playing a mussel shell like an almost silent castanet. Each man's face was a thing of fire and shadow.

'What about you?' said Calley. 'You must have been a soft boy.'

'Soft?'

'Had friends.'

'Yes, I had friends. And some of those I played with as a boy are my friends still. Some are in the army with me. If I am still in the army.'

'The famous Spanish cavalry,' said Calley.

'Yes. The famous Spanish cavalry.'

'With no horses.'

'With no horses.'

'I once saw a whole field of horses,' said Calley, 'left behind by the French. They'd all had the strings cut in their back legs. So they couldn't be used by us.'

'The war,' said Medina, 'is very hard for horses.'

'I'm not saying they did wrong, mind. We did the same on the way to Corunna. What couldn't be moved had to be tossed. Rules of war. Horses, cannon, wagons. All sorts. I saw a pair of commissary clerks throwing bags of money down a ravine. Spanish dollars. Swinging big bags of it down the ravine. I mean they were drunk as fuck but they were doing what had to be done. And I'll tell you what, if they'd tried giving it away no one would have touched it. No one wanted money.'

'The retreat,' said Medina.

'Your lot were useless,' said Calley. 'Worse than useless.'

'We had difficulties of our own,' said Medina. 'The Army of the Left, the Army of the Centre . . .' He shrugged.

'Your irregulars were more trouble to us than the French. Savages.'

'I fear we might say the same of the British army.'

'People closed their doors on us,' said Calley.

'So you broke down their doors and hanged the men from a tree. As for the women—'

'Fuck off.'

'We were both at the inquiry,' said Medina. 'Or have you forgotten that is the reason we are here?'

Calley said nothing. Neither man was particularly excited or angry. There was nothing important to be settled between them.

'In the morning,' said Medina, 'we will find a boat.'

'You know where to look, do you?'

'It is an island. There will be a boat. It is the law of islands.'

'Bollocks,' said Calley.

'Even so,' said Medina. 'I believe we will find one. We will be lucky.'

They cleared spaces for themselves either side of the fire, lay under their coats with their heads on their packs watching sparks lift into the night's velvet.

'What are you called?' asked Medina. 'Your Christian name? You cannot be just Calley.'

He waited. There was no answer. He had not been heard; it didn't matter. Then, tossed over the fire as earlier they had tossed away their shells: 'Andrew.'

Medina pushed himself on to an elbow. 'Andrews?'

'Andrew,' said Calley. 'There's no fucking s. If it was *Andrews* there'd be two of me.'

Medina tried the name again.

'They called us after the parishes where we were found,' said Calley. 'George for St George's. Giles for St Giles. Girls called Agatha, Mary. We even had a Barnabas, a little red-haired cunt they 'prenticed to the sweeps. No way *he's* still living.'

'I am Ernesto,' said Medina.

'You what?'

'Ernesto. Also, of course, a saint.'

Somewhere in the last of the night Medina rose and stood by the embers of the fire. He had got up quietly but knew Calley would be aware of him.

'Nothing,' he said. 'It is nothing.'

He went out, bowing under the stone lintel, and though he had slept in a roofless house under the dragged light of the moon, he felt at once a new sense of space, the vast suggestiveness of the coming day. He walked down to where he had collected water for their supper, found the water with his fingers, cupped his hands, drew the water to his mouth and drank (it tasted of liquid stone). He was trying to reassemble his dreams but they slipped away like the water between his fingers. Friendship had been part of it. Had he not glimpsed the faces of his friends? But he had not been able to address them, to touch them, either because they were ghosts and he still living or they still living and himself a ghost. And now, he thought, my only friend is Corporal Calley, a lunatic from where they grow thieves like saffron. He grinned, then finding a grin was not enough he leaned back his head and laughed, silently.

After that, in the stillness that followed, two truths arrived with equal force. The first was that he wanted, very much, to smoke a cigar (though he had none and had not smoked since Glasgow). The second was that today would be his last with Calley. They could leave the island together, he had no objection to that, but then their ways must part. There would be some fuss, some name-calling. He would be reproached. But he would remain calm; he would be immovable. They might even shake hands, nothing *warm* of course, but a recognition of what they had shared, the strangeness of their journey, the fate that had thrown them together. And after that, well, Calley could do as he wished, could find the English officer and carry his head back to Lisbon in his knapsack, a thing he was, in fact, quite likely to do. As for his own path, he had no money and was unlikely to be offered any, but it was harvest time and with so many men at the war help would be needed in fields and barns. He would work his way, farm by farm, back down the road they had come. And somewhere on that road he might hear of Phyrro, of the men he had swum with in the river, the women with their sunburned arms and dusty boots . . .

To this – the vision of his figure on the road, free as a boy – he gave a single vigorous nod of assent, then set off for the beach, seeing, as he worked his way down, the rim of the rising sun a finger's width above the horizon, already too fierce to be stared at.

When he reached the shore he sat on the sand, took off his boots, peeled off the frayed mess of his stockings and walked into the sea, standing with the surf around his calves until his feet throbbed with the cold. He came out, picked up his boots and walked – sauntered – to the western end of the beach, stepping from sand on to stones shaped like giant turtles, then up on to the plateau where, after losing his bearings (distracted by the setting moon) he came again to the rock with the mussels on it. He squatted, picking off a dozen of the smaller shells and eating them where he was, dropping the shells into the water. Further off, the sea seemed hardly to move at all. He saw other islands, small ones, inhabited, surely, only by birds. No fire smoke, no black speck of a boat.

He span away the last shell and turned his back to the sea. The sun was rising swiftly and he saw that he was standing at the edge of a meadow, the grasses growing from sand, and in the grass myriad small flowers he had not been aware of when he came the first time, that must have been closed against the weather, the chill of evening. Now, discovered by the sun, they ignited, one by one. The yellow and the white, the gold and the red, so that he seemed to be looking across a field of small lights afloat on the shallow water of morning shadow. Under his bare feet the ground was fibrous with a structure of endless soft branchings. It was odd to take in the world through his feet, the soles as sensitive, as inquisitive as a tongue. It was like that game children and lovers play, sketching words on each other's back with a finger, half caress, half riddle. His movement woke a bee, sent it zagging, almost too heavy for flight, over the tips of the flowers. He apologised, out loud, in high Castilian.

He considered how he would describe all this to one who had not seen it – that one being all the world but himself. Start with the flowers? With the sea? With the sun whose warmth he could feel now against his right cheek? He had the desire to pray but let his prayer take the form of a slow walking over flowers. Someone, he thought, someone should have taught me how to meet joy better. He raised his arms and tried moving in a dance, had it for a moment, a slow, courtly turning, his feet brushing the grasses, the stems, the petals. Then he dropped his arms in a fit of laughter, took off his coat, his jacket (how ragged he'd become!) and lay down, heavy with gratitude, heavy too with a month of nights broken by foxes and owls, and by other creatures – men perhaps – less easily known.

Like this he slept off the first portion of the morning, a shape in the grass, perfectly at home, perfectly ignored. Birds in low flight flicked their shadows across his shirt. A small topaz beetle climbed the slope of his wrist. When he woke, and before he opened his eyes, he wondered if it would be the same, if the intoxication of the dawn had been no more than that, a passing excitement, but when he sat up and looked around he found that though the light was different (the sun pouring from a sky almost cloudless, so that the meadow had exchanged a quality of water for a quality of glass) the morning was intact, had lost none of its enchantment, and he climbed to his feet ready for anything, any extravagance – a whale the size of Gibraltar, a parliament of drowned men, some green-eyed Christ patiently stripping religion from the land . . . Instead, he caught sight of Corporal Calley climbing up from the beach to the plateau. He was wearing his coat still, while he, Medina, stood perfectly warm in breeches and shirt. As he watched him come there was a moment of misgiving, a second, the fragment of a second, like a stumble of the heart, but it changed nothing. In truth, it felt that nothing could be changed.

'I've been looking for you,' said Calley.

'And I have been here,' said Medina, spreading his hands as though to welcome Calley to what he had found, his half-acre of the beautiful.

'Doing what?'

'Sleeping.'

'Well, that's fucking useful. Have you found a boat?'

'I have not. Have you?'

'This is the wrong side of the island,' said Calley. 'This is south.'

'And you wish to go north.'

Calley looked at him. He came closer. Six, eight steps between them now. 'What the fuck is wrong with you?' he asked.

'Nothing is wrong with me.'

'No?'

'No.'

'Then why are you acting like a cunt?'

'To you,' said Medina, 'most people are acting the cunt.'

'Put your boots on.'

Medina did not move.

'I said put your boots on.'

'I will put my boots on,' said Medina. 'But first I will tell you what I have decided. What I decided this very morning. I will take no more orders from you. I will have no more insults. The story between us is over. I am going home. Or I am going . . . somewhere. I have not yet chosen the place or the route but I am going where you will not be going. That I do know. ' He paused, trying to judge the effect his words were having. That Calley was listening to him and listening closely, he had no doubt. Beyond that . . .

'This man you are hunting,' he continued, 'does he even exist? Why have we not found him? And if he does, let us suppose that he does, can you believe, in truth, they intend to let him be killed? One of their own? By *you*? Their mistake was to send a man who does not know when to stop, who continues to act even when the theatre is dark. If you kill this man and go back to Lisbon, you think they will say thank you? You think they will give you a medal? I will tell you what will happen. You will be found in the Tagus with your throat cut. And let me assure you there will be no inquiry to discover the fate of Corporal Calley. A man without family, without friends. So this is my advice to you. Disappear. Forget the army. Forget the war. Disappear. Become someone else.'

Calley unbuttoned his coat. 'You finished?' he said.

'Oh yes,' said Medina. 'I have finished.'

'That's good,' said Calley, 'because I'm going to tell you now what I know. What I *know*. First off, this man we are hunting. I have seen him. Remember? We have been to his house. We have been to his sister's house. He exists. Of course he fucking exists. Second, you and me are soldiers in the field and we will do what we have been ordered to do. And I'm not talking about that streak of shit Don Ignacio. I piss on him. No one cares about him. I'm talking about someone you can't even fucking imagine. A man who cannot show himself because his face would blaze like the sun. A man whose word cannot be gainsaid. And though I will not hear his voice again, and I am sorry for that, very sorry, he has placed his trust in me and I will not fail him. So we will do the job, you and me, and we will go to Lisbon and you will tell them what you saw. That is what you are going to do.'

'No,' said Medina, '*No es asi*. I will find a boat with you but nothing more. The rest is for you, Señor Andrews. Alone.'

Calley reached inside his coat, unslung the carbine, cocked it. All smoothly done. 'It's like I said, I know what you are going to do. Now put on your boots and pick up your coat.'

Medina nodded. He glanced over to his boots then back at Calley. 'My friend,' he said, 'you say you know things but the truth is you know very little. You are, I believe, the most ignorant man I ever met.' He bent down to pick a flower by his bare feet, a yellow flower the length of his little finger. 'Do you know this? Do you know what this is called? No?' He bent down again and picked another, a purple flower or, arguably, a blue one. 'Or this?' he said. 'You know what this is?'

As he stood with a third flower – it is difficult to stop these things once you start – he felt himself lifted and saw the flower, or something he took for the flower, flash past his face. Then he was gazing up at the birds. There were thousands of them, their dark forms in frantic movement so that it seemed incredible they did not collide with each other. Calley came into view and looked down at him. The birds circled his head like a crown. His mouth was moving but whatever he was saying Medina couldn't hear him. More surprisingly, he could not hear the birds either. He wondered if he had become deaf. But then he heard the slow rush and roar of the sea, and he knew that all was well.

19

The Oban coach should have left at two o'clock but some trouble with an axle delayed it. For this reason, Emily and Lacroix, reaching the coaching office at a quarter past, were able to buy tickets, though there was only one place left inside. The other passengers looked out with deep interest at the sight of a woman with her head bound in a grey silk scarf. Room was made for her next to the window on the side facing the horses. A man – fatherly, red-faced, slightly drunk – spread a page of the *Dundee Courier* across the seat, explaining that the windows of coaches could never be made to shut securely and he feared the leather was somewhat damp. Lacroix thanked him, nodded to the woman who was to be Emily's neighbour, then climbed up the back of the coach to his own place on the roof. There were two others up there. One man was tying on his hat with a ribbon; the other had the look of a poor poet, a man uselessly exulted and who would perhaps, at some point, begin to babble about the moon.

Ten minutes later, the axle declared safe, a horn was blown, and a minute after that they were rattling through the streets of Glasgow, the outside passengers returning the waves of small boys, old men and the city's population of inebriates and gentle idiots for whom a common coach was a masterpiece of human excitement.

Two hours out of the city they stopped to stretch legs and empty bladders. Lacroix stood with Emily beside one of the coach's yellow wheels. Was she comfortable? Did she need anything? Had she been able to sleep a little? They had not, since their encounter that morning with the master, had any opportunity for a conversation of the sort both knew must come, and soon. This left them strangely free, all large questions, the answers to those questions (if such existed) postponed until the conclusion of the journey. In the meantime they could simply loiter in the moment. He described a cloud to her. She told him she could hear a blackbird singing.

The coachman rounded them up. They resumed their places. On the roof the poet addressed Lacroix in schoolboy Latin; Lacroix responded (he had schoolboy Latin of his own). The man with the ribbon under his chin talked about the weather. He could, he claimed, smell a change on the way, and though to Lacroix the weather seemed exactly what it had been for hours it turned out the man knew what he was speaking about. The western air began to have a hazy appearance. They passed by coils of smoke, sea-flavoured, that spread and grew denser until the scenery on either side, the grand vistas, was entirely lost in it. In the high places they were above it and looked down at a white sea they would, shortly, plunge into again. Lacroix, gripping his strap, sought to ignore it, the odd spectral loveliness of it. He was concentrating. He was trying to think. And he made good beginnings, recalled in detail the whole of the master's narrative, examined it with a thoroughness quite impossible when he first heard it, the master staring at him like a one-eyed Torquemada.

But after each good start he came up against what he could not make sense of and he faltered and fell into fancies, and into one in particular in which he advertised his whereabouts in a newspaper – the *Dundee Courier*? – then went alone, north after north, to Iceland, to Greenland, all the while drawing the master's assailant after him and away from Emily, from everyone. And then he would wait, sitting in some ice cave, ice crystals in his beard, until he saw, in all that whiteness, the tiny black upright of the monster's approach . . .

This daydream, ever more detailed, engrossed him for miles and might have done for miles more had the poet not let go of his strap to point at a pink moon rising above the mist's horizon. His cry of joy turned to a yelp of terror as he tumbled backwards into the luggage basket. He was in the midst of a somersault that would have ended in the road when the man with the ribbon caught the hem of his coat and clung to it until Lacroix found the poet's hand and together they dragged him back to his place.

I will have to be quicker than that, thought Lacroix. I will need to be more awake. Enough of this dreaming. Live in the world, man!

At half past eleven they were above Oban, though only the church spire showed clearly – an old black piling in a moonlit sea of milk and purple. They descended, were swallowed up, and came to a final halt in the deadened air between rows of ghostly houses and the yardarms of ghostly ships. The coachman held up his lamp, a thumbprint of yellow light. Lacroix and the others on the roof helped hand down the luggage. It was, generally, how outside passengers regained the use of their limbs.

Emily waited with the woman who had sat beside her on the journey. Lacroix, still unsure where in the town they had stopped, asked the way to the Russian Hotel. The Russian Hotel was not its name but everyone, even the poet, knew what he meant, and three or four of them, more familiar with the town or less easily disorientated, pointed the way.

'But you'll be lucky to find a room,' said the man with the ribbon.

'Why?' asked Emily.

'The ship,' said the man, 'the *Chiron*. Due in three days. The town will be filling up with passengers. Poor devils.'

Lacroix caught only 'ship' and 'poor devils' but it was enough. He understood. 'We shall have to take our chances,' he said. He collected their bags, and with Emily's hand on his shoulder, started out, aware their backs were being watched, that the moment they were deemed to be out of earshot there must be some discussion of them.

It was not far to the hotel, a ten-minute walk, but they passed on their way a number of small camps, families bivouacking under shelters of canvas or cloth or nothing at all. The more fortunate had small fires in makeshift braziers and by the light of these could be seen men and women and children. The displaced, the chased-off, or those with an uncle or brother in the New World, someone who sent letters about a land that had no end to it and where you would not be robbed by laird or tacksman.

In the hotel parlour the air was a fug of tobacco fumes, and under that the slightly sweet, slightly pissy scent of island tweed. The company was mostly men. One of them was singing and Lacroix thought it was a song he had first heard the night he wandered into the house at the bottom of the hill, the night Ranald sat beside him in his red coat asking if he had come far.

When it was finished, people began to notice the newcomers. They glanced at Lacroix but at Emily they stared. It was as if, in

364

their heightened mood of parting they felt themselves visited by a figure from one of their tales of misfortune, one of their endless tales of misfortune. Lacroix thought he might need to say something – an introduction, an explanation – though feared he would sound like the manager of a fairground sensation, that they would expect him to promise she would tell their fortunes or stand unflinching against a door while he threw knives around her head. Then he saw Spinkey crossing the room in his gear of 1780, and it was clear from the way the Russian held out his arms that he was equal to the moment, that a show of largesse was in the offing, that it would be quietly approved of by the company, and that they would not need to spend the night camping beside the water. He greeted Emily like a fellow exile. He looked at her, held her sightless gaze without a trace of awkwardness, as though his work had somehow habituated him to the appearance of blindfolded women. There *was* a room. The very last he had. It was on the top floor of the hotel. It was simple, bare. He was ashamed of it. It was where the cats slept. But if they thought such a room would not insult them he could make up a fire, bring up hot water . . .

A girl was summoned, the same one who had shown them to their rooms the last time they stayed, the putative daughter. They went up the stairs with her – the girl first with the candle, then Lacroix with the bags, then Emily holding on to a fold of his coat. Over four flights of stairs she stumbled only twice. The room was, as they had been told, a dormitory for cats. It smelled of cats and of what they had brought up there but it was, otherwise, a perfectly good room with a window that looked out over the harbour. Lacroix, after a certain amount of struggle, got the window to open. They were, on this floor, just above the fog. The moon was directly ahead of him. A fist's width to the left of it was a star or planet, blue and trembling.

When he looked round into the room an old man was tipping live coals into the fireplace and the girl was flapping her apron at the cats who departed, rubbing the edge of the door with high backs. The fact that there was only one room rather than two, well, it was a fact and they would deal with it later. There was a chair, vaguely French, where a last cat was still asleep. Lacroix thought he could manage on it quite well. The cat could share the bed with Emily.

A candle, a fire, a room. And later, Spinkey himself brought up a tray with two bowls of hot negus, two hard-boiled eggs in their shells, some bread. He apologised again for the room. Lacroix said they were deeply grateful. They had forgotten about the emigration ship. Were all those in the parlour passengers?

'Some are to voyage,' said the Russian, 'some to say adieu.'

'Mr Spinkey,' said Emily, who was sitting on the bed, who looked exhausted, 'we need a boat tomorrow. Tomorrow morning.' She told him where they were headed. That the matter was urgent.

'Madam,' said Spinkey, the fixer of all things, the soother, 'the people have all been delivered by boats from the islands and the boats must return. There will be no difficulty finding what you need. In the morning I will send out Sasha to ask among the captains.'

He put one of the bowls of negus into her hands. He wanted her to blow on it a little. She did, and sipped from it and swallowed and was very still.

'*Vous l'aimez?*'

'It is perfect.'

Spinkey smiled, bowed to them both, and left them. They emptied their bowls. Spice, wine, heat. Lacroix peeled an egg by rolling it between his palms. He gave it to Emily and she ate it as though asking questions of it, as though devouring it with curiosity. Because the bed-frame was high, appeared to stand on its tiptoes, her boots did not quite touch the floorboards.

'What time is it?' she asked.

'Late,' he said. 'Midnight at least.' He squeezed a scrap of bread, made a pellet of it. 'Emily,' he said.

She nodded. 'You have things you wish to tell me.'

'Things I must tell you. Though now I suppose is the wrong time. You are tired. You should sleep.'

'And delay some more? I *am* tired, John. But I do not want to wake in the morning without there being some truth between us.'

He was surprised how much the remark distressed him. What of their travelling together? Their wait in the cathedral, the vigils at the hospital? Had there been no 'truth' in any of that? For two, three seconds he stared at her, then crossed again to the window. He knew he would not be able to talk while looking at her. The nature of what he had to say, of course. But also the blindfold, that half-yard of grey silk Rizzo had given as a parting gift. Even more than the dressings it had replaced it made her . . . what? Allegorical. A figure from a masque, a pantomime. Like sharing a room with the Oracle of Delphi.

Through the window, through the thinning fog, he could see the flickering of the emigrants' fires and imagined for a moment the state of their hearts. Then he began to speak.

'Did you follow the war, Emily?'

'You mean did I read about it in the papers? Did people talk to me about it?'

'Yes.'

'I heard things,' she said. 'One could not avoid Trafalgar.'

'The business in Spain,' he said, 'it was a great ... muddle. It is not even clear they wanted us there, the Spanish. Certainly I cannot believe they would want us there again.'

'They can manage on their own?' she asked.

'Their what?'

'They can manage alone?'

'No. Not really. They had some success at first but the French have been fighting for years against armies vastly superior to anything the Spanish can put in the field. In Spain you see generals dressed like emperors and soldiers carrying, I don't know, billhooks from the time of the Armada. It's not a lack of spirit. They've plenty of that. It's a lack of everything else. And it was not just the army. The whole country. No real order. Bad kings and bad governments. Centuries of it. And then there's the nature of the physical country. The only decent roads are the ones the Romans left behind them—'

'John?'

'What?'

'Is this what you want to tell me? About the roads?'

He started again. 'I went out to Lisbon in the summer. We sailed in convoy from Falmouth, were nearly wrecked in the Bay of Biscay, arrived at the mouth of the Tagus on the 29th of August. I don't think you've been anywhere like that. Lisbon, I mean. I know I hadn't. Lovely from the water but to walk through the middle of it ... Heat, stink. Most of the buildings are whitewashed so you can hardly look at them in the full light of day. A church on every street corner, their steps covered with beggars, the beggars covered in flies. Feral dogs. Ten thousand cats that look too thin to be alive but somehow are. For a week we loathed the place, then began to see something else in it. I'm not sure what to call it. You rest your hand on a stone at midnight and the stone is warm. You see a street lined with orange trees and imagine all your life you have been waiting to see exactly that.

'Anyway, our lives were pleasant enough once we grew used to the heat. And my duties were much the same as those I'd had in England. Exercise the horses, drill the men. We went sightseeing. We went to routs. We invented card games. It was not unpleasant at all, though I suppose we were all chafing a little. Soldiers must at least *appear* as if they wish to fight, so when November came and we received orders to make ourselves ready to go into Spain I remember three or four of our people giving the hunting cry. There was a lot of talk about tactics, fighting spirit, the superiority of our horses, our swords, our guns. It was also when we had our first taste of the confusion that in the end overwhelmed everything. The rains were due, no reliable maps were to be had and no two Portuguese could agree on the best route to the border. To spread the risks the army was divided. I went on the road through a place called Elvas. We had some of the German legion, some dragoons, six batteries of guns. Highlanders too, the 71st, and it was on the road to Elvas I first heard Gaelic spoken, spoken and sung. The intention, as I understood it, was to defend Madrid, but by the time we had any degree of readiness Madrid had fallen, gone without a fight, the government fleeing south as fast as their mule cars would carry them. As for where the various French armies were, what their numbers might be, their dispositions, I had the impression that no one, from General Moore down, really had the least idea, and as the French were equally ignorant about ourselves we were all of us reduced to moving about the country in the hope of hearing something. Thousands of men in bright coats on beautiful horses looking for each other in the rain! And when the rain stopped the snows began. Spain in winter is a cold country, Emily. A cold country and a hard one.

'At last we did stumble across them, the enemy. A dispatch was intercepted and we learned of a body of their cavalry in a town five leagues or so from where the regiment was quartered. We set off at midnight, travelled through the dark, but as we came close we were challenged by one of their patrols and when we reached the town they were ready for us. Heavy dragoons, Chasseurs. It was first light, misty, not like today, but enough to make the ground uncertain. We wheeled into line. The charge was sounded. I was on the far left of the line and after galloping through a vineyard with my sword stretched out ahead and yelling like the best of them I found nothing in front of me but mist and snow. I gave the order left shoulders forward, the one you said I spoke in my dreams that night, but by the time we joined the others it was almost over. The first shock had been enough. The French were scattering. I fired my pistol at one, his back as he was riding away. I missed him, I probably missed him by yards. I don't think I was sorry for it. They lost above twenty. We lost six. We took prisoners, including a pair of colonels, captured a good many horses, good horses too, none of them less than fourteen hands. It was our great moment. Everyone telling everyone what everyone had seen for themselves. This was what we had come for! *This* was war! You should have seen us swagger. Well, there was little enough time to enjoy it.

'On Christmas Eve the retreat began. Not back to Portugal as we had hoped but north, into Galicia. We crossed the River Esla on the 28th, reached Bembibre on the 31st, Villafranca on New Year's Day. The French were never far behind us, Marshal Soult, possibly Bonaparte himself. There were always rumours about him, sightings. The general staff were in a panic and the men were pushed on at a rate they could hardly bear. On one occasion we marched thirty-six hours without pause. Even on horseback that was hard. On foot it must have been torture. We were not equipped for the mountains, not the mountains in winter. Soldiers roamed in gangs hunting for food. We began to view the Spanish as much our enemies as the French. Why did they not help us? Why did they not provide us with what we so desperately needed? The answer of course was that they could not, they had not the means, but that did not stop us from hating them.

'Each morning we left behind those who had not survived the night, and if we buried them at all we buried them in snow. Discipline fell away. People . . . altered. You could see it in their faces, a confusion, as though they were searching for what they might trust in, something to guide them, but everything that could be brought to mind was false, dust, nothing. I cannot say when it started with me. It might have been when I saw the commander of our cavalry led past with his eyes covered much as yours are. He had opthalmia. It was common enough. A trooper was leading his horse by the bridle. They went by in perfect silence. I know I was *physically* ill by then. I had the flux. I also had violent pains in my head, a neuralgia of some sort, and I had taken to pushing balls of cotton into my ears to stop the wind from piercing them. I have sometimes thought that is the cause of my deafness, that there is still some of the cotton in there. I should have had Rizzo look in with his glass.

'But in the midst of all this we were still giving and receiving orders. I suppose it gave us a sense of things going on as they should, of normality. One evening when my squadron were trying to build shelters at the side of the road, a cornet rode up with a dispatch from Major Leitch informing me I was kindly to remain behind in the morning when the army moved north and to collect stragglers. Collect them and form them into something of a vaguely military character. This was laughable, of course. Completely absurd. The stragglers were the most dispirited, the most afraid, the most desperate. I was to make a fighting body from such men? I think now I could safely have ignored the order. I doubt anyone would ever have known or cared. But a soldier who does not obey orders has ceased to be a soldier at all and it seemed I was not quite ready for that. So I stayed. The army marched away and for a while I was entirely alone, a horseman on a road of churned snow, the last man in Spain. How long I was to wait there had not been specified. An hour? Two? And what if instead of British stragglers it was the French vanguard that came over the rise? I even began to wonder why they had chosen *me* for such a duty. Was it a recognition of my competence? Or was it that I was considered the most dispensable? The officer they could most easily do without?

'Then the first of them appeared, four men, bowing into the wind, shuffling. They did not see me until they were almost upon me and when they looked up they looked up like children. Was I there to save them or to kill them? Others came. Men with beards, boys who could not have grown a beard had their lives depended on it. Some of them called up their names, their regiments. No two seemed to be from the same outfit. I am not even sure they were all British, that I didn't have some of General Romano's men. You couldn't tell from the uniforms because there weren't any, or rather there was a complete muddle of uniforms, anything at all as long as it gave some protection against the cold. One man had on the brass helmet of a French dragoon. God knows where he found it. I thought of telling him to take it off but I didn't. I couldn't be bothered. I didn't care.

'In all I collected close to thirty. Some still had weapons. Most could have done nothing but throw snowballs at the French. It had been common practice for some time to use musket stocks for firewood. Well, I formed them into a column and we set off in search of the army. It was not that far ahead of us, couldn't be, and the sooner I caught up with it the sooner I could be rid of my charges. It was necessary however to keep stopping. Had I not done so I would soon have had to commence the whole business over again. So we stopped every hour then every half-hour, all the while widening the gap between us and the army. The snow came horizontally. I remember leaning on my horse's neck trying to see the road. I had no sense of progress, no notion of our coming closer to anything other than our own extinction. For three days we went on like this. Three days does not sound like a long time but to us it began to seem we had never known any other and never would. Some gave up, walked into the forest or lay in the snow to sleep. Others joined us, fell in with the column. I followed the road and they followed me, their officer. Not out of any respect or fear. There was nothing of either. Very likely they followed because I was on a horse and had I toppled off the horse, as I often thought I might, they would have taken my boots, my cloak, left me where I was, dead or dying. I would not have blamed them. I would have understood . . .'

He let himself falter, let his gaze settle again on the moon, which had slid perceptibly westwards since he started to speak. Behind him in the room he could hear nothing. Was she asleep? Was he confessing to a sleeping woman? A sleeping woman and a cat? He could look round but he chose not to. To start all this again, later, tomorrow, the day after – an intolerable thought.

'At dusk on the fourth day we came to the village. I had sent off some of the stronger people as scouts, more for form's sake than out of much hope they would find anything useful. But they came back with news of the village and we turned off the road towards it. It is a place called Morales. Hard to believe you'll find it on any maps. A church, a square with an old twisted tree in the centre, perhaps thirty houses. They did not welcome us. It may be they thought we were the French, though most had not stayed to find out. By then the snow had stopped and I could see a score of them disappearing into the treeline above the village, men and women, running away. Well, it turned out, of course, they were very wise. There was a moment then, I believe there was, when I might have called the men to me, drawn them up in the square, spoken to them, reminded them we were there on sufferance, that these people were our allies, that property was sacred. I did nothing of the sort, of course. I rode to what seemed one of the better houses, rode up to the front door, knocked with my boot, received no answer, dismounted, went around the back of the house, tried the door there, pushed at the shuttered windows and finally discovered one I could force. It was dark in there, silent. I don't know what sort of room I'd climbed into, I couldn't see enough of it, but I felt my way to a door and through it into another room where there were the embers of a fire. Immediately I looked for something to burn on it. There was probably a wood store under the eaves but I wasn't going outside again. I broke up a stool by swinging it against the floor. Furniture usually burns well, that was one of the lessons of the retreat. I laid the pieces on, they caught. Soon there were flames, beautiful flames, and the room took shape around me. There was a table where the family must have been eating when news of our arrival reached them. Three plates on the table, meals abandoned before they had been quite finished. Beans, bread, oil. I tugged off my gloves with my teeth, picked up the first plate and stood there scraping

374

the food into my mouth with my fingers. It was a reprieve, a marvel. I was, quite suddenly, intensely happy. An hour earlier the world appeared determined to be rid of me. Now it had reached out to save me.

'I was still eating when I heard the first shots. I listened of course. I may even have stopped chewing for a few seconds. But the shots were irregular and seemed only to come from one place. I did not think it was contact with the enemy. Apart from anything else neither we nor the French were much inclined to fight in the dark. So I went on with my supper then got on my knees to search the floor for what might have been dropped. I hope you can picture that. The captain of hussars snuffling like a dog under the table. But soon there was a new disturbance and harder to ignore. The main door of the house opened into the room I was in, or would have done had it not been barred on the inside. A fist hammered at the wood, a voice called out for me. Sir! Sir! Sir! I kept silent but he kept knocking, kept calling. In the end I realised the only way to get rid of him was to ask who he was and what he wanted. He said he was Thompson. I recalled him, just about. A boy soldier and among the first who came to me along the road. He said that the others had gone berserk. Or they had gone mad. I forget the exact word he used. He had seen them shoot a man, a villager. He had seen them taking women away. He feared they intended to set the church alight. None of this amazed me. None of it, I think, meant anything to me at all. I called back that he should stay out of their way, that I would come and see for myself. He begged me to come soon and I assured him I would.

'When I was certain he had gone I climbed out from under the table. I stood, drew my sword, and started poking the thatch above the rafters. We knew this was one of the places they liked to hide things, the Spanish. It was always good to search there. And sure enough, after walking up and down the room a few times stabbing the straw I had a success. I punctured a wineskin. It startled me. I thought I had run through something living. Then I could smell what it was and stood beneath the stream and opened my mouth. I washed my face in wine, it ran into my eyes, but most of it I managed to get down my throat. I could still hear shots, and there was some shouting, but it wasn't directly outside, it wasn't close. When I had drunk all I could I lay by the fire, as near to it as I dared. I can hardly tell you the pleasure I felt. The warmth of the fire, the warmth of the wine. I slept. I have no idea for how long. It might only have been ten or fifteen minutes but had I not been woken by more beating at the door I would, I suppose, have slept on until the French arrived or the house-holder came back to wake me with the edge of his axe.

'It was the boy again, Thompson. He was more urgent now, his voice shrill. I hated him. I wished him dead. But at last I got to my feet, went to the door and unbarred it, my one honoura-ble act of the entire campaign. The instant the door was open I could see the fires. The houses had thatched roofs and even with snow on them they burned well. The light must have been visible for miles. Well, I was sober enough then, sober and awake. The boy ran, I followed. He led me along the edge of the village to a large house beside the track we had come in by. The door was open and we went inside. It was a room much like the one I'd been sleeping in, though this, I remember, had a large crucifix on one of the walls. The men were in there, about half our company. A few of them carried burning sticks, though most of the light came from the flames on the roof of the house opposite. They were gathered in a circle and in the centre of the circle were two chairs. On one of these a girl was standing. She had on a petticoat but above her waist she had nothing and had crossed her arms to cover herself. On the other chair, a little behind her, was a soldier with a pair of shears, sheep shears, I think, though they might have been for cloth. He was cutting off the girl's hair, cropping it close to her scalp, one hand working the shears, the other holding her head still. Most of her hair had already gone, black hair in a pile on the floor, enough to stuff a bolster with. Her eyes were shut. She did not weep or call for help. She had withdrawn herself, had sent her spirit away somewhere.

'The men, when I first went in, were rapt. They had foolish grins on their faces and yet they looked horrified. As they became aware of me, my presence, so their expressions changed. They started to be uneasy and looked about themselves like people waking from a dream. But not the soldier on the chair, not him. He was one who had joined us the previous day, met us on the road, alone. He had been wearing a greatcoat then. Now he had taken it off and I could see his tunic and his corporal's stripes. When at last he did look at me it was because he was ready, because he chose to. Looked, looked away, went on with his cutting.

'It was Thompson who shouted that he should stop. The girl on the chair was probably his own age. I'd say she was. And it was that, the boy's protest, that finally woke in me some sense of duty, of decency. I made to draw my sword only to realise I had left it in the house where I had slept. My pistol, thank God, I did still have and I would have been entirely within my rights to have used it on him. He was only a few feet away, I could hardly have missed. He looked at me again. I think he was surprised though he was careful not to show it. He brushed some hair from the girl's shoulders, dusted it away. Here, he said, is one who will remember the British army. Only then did he come down.

'I ordered them out, all of them, told them the French would be on us at first light. Thompson hung on my sleeve asking about the girl. She was still on her chair. He wanted me to do something for her. I made some promise or another, shook him off, went back for my horse. I didn't go into the house for my sword and so lost it, itself a shameful thing to confess. But there was more, there was more. When I rode into the square I saw, by the light of the burning church, the use they had put the tree to. Firelight on bare feet, bare feet floating a half-yard off the ground. I did not stop to count them. I did not want to risk seeing their faces. I did not even look round to see if the others were following me. For the villagers watching from the hill I must have looked like Death himself riding out of the village.

'After that . . . well, after that nothing matters very much. The last forty-eight hours into Corunna I walked. My horse had gone lame and the ball I should have put through the corporal I put through the animal's head. I did not take part in the battle where General Moore was killed. I was already in the transports in the bay, delirious. Two weeks later, having failed to die, I was at Plymouth. Some time after that, though I have no recollection of it, I was delivered to my house in Somerset where our servant, Nell, tended me with a devotion entirely at odds with what I merited. I recovered. I could not quite keep myself from it – from life, from living. The name I assumed, Lovall, belonged to a blameless young officer who died of a fever on the road out of Portugal. I hope to God I have not disgraced that name, though I suppose I have. I must have. Even more, I fear I have disgraced you and your family. By association, I mean. Certainly I seem to have put you all in danger, though who he is, this Henderson, what he wants of me, why he has pursued me here, that I still do not understand. It is to do with Morales of course, it cannot be

378

otherwise. Some sort of reckoning. Anyway, I have a scheme of sorts. I was piecing it together on the coach today. I will find the means to make my presence known to him. I will advertise myself and draw him away. Away from you, your family, from everyone. He will have no reason to trouble you then. And you will be free of me, Emily. Your life, I think, was a good life before I—'

She stopped him, mid-sentence, with a touch. He had not heard her cross the room. She was standing directly behind him, had walked up the sound of his voice and found him. She had her fingers on his shoulders, then she leaned her head against his back, her forehead pressing between his shoulder blades. When she spoke her voice was a trembling in his chest. What he heard, and he heard it clearly – the connective power of bones and blood – was like the speaking of his own heart.

'I do not know how to judge any of this. It is not for me to judge it. I suppose you must go on living with it somehow. But I do not feel disgraced by knowing you. Nor do I wish to be free of you. I began to love you as John Lovall. I shall love you still as John Lacroix.'

He guided her to the bed. She sat and he unlaced her boots, took them off, took off his own. They lay on the bed together holding hands. He tried to think back to the day's beginnings; it was like trying to think back to his own infancy. On the ceiling the light moved like water, was restless as water. He heard her say he could kiss her if he wished to. Or that he should? He propped himself up, looked at her, could not quite shake the feeling she looked back at him through the silk. Her lips were dry at first and tight, as were his own. Kissing was a strange thing to do, awkward. Then his hand found one of her breasts, seemed to stumble over it, and through the cloth, through layers of cloth, he felt the hard, impersonal life of her. After that it was easy. A mutual falling, the grief of appetite. And in between the touching, the tender manoeuvres, the new knowledge, he had calm thoughts, grammatical, useful, and remembered even when it was over. One was, what I have done in Spain I cannot make good, and telling it changes nothing. Another was, she does not especially mind what I have done, is not, perhaps, particularly interested. It is what she expects of soldiers. A third – she knows more about this thing we are doing than I.

He must have cried out at the end. There was a shattering of china. The cat had been on the table drinking the dregs of the negus and had been startled into a clumsy jump.

'He'll want letting out,' said Emily.

'Want what?'

'Letting out, John. The cat.'

He got off the bed and crossed the boards to the door. He was wearing only his shirt and a single woollen stocking, ravelled round an ankle. As soon as the door was open the cat darted past him. The stairs were dark, the hotel silent. He waited there, hanging on with some sense of offering himself as a target to whatever – whoever – might be standing in the throat of the stairs. But it was only a game; he had no intention of sacrificing himself. He shut the door, worked home the little bolt, snuffed the candle and went back to her.

20

He was on a beach at the island's northern tip. Facing him was another island, so much like the one he was standing upon – the beach, the bay, the rocks, the pelt of brown and green, the absence of trees – it was like a mirror, though a mirror that did not, of course, include him, the one who looked, who stood alone and gazed out.

The distance was not great. He gauged it at half a pistol shot, probably less, and a man who knew how to swim might be tempted to try it. That man would not arrive. An entire ocean pushed its wild green arm between the islands. Ten strokes out and you'd look up with a gasp to find yourself somewhere else entirely. Human strength would mean nothing out there. Even in a boat it was hard to see how you'd do it. Not, he thought, in a straight line.

He walked away from the sea, sat in the sand between tall spikes of dune grass. All day, scrambling around the island, he had waited for himself to come right but he hadn't. Not right as rain, not the old Calley. There was the sense of a misstep. The sense of being given the kind of lesson he would not recover from.

He picked a piece of grass, picked another, started winding them together. I'll make a rope, he thought, but what would he do with it? There was no one to take the other end. There was not even a tree he could hang himself from. That little pine tree, you'd have to be a midget to hang yourself from that.

Anyway.

The point is.

What I'm *saying*.

He spoke to Medina. It had taken hours to find the right voice and he had settled on something that drew on their better times together, like when Medina brought him the soup those clowns in Wales brewed instead of tea. Or that night after they found the tattooed sailor and thought they were closing in on Lacroix. Or sitting on the harbour wall at Mull. Or eating mussels, last night.

What's your name?

Andrew.

And when Medina repeated it he got it a bit wrong, said Andrew with an s. Andrews. That didn't matter though. He didn't mind. It was funny because Medina didn't make mistakes as a rule, could speak the king's better than a lot of men Calley had served with. So it hadn't mattered, he didn't mind. And that was what he'd been trying to say, how much he hadn't minded things and hadn't even minded that thing with the flowers, not really, and if you'd stopped at two, well, you dozy cunt, we'd be sitting here on the beach together having a chinwag.

He tossed the grass away, his little rope. The shadows were long now. On the water the light was a slowly deepening gold. An hour of light left; half an hour of good light, of useful light.

He dug deep in one of his many pockets, pulled out the brass case, fiddled with the catch, opened it. The blonde curl, the woman's eye, the two grey tears. He was not sure if Medina had seen him palm it. 'Did you?' he asked, his voice part of the night breeze through the marram. 'Did you see me, you sly dog?' And he grinned and thought, I'd give it to him now, if he was here, if he wanted it.

He wound himself down into the sand. It wasn't cold, or not especially so. He held the brass case in his hand. The painting was of some dead man's squeeze, the woman dead herself no doubt, hence grief, hence the cutting of the neck, hence a grave at the edge of nowhere. But she looked on him with a kindness he relished and he gazed back until, fading with the fading light, the eye seemed to close. He pulled his coat up around his cheeks and closed his own eyes. He readied himself for a dream of his mother – not his actual mother, about whom he knew nothing at all, but one of that troupe of dream women who, once or twice a year, stood over him in sleep. Tonight, perhaps, she would walk out of the sea. She would cross the beach and find her son sleeping in the open without as much shelter as a dog. She would bring him something, a gift, he didn't know what, a suit of magic armour perhaps, leave it heaped on the sand beside his head. He readied himself, he thought he was probably lost enough, that he'd earned it, the apparition, the ghost mother with her ghost love. Instead, he dreamed, briefly and powerfully, of Ernesto Medina stretched out on the grass and through his white shirt, the skin of his face, two dozen crimson flowers coming into bloom.

When he woke he lay in a perfection of readiness, eyes wide, breath slow. With finger and thumb he tested the darkness like a cloth. Not quite night, not quite day. The edge of both.

He listened, leaned himself against the door of the world, heard all the subtle graduations of nothing. Then he heard again the voice that had woken him. The rising and dipping of a song. Some man flying his voice like a kite.

Where was he? Measure distances, Calley. Be certain.

He shifted in the sand, raised his head so that he could turn it – a little this way, a little that. The voice was not behind him, where he might have expected it, nor was it on the beach in front of him.

He sat up. Glimmer of sand. Late stars. A breeze in which he seemed to smell the salty fish-head muck the world was made of, half Billingsgate, half sex. Out in the channel was a small light. It was hard to say at first which way it was headed or if it was headed anywhere, if, perhaps, it was merely floating out there. But after watching a minute, unblinking, the light grew brighter, the song clearer, and there could be no more doubt.

Whatever was coming it would touch the beach no more than thirty yards from where he sat. He undid his coat. The carbine, faithful dog, fell under his touch, but as his fingers slid towards the lock, the hammer, he realised he had not loaded it again, not since. And this was remiss and strange, some foolish symptom of the previous day's confusion. Anyway, the look of it was usually enough. The look of himself. Usually.

The singing stopped. You might imagine the world's turning stopped with it. Then the light was raised and Calley saw the form and figure of a man, though one so encumbered with what he carried – a great shadow on his back – he was more a type of beetle than a man. A beetle that crossed water without the need of a boat.

He let go of the carbine and buttoned his coat again. Anyone who could cross a torrent in his boots, singing, was not to be frightened off with a gun. He walked down to the shore and stood there waiting as the light came closer. Another stop, another raising of the lantern. They were only ten yards apart now.

'Good morning to you, brother,' said the voice in what might have almost been a continuation of the song. 'You are a man and not a spirit, I suppose?'

'Flesh and blood,' said Calley. 'Though I do not yet know what you are.'

'One who would come ashore if you have no objection.'

'I have none,' said Calley.

'The crossing time is short,' said the man, walking again, walking where, when Calley lay down to sleep, the sea had been.

A minute later and they stood together on the beach. The beetle was plain enough now, a man about Calley's own build, and on his back a frame to which a vast number of objects were attached. He had a stick in one hand, the lantern in the other.

'You're a pedlar,' said Calley.

'*The* pedlar,' said the man, 'or so I like to think of myself though there are one or two others who walk the islands. May I raise my lamp, brother, and see you more clearly?'

He raised it, looked, nodded, lowered it again. 'I did not know we had soldiers here,' he said.

'Are you alone?' asked Calley.

'I am,' said the man, 'for the moment. And you, brother?'

'Yes,' said Calley.

There was a pause. The man came a step closer. When he moved you could hear the creak of the frame, the soft shifting of the things attached to it. He wore his boots around his neck. His feet were bare.

'You are wondering,' he said, 'how I did that. How I walked across. You are wondering if it was some enchantment.'

'Where has the water gone?' said Calley.

'The moon has it in her pockets,' said the pedlar.

'How's that?' asked Calley.

'Tides, brother. On certain nights there is an hour at the ebb when you can cross. A bare hour, mind. You have to know what you're about. When the water starts to come back you could not outrun it on a horse.'

'How much of the hour is left?'

'Tonight?'

'Tonight.'

'I'd say half. A little more, a little less.'

'And how long does it take to cross?'

'Half an hour. More or less.'

'And when does it come again?'

'Like this? Two weeks, I'd say. Depending on her Lunar Majesty. She has her moods.'

Calley stepped away, got himself apart from the man's light and stared out into the channel. He chewed his lip, made calculations that had little to do with time and distance and much to do with luck. How much he might have used, how much remained.

'I'll go,' he said.

'I believe you will,' said the pedlar.

'I need a light.'

'Well now,' said the pedlar, 'it so happens I am in a position to meet your needs.' He shrugged off his frame. He did it well, seemed to dance it down on to the sand. Then a moment of search, of rummage. 'One like this?' he said.

'Yes,' said Calley.

'And you'll need a candle. Do you have a candle?'

'A candle too,' said Calley. 'You got any food?'

'Now food is a thing they do not really need me for. I have tobacco, a little brandy. I have fifteen different clocks. Recently the islanders have become interested in time.'

'I don't want a clock,' said Calley.

'You might pick up a lobster on your way over,' said the pedlar. 'Listen out for them. Clack, clack, clack.'

'Light the candle for me,' said Calley.

'You have something for me I hope?'

'I have money.'

'Money is good,' said the pedlar, lighting the candle from his own and placing it inside the lantern, shutting the little door. 'Though sometimes I prefer items of value I can trade in. You have some trinket on you? A watch? A watch would get you the lantern and candle, a pipe and tobacco.'

'I have no watch,' said Calley. He reached into his pockets. His right hand touched the brass case, the little painting; his left skimmed one of the items he had taken from Medina's coat before making the coat into a shroud, weighting it with stones and rolling the Spaniard into the sea. He took the item out and showed it. It was Medina's uniform collar badge, a sabre crossed with a palm branch, brass. Medina must have carried it to prove what he was in the event they were taken. To prove he was a soldier. As if that would have helped.

'Now that's a curious piece,' said the pedlar. 'It could almost be a lady's brooch. I know a man clever with his hands who could put a pin on the back of it. Pin and clasp. Very well. This and five shillings gets you the candle and lantern.'

'That's fucking steep,' said Calley.

'You could always go to the other fella,' said the pedlar. 'See what he'll offer you.'

Calley paid. Five shillings left him with only two but there was no time to haggle. No time even to thrash the man.

'You should take off your boots,' said the pedlar.

'Don't worry about my boots,' said Calley. 'Point the way with your stick.'

The pedlar raised the stick, held it out. 'Halfway across,' he said, 'you'll begin to see where you're going to. But don't stop, don't change your course even if you hear the water. Keep going, straight as an arrow.'

Calley put his knapsack on his back, picked up his new lantern. 'Why did you come here?' he said. 'There's no one here.'

'You were here,' said the pedlar.

Calley began to walk. Dry sand, damp sand. Then sand and weed and pools of water, not deep. For the first few minutes he knew he would be able to run back to the beach. After that he would be a man committed. The air was cooler out here, colder. It was like walking into a cave. Then he stopped. He turned a careful one hundred and eighty degrees until he was facing the path he had just walked.

'You are doing grand,' called the pedlar. 'But it's not wise to stop out there.'

'I'm looking for someone,' said Calley. 'On the islands somewhere. English. Army officer. Lovall or Lacroix. Plays a fiddle. You know him?'

'English? The only English I know are in a house two days' walking from where you're stood. Two sisters and a brother. But now that I think of it they may have a man staying with them. A visitor. Came to the island on the back of a cow, they say. Might he be your officer?'

By the light of his lamp, Calley saw the water riddling round his boots, felt, even through the leather, some small shifting of its force. 'Two days' walk?' he said.

'The family, name of Frend,' called the pedlar. 'A white house near the western shore. A place on its own. You can ask for Ranald if you want to find them.'

'Ranald?'

'Has hooks for hands. Everyone knows Ranald. But if you stand there much longer you'll have to look for him in America.'

Calley shut his eyes and turned back the same careful half-circle. 'Advance in line,' he said softly, 'by the left . . .'

He went as quickly as he dared, stone and slither under his feet, sucking-mud, black-shine. He imagined finding Medina, his body washed around into the channel, imagined stumbling over him, his white face, his hair plaited with ribbons of weed. How wide the channel was! Wide and cold! And why could he still not see the far shore? Had he curved away? Fallen into the foolish error of following his own light as though it led him?

He lengthened his stride. The lantern swung, the candle flame flying within the glass like a terrified bird. All the voices in his head fell silent. He had neither name nor history. He was a shadow. A ghost fleeing before the dawn. He was the done-with, the uninvented. A freedom of sorts? Then his heel glided on something slick and glabrous and he went down heavily with a grunt, lay a moment in the water, stunned, feeling the water shove at him. The candle was out. He got to his feet, threw away the lantern and ran.

21

The boat that took them was called *Halcyon*. Two days earlier she had delivered four families bound for the emigration ship. Now, loaded with timber and a hundred blades for sickles and scythes, a bolt of pink-striped cotton for a customer in Tarbert, the boat was ready to depart. The crew untied from the quay as the church rang ten. Spinkey himself came down to wave them off.

'I appeal,' said Emily, 'to his Russian sense of the tragic.'

'That may be,' said Lacroix, 'but he has played a part now in the lives of both sisters.'

She nodded, blushed a little. Lacroix liked her blush but wondered if he had been indelicate. Hard to know what was permitted, what could be spoken of, what merely known. They were as new to this as the day was new. Ten o'clock marked the entire history of their . . . whatever it was. Was it an engagement? Was it? What did *she* think it was?

'He is still waving,' he said.

'Are you waving back?' she asked.

'Yes,' he said. And waved.

*

The day was breezy but the breezes fitful. High cloud, slow-moving, no swell to speak of, the colour of the sea a rich impenetrable green. Emily and Lacroix were the only passengers. They moved freely around the deck, Emily's arm wound tightly through Lacroix's. After the hospital, the long cooping-up of the carriage ride, she declared herself relieved to be out in the air. He told her she should have tried travelling on the roof of the coach, that he had felt himself inflating like one of Montgolfier's balloons.

'I would rather have been up there,' she said. 'I would have been with you and you would have held on to me.'

'Yesterday,' he said, 'we were still simply friends. Travelling companions.'

'Nonsense,' she said.

'Hmm?'

'You know it's nonsense, John. Do you not remember our walk on the beach?'

'I remember every moment of it,' he said. 'I remember you being very angry with me.'

'That part you may forget,' she said. 'And I wasn't angry with you. I was angry with how little men understand the lives of women. And not because they cannot understand but because they will not trouble to. They will go to the greatest lengths to understand rocks or the smelting of iron. They will speculate endlessly on the nature of the divine and how we should say our prayers. Women they only pretend to give their attention to.'

'Is that true of Thorpe?' asked Lacroix.

'You should not think of Thorpe any longer,' she said. 'He was never your rival.'

'You knew him first.'

'Yes. And liked him. As you will like him, perhaps.'

'I hope I will,' he said, 'for Jane's sake.'

'My rival,' said Emily, 'was my own sister.'

He denied it, as vehemently as he dared.

They crossed the firth, entered the sound between Mull and the headland. The day was half warm, half cool. When the bows raised spray the water wore a crown of coloured light. Out of earshot – they knew there were English speakers on the boat – they set themselves to be practical, to try, in to and fro, to sift what they knew from what they didn't, what they could guess from what they could not. Emily started with the master. Were not all seamen notorious for their yarns? The simplest explanation for the strangeness of his story, its character of the incredible, was that it was, in part or in entirety, made up. Lacroix shook his head, said that could not be. Everything he had seen of the master, and he had seen a good deal of him on the journey up from Bristol, convinced him of his honesty. A scrupulous man, a plain speaker. And what of his injury? That was no invention.

This brought them to his assailant.

'When I think of him,' said Lacroix, 'when I picture him . . .' He faltered. She heard him shrug.

'What?' she asked. 'You know him after all? You have guessed him?'

'I do *not* know him,' he said. 'I have sworn to you and to Captain Browne. I do not know him.'

'But something,' she said. 'When you picture him you see . . . who?'

Lacroix was silent a while, however long it takes the unvoiced to thicken into language. 'The master,' he began, 'told us Henderson had bow legs. Bandy. The corporal in Morales, the one who cut off the girl's hair, he had them also.'

'So have a great many,' she said. 'My father's friend Smith looked like a pair of egg tongs.'

'But the way he was in the master's house,' said Lacroix. 'The coolness of it.'

'You mean the cunning of it.'

'The what of it?'

'A cunning man. A shameless one.'

'Exactly.'

'But you cannot remember the soldier's name?'

'No.'

'Or you never knew it at all?'

'That is possible. Likely even.'

'In which case—'

'In which case,' interrupted Lacroix, 'there is nothing to say he was *not* Henderson. But if it is the same man, suppose for a moment that it is, why pursue me? An officer who barely knew him, who did him far less harm than he might have . . .'

'You saw him in his crime.'

'He saw me in mine.'

'They are not the same, John! Not at all!'

'I suppose,' said Lacroix, 'if they wished to have me brought before a court he would not be the worst they could send. A man who could recognise me . . .'

'That cannot be right,' said Emily.

He didn't hear her; the breeze scattered her words. She leaned in closer. 'He has not come to arrest you,' she said. 'A man who behaves as he has done does not act for any court. And did he not say to Captain Browne he was outside the law?'

'He also said he was sent by one whose word could not be gainsaid.'

'And you answered it was a fantasy to justify his violence.'

'I did.'

'But now you think differently?'

'I do not know what to think. I start to make a path, to see one. Then I lose it, or it was no path at all.'

'Well,' she said. 'If we do not know all we know enough. We have been warned. That is what counts. We will fetch Jane and Cornelius and then all of us will go where this man, whoever he is, can never find us.'

'And where is that?' asked Lacroix. 'Shoreditch?'

For the moment there seemed no more to be said. They were caught in the space between two stories, between the sweetness of what they had, (their half-night at the hotel, souls and bodies bared), and what still lay at a distance, the outer world that signalled to them but whose message would not harden into sense. They stopped their parading of the deck and settled themselves, hip to hip, in the lee of a cord of timber. The smell of forests settled on them. She said it reminded her of her father's workshop. 'By ten,' she said, 'I knew wood well. I could tell you the difference between rosewood and maple. Oak and sycamore.'

'You helped him with his work?'

'I remember,' she said, 'Jane and Cornelius and myself squatting like Chinamen lining hatboxes with scale.'

'Is that a happy memory?' he asked.

'It is today,' she said. She shifted at the side of him, felt for his face and kissed him. A sailor, tying off a halyard to a pin, glanced at them and looked away, as if he were the world's observer and had towards them some duty of tenderness.

They crept up the sound. On the water the cloud-shadows were almost stationary. Another hour and a town of brightly painted houses showed on the port side; an hour later and it was still in view. Lacroix spoke with the captain. 'When we come out of the lee of the island,' said the captain, 'we may find the wind again.' But they came out and the wind was less than before. They were carried north on the current, cleared the headland at Ardnamurchan under the shadow of its cliffs, the crew fretting the sails to pick up whatever scraps of wind might give them sea room. It was already late afternoon. Ahead of them was a small island with a curving high ride of bare rock along its back. This, Lacroix and Emily were informed, was where the *Halcyon* would spend the night. In the morning they might have better luck.

They closed on the island, drifted into a bay. The anchor was let go and the *Halcyon* found her angle and was still. The captain asked if they cared to go ashore. They went, rowed over by a straw-haired sailor who told them he had once, on the beach they were rowing towards, found a coconut shell that must have been washed all the way from the Indies.

'Where are you from?' asked Lacroix.

'Friesland,' said the sailor. 'Or an island near the coast. Ameland.'

'Is it like this?'

The sailor shook his head. 'We have no mountain in Ameland. There you are born with your feet in the sea and you can never make them dry again.' He laughed, shipped the oars, stepped out of the boat and drew them on to the beach. He and Lacroix – one elbow each – lifted Emily down to the sand.

'I will wait for you here,' said the sailor. 'I will smoke my pipe.'

They walked the curve of the bay. Lacroix described what he could see. He said he thought reading Hutton had made him into a better observer, more exact.

'I cannot stop thinking,' she said, 'of where he is. I seem to see him sometimes.'

'I assume you mean Henderson rather than Hutton.'

'When I see him he is running.'

'He cannot run over the sea.'

'What if he does not need to?'

'These are imaginings, Emily. He may be a hundred miles away. He has returned to England perhaps. For all that we know he is back in the Peninsula.'

'I do not believe it,' she said. 'And neither do you.'

He looked at her. With her eyes covered was she developing other ways of seeing? He thought not, told himself not (apart from anything else soldiers generally did not run unless they were ordered to). Still, it unnerved him. Emily was also Basemath, daughter of Solomon, dreamer of dreams. As Emily, she was for the moment almost helpless. As Basemath he did not know what powers she might yet have, what her limits were.

He sat her on a rock and settled beside her. They were in the shadow of the ridge but ahead of them the ship floated in a light so pure and perfectly clear he could fancy he saw, across three hundred yards, the glint of a gold ring in a sailor's ear. A woman approached them. She was young, sturdy, carried a basket and addressed them in Gaelic. She showed Lacroix what was in her basket. Eggs, oatcakes, a ball of red wool, some combs and spoons carved from horn. She could not keep her gaze from Emily, and when she looked at Lacroix her expression was part fierce, part fearful, as if she wondered what manner of man travelled with a woman like this, her eyes bound. By tomorrow, thought Lacroix, Emily will be a story. Over time she might be folded into song. He bought two eggs from her, two of the oatcakes, then, for its redness, and because the woman's appearance felt like part of the theatre and fate of these days, that he was in the presence of not one but two creatures touched by the uncanny, he took the skein of wool. He had no idea what the price of these things might be and if she was telling him she may as well have saved her breath. He held coins on his palm and she picked among them. The deep, deep seriousness of her! She spoke once more – a blessing, he hoped – then walked on down the beach towards the sailor.

'What's this?' said Lacroix, and touched Emily's face with the wool. She took it from him, sniffed it, pressed it in her hand.

'Lovely,' she said.

'And can you tell its colour?'

She said she could and that it was blue.

They slept in hammocks and in the morning were woken by a chain rattling into a locker a yard from their feet.

'The anchor,' said Lacroix, when Emily raised her head above the canvas. They waited, two risen spirits, listening to the movements of the crew overhead, the dull slap of bare feet on the wood. They waited, then felt the water tighten around the keel and the ship begin to work, to live, to make the air around them live. Something fell; someone laughed.

'The wind,' said Emily.

'Yes,' said Lacroix. 'The wind is back.'

He helped her down. The helping ended in an embrace. He thought how much he would like to begin every morning for the rest of his life with such a moment. Thought also that he was glad to do it once.

The wind was a southerly. It took them towards the hills of Skye where they turned, swung west, and beat out into the Minch. Lacroix, leaving Emily eating the oatcakes he bought on the island, her back safely against the timber, went to stand beside the captain. They would, said the captain, make landfall by the middle of the afternoon. In a few hours they would have the tide with them.

Lacroix thanked him. He scanned the sea for other boats, saw two, three. He borrowed the captain's spyglass to look at one he fancied was on the same heading as *Halcyon*. In the glass bobbed four bearded heads, and so alike they had to be brothers. They had no stranger with them.

He went back to sit with Emily. The knowledge that they were only hours from their destination, that they could – should – be at the house by the shore long before dark, did not soothe her. Every fifteen minutes she asked him what he could see, how close they were, how soon he thought they might arrive. She was so agitated he wondered if she was in pain. He asked if her eyes were troubling her. Would she like him to examine them? She frowned at him. She was getting more accurate, did not waste many expressions on empty air.

'It is not my eyes. Use *yours*.'

'I will,' he said, 'when there is something to use them on.'

They sat without speaking, two stiff figures rolling with the rolling of the boat.

'You are already tired of me,' she said, but he didn't hear her. A half-minute later she felt for his hand, squeezed it. 'John,' she said. 'Will you do something? Will you sing? It need not be loud. The others need not hear you.'

'Sing?'

'Yes.'

'Sing what?'

'Sing anything.'

He sang her 'Greensleeves'. He sang 'As I Walked Forth'. He sang 'Black-eyed Susan'. He sang close to her and quietly. She listened to him like a bird enchanted, a child. When he finished he asked her to take her turn. She said she could not, not now, she was too uneasy, but after a minute, without warning, she opened her mouth as though to speak and sang instead. 'The Lass of Richmond Hill', 'A Sailor's Life', then 'Fare Thee Well', though in the last verse her throat was tight and from under the scarf, in the groove between cheek and nose, a tear came. Lacroix, wiping it with his thumb, said it was a good thing her eyes still did what eyes could do, that he was sure now she would see again, and soon. He said if he had wine in his hand he would drink to Rizzo.

'We will do so,' she said. 'All of us together.'

This thought gave them, perhaps, ten minutes of calm, then it was back to willing the ship forward, to a kind of scratching at the interiors of their own heads. The land hung back. The sea was leisurely, indifferent, lost in a slow green dreaming of its own. He wished she would sleep. A bare six days since she had been on the table under the glass roof! What if the fever returned? Rizzo had spoken to him about it in the few minutes there had been to discuss anything. The importance of keeping her eyes clean. Clean water, water that had been boiled, perhaps with a little vinegar. Plain food, rest. The avoidance of dust and smoke, the fumes of anything. The avoidance, where possible, of whatever might agitate her, physically or mentally.

She sent him to speak to the captain again. The captain looked amused.

'Your lady is very anxious to be ashore, sir.'

'We are both,' said Lacroix.

The captain took out his watch. He flipped up the lid with a thumbnail, looked at it, looked at the set of sails, at the land. 'It is five minutes before four o'clock. If we are not tied up by half past five you may tell me I do not know my business.'

Lacroix leaned at the rail. They were not, he knew, going to come in by the narrow opening the cattle boat had carried him through when he first arrived. They were going further north – were already further north – and would make their entrance through a labyrinth of islets that stood at the mouth of a loch better suited to a vessel the size of the *Halcyon*. It would make the land journey slightly longer but all distances on the island were small enough. They would sleep at the house, and in the morning ... what? Leave with what they could carry? Get Ranald to borrow one of the kelper's carts, return to the coast? If they left before it was light they might even get aboard the *Halcyon* again. But could so much be done so quickly? One sister pregnant, one blind or as good as. Not to mention Cornelius and the condition he might be in. And something in him jibbed at the thought of running from this Henderson. He was – unless he was already marked down on the muster roll as a deserter – still an officer in His Majesty's Army, a regiment that thought itself among the best. He had charged French cavalry (only once, but he had done it). He had worn the uniform, the blue and the silver. Yet now he was planning to hide from a man whose idea of valour was the bullying and assault of an unarmed sailor in his house at night.

He found himself wishing – absurdly! – that Thorpe was present. Thorpe might have interesting ideas. And two men could mount guard in a way one could not. Cornelius would be useless, and Ranald, a man with no hands, should be kept well clear of it all. But Thorpe! His opinion of him was that he was a version of the mad cabinet-maker Emily had had for a father, a spouter of cod-wisdoms, a snare for credulous women. Or that was the opinion he would have offered to a stranger. Beneath it – the underweave – was some idea of him as remarkable, someone you gave the first place to, gratefully. A man who did not doubt himself.

They were close now. He went back to Emily, stood her up beside the ratlines. What he saw and recounted, she listened for.

'And are there people, John?'

'People?'

'Yes.'

'Two women in the company of a cow. And there's a man on the pier. To take our ropes, I suppose. No one else.'

They were sliding in, the mate at the bows, the captain back by the helmsman, all others, the cook included, dropping sails or standing by. Lacroix had spent enough time at sea these last months to know where to be out of the way. The man on the pier moved like a somnambulist, but when the first coiled rope was thrown he was in precisely the place to receive it and as the *Halcyon* drifted the last yards he turned the rope around an iron bollard then ambled back to take the stern line. This was the perfection of repetition, the power of not-much.

With the Frieslander's help, Lacroix and Emily got down on to the jetty with their bags. The captain held up his watch and tapped its face. Lacroix mouthed 'yes', and bobbed his head, sorry, now they were here, to leave the company of these men who knew so well what they were about.

With Emily he took up the usual arrangement, the bags in his hands, her left hand on his right shoulder. They could not hurry on the planking of the jetty but once they reached the road it was easier, slightly. They headed for the inn, the only building of any substance, certainly the only one with an upper storey and a slate roof. The people there kept a gig and pony and Lacroix meant to hire them, but when, hot and midge-bitten, they entered the dark of the parlour, they were told the gig had a wheel off and the pony was out to a man called MacRae who wanted it for the harvest. It would be back in a week, though it would probably need to rest then.

'That is no good to us,' said Lacroix. 'You might as well use the gig for firewood.'

Emily pinched his arm. She spoke to the innkeeper. She told him – reminded him, for he certainly already knew – about her sister's condition, hinted at developments that made her presence at the house a matter of urgency.

'You could take old Tom,' said the innkeeper.

'Old Tom?'

Lacroix and the man went out together. They walked across the unfenced land in silence, walked twenty minutes before coming upon a big horse, his head down and grazing on sea pinks. He came with them easily enough, and in a lean-to at the rear of the inn Lacroix picked through tangles of old tack. There were no saddles. He rigged up a kind of bitless bridle with the parts of two head collars, then climbed on to the horse's back from a stool before lifting Emily up behind him.

'Did you not ride a cow before?' asked the innkeeper. He seemed to intend no disrespect. 'Old Tom should be easy enough.'

It took Lacroix a full mile to find the horse's mind, to establish some understanding between them. At certain places, entirely of the horse's choosing, they trotted. For the rest they plodded, ambled, the motion easier for them all. They rode towards the sun. Emily, side-saddle, rested her head against Lacroix's back. Her bag was in front of him; his own bag he had left at the inn to be collected when he returned the horse. He wondered what the innkeeper would have said if they told him the truth of their journey. Where would it fit among the strange, even fabulous things, the man might know? An innkeeper on one of the edges of the world! And these people, the Gaels, were a curious mix, rooted and practical, but living easily among dreams and stories and superstition, one ear always pressed against the night-world, or whatever it was, the correct name for that part of life people were forgetting how to address.

'I can smell the burning,' said Emily.

'A turning? Here?'

'The kelp, John. We cannot be far off.'

He had done no more than follow the road. Now, as the road became uncertain, became a track, became two paths, paths that soon guttered out in the grass, he began to recognise the landscape. He tapped old Tom's flanks with his heels. The horse looked up, caught something of the new mood of purpose, and went on at a smarter pace. Smoke to the south, grey smoke and the haze of heat from the trenches. Then the sea was in view, dark under the blaze of a low sun. Another half-hour and a patch of white became the facing wall of a house. Fifteen minutes after that and both house and boat shed were in plain view, and not smouldering ruins but exactly as they had left them. Lacroix tensed his gaze, trying to pick out the human upright, a moving figure. He could see Emily's garden, the path to the well . . .

'They will be amazed to find us suddenly in front of them,' he said. For a moment he had put aside the reason for their return. This was a homecoming. Emily had been placed in his care and here he was, returning her, unharmed and perhaps soon to have the use of her eyes again.

'Jane is in her room,' said Emily. 'She is sewing something. Not very well.'

'And Cornelius,' said Lacroix, 'is uncovering the last blackened toe of the Caledonian Achilles while poor Ranald pretends to take an interest.'

'Yes,' she said, 'Ranald. There's a voice I have missed.'

They came down a long, gentle slope, through grey stone and flowering heather. They had momentum now. The horse lifted the great brown bells of his hooves and the ground slid comfortably beneath them, but fifty yards from the house Lacroix tightened the reins and they stopped. He did not know why, and when Emily asked what it was he said it was nothing, nothing. He started the horse moving again but he felt different now, as though his eye had registered some flaw in the pattern of things he could not yet name. The green front door was shut, the windows coloured with the flat glare of the sun. Anyone inside the house would be able to see out easily enough but you could not see in.

He rode up close to the door, swung Emily down then climbed down himself. For a moment he considered the wisdom of leaving her outside while he went into the house on his own but she held his arm tightly and they went together. The front door opened at the turn of the handle. (The door had a keyhole but if it had a key Lacroix had never seen it, nor were there any bolts on the back of it.) The second door, the door into the big room, stood wide. They paused at the threshold. Lacroix looked in. The ottoman, the stairs. A shawl on the floor by the bottom of the stairs where perhaps it had slid from the banister. The dining table was spread with sheets from a newspaper and on the paper were pieces of shaped stone and pottery. The kitchen door was shut, the door to Cornelius's room partly open.

'Jane?' called Emily. 'Cornelius?'

They went to the kitchen. The door to the outside – another unlockable, unboltable door – was shut. Two pots with some congealed matter in the bottom of them stood on the range. There was no fire and no embers. They returned to the big room.

Lacroix sat Emily on the ottoman and went up the stairs to Jane's room. He knocked, entered. The bed was unmade, tousled. He touched the sheets as though hopeful they might still be warm. For several seconds he stared out through her window. When he came down the stairs he picked up the shawl and put it around Emily's shoulders.

'It is us who will welcome *them* back to the house,' he said. He pressed the wall by the ottoman, moved along a little and pressed again. The door of his room swung open. Emily's guittar, his fiddle case, the bed with his little pile of possessions on it, the uncurtained window.

'I know where they are,' called Emily.

'Yes?'

'They will be on the hill watching the sun set.'

He went and crouched by her knees. 'At the excavation?'

'You could fetch them,' she said.

'The sun will be down in a couple of hours. They'll come back then.'

'But I am anxious to see them, John. It will not take you long.'

'You mean I should leave you here?'

'We are at the house now. I feel perfectly safe. And I have done enough for one day. I would like to rest. I need to.'

He looked up at her. It was suddenly obvious to him that she could not be expected to do any more. 'Well,' he said. 'I suppose. If you wish it. And if I do not find them I will turn around and come straight back.'

He asked if she would like her guittar for company. She said she would. He fetched it from its peg, dusted it with his sleeve and settled it in her lap.

'It will need tuning,' she said, her left hand already sliding up the instrument's neck towards the brass box and the little key.

He went out. He looked at the horse then decided to walk. He could stride now, unencumbered by luggage, by a woman in a blindfold. He thought, my sword hand is free, then thought of his sword left lying in a room in Spain, and of the fact that there was not even a branch of wood on the island he could use in its place. After a few minutes he halted to look back at the house. He fancied he could hear the guittar but knew he could not, not really. What could he hear? Birds. The sea. The sea perhaps. That too he might be imagining.

He went on. The air had a scent, a herbal sweetness, his own walking gave rise to. Heather, wild thyme, clover. But how open it was here! No hiding place for anything bigger than a lapwing. He was, he realised – had been since that moment on the ride down to the house – moving in two realities at once. In the first, everything was perfectly ordinary and just as it appeared, the island as he had come to it in the beginning. In the other, he had to resume the habits of active service, the scanning and reading of the land, the making and remaking of schemes with which to meet what could only be guessed at. If he had poor Ruffian under him! A man on a cavalry horse is a powerful man. On foot he is nothing but himself, the bare creature, unresourced. And into his mind came the face, the scarred arms, of the gunsmith in Bristol, his quip about infantry officers always trying to see over the top of something. He remembered it but it did not make him smile.

He walked hard, leaned into the air ahead of him, but as he neared the bottom of the hill, walking his shadow into the hill's shadow, he slowed his pace. He had, he realised, no clear idea what he was going to say if he found Jane and Cornelius sitting on the far side. Cries of surprise, hearty handshakes. And then? They would be expecting a story about eyes, operations, a hospital. About Rizzo and Glasgow. Jane might be expecting a story about himself and Emily. Instead, they would hear a tale about some soldier run amok and searching the islands to do God knows what. All too easy to picture the confusion, the exchange of glances. Cornelius would laugh. He would think it was a joke. And even if he managed to persuade them, why should they not simply refuse to go anywhere? They were not old friends. They had between them half a summer. And it was *he* who this man was after. Lacroix who had called himself Lovall. The dubious stranger. The liar.

Ten strides from the brow of the hill – he had begun to settle on a scheme of saying as little as possible, of leaving the bulk of it to Emily – he noticed an object lying, casually, in the grass a short way to his left. A thing dropped, an object out of its place. He went towards it (already he seemed to know everything), and crouched beside it. It was one of Ranald's hooks. He touched it, solemnly, as though touching flesh rather than iron. Then he looked up, swiftly, to where the evening sky stood on the hill. His mouth was very dry, his breath in his throat like a feather. He picked up the hook, held it by the leather sheathing. It was the closest thing he had to a weapon. It was the only thing.

He covered the remaining yards at a crouch, his free hand brushing the grass-tips. He wished to Christ he could have more faith in his hearing. At the top he readied himself but when he stood he saw only the cropped blue slope, the empty sea. Ahead of him was the trench he had worked in with Cornelius. Beyond it were two new trenches, one smaller than the other, each with its pile of excavated peat and rubble. He walked down to the old trench and looked inside. It was dark in there, the dusk light already brewed into night, but he could see at the bottom the soft petal of a man's face, and after staring at it a while not knowing if he should weep or roar or simply run away, he dropped the hook on to the grass and climbed in. He knelt by the man's head, put a hand against his neck. The skin was warm and he could feel the movement of the blood.

'Ranald! Ranald, man!'

An eye opened, peered up at him.

'Ranald. It's Lacroix. Lovall. Listen. I am going to lift you. Yes? Lift you out of here.'

The eye seemed to give its assent. Lacroix manoeuvred himself along the trench until he stood at Ranald's side, then slid down as low as he could go, pushed one arm beneath Ranald's knees, one beneath his shoulders, pressed his own back against the earthen wall, and lifted. No groan from Ranald, or if there was he did not hear it. He raised him high enough to clear the lip of the trench, then scrambled out himself, came round and lay on the grass beside him. He had taken a tremendous beating. You could still feel the heat of it. On the left side of his face the skin was tight and purpled, his left eye lost in the swelling. A long gash from his left eyebrow to his hairline. Left ear ripped. Part of it missing perhaps. A good deal of drying blood around his mouth.

'Ranald! Can you hear me? Ranald. Think of Aboukir, man. The beaches.'

'I had not forgot them,' said Ranald.

'No, you have not, I know it.' He could have embraced him then. A depth of relief that felt not importantly different from love. 'Ranald. The one who attacked you. A soldier? A soldier with bandy legs? Calls himself Henderson?'

'He did not offer me his name,' said Ranald. 'But it was him.'

'And Jane? Cornelius?'

'Gone.'

'What?'

'They had . . . word of Mr Thorpe. They have gone to meet him. They will not be back today. Nor tomorrow I think.'

'Ranald. This man. He knows where the house is?'

'He will find it.'

'Listen, listen. Emily is there. She is alone. I have left her alone. I will come back for you, I swear it. As soon as I can.'

He tore off his coat and spread it over the damaged man. Ranald was speaking again. Lacroix watched his lips but it didn't help. He lowered his head, turned it until he felt Ranald's breath against his ear.

'He means to kill you, Mr Lovall. He made that plain enough.'

He ran. Ran and stumbled and ran again. It was clumsy to run in boots. He sat, dragged them off, left them on their sides in the heather. He pushed himself, ran right at the edge of nausea. When the house was in view he stopped again, bending forward, hands pressed against his thighs, heaving in the air. He could not see the horse, then saw it had wandered down to the sea and was standing there, gazing out like an old man lost in the contemplation of wonders.

He ran again. No thought of stealth now. At the front door he paused to look over his shoulder. From inside the house came a steady hum of silence. He went in. Emily was lying on the otto-man, the guittar held in her arms like a sleeping child. The room was cut with light and she lay just beneath its surface. He woke her.

'Jane?' she said.

He pulled her to her feet, held her upper arm with one hand, took the guittar with the other. 'He's here,' he said. 'Henderson.'

He went with her into his room, sat her on the chair at the far end, hung the guittar on its peg beside her, then closed the door and looked for something to secure it with. There was nothing, or there was only the bed. He put the small pile of his things on the floor and pushed the bed up hard against the wood. He thought it was probably useless, would keep someone out for no more than a few seconds but at least the door would not now give at a touch.

He squatted on the floor under the window and took the wrapped pistol from where it lay on top of Lovall's writing case. He began to unwind its swaddling.

'Jane and Cornelius are safe,' he said. 'They have gone away. Ranald is hurt but will live. We cannot speak now, Emily. We will listen. We will be still and we will listen.'

He threw the oilcloth aside and drew back the hammer to half-cock the pistol for loading. He knew – remembered clearly, could see his hands at the work – he had made up cartridges on the *Jenny*. He could not, however, remember where he had put them. Were they in the bag that was stolen? He stared at the gun as though it might inform him. What was this? Some effect of fear? Some mental locking brought about by fear? And why was he bothering with the pistol at all? Did he seriously think he was going to *shoot* anybody? They would be better off hiding themselves among the dunes. Or in the house? There must be some chest or deep cupboard they could lie in together, play dead . . .

He was, in his confusion, starting to look for it, the hiding place, when he saw, on the other side of the chair where Emily was sitting, the scuffed leather nose of his fiddle case. He crawled to it, unbuckled the straps, lifted out the fiddle, opened the lined box below, took out two of the cartridges. He glanced up. The top of a man's head passed the window, left to right, a distance of five yards or so. Lacroix touched Emily's hand. 'Not a sound or a movement,' he said.

Then the head was back, the head, a face looking in at the window's edge, but it was the wrong edge for any easy view of Emily and Lacroix. He did not see them, or if he did he gave no sign of it. He dropped away. Lacroix crawled back to his place under the window, took up the pistol and bit into one of the cartridges. He had recognised that neat and narrow face perfectly well, for though they had been in company together only a short time – hours more than days – it was a face he would remember for as long as he remembered the village of Los Morales. Not Henderson though. Never that. His name – the one he had called up in a clear voice from the frozen mud of the road that day – was Calley. Corporal Calley. Calley who cropped girls' heads so they would not forget the British army.

He tapped powder into the pan, closed the frizzen, tipped the remaining powder into the barrel, dropped in the ball, pushed in the cartridge paper with his thumb. He could not get the ramrod loose. He let it alone, breathed, tried again, freed it. He thrust paper and ball down into the breech, swung the rod back to its place beneath the barrel. Prised the hammer to full cock.

Emily had raised her left hand. She was pointing to the wall dividing the room they were in from the big room. He watched her. For two or three seconds he had no idea what she was doing, then he understood. Slowly, her finger moved in the direction of the door, stopped, and moved back towards the stairs. Then up, up, until she was pointing to the ceiling. Lacroix thought he heard the complaint of a board in the corridor but it was Emily's finger he trusted in now. When she drew it back along the ceiling to the top of the stairs he got to his feet, went to her and, as gently as he could, raised her off the chair. As she stood, her shoulder knocked the guittar and it gave out a small, sighing echo of its strings, a ghost chord. He walked her to the centre of the room. For a moment her hands hung idle – she had lost him – then she raised her right hand and traced a line back down the stairs.

'Captain Lacroix, sir? I think you are hereabouts somewhere, sir. I have a message for you. It won't take long. A military matter. From the top. Very pressing.'

He was, according to Emily's finger, speaking from near the bottom of the stairs, somewhere between the stairs and Cornelius's room.

'You don't want to go worrying about that business on the retreat, sir. That's all forgotten now. No one even remembers the name of the place. It's all forgotten. The war's moved on, sir. No need for you to be uneasy. Same for the lady who's here. Nothing for her to worry about.'

Emily's finger began to shift to the right, away from the stairs. There was a tapping on the wood of the wall that even Lacroix heard, though Emily's finger pointed eighteen inches further to the right from where he would have placed the sound.

He has looked in the window, thought Lacroix. He knows there is another room, a room unaccounted for. He has only to find the door.

'I've come a long way, sir. Had a weary old time of it, I have. Even lost my mucker on the road. My friend. No one to blame, sir, not really. Though I won't pretend it has not made me sorry.'

More sounds. He was . . . dragging something. The ottoman? Lacroix edged half an inch closer to Emily. He settled his left hand on her shoulder, very lightly. Through her shoulder he could feel the pulsing of a heart but could not easily have said if it was his or hers. Her finger moved right, stopped, moved back, stopped, moved right again until she was pointing at the wall directly ahead of them. Could Calley *see* them? Was there some fine crack in the panelling he could see them through? Was his eye pressed to it even now? Her finger was steady as a compass needle. It was a truth of sorts. Lacroix reached out with the pistol, its barrel as close as he dared to the side of her hand. You will have one chance, said the master, one only. Hesitate and you are lost.

The trigger – he seemed to crush it in his fist. He saw the hammer go, saw sparks in a dance, but felt no strong push-back, no arm-shove. A misfire? If so, he was dead, they both were. Then a curl of blue smoke cleared from in front of his face, parted like blue yarn, and he realised he was looking through a jagged star of shattered wood into the big room, and through the width of that room to the window and out to the land beyond. He walked to the wall, looked through the hole, looked down. The ottoman was at right angles to the wall and pulled a short way back from it. A man's leg – his boot – was lying on the silk, the rest of him in the deep shadows of the floor. He watched the leg on the ottoman for a while, how it seemed to be resting there. When he was satisfied he turned back to Emily. She was still pointing, her arm rigid. He touched her hand and very slowly lowered it.

22

He spent most of the night by Ranald's side, had carried up water for him and a cloth wrung out at the spring to cool his swollen face. Three or four times in the dark, Ranald addressed him, or some figure from his dreams, in Gaelic, and each time Lacroix replied, *'Orra bhuinneagan, a ghaoil, Orra bhuinneagan, a ghràidh . . .'* It was from a song about potatoes and it was, on his tour of the north, all the music he had managed to collect. He hoped the sounds would be comforting.

He did not dare to sleep. He watched the starless sky, smelled the ground, curled and uncurled his fingers, and in his head made passionate speeches to uniformed men in a large room he did not recognise. The men looked on impatiently. They had heard it all before, many times.

At first light he lifted Ranald on to the horse's back. He did not look into the small trench, did not tell Ranald who was in there. He led the horse to Jesse Campbell's house, kept his distance from the kelpers, found the old man milking his fettered cow. Together they carried Ranald inside and laid him on the bed where, immediately, the old man began to tend to him, to tend and to sing. The hook Lacroix had found in the grass he left on a table where it weighed down three of the blue Glasgow notes, money he hoped would be of use to them, feared would not.

Then back to the hill for Calley, who lay in the trench, rigid and boy-small, his pack at his feet, the sawn-down carbine across his chest. There was a black rose between the second and third buttons of his coat, something much bigger than that on the other side. At the house, while the body was still warm, that hour of perfect strangeness that followed the firing of the gun, he had searched Calley's pack and pockets, hoping for something that would explain him, but all he had found beyond the ordinary, the predictable, was a piece of paper with a list of islands on it, their names strangely mixed in with Spanish names, and in a brass case in one of the coat's many pockets, a lover's eye with two grey tears at the crease and certainly stolen . . .

Now – no words, everything businesslike, orderly, frantic – he put on top of Calley all that was piled at the side of the trench, shoved it in with his hands hoping to fill the trench completely, but some of the peat must have been taken away, perhaps to be examined by Cornelius's trowel, and he fetched more from beside the other new trench and made the ground level by stamping on it. Then he stood, staring at the earth between his boots, panting and wiping the dirt from his hands. He wept. It came on him like a shift in the weather, a vertigo, moved through his chest, his throat, convulsed his face. Who was it for? He hoped it was for the girl on the chair in Morales but feared it was only for himself. As for the man he had just buried, who would shed tears for Corporal Calley? Would anyone miss him? Did he have family? A sweetheart? A friend? Had he not, at the end, boasted of a friend?

For a dozen terrible seconds Lacroix thought he was crossing into madness. He could not understand how he had done so much with so little intention. As if his life were not his own, as if he lacked the will, the discipline to make it so. Where to begin? Where to begin *now*? Voices mocked him, his own among them. He wondered suddenly if his father had been mad, if that was what the doctor's calls had been about. Were the music books, the dried flowers, simples against madness? He gripped the sides of his head, squeezed it in a way he knew must have looked comical to anyone who had been there to see it. And it was then – lost to a degree he had not imagined possible – that he looked up and saw, right at the edge of what sight could bite down and faint as brushstrokes, the mast-tips and royals of a ship, something big, broaching the northern horizon. He was stunned. It was as if the world had agreed to look back at him, had met his gaze. He waited, breath stilled, life stilled, until he was sure he was not seeing clouds or sea-smoke, that it was not a vision, something he himself had placed there. He watched it rise, waited until the hull rode over the horizon, until sunlight touched some bright thing on it and made it signal, faintly, its existence. Then he broke away, seemed to fall into the air behind him, called to old Tom (what had they not been through together, these last twenty hours?) and led him, as swiftly as the horse's bulk would allow, back to the house on the shore.

He found Emily in the kitchen. She was sitting at the table facing the door to the outside. She had dressed herself in clothes and colours he did not think were meant to live together. She had misbuttoned the neck of her dress. Once she knew it was him, that he was alone and not accompanied by some official propelled on to the island by news of a stranger, a gunshot, she wanted to know about Ranald. He told her. 'Oh Ranald,' she said. It was her turn to weep. He watched her with the openness that had become habitual, the way her tears darkened the silk. When she was easier he told her what he had seen from the hill. He said he thought it was the emigration ship, the *Chiron*, and that she would pass the island as the other had, a mile or so from the shore. The timing was right, the heading. What else could it be? She nodded – a slow, blind, feeling-out of his voice.

Then, after a pause during which the cat sauntered between them, hopeful perhaps that normal life was about to be resumed, its old paradise of spills and splashes, he told her he did not believe any more that Calley was merely some deranged, solitary assassin. Calley had followed orders; that was what men like him did. It didn't matter whose orders. He would not be the last to come, he would not be the end of it. Then he told her what he intended to do. He gave to it the character of a revelation, knowing she was used from childhood to the authority of such moments (and had it not, in its suddenness, its completeness, been very like a revelation?). But for several seconds she was silent and he began to think she could not have understood him. He was about to repeat himself when she said, 'And me?'

'You?'

'Yes.'

He said he could not ask her. That he had no right to.

'No right even to offer me the choice?'

'But your sister. The child. Thorpe!'

'Thorpe is the last person I wish to see. Do you not know that?'

He shook his head. He did not.

'John,' she said. 'Ask me. *Ask me.*'

So he asked and she answered. There was no delay in it. Nor did he fail to hear it, or mishear it or imagine he had. She stood from the table. He reached across to touch her cheek, her hair, then they went together to the stairs and up the stairs to her room where she sat on the bed telling him what to pack. For his own things he borrowed a bag out of Cornelius's room, the initials O.T. painted on the side. (He decided not to inquire if Thorpe was an Osbert, an Oliver.) When both bags were ready they sat at the table downstairs and she dictated to him a letter for her brother and sister, which he wrote with pen and paper from Lovall's writing case. It explained what there was time to explain, offered love, promised a return. At the bottom of the letter he added: *For God's sake do not dig in the small trench. Leave it be!*

He then scratched five lines to his sister. He hoped she was well and the children and William. He might soon be in Ireland. He might be in Canada. He would write again when he could. She did not, he said, need to keep a lamp in the window any more.

He addressed the letter and left them both on the table in the big room, propped against a shape of grooved and bluish pottery, a fragment as beautiful as it was broken.

Since seeing the ship from the hill he reckoned a bare hour had passed, no more.

They went down to the boathouse. It was early afternoon, the day was mild and clear – though less mild and less clear than it had been. Lacroix carried the bags and his fiddle case. Emily clutched the sleeve of his green coat with one hand, carried her guittar with the other. At the boathouse he put down the bags and opened the door with a series of shoves. He had imagined something flying out – or running – but nothing came out and he looked through to where the boat floated on its bed of silky water. He left Emily sitting on one of the bags and went inside. Odd acoustics in there. He crouched to examine the interior of the boat. There was water, two inches or so over the keel-line. It could, he thought, be rainwater. He looked for something to bail with and found a wine glass sitting on its own on the wooden walkway by the bows. He sniffed at it. Dregs, ancient lees. Had someone poured a libation to the gods here? An offering in hope of a safe crossing, a successful fishing trip? Or did Cornelius sometimes come in here to hide from his sisters?

He knelt and used the glass to empty out some of the water, then gave it up. He had killed a man the night before. Why worry about damp feet? He went out to collect the bags and the instruments, loaded them into the stern where the wood was drier. Then he picked at the rope that secured the boat to its post, loosened it, undid it, looped it around the post again and went to fetch Emily.

Getting her into the boat was nearly the end of it all. The boat moved like a thing shocked by contact, and Emily, scrabbling at shadows, staggered and made a sound that was the echo of her gasp in the room in Oban, though it had not been fear then. He caught her hand, helped her to sit. The boat grew steady; the water ceased its slopping. He slid the oars from their place on the beams, stripped away stubborn layers of cobweb, slipped the rope from the post, got into the boat himself and sat on the middle thwart. With the blade of an oar against the boathouse wall, he pushed them backwards into open water, into the full silver of the afternoon, then moved around on his seat until he was facing Emily. He fitted the oars to the rowlocks, braced his feet either side of hers, looked over his shoulder and readied himself. He had rowed a boat before. He had, he thought, done so twice – once on the River Fal, once on the Tagus, both times for fun. His first stroke skimmed the top of the water, feathered it. The next was so deep the water was solid, a wall. He lifted the oars clear, let them shine and drip in the light, started again. After the eighth or ninth stroke he felt himself finding a rhythm. He pictured the Frieslander rowing them from the *Halycon* to the bay, tried to imitate what he remembered seeing, the swing and push of it, the whole of the body engaged. He took his bearings from the land behind Emily's head. He watched the white house dwindle. He watched old Tom, who seemed to be watching him. In time the innkeeper would come for him. Until then he could eat all the sea pinks he could find.

At what he reckoned was a good half-mile from the shore he saw that the water in the bottom of the boat was now deeper by about an inch. Perhaps two. Did it matter? If they were sinking they were sinking very slowly and would have time to row back to safety. What bothered him more was how the air was closing in. Not a mist yet, not a fret or a fog, but enough to make the distances hard to gauge. And where was the ship? *Where was she?* She could not have passed while they were packing, he did not believe it. Had she called in somewhere up the coast? Or would she burst out of the thickening air, gleaming, horribly real?

He began to row again, pulling steadily for another ten minutes, pulling hard, then drawing the oars in and crossing them over his thighs. He was thirsty but they had not brought anything to drink.

'Is she close?' asked Emily.

'Not yet,' he said, 'though she cannot be far off.' He asked her to reach into the top of his bag for the pistol. He told her to be very careful with it. The gun was loaded. 'When I see her,' he said, 'I will shoot to get their attention. Then they will know what we are here for.'

'Can she stop?'

'She will heave to,' he said. It was a term he had heard several times on the *Jenny*. He was fairly confident he had understood it.

She twisted in her seat, felt for the bag, found it, opened it, lifted out the pistol and passed it to him, barrel first.

420

'Christ, Emily!' He pushed the barrel aside and took the gun from her, though he found it almost funny, the idea of her shooting him out here, then floating around, a blind woman in a sinking boat . . .

They had, it seemed, now entered a current, a sea-road. It carried them gently southwards, parallel to the coast. He could see strands dotted with cattle, hills like sleeping men or men at prayer. He could see the smoke of the kelpers but nothing of the kelpers themselves.

The sea around the boat was very clear – much clearer than the air – and though the surface was patched with shifting brilliances of copper glare, he found that between these he could peer down into a kind of spacious upper room of well-lit water. There were creatures in there! Small, with bodies like globes of purest glass, their legs trailing under them like ribbon, like soaked cotton. He did not remember seeing these before. He had been unobservant, perhaps, or had simply not been in a boat like this, so close to the water, getting closer. And once he started to watch them he could not stop. They were immensely restful (he was immensely tired), and as he followed them, saw one rising into view, another sink into obscurity, he felt the moment's circumstance – the circumstance as you might describe it in, say, a court of law – start to loosen, to slide. The creatures, animate bubbles that fed, quite possibly, on light itself, were trying to teach him something he did not know he would be able to bear. He looked up at Emily, but before he could speak she leaned forward, startling him, finding his knees, clutching them. She had, quite unseen by him, removed the grey silk. Her eyes – pale, pale lids – were shut, and on her face was an expression of deepest joy, the same face she might have shown the congregation at her father's house in the days before the dreams turned sour.

'John!' she cried. 'John! Now we shall be entirely free!'

Acknowledgements

I would like to acknowledge the generosity of Drue Heinz and the Hawthornden Foundation at Lasswade. Hard to imagine a more perfect place to work. And heartfelt thanks to Frieda and Rachel for putting up with my absences and occasional derelictions of duty. Also to Jon and Mary Pritchard, who led me, very gently, towards the playing of music.